L.C. Moon's

A BEDTIME STORY

A BEDTIME STORY

By L. C. MOON

Cover art by Dominique Blais

Les Éditions D. A. D. inc
D. A. D. inc Publishing

Head Office
1637, rue Des Clapotis
Terrebonne, Qc, Canada
J6X 4N4

ISBN: 978-0-9938655-0-3

theBTSproject.com

Know who you are, and they will too.

Lev Malkin

Acknowledgments

To Claudia, truth be told, if it weren't for you, *A Bedtime Story* (*BTS*) would have forever remained my personal "bedtime story".

To my sister, Lana Chacra, a.k.a. Sissi, and most likely my (evil ;p) twin in another life. You understood *BTS* more than I did at times and did not shy away from putting me back on track (in harsher ways than I expected :s) when I got lost. Your unwavering faith in me, in *BTS*, is what got me to the finish line. I will never forget our daily e-mails and their endless "last version!" I will never thank you enough for your support and for all the memories we created, caught up in *BTS* world, story, and music. Thank you. Most of Laura and Kayne's story was written with the songs you composed for them playing on a loop. In the most excruciating moments of doubts, I only needed to play their theme song again, and I would think to myself, BTS *has to be good if it can inspire such hauntingly beautiful melodies.*

One cannot mention *BTS* music without mentioning Brent Bourgeois. Brent, thank you. Listening to what you have done with *BTS* is a very humbling experience. Some encounters are meant to be, and I believe Lana and yours was among them.

To Cam, my VERY OPINIONATED… interested party ;). I love you and could not have asked for a better brother-in-law. You are more than family, you are a kindred spirit. Thank you for your devotion, from the amazing lyrics you wrote for *BTS* to the time and dedication you have given to the book and music. I would not trust *BTS* in anyone else's hands.

To my editor, Natalie Najarian (a.k.a. Bubbles). I took over your life. Shamelessly, one might say (though not me… lol). I will always cherish our two-hour long (almost daily) conversations and heated debates over (grammatically questionable) "AUTHOR INTENT!" lol. I have grown as an author under your care and patience. Our friendship was way overdue but will pass the test of time.

To my best friends and "FA-MEL-LY", you are few and irreplaceable. I could not have chosen better mates to travel this road.

To my friends and Beta readers, ML, AS, and SP, and a special thanks to Tina E., JG Faherty and Donna J. Thank you for all your help and support.

To Dominique Blais, a.k.a. Doom, I have always loved your art and knew from the get-go that it had to be you and no one else. My expectations of you were tremendously high, and you surpassed them by a mile. Thank you.

And lastly, to my husband, my best friend, the love of my life, and always, my partner in crime. You know me like no one else on earth. You are the protective older brother I always craved and the ally I always needed. Boubounet, we have created our own little world. I look forward to growing old with you. Bald and toothless, still goofing around, cracking up at each other's jokes under our friends' discouraged headshake. It amazes me. Two accidents... and yet fated in the stars. Je t'aime, plus qu'hier, moins que demain... 10-5 20-1-9-13-5.

Table of Contents

Day-0

She was standing still, amidst the chaotic music and frantic crowd, holding a Long Island Iced Tea she had been absentmindedly sipping for the past half hour. She had her back to him, and he was willing her silently to turn around. He'd been watching her for two weeks now, keeping track of her routine, her habits, and her correspondence. She kept to herself, no friends, no pets, little to no contact with the outside world. She went straight home after her shifts, bussing tables at the local deli where the obese, middle-aged manager obviously kept her for ulterior motives, considering the amount of dishes she broke in those two short weeks. He liked watching her. She was young, innocent, and pretty. *Very pretty.* She looked even prettier in a grey chiffon cocktail dress and nude stilettos. It was certainly a change from the jeans and hoodies he'd gotten so used to seeing her in. But he wanted to see her face again, to take in her delicate features and stare into those big round grey eyes. Maybe if he was lucky, he would get a glimpse of one of her scarce but impossibly sweet smiles. He was excited, tonight, he would finally make contact. And yet he felt slightly nostalgic, tonight, the job was over.

She finally turned her head, only her head, with her back still facing him, as if sensing his stare. Straight brown bangs framed her eyes. Her long chestnut hair, usually in a ponytail, hung loose below her delicate shoulders, contrasted against her porcelain skin. She looked sophisticated, far beyond her years. He almost felt reluctance at what was to come, she was so pretty. Under different circumstances, his plans for her would have been as sinister, though designed for his own depraved pleasure. *But no, Laura Spencer was a job,* and an important one at that.

* * *

It was supposed to be fun. The first warm night in early spring had all of Montreal buzzing with life and excitement. Restaurants and clubs were packed with the overjoyous liberated hibernators. Laura regretted the decision the moment she stepped out of her door. Pamela, her overfriendly coworker, had finally worn her down and convinced her to come out. "It's a new club, classy, you'll love it! Besides, girls need to stick together. You can't let me meet this guy alone!" And her personal favorite, "He's *soooooo* hot!" *Uuughhh.* Pamela seemed awfully fine, flirting up a storm with the hot customer she had given her number to, earlier that day. It didn't take Laura too long to realize she had become a third wheel, and she remorselessly wondered off to get herself a drink. She was tired; she was always tired. She just wanted to go home. Tomorrow, a new postcard might be in the mail. For the past six months, one card was delivered to her mailbox every other week. She lived for those deliveries.

A few men had tried approaching her, and she gently brushed them off. Suddenly, she felt a prickle down her spine. Turning her head around, she noticed him. He was wearing jeans and a black shirt. He was tall, dark, and handsome, very much so. She surprised herself by noticing it. She was barely aware of her surroundings and the people in it. She often got in trouble at work for it, too distracted to notice clients, bumping left and right into waiters carrying hot plates, breaking a few too many plates herself. How she wished to be graceful and elegant; she consciously tried to be aware of her movements. In the end, she resigned herself to losing a tenth of her paycheck every other week to compensate her employer for her clumsiness.

He was staring at her, very intently. *Not the typical stare you'd expect from a man on the prowl.* She held his gaze for an instant before her eyes instinctively fell to the ground. She didn't dare look in his direction again, *knowing* his eyes were still glued to her. She gulped the remainder of her watered-down drink in one shot and headed to the bar for another.

The very sexy, platinum blonde, miniskirt-sporting bartender was evidently more interested in serving the male clientele. After a few failed attempts at waving her down, Laura was about to retreat in defeat when a freshly made Long Island Iced Tea miraculously appeared in front of her. Her heart skipped a beat, in excitement, and in fear. *Could it be the incredibly handsome, slightly creepy mystery man?* She was relieved, if not disappointed, to find out it wasn't. One of those overconfident corporate-looking guys was smiling at her, wearing the typical stare you *would* expect from a man on the prowl.

"So… did I get it right?" He shot her one of those cocky smiles.

"Yes… hmm… I mean no… Sorry, I can't take that."

"Ah c'mon, don't be like that. It's just a drink. I saw you there downing the last one pretty fast, seemed like you really could use another."

She giggled awkwardly. "Sorry… I really can't… I have to find my friend. Thank you though…" she mumbled the last part nervously, as she quickly turned around to make her exit, chiding herself inwardly for her lack of cool composure. Before she knew it, she ran into a wall of flesh and was about to lose balance when two firm hands caught her on either side.

"Easy there… you okay?"

It was *him*. She remained mute, simply staring up wide-eyed at him. He was even taller and better looking up close. He was light tan with deep brown eyes and dark wavy hair that fell to his chin. She gulped as he leaned in, facing the square jaw, full red lips, and very strong muscular body, which at the moment were too close for comfort.

"Are you okay?" he repeated himself slowly, speaking softly in her ear. She could feel his breath on her face, feel her heart racing, and for some reason, red flags going up all over the place.

"Yes… Thank you… I have to go…" she managed to blurt out before she broke free of his hold. She looked around desperately for Pamela. She wanted to leave. *Now.*

She found Pamela making out in a corner with Mark, *because now he's just Mark*, not the stranger for whom Laura had to play chaperone. Pamela frowned at Laura when she voiced her aggravation at the disappearing act. *She was just with Mark, it's okay, don't freak out,* like she'd known him her whole life. "Just fifteen more minutes? Pleaaaaaaase, pretty pleeeeeeaaase?" She even threw in with eye batting and the whole hoopla. Rolling her eyes, Laura warned her coworker, *not friend*, definitely not in that moment, that she would go outside for a cigarette. Fifteen minutes. Not. A. Second. More.

He was already outside by the time she made her way to the street. He was alone, and he spotted her. It was too late to turn back now, no matter how badly she wanted to... or not. She smiled politely at him and stood at the opposite side of the door. He nodded his head to her, an imperceptible smile crossing his lips as he took another drag of his cigarette. She was waiting for him to speak to her, initiate small talk, but he didn't. She was halfway through the cigarette, the silence making her uncomfortable, even more so when confronted to his relaxed posture. She was unnerved by his actions, or lack thereof, but reminded herself of the way she had treated him earlier. He was only being gentlemanly, and she'd brushed him off. It was up to her to make the next move.

"Hey... sorry... about earlier... I didn't mean to be rude..." She flashed him an honest smile. She did feel bad.

"It's okay, no harm done." He offered her a charming smile, a heart-melting, teenybopper-mania-inducing, guy-next-door smile.

Her heart fluttered and she couldn't stop smiling herself. "I just... I really suck at these things... and by things, I mean most social interactions..." she blurted out nervously, as she always did in these situations. Why couldn't she be the composed, self-assured, aloof type? Even her voice went up a few octaves, the sound grating her ears. This man was in his late twenties at the very least, and there she was sounding like a high schooler on her way to the prom.

"You doing all right," he said with a knowing, indulgent smile as he flicked away his cigarette. He then added, "Take care of yourself," brushing her elbow with the tips of his fingers as he made his way back in.

She was floored. He might as well have slapped her in the face. She felt rejected, and yet she couldn't help rubbing the spot he had just touched, smiling to herself. She was still daydreaming, a telling smile on her face, when she remembered hunting down dear Pamela so they could finally get out of there. As expected, Pamela was found in the same corner, though the situation seemed to have escalated. Looking away, Laura tugged at her friend in a vain effort to detangle her from Mark. Annoyed, even more so than the previous time, Pamela informed her that she would be leaving with Mark, adding in a gentler tone, "Is it okay?"

"Yeah, don't worry. I'll be fine. I'll just take a cab." *Of course it's not okay. I came here for you.*

"Oh really? Yay! Thanks, you're the best!" Pamela clasped her hands.

"Yeah, you're the best, Lisa!" Mark agreed.

She didn't bother correcting him. She'd be impressed if he remembered Pamela's name come morning. She headed outside, relieved to have survived the supposedly fun evening out. She was looking through her purse for her cellphone to call a cab when she realized her wallet was missing. *Could this night get any worse? Emotionally coerced by friend/coworker to go out? Check. Rejected by handsome stranger totally rocking mixed signals? Check. Ditched by said friend/coworker for obvious douche bag? Triple check.* As for the icing on the cake, the case of the missing wallet… Laura would have gotten much more irritated if she hadn't been used to so much worse. As she lit a cigarette to weigh her options, *and walking was not one of them*, he reappeared again.

"You're still here."

It wasn't a question, more of a happy observation. And just like that, her insides were swarming with butterflies.

"Well… I wasn't here the whole time… I went to look for my friend inside… Turns out she's ditched me."

"I meant at the club."

"Oh… yeah, of course… I mean no, I'm leaving, or I'm trying to. Turns out I lost my wallet too." She offered him a self-deprecating smile.

"So… a great night."

"Yeah, you could say that again." She let out a soft chuckle under his amused gaze.

"I'm Kayne." He offered his hand.

"Laura, nice to meet you." She shook his hand, reminded of its warmth and firm grasp.

"Do you need money for a cab?"

"Oh no… I couldn't possibly. No, I'll just walk… It's not that far…" she said unconvincingly.

He just gave her the look, like even he knew she didn't believe that for a second. He shook his head with playful disapproval and, reaching into his wallet, pulled out a fifty-dollar bill.

"That should cover it," he said, handing it to her.

"No. Seriously, I *can't* take your money," she said adamantly, almost offended. *Why couldn't he just offer her a ride… like normal people?*

"Where you heading?"

"Close to the university. It's not that far. Seriously, I *could* walk…"

"Hmm…" he uttered, unconvinced, and visibly entertained as he put the money back in his wallet and turned around. He pressed his car starter and started walking toward a granite Audi SUV, leaving Laura feeling abandoned and confused on the sidewalk.

"You coming?" he asked, barely turning his head back to her, showing her a glimpse of his smirk.

Thank you! She thought he'd never offer, and *damned if she asked*. She caught up to him, smiling away. "Are you sure you don't mind?"

He responded with a sly smile, offering her his hand to help her into the car. He turned on the radio once they were inside. She began to chat away, jittery, the entire time, wondering if he would ask for her number. He turned to her from time to time, restraining a smirk, amused by her nervousness. At some point he made a turn off route then turned to her, resting his hand very gently on the top of her knee, for just a few seconds.

"Listen, Laura, I have to drop off something. It's literally two blocks down. Do you mind if we make a quick stop?"

"No, no, of course not. Please, go ahead." She was still giddy from his touch, from all the possibilities playing in her head, and honestly, she welcomed the delay if it meant more time with him.

This neighborhood wasn't the best, and the street he parked on looked even shadier. He smiled warmly at her. "Well, it's here. Do you want to come with me, or would you rather wait in the car?"

She looked around wearily. She didn't want to be alone. "Hmm… I'll go with you. If that's okay?" she asked uncertainly.

He answered with a soft chuckle and, after opening the door on her side, offered his hand.

* * *

He had never seen her smile as much as she had in this past half hour. She really had a gorgeous smile. He took some pride in knowing that he'd gotten so many out of her for himself. He felt her tense from the moment they entered the building. He was walking fast, and she was struggling to keep the pace. The charade would be over soon. They got to a double door, and she threw him an inquisitive look. He could tell she knew something was off. For starters, he wasn't carrying anything, but she made no mention of it. He did feel a few furtive stares burning his back on the long walk down the corridor. By that point, he knew she had followed him against her better judgment. He opened one of the doors and ushered her inside, with a *ladies first* kind of gesture. She smiled nervously but obeyed.

There were three men already inside the room. A short stocky one in a pinstripe suit sat behind a massive mahogany desk facing them. He immediately stood up to greet them, an ugly sneer marring his face. The other two could have passed for Secret

Service agents, complete with black suits and earpieces, if not for the AK-47s they carried. They stood stoically against the walls on either sides of the room.

She stopped right in her tracks and turned to Kayne abruptly. "What is this? What's happening?" she hissed through clenched teeth.

His expression was detached, his eyes cold and intense, just as they had been the first time she noticed him. A shiver ran down her spine. He didn't answer her. Never breaking eye contact, he slowly shut the door. With his hands behind him, he leaned back into it, effectively blocking the only exit. He simply nudged his head in the stocky man's direction, who was unsuccessfully trying to get Laura's attention.

"Miss Spencer, how lovely to finally meet you. Let me introduce myself. I'm Maxwell Bane. Please, have a seat."

Laura quickly turned her head to Maxwell at the mention of her name, then right back to Kayne, bewilderment now in her eyes.

"Kayne, what is this? How does he know my name?" Her breath quickened, her voice barely above a whisper.

"He just wants to talk, Laura. Have a seat." His voice was commanding, devoid of any sympathy.

Maxwell began again, this time, the gentleness in his tone more forced, his words articulated. "Miss Spencer, please have a seat. All I am asking is for a little friendly talk. Let's keep things nice, shall we? I would hate to resort to more… persuasive methods…"

Laura finally turned to face him. "Please… Mr. Bane… I am sure this is a complete misunderstanding…"

"Is it? Are you not Miss Laura Spencer?"

"Yes… but—"

"*Sister* of Peter Spencer?"

Her face instantly paled, her mouth opened then closed, without releasing a sound. So *this* is what it was about. *Oh, Peter, Peter, what have you done?* She knew he had gotten involved with bad things, bad people. He had been doing drugs for as long as she could remember, but it was only in the last few years he had gotten seriously into the harsher stuff. He completely changed, became paranoid, she barely saw him anymore. But she held on to what she had, he was her only family. About eight months ago, he had come to see her at her apartment. He was acting very weird, thought he was being followed. All he said was that he had to disappear for a while, *until things blow over*. He had told her how much he loved her and how sorry he was, that he would write to her so she could know he was alive and well. He proceeded to explain to her a secret code he'd constructed to ensure a *secure communication*. She started receiving his postcards about two months after, every two weeks, sometimes three, never more than that. She never believed anyone was after him. But she didn't have it in her to fight his drug-induced paranoia, and so she resigned herself to kiss every postcard and burn it after reading, as instructed.

"What is this about? What do you want with him?" Her voice was firmer, her tone defensive.

"Miss Spencer, please have a seat. We just want to ask you a few questions about Peter."

"I don't know where he is. I haven't spoken to him in almost a year."

"Oh, come now... We know that's not true. We know *for a fact* that you know where he is. We just want to talk to him, that's it."

"Bullshit," she mumbled to herself. "You're wrong. I don't know where he is. I'm sorry."

Maxwell squeezed the top of his nose with two stubby fingers, clearly starting to lose patience. "Miss Spencer, I was hoping we could be civil about this. I don't think you understand the severity of your situation. Maybe my friends can help." He waved his arm toward one of the men by the wall.

She shuddered with dread. She did understand, she understood too well. What *they* didn't understand was that she would never, under any circumstance, betray her brother. Peter, her brother, her only friend, her only family. Peter, who bandaged her wounds when she was still a child and held her at night when she had nightmares. Peter, who taught her how to lie so they could stay together when they were minors, who skipped supper more than once so she could get dessert to finish off her meals. Peter, who sacrificed everything, for her. No, she understood. Tonight, she would not leave this room alive. A whimper escaped her lips. She turned back to Kayne slowly, the familiar sadness back in her glistening grey eyes.

Her voice was soft, wavering. "Please… please… I really don't know… You have to believe me."

He remained unmoved, staring her straight in the eye. "I'm not the one you have to convince. My job was just to get you here."

She just stared at him, hurt and betrayal in her eyes. "How could you do this to me?" It was so silly, and yet she couldn't help herself. "So… that was your plan… the entire evening?"

The faintest smile crossed his lips as he reached into his back pocket and pulled out her missing wallet.

"You're a monster…" She wasn't saying it out of spite, just acknowledging it quietly to herself, amazed at the realization.

He didn't respond. Instead, he stepped forward and grabbed her firmly by the arm, though not unkindly, and pulled her toward the chair. She didn't resist, simply allowing her limbs to be dragged. As he sat her in the chair, she looked up, her eyes reflecting a mix of pleading and panic.

"So that's it? You're just going to leave me here with them?"

If only for an instant his eyes softened, his tone remained impassive. "Do you want me to stay?"

She realized the perverse irony. He had brought her here. He was the reason for all of this. But right now, *yes*, she wanted him to stay. Somehow, she felt safer with him around. Her voice broke into a little sob, and she nodded shamefully, letting out the faintest "yes."

He nodded his head slowly, then with the tip of his fingers, he lifted her head ever so gently to force her to look him in the eye. "Okay. I will."

He walked to the back of the room and took a seat facing her, backing the chair against the wall. The two men in black closed in on her, proceeding to handcuff her hands and feet to each side of the chair. Her breathing quickened. Maxwell was grinning perversely, waiting for her to be settled. He looked back at Kayne, with a casualness reserved for old buddies.

"So you'll be joining us? Ah, just like good old times." He winked. "Nostalgic, are we?" He let out a sickening chuckle to which Kayne responded with a cold smile. Maxwell then turned all his attention back to the helpless girl tied up in front of him.

"It saddens me, Miss Spencer, to have to resort to such measures. This could have been easily avoided. I do not wish you harm, but let me make myself clear: I will get my answers. You will talk, one way or another."

"But I swear... I don't know..." She sobbed quietly.

"Very well then. If that's how you want to play, have it your way." His voice was stern as he motioned to the man identified as Carlo to bring some sort of medieval-looking iron instrument seemingly straight out of the Spanish Inquisition. Removing her left shoe, Carlo then proceeded to insert her foot in the contraption.

He began twisting one of the dials. A sharp pain shot through her entire body. She screamed in agony as her sobs intensified, repeating over and over again the same few words: "Please, I don't know, I swear." But the dial kept twisting, intensifying the pain. She thought she might pass out. She could barely make sense of what Maxwell was shouting. She threw a look in Kayne's direction, her vision blurred with tears. He was sitting calmly, his legs spread wide open on the chair, leaning forward, with his elbows resting on his knees. He was slowly inhaling a freshly lit cigarette. He returned her stare, emotionless.

He truly was a monster. How naïve she was to think his presence would benefit her condition. Despair began to invade her thoughts, and she prayed she would pass out soon. Without warning, the pain stopped. Maxwell kept repeating her name, seeking her attention. He insisted on calling her Miss Spencer, with his eloquent speech and gentleman mannerisms. It was all a farce, a cruel joke she had walked into of her own accord. And why? Because a handsome stranger had also played the gentleman.

Just as she was starting to catch her breath, she felt the sting of cold metal on each side of her little finger. Carlo was holding garden shears, trapping her left pinky in between the blades. Awaiting Maxwell's instructions, he applied just enough pressure that she made no attempt to move. With cold terror in her eyes, she looked around frantically, resembling a cornered wild animal. She repeated the same words, even screaming, her vocabulary dwindling to *please* and *no*. Maxwell's smile was full-on sadistic. There would be no mercy there. *Was there ever?* No, he was taking pleasure in this. It was more than a means to an end. She instinctively fell back to Kayne, pleading with all she had, her words, her tears, her eyes, her uncontrollable heaving.

"Enough." His voice echoed in the room. In response to Maxwell's inquisitive look, he finally broke eye contact with Laura long enough to tell him to leave them. He wasn't asking. Maxwell seemed displeased with the turn of events but also seemed to know better than to defy a direct order. He gestured to his men, and they all left the room quietly.

Kayne got up, unhurriedly making his way over to face Laura. Resting slightly on the edge of the desk with his arms crossed, he patiently stared at her, waiting for her to regain some kind of composure. He only spoke to her when her heaving stopped and she finally lifted her head to meet his eyes.

"You love your brother very much." He waited for her to nod in agreement before continuing. "And you are very loyal to him, I can respect that. You think there's nothing we can do that will make you talk, that you'd die for him if you had to. But that's not how it goes. Trust me, Laura, *I know*. Everyone has a breaking point. Everyone talks. The only thing that ever changes is the state they're in when they do."

She broke down again. "What do you want with him?" she sniffled, her nose running.

"Information. Information he stole." His voice remained calm.

"You're going to kill him… and you'll kill me regardless of what I say…" she whispered softly, still gasping for breath.

"Cooperate, and I give you my word. You will leave this room alive."

She laughed sardonically. "You give me your word? Oh, what a relief!"

"Think about it, Laura, I haven't lied to you once. I don't lie."

"Seriously? You're gonna pull that—" Before she could utter the word *shit*, he raised his brow at her. *He apparently didn't like cursing.*

"You said you had to drop something off."

"I did." He grinned wickedly.

Of course, she was the *thing*. She felt her Long Island Iced Tea coming back up. "I followed you here… You didn't even have to drug me or force me…" Her disbelief and bitterness bled through her words. "Why go through this charade?"

He actually smiled at that. "Don't beat yourself up about it. I would have brought you here one way or another. I thought you'd prefer my way," he taunted.

"You really are a monster." This time, she was saying it to his benefit, her soft voice cracking. She broke down again, muttering to herself, "Oh god, oh god, please help me."

"You think God can help you? No, Laura, God can't help you. I may be a monster, but I'm the only one who can help you right now."

She didn't respond, didn't know how to respond. So she lowered her eyes to the ground and repeated the same words, caught in a hellish loop. "I don't know where he is."

He approached, kneeling down on one knee so he was at eye level with her. He lifted her head, in the same gentle way he had done earlier. "Look at me." He waited until she did. "I'm offering you help. I understand you want to protect him, but don't *ever* lie to me," he spat, his stare cold and ruthless, making her shiver.

"Here is what I am offering you, Laura, I don't want you to tell me where he is."

She remained quiet, opting for the safety of silence. She held his gaze as he stood back up, a lingering hope flickering into her eyes.

"What I want is for you to tell me something, anything, to lead us in his direction. I don't want his specific location. Just the city he's in."

"So you can find him and kill him."

"Or not. It could take us over a week to track him. He might even be gone by then. Don't you see what I'm offering you? I'm offering you a chance to get out of this alive while still being able to live with yourself." He could see her thinking it over, hundred thoughts racing in her mind.

"But—"

"No buts, Laura. It's a good offer. It's a *very* generous offer. And it will expire soon. I'm going to count to five. If I don't have the name of a city by then, I'm walking out of here. And no one, not God, not anyone, will stop what's to come. Do you understand?"

She nodded nervously. As he began to count, she stopped him at one, anything to bide her time. "I could lie, how would you know?"

By the way his eyes narrowed and his jaw tensed, she instantly regretted the words that had just left her mouth. She cringed as he approached, leaning into her ear, his voice deceptively soft. "You could. But I would *strongly* advise against it. I *will* find out. And when I do, I will *personally* continue what they have started. Not for answers, not for the truth, but for the sheer joy of it. I will make a masterpiece out of you. Do you understand me, Laura?"

She nodded her head frantically, terrified.

He grabbed her chin tightly and forced eye contact as he uttered his warning. His voice was harsh, as he emphasized each word.

"Whatever you do. Never. Lie. To me." And then he resumed his count. "Two, three, four—"

"Boston! He's in Boston." Devastated, she broke down, her body barely supporting her. He grabbed her by the chin again and studied her features, trying to read into them. Her mascara was running down her cheeks, her face contorted in pain. She was a mess.

He knew from the torment reflected in her eyes, she told the truth. Still, he asked, "Boston, are you sure?"

"Yes…" she wailed, her body shaking uncontrollably.

He left her side. The next thing she knew, she was alone in the room. She could hear voices on the other side, as if Maxwell and Kayne were arguing, their tones restrained.

They eventually reentered the room. Kayne walked straight to her, determined, followed by Maxwell, venom dripping from his strained features. Kayne briefly looked her in the eye then proceeded to unshackle her. She was confused. Were they going to kill her now? But then why unshackle her? Kayne lifted her to her feet with a firm hold, ignoring Maxwell's presence.

"You're coming with me," he answered her questioning look as he dragged her impatiently out of the room.

"Where are you taking me?" she asked softly, the fight in her long gone.

"To my home. You'll be under my supervision." Sensing her hesitation, he snapped at her, annoyed, "Unless you would prefer me to leave you here?"

She shook her head vehemently in response.

"Good. Let's go." As they were about to pass through the door, he stopped, turning to face her. "It's a long drive. I expect you to behave. If you try to reach out to anyone, even just to make eye contact, I will kill them. And you will finish the ride in my trunk. Understood?"

She nodded, her eyes wide with alarm.

"I want to hear you say it."

"I understand," she quivered.

He nodded his approval, smiled, and brushed her cheek with the back of his hand. "Good girl."

She remained perfectly still. If this gesture was meant to be soothing, it had the total opposite effect. She felt her insides churn with revulsion. To think that not so long ago, a couple of hours actually, the same touch would have had her dreaming for days. That already seemed so long ago, like another life, one that was never really hers. It was funny, she thought, this should feel surreal, but it didn't. Everything leading up to this ill-fated room was the dream. The nice club, the flirtations with a handsome stranger, those were the illusion. The nightmare that followed, that was reality.

He opened the passenger door for her and helped her in, always the gentleman. The drive was quiet, the roads empty. Dawn was creeping in. It was past five in the morning, and she was exhausted, but she refused to shut her eyes, wanting to maintain some type of control, however small, in her life. About twenty minutes into the drive, as she was losing her battle to fatigue, the sound of his voice startled her.

"While you're under my roof, there are three simple rules you need to follow, the first you've already been warned of. Never lie to me. Never disobey me. Never disrespect me."

The warning snapped her senses fully awake, and she nodded her head meekly in response.

"Here, wipe your face." He handed her a tissue, which she tentatively reached for. He then proceeded to place a call via the Bluetooth in his car. A gentle female voice came on the speaker, with the unmistakable patient and kind tone older women adopted when speaking to their offspring.

"Master Kayne."

"Hi, Olga." His voice was soft, in a way Laura didn't think possible. "Olga, please set up the bedroom in the eastern wing. We will have a… *guest*… staying with us…" He eyed Laura with an indiscernible smile.

“Yes, Master Kayne, anything else?”

“Yes. Please ask Lucas to set up the B security system.”

“Yes, Master Kayne. Will that be all?”

“Yes, thank you, Olga.” He was smiling to himself, a true warm smile, like the million-dollar one he flashed her at the club. *So if it wasn’t all an act, who was that man? She was getting a room?* That was a good thing, she assumed, hopefully with a lock on the inside. It hadn’t even crossed her mind to worry about her new living conditions before, she was so glad to be out of the room.

They kept driving silently. Laura was looking out the window, pondering about the meaningless life she led up to this point. Did she ever truly live? And now it was too late. Worse than the fear of the life awaiting her, it was the stab of knowing she was leaving nothing worthy behind that hurt the most. Eventually she noticed a car fast approaching. For the two seconds they were side by side, Laura chanced a side glance and noticed it was a woman at the wheel. Her heart started racing. *Could she try anything?*

“Don’t even think about it.” His calm voice conveyed the threat.

“Of course I’ll think about it!” she snapped back before she could think her response through.

“Careful, Laura…”

“Well… you said to be honest…”

He gave her a long measured look, a smile curving on his lips. “I also said to be respectful. Watch your tone.” His voice was stern, but she could feel the smile he repressed.

The sun had risen by the time he finally turned into a long cobblestone driveway with cedars planted on each side. It was an imposing estate in a very secluded area. They passed electronically controlled gates, to continue the long drive up to a huge white stone mansion. Men dressed in black, not unlike the ones she had seen earlier, were spread throughout the premises. Kayne turned to face her and with the same sweet smile announced, “Here it is, home sweet home.”

He got out and once again walked over to her side, opening her door and offering his hand.

She remained frozen in place.

"Get out," he ordered, all traces of the sweet smile evaporating into thin air.

She gave him a feeble hand, but when her feet hit the ground, they refused to move. She knew, once she entered this house, she would never leave. Impatiently, he dragged her forward. She stumbled, her knees weak, her ankle still torturing her at the smallest bit of pressure. Kayne wrapped his right arm around her back, keeping his left hand firmly gripped to her arm. They climbed the few marble steps leading to the massive French doors at the main entrance where one of the security men held the door open for them. They walked in to an opulent vast room, high ceilings and all. A slightly overweight older woman in uniform was waiting for them. She had greying hair tied in a low bun, and her fingers were laced in front of her, as she offered them a kind smile.

"Master Kayne." She respectfully bowed her head.

"Olga, this is Laura Spencer. She will be staying with us."

"Nice to meet you, Miss Spencer." Her smile seemed genuine, but she showed no reaction to Laura's pathetic appearance. Laura would not find an ally in her.

Unsure how to react, she nodded quietly. It was in this moment that the absurdity of it all started to dawn on her. This was it, it was really happening. But she wasn't freaking out, she just felt numb.

"Laura, this is Olga. I trust her with my life. While I am not here, she will see to anything you may need." He looked at his watch. "She'll show you around tomorrow. Feel free to go wherever you want and use anything at your disposal on the first floor. Just don't go downstairs, upstairs, or outside without my direct consent. Understood?"

She nodded again, her stare blank.

"There is no Internet. The phone lines will connect you to Lucas, my head of security. If there is an emergency, simply dial *9*. You will not be able to make any other type of calls. There is security outside the house 'round the clock and cameras in every direction. All the windows and outside doors are equipped with alarms. My men were given my instructions. Please don't try anything stupid... I think that about covers it for now." He paused then surprised her by adding, "Are you hungry?"

She wasn't hungry, just tired, so incredibly tired. All she wanted was to curl into a ball, cry herself to sleep, and hopefully never wake up.

Day-1

Olga led her to her room. It was very pretty, and girly. A woman had obviously lived there, a woman with expensive and elegant taste. *Who was this woman? Where was she now?*

Olga politely asked her if she would need anything else before excusing herself and closing the door. The door did have a lock, but the old style, with a key, which Laura doubted would ever be given to her. It could have been worse. She felt an urge to investigate her new living space, but her tiredness took over in one swift wave. She barely had the strength to kick off her heels before collapsing on the big fluffy bed, still wearing the grey chiffon dress.

She slept deeply and had many dreams, mostly about her childhood, mostly about Peter. By the time she woke up, the sun was high in the sky. She opened and shut her eyes a few times. She had almost forgotten… She decided she would not move from the bed. She would stay there, right on that spot, and not move a muscle until she died. The thought almost made her smile.

Olga came in a short while later, pushing a metal trolley bursting with appetizing scents. "Ah, Miss Spencer, I'm glad to see you're awake. I hope you slept well. I would have knocked, but I didn't want to wake you."

Laura barely moved her head in her direction, tucking the sheet further up to her neck.

"Well, I don't want to disturb you. Master Kayne will be home for supper. It will be served at seven, but I thought you might be a little hungry."

Laura cringed at the mention of his name. How could this woman seem so casual about the situation? Did she not know who her employer was? He was obviously part of a criminal organization.

Did she not care? Was she some type of Mafia-wife nanny turning the blind eye?

"Supper…? What time is it?" she mumbled, her voice raspy from sleep.

"Four thirty in the afternoon." Olga was always smiling that kind smile of hers.

"Uh, okay, thank you."

"Well, if you won't be needing anything else, I will be in the kitchen. I can come back later if you like and give you the tour?"

"No, thank you. I'd rather stay in here, if that's okay." Laura wasn't rude, just cautious. A small part of her, her apparently very off intuition, led her to trust the woman, while every other logical and pragmatic part of her screamed *caution*.

"As you wish." Olga smiled again before heading out, leaving the trolley in the room.

Laura was weary to touch the food. What if it was drugged? But what would be the alternative, starve to death? She actually considered the option for a moment, but dieting was never her strong suit. She seriously questioned her willpower in the face of famine.

She slowly made her way out of bed, as if being observed, careful with every move. Her ankle was still swollen and hurt the moment she tried to stand on it. She limped to the trolley and dragged it close to the bed to sit back down. The bed was safe, she had claimed it. The rest of the room was still hostile territory.

She opened the metal dome to find eggs Benedict. She would have usually been thrilled, but her stomach turned at the first bite. It was too heavy, and her fragile nerves were affecting her appetite. She closed the dome, subdued, and crawled back under the sheets. Silent tears rolled down her cheeks. She closed her eyes and waited for sleep to come again.

It was six fifty when Olga come to fetch her. Laura had finally taken notice of the grandfather clock in her bedroom. She had spent the day between the bed and the en suite luxurious marble bathroom, which had proved very useful after she got sick repeatedly, dry heaving into the toilet.

Olga rapped gently at the door. "Miss Spencer?"

"Yes…"

Opening the door halfway, just enough to peek her head through, Olga took care not to enter the room. "I just wanted to tell you that supper will be ready in ten minutes, in case you need to get prepared. I will come back in a few minutes to take you to the dining area."

"Actually, can I stay here, if that's okay? I'm not really hungry. I don't feel very good. I'd rather stay in bed."

"Oh? Is something wrong? Can I get you anything?"

"No, no, thank you. I would just like to sleep."

"Very well. I'll advise Master Kayne you are feeling ill." Her words feigned concern, but her tone seemed anxious, if not vexed.

* * *

Olga hurried apprehensively to the master of the house. She was all too aware of his bad temper; you simply did *not* disobey Kayne Malkin. He had inherited his mother's wild Italian temper. Thankfully he also possessed her good humor, some of her kindness, and all of her charm. His father's heritage was more sinister. From him, Kayne got his eyes and good looks, his ability to manipulate, his need to dominate, and his very blurry sense of morality. Lev Malkin was of Russian origin, born in his homeland. He had left his country at a young age to immigrate to Canada with nothing but a picture of his family and the clothes on his back, as was most often the case in those days. He was a serious man, cold and calculating, even heartless when needed. Yet he was fair. He looked after his own, rewarded loyalty generously, and dealt with betrayal swiftly. He followed his own code of ethics and didn't make any exceptions or excuses, *for anyone.*

He soon found out how to put those traits to good use and rose quickly to high ranks in the Organization. They didn't have a name, though members referred to it as *the Family*. Lev met and impressed the right people. Though mostly composed of Russian expats, the Organization saw its members diversify over the years. Its core and highest positions, however, remained exclusively in the grasp of the *true blood*, Russian born, or descendants. In this strange new land, they flocked to each other and looked out for their own. When Lev met Olga, she had nowhere to go. He took her in and gave her a job. He was a fair employer, strict, demanding, but never inappropriate. That alone earned him her complicit silence.

When he met Kayne's mother a few years later, it was love at first sight. It took him over a year to convince the beautiful Italian student to give him the time of day, but eventually, he succeeded. He always got what he wanted. They had a whirlwind romance and were married within the year. A beautiful boy followed. How Olga loved that boy, that quiet boy, so determined, even at a young age.

Olga knew, she didn't delude herself about what type of man that boy grew up to be. But she loved him as a son. He was the only son she ever knew, and she was the only mother he'd ever have. She watched him grow up, shaped in his father's mold. Lev would have been proud. Kayne was ruthless, calculating, and cautious, never flashy. And yet he could still show kindness, and that by itself was a miracle. When his mother died, he was still a toddler, and Olga knew right then that she would never give up on him, that she would always love him, no matter what. If his father earned her loyalty to the Organization, the boy ensured her devotion to the Malkins.

He was already sitting at the dining table, head hanging back and eyes closed when Olga walked in.

"Master Kayne…"

He opened his eyes tiredly and his stare immediately darkened, sensing her nervousness. "Where is she?" he snapped.

"That's the thing… She says she is not feeling well… She asked to stay in her room to rest."

"Did she now…" He exhaled slowly, bemused, tapping the fork absentmindedly against the table.

"You technically haven't requested her presence, and she *did* ask if it was okay…"

He looked her straight in the eye, he knew where this was going. She was pleading her case to avoid her any reprisal. He had already known when he brought her to the house that Olga would take her under her wing. She had always been the nurturing type, and he loved her for it. He wasn't even sure he even knew what love was, but what he felt for Olga was probably the closest thing. He gave her an indulgent smile.

"Fine, let her be."

Olga smiled at him gratefully, approvingly, and excused herself.

He ate alone, reviewing the events of the past twenty-four hours in his head. He wondered when his mind changed. She wasn't the first pretty girl he delivered to the wolves. *Hell, he had done far worse.* What was different that time? He surprised himself; he took a big risk for her. Maxwell was not happy about the arrangement at all, but Maxwell was not to be worried about. Though he had gained considerable power and prestige in the Organization over the past years, Kayne still outranked him. Dimitri Drugov, the big boss and the only one above him, was the worrisome one. If he couldn't convince him, it would not end well, for anybody.

Why couldn't he just leave her in the room? She would have talked, he had no doubt. He thought back to her big teary eyes supplicating him quietly, desperately, and he could feel himself harden. No, he hadn't saved her out of mercy. He saved her because he wanted to be the one to make her cry and beg. He saved her so he could be the one to break her and have her in all the ways he wanted. But first she would have to surrender, willingly, and he would have to make her. He wondered if it was even possible at all considering the situation. Kayne had never personally held a woman captive before. But she was attracted to him. He smiled to himself as he replayed scenes from the club in his head, remembering her bashful ways, her nervousness. He would just need to buy himself some time, but he would have her, powerless and at his mercy.

* * *

It was past one in the morning when Laura woke up with her stomach growling. She got up and paced in her room a little, eyeing the door hesitantly. Her ankle was feeling a little better. She decided on conquering her quarters before venturing further in the house to appease her hunger. The closets and drawers were bursting with all types of clothing, from casual to formal wear, most with the tag still on and in her size. The vanity contained all the beauty supplies a girl could ever need. She wondered if they were purchased for her, but that couldn't be. He never meant to bring her back to his home. He was ready to walk out on her in that room. She wondered if she would still be alive if he had. Would she be mutilated? How much pain would she have endured? She shuddered at the thought. Her hands were still shaking when she finally reached for a pair of comfortable grey sweat pants and a cozy purple hoodie. Her eyes fell back to the clothes, and she wondered what fate had befallen the mysterious tenant.

Laura lingered behind the closed door for a few more minutes, gathering courage before she cautiously pulled the handle. It swayed open without a sound. The house seemed deserted, all the lights off. She breathed a little easier at the observation as she tiptoed down the hall, her eyes adjusting to the darkness. Passing a few closed doors on each side, she finally made her way back to the grand entrance area containing the double stairs leading to the ominous upper level. Anything beyond that point was stepping into new territory. But he said she could go as she pleased on the first floor, and so she reassured herself that she wasn't breaking any rules. The affirmation, along with her howling stomach, strengthened her resolve. She marched on, in her quest to find the much-sought-after kitchen, regretting for a moment turning down Olga's offer of giving her the tour. The truth was, she was just too terrified of running into him.

The kitchen was fortunately right behind the wall, to what she presumed was the western wing. It was huge, with the big marble island and countertops displayed in all the magazine kitchens. It had an open concept layout with a spacious dining area in the front. It was dimly lit by spotlights in the ceiling. She rejoiced in her small victory and headed to the double-door stainless fridge to reap the fruits of her conquest. It was packed full. She didn't want to move too many things and risk waking someone with the noise. Clumsy as she was, better safe than sorry. She opted for the first loaf of bread she saw, carefully taking out a slice from the package, grabbed a piece of ham, and thanked her luck when she found plates in the first cupboard she opened. As silently and swiftly as possible, she slapped the piece of ham on the bread and headed out of the kitchen, looking back to ensure she left no trace of her nighttime excursion.

The lights suddenly shone to their full brightness as she found herself face-to-face with *him*. Startled, she let out a scream, dropping the plate to the floor. It shattered at her feet, her nerves crumbling along with the porcelain plate.

"I'm so sorry, you startled me. I… I'm really sorry. I'll clean it up." She bent down to pick up the mess she just created.

"Leave it."

She looked up, terrified for an instant, and obeyed, remaining still with her eyes nervously traveling from his face to the floor. His expression was hard to read, though he didn't seem angry. He looked down at the mess, then back at her in one slow motion.

"So… of all the choices, you went for a ham sandwich?" he asked her, the corner of his mouth curving into a smile.

"I didn't want to make noise and disturb anyone…"

"Relax, have a seat." He pointed to one of the stools with a tilt of his head. "Let's see if we can fix you a little something." He walked leisurely to the fridge and opened the door to consider the available options.

She hurried to the stool, sitting with her back straight and her hands properly crossed on her lap. Good girls with proper manners were always treated better, she recalled her second-grade teacher saying. She was a good girl. She would always do what she's told, always looked to compromise and please, hoping her fate would be the better for it.

"So I see you're feeling better," he added without looking at her.

"Yes. Thank you," she managed sheepishly.

He stopped rummaging in the fridge, popping his head up to stare her up and down. "Hmm," he uttered, unconvinced.

She immediately lowered her eyes. She would have done anything to avoid his stare. Her heart was racing. She was terrified she had gotten herself into trouble getting caught in the kitchen when supposedly sick in bed. She would pull all the *thank yous* and *pleases* necessary and remain on her best behavior facing his suspicious good mood.

"How about chicken?"

"That's perfect, thank you."

He proceeded to pull a few things out, chicken, salad, some rice, then heated her meal in the microwave. "What do you want to drink?"

"I'm okay, thank you."

"I have Diet Pepsi… Don't all girls drink Diet Pepsi?" he tempted her, offering her an impish smile. She loved Diet Pepsi. It was, in all truth, the only nonalcoholic beverage she drank.

"Oh… Yes, thank you."

"Ice?"

She was confused by his considerate-host act but knew better than to let her guard down. "Hmm… yes, please. Thanks."

"Just like Olga. She makes me buy these things by the cases." He shook his head indulgently. He brought her the mouth-watering plate and put the glass down next to it.

"Here, bon appétit."

"Thank you."

He took a broom from the closet and cleaned her mess while she devoured her meal. When she was done, he took her plate. "Was it good?"

"Yes, thank you." She didn't think anyone's ever said those two words as often in this amount of time. She felt like a broken record, her vocabulary reduced to *thank you, please, I swear, I don't know*... the last part made her eyes water.

No one spoke for a while. She was tracing circles on the counter with the tip of her fingers. He was leaning back against the closet where he just put away the broom, openly watching her with an amused smile. She could feel his stare, but refused to look at him unless specifically told to do so. The felt silence was marked by the incessant ticking of the metal-plated clock on the opposing wall. Laura thought an eternity passed between each swipe of the pendulum, its ticking sound increasingly louder in her ears. Unable to bear the heavy silence any longer, she finally spoke up.

"May I be excused?" She felt pathetic, like a child requesting permission.

His smirk broke into a full grin. "Yes, Laura, you may be excused."

He had barely finished uttering the words and found her already up on her feet, rushing out of the kitchen. He watched her leave, almost breaking into a run. He'd let her run and hide, *for now.*

Day-2

That night Laura dreamt of Peter again, but not the Peter she remembered. He didn't resemble himself, though she knew it was him. They were alone, surrounded by darkness as violent winds roared all around them. Nothing but empty black space except for a bright light illuminating their faces, as if a spotlight shone on them, its source, invisible. Peter was calling out to her, his face distorted in pain as he was being sucked into some kind of black hole. She couldn't see the lower half of his body anymore. She was gripping his hand with both of hers and pulling with all her might. Her entire body hurt, but she refused to let go. She could feel him slipping away, his hold loosening. She kept screaming for him to hang on, but she could barely hear herself through the howling winds. He looked up at her, looking like himself again. He seemed serene, his face relaxed and his eyes kind. He smiled at her, tender and comforting, mouthed *sorry*, and let go. He was immediately sucked into nothingness. The force threw her back to the floor. She called for him, screamed his name, over and over again, breaking down into sobs.

Her tears were still fresh on her face when she woke up. She opened her eyes, long enough to confirm the nightmare was still real, and cried herself back to sleep.

The next morning, Laura rebuffed Olga's few initiatives to get her out of bed. Not even the appetizing trolley lured her out of the sheets. Olga graciously gave her space but emphasized that Master Kayne had specifically requested she join him for supper, which would be served at seven. Laura dismissed her concerned efforts. She had no intention of leaving her bedroom, come what may.

At six fifty sharp, just as the day before, Olga knocked at her door. When Laura didn't respond, she opened it partially, her alarm apparent at finding Laura the way she had left her.

"Miss Spencer… Please, you must get ready. You must eat something." She tried to reason with her.

Laura didn't even move a muscle.

"Master will not be happy…"

For some reason, the words made Laura snap, with a fury that betrayed her previous apathy. "Master will not be happy! Master will not be happy?" In one movement, she was up on her feet, almost screaming.

"Miss Spencer, please, I beg you, calm yourself…" Olga was beyond nervous.

"No! I will not calm myself! Do you even know why I'm here? Do you even know who you work for? Who you're asking me to have supper with?" Her voice faltered, as a lump rose in her throat.

"Oooh, Miss Spencer… please…" Olga appeared to be on the verge of tears, her eyes flicking behind her constantly. Her fears realized as loud steps approaching echoed throughout. While Olga closed her eyes, Laura kept hers wide open, her posture firm and ready for battle.

"What's with all the commotion?" Kayne slammed the door open, passing Olga, and in a few steps, he faced Laura.

"Is there a problem, Laura?" His voice was chillingly calm.

"No, Master Kayne, no problem. I was just about to get Miss Spencer ready…" Olga threw to his back.

He ignored her. His eyes were burning into Laura, daring her to defy him. She gulped but held his stare. She'd take the bait, gladly.

"I would prefer staying in my room." Her voice was just as calm, though her heart beat so frantically in her chest, she feared it might explode. She knew it was madness, but she couldn't back out now, and she was in no mood to spend another supper as his obedient pet.

"You would *prefer* staying in your room?" he hissed. He then sneered at her, a wicked gleam in his eyes as he lifted a hand to her face. She flinched, but he gently brushed her cheek with the back of his hand. "And here I was thinking we were off to such a good start," he said mockingly.

With no other warning, he grabbed her by the arm and dragged her forcefully out of the room as Olga watched silently, looking miserable, her head bowed. He dragged her down the hallway and through a small room in the western wing. He only stopped when they reached a door at the back of the room. Laura had maintained her composure until that moment, until he opened the door to reveal the downward spiral staircase it led to. Something about those stairs, the black iron ramp, the steep steps too close to one another, the damp air that reached her nostrils, raised every hair on her skin.

"Where are you taking me?" she breathed, fear stricken.

He looked her over very briefly, his eyes cold as ice. "You'll see."

As they reached the sublevel, he pushed her to the left, stopping in front of a metallic door with a keypad on the side. He pushed a few buttons, and the door opened, revealing a concrete holding cell. It was tiny. There was a toilet, one roll of toilet paper sitting at the top, a sink, and one plastic cup. There wasn't even a dirty mattress on the floor. He offered her a sinister smile as he urged her inside with his typical *ladies first* gesture, the same one he used when he lured her in the interrogation room.

Laura blanched, beginning to shake her head violently. "No... no... Please... no, please..."

Seeing his stoic face, she grabbed his shirt in anguish. "Please, you don't understand... anything, but not this, please, I'm sorry, I'm sorry, please..."

"It's a little late for apologies, Laura," he said coolly as he firmly removed her hands off him.

"No... Please... you don't understand... please... not the cage, not the cage! I'll do anything!"

Her desperate pleas fell on deaf ears. His eyes were cold as ever, as he pushed her in and locked the door.

* * *

He could hear relentless banging and desperate sobs as he walked away. He had never utilized the cell in that fashion. Mainly, he'd used it for its intended purpose, bringing in countless men for interrogation and holding them prisoner when necessary. A few times, he had even locked away some of his submissives as punishment when they misbehaved. It was all part of the game though. Never had he forced a woman in against her will, let alone one he was intent on seducing. He shook his head, all too aware of how detrimental to his cause his action had just been.

He couldn't help it, he was still livid. He would not stand for such behavior. She had to pay for her impudence. However, he did not expect such a violent reaction. Did she just call it a *cage*? *Interesting...* He didn't want to traumatize her, but he couldn't soften up. Empty threats were death. She had to learn; her actions would have consequences. Tonight had not gone according to his plans, and that alone was a very strong irritant. He did like her spirit though. He hadn't thought she had it in her. He smiled to himself. The perfect combination of pride and submissiveness.

* * *

Laura banged on the doors until her knuckles bled, screamed until her lips moved, but emitted no more sound. She let herself fall to the ground, wrapped her arms around her knees, and rocked herself, just as she had when she was a little girl. She cried and cried, pleaded and begged, but Peter couldn't let her out of the cage this time. She called out to him nonetheless. Peter had always come and saved her. Regardless of the beatings that followed, he would find a way, and the door would magically open after she could hear her father's drunken snores. Peter would crouch next to the open door holding up the key, grinning from ear to ear. They would chuckle silently, with their hands covering their mouths. It was a game.

She didn't know how long she'd been there; she'd never been in the cage for so long. She was numb, cradling herself in the corner, her fingers gliding over the concrete wall forming random patterns. She wondered where he was. She thought back to the interrogation room and, with a manic twinkle in her eye, chuckled quietly to herself, her hands covering her mouth, just as she had as a kid with him. The game was still on, still outwitting, outrunning the villain. By this time, Peter would be long gone. He never stayed in one place for more than two weeks. She had been expecting a postcard the very next day. But what if this time he had, what if they found him? With only time on her hands, her thoughts quickly turned against her, swaying back and forth from arrogant optimism to utter despair.

Day-3

Olga wouldn't let up; she had pleaded the girl's case incessantly since the previous night.

"But she is just a terrified little girl… what did you expect?"

"No, Olga, she is a twenty-three-year-old adult," Kayne said, refusing to yield.

"Exactly. Twenty-three, do you even remember how you were like at that age?" She made her point.

He let out a long sigh. "Did you check up on her?"

"Of course I did. I brought her a meal at two, just as you asked. Soup and bread." Her voice was polite, though barely masking her disapproval, if not blatant hostility.

"Did she eat?"

"No, Master Kayne. She hasn't moved from the corner since last night. She didn't look well."

"What do you mean?" The hint of concern in his voice wasn't lost on Olga, an emotion he tried to pass off for irritation.

"She seemed… I don't know… disconnected… like she wasn't there. She was very pale. She hasn't eaten in two days…"

"And whose fault is that?"

The scowl she threw him hit its mark. His eyes softened. "All right… what time is it?"

"It's almost six."

He sighed. Without another word, he got up from the dining table and made his way down to the holding cell.

Olga hadn't exaggerated as he suspected. The girl looked pitiful, scooped up in the corner, with her head resting on her knees and her arms hugging her legs. He had a sudden impulse to pick her up and hold her in his arms, which he dismissed just as suddenly. With his voice low, his tone measured, he finally spoke to her. "Supper will be served at seven. I will expect your company."

He left right after, leaving the door wide open behind him. Olga appeared not long after, rushing to Laura's side. "Oh, Miss Spencer..." She shook her head sadly. "Here, let me help you."

She helped her to her feet, gently up the stairs, and into her room. She smiled compassionately to her, a kind heartbroken smile. Laura obediently sat as Olga fixed her hair, picked her clothes, and helped her into a nice dress with a matching cardigan. She felt like a doll but didn't mind. She just went through the motions as an unaffected spectator. She did think a shower would have been in order, but Olga didn't bring it up, so she let it be. She barely had the strength to form cohesive thoughts, let alone full-on sentences.

At five to seven, Olga clasped her hands. "Well, we should get you to the dining room. You look beautiful, Miss Spencer."

Laura nodded, offering a faint smile. She followed Olga down the corridor into the dining area. He was already sitting at the table. He stared her up and down, his expression unreadable.

"Glad you could finally make it..." he said after a while, his eyes remaining on her, as a cryptic smile formed on his lips.

Laura was feeling weak and light-headed. She smiled back at him, a genuine smile, devoid of malice or sarcasm. It was the kind of smile good-hearted people offered strangers, sweet and impersonal at the same time.

Her smile both surprised and concerned him. He leaned forward in his chair, as if physically trying to get closer to her, sensing a danger. He barely finished the thought, when he saw her eyes slowly roll backward, her muscles going limp. In an instant he was at her side, catching her as her frail body went slack in his arms.

He carried her to the couch in the adjacent living room, calling out for Olga. He laid her down gently, fluffing the pillow Olga had brought along with the covers. He tucked her in, took a seat on the La-Z-Boy next to her, and watched her sleep.

She looked peaceful. He wondered if she was dreaming. He had to restrain himself from touching her, not in a sexual way. He just wanted to caress her face, brush away the strands of hair causing the little beads of sweat slowly dripping to her lips. She was beautiful when she looked serene, she was beautiful when she looked sad. She was striking when she was furious. He had gotten a taste the night before. Something told him there would be many more of those to come. A devilish grin formed on his lips. His mood shifted at the thought; long gone were the sweet caresses he yearned for a few moments ago. But his fantasies were wasted on an unconscious body, as enticing as that body was. He had never been the type to force himself on a woman. He never had, not out of a misplaced sense of morality; it was just not his thing. Granted, he understood, felt, the exhilaration that came with a beautiful woman's tears, the terror in her eyes at the realization of her powerlessness, despite her vain efforts to resist. But the similarities ended there. To overpower a woman physically was no great task, even less so if she was unconscious; what a bore that would be. They say rape is about power. The truth was all sex is about power. The power he sought was just of a different nature. It was a battle of the mind, of the soul, where his ecstasy could only be found at the deliberate and complete surrender of the object of his desire. Her tears would taste sweeter as he pushed her toward orgasm, the horror in her eyes not directed at him, but at her body's reaction to him. Her powerlessness, only understood after a long battle lost within herself.

* * *

Laura awoke sometime after. She opened her eyes, looking around silently, taking in her new environment. She was on a comfortable couch. The lights were dimmed, but she could make out a large rectangular table with a glass top just in front of her and a big screen TV hanging on the wall surrounded by the usual yet imposing TV stand. She didn't venture to move her head to check out the rest of the room. She had a splitting headache and her limbs refused to move, as if weighing a ton each.

He had noticed her slight movement. He was still sitting on the La-Z-Boy next to her, a laptop in his lap, illuminating his face.

"Well, good morning, Sleeping Beauty," he greeted her in a playful tone. His stare, however, was still reproachful.

She nudged her head barely an inch to see him and instantly brought her hand to her forehead, a cry of pain escaping her lips.

"Don't move." He slowly put the computer down on the table, throwing her another look before he disappeared. He returned with a glass of water and two pills, which he offered her, crouching on the floor by her side. "Take this."

"What is it?" she whispered apprehensively.

"Cyanide."

Her eyes instantly shot up to meet his.

He rolled his eyes, smiling. "It's aspirin, Laura."

She hesitated for a second, then reached her hand out. He watched her swallow her pills, like a parent would to a rebellious child. Satisfied, he disappeared again. He came back a few minutes later with a hot bowl of soup and some crackers.

"Eat this, it'll help."

She pulled herself up, resting on her elbows, eyeing the platter in front of her suspiciously. She knew she was famished but had no appetite, and a part of her didn't want to eat simply because he had said to.

"If you want to defy me, Laura, at least make it worth your while," he said as if reading her mind, while he stood over her with his arms crossed casually, an amused smile on his face. Then in a commanding tone, he added, "Eat."

Begrudgingly, she brought herself to a sitting position and obeyed. It did make her feel better, the headache faded, and her strength returned slowly. When she was almost done, he returned to claim his seat. With a veiled expression, looking in her eyes, he softly said, "Good girl."

Her stomach turned at the words, at the way they were said, and she blushed. Never once, since that night at the club, had she thought of him as anything but a monster, but he was also a man, she would do well to remember. *Very much a man.* She could feel his predatory eyes linger on her body, and she shifted in her seat uncomfortably. He went back to his laptop and didn't even look in her direction after that. She remained seated, quiet, too afraid to remind him of her presence, desperate to get back to her room, wondering if that was even an option.

At last, she cleared her throat, her voice tentative. "May I… Would it… be okay… if I go back to my room?"

He stopped typing to look at her. "I understand you don't leave your room in the day?"

She didn't answer.

He sighed. "Have Olga give you the tour tomorrow, okay?"

"Yes… sir." The word just slipped past her lips. She wasn't sure why she called him that, but calling him by his name felt even weirder. *Master Kayne* wasn't even an option.

He lifted his brow, his expression slightly surprised, however pleased. He stared at her pensively then nodded. "Good night, Laura."

Day-4

Laura lay awake for a long time in her bed, tossing and turning, his face imprinted on her mind. She had the weirdest nightmare. She was running desperately in a labyrinth made of stone, and the Secret Service-looking men were hunting her down. She was carrying a torch, running randomly down unknown paths until she turned into a dead end. He was already there, as if expecting her, dressed in black and looking strikingly devilish. He smiled seductively at her and crooked his finger, beckoning her to come to him. She wanted to turn back; she stumbled backward before noticing the security men had caught on and blocked the way behind her. Her eyes rounded, realizing too late she was already walking to meet him, slowly but surely, as if hypnotized. He pulled an arm out to her and brought her to him, enveloping her with his whole body. She leaned into him, into the warmth of his embrace, a sense of safety washing over her.

Everything vanished around them, and it made her giggle. They were the only two people left in the world. The idea was strangely comforting. She looked up and smiled at him. He smiled back, lowered his face to hers, and huskily whispered in her ear, "Everything is going to be all right." Her voice throaty, she obediently replied, "Yes, Master."

She closed her eyes as he pulled her even closer, holding her so tightly in his arms she couldn't move. He started kissing down her neck, his hands caressing her arms, then lightly trailing down her back. She wanted to tell him something, tried to open her eyes but couldn't. She couldn't move a muscle, could only feel his hands all over her body, everywhere at the same time, as if he had a thousand of them, just like the mythical Greek giants. Panic took hold of her, and yet every sensation was heightened, every caress echoed throughout her body, and she didn't know if she wanted it to end.

She woke up panting, sweaty, and distraught. And much to her dismay, wet, in places she shouldn't be. She tried not to analyze what it meant, just blocked it out completely. She couldn't catch any shut-eye for the rest of the night, staring out the window until the sun crept up.

When Olga came in to serve her breakfast, she seemed pleasantly surprised to see her sitting up in bed. "Good morning, Miss Spencer, you're up early this morning. I hope you feel better. You gave us quite a scare last night."

She wondered why Olga would bring her breakfast if she thought she was asleep. Laura thought back to the previous night, to why she was up so early and blushed. She questioned Olga's choice of the word "us". Was she expected to believe *he* worried for her well-being?

"Well, if you're up to it, I can come back after you've finished your breakfast and give you the tour of the house?"

"Yes, thank you, Olga," Laura answered, attempting a feeble smile.

Olga smiled back at her, visibly pleased.

She returned about half an hour later. Laura was dressed and ready and actually quite anxious to leave her bedroom, eyeing the traitorous bed resentfully. In fact, for the first time since her arrival, she thought of escape. She knew it would be near impossible and shivered at the consequences she would face in the event of a failed attempt. Even if she succeeded, where would she go? They surely wouldn't have trouble tracking her down. She didn't have Peter's skill, knowledge, or paranoia to survive so long on the run. Still, she needed to maintain the hope that she would one day leave this house, but first she had to know her enemy.

The house looked different in the midday light. She noticed the security men roaming outside the house; she tensed, glad not to run into any of them inside. She followed Olga around quietly in and out of every room. There was a cozy small room in the eastern wing with a fluffy red couch, a small table, a desk, and a big TV. There were plants by the wall near the window. She immediately decided to claim it. The rest of the tour was uneventful, many rooms, bedrooms, more media/living rooms, although they looked more modern than *hers*. There was even a ballroom. *Did people even throw balls nowadays?* As they didn't run into anyone else, Laura wondered if Olga did everything alone. Olga pointed out that a cleaning crew came by weekly and advised Laura it was best to ignore them, and they would do the same. In any case, they were Russian and didn't speak English or French.

In the western wing, Olga opened French double doors to a grandiose library. Endless books from ground to the ceiling filled every wall. Crafted within the high ceiling was a big glass dome made of churchlike stained glass, making the sunlight shine in vibrant hues. The bookshelves were made of intricately carved wood. Inner marble stairs circled around to the higher level with a finely sculpted ramp. It truly was breathtaking. Laura loved books, more than anything else in the world. She loved the escape they offered, the teachings they generously imparted, and most of all, she loved the promise each book held of a unique journey.

She breathed "wow" as she rushed into the room, looking around excitedly. For a moment, she forgot where she was. She practically ran to the nearest row of books and started reading the titles, moving excitedly from one end of a shelf to the other. The books were classified by language. Most were in English, but there was an imposing section in Russian, Italian, and a good few in French. She recognized a few French classics, as she was fluent in French herself, being a Quebec native.

She felt exhilarated and, for the first time in a long time, safe, amid old friends and wondrous suitors. She smiled as she languidly caressed the covers of beloved novels, elated with each title she recognized, past lovers she still cherished, Salinger, Steinbeck, Hugo, Sartre… There was even her first love, Emily Brontë's *Wuthering Heights*. Between the Brontë sisters, she was definitely *Team Emily*. This was not a man's library, she noted. A woman surely contributed to the inventory. She was suddenly flooded with the image of *her*, Kayne's girlfriend, tall, breathtakingly beautiful, elegant, cultivated, graceful… A girl he might have loved, who had lived here, in her room, and whose unworn clothes Laura had now inherited. The idea bothered her. She wasn't sure why, and she quickly dismissed it. She wouldn't let anything taint this magical moment. Who knew when would be the next, if ever.

The moment the thought entered her mind, Laura went on a mission to find it, *her* book, her greatest love, her one true love. The book that had saved her life many years ago when she was just a teenager, after Peter had left, and she was all alone in the world. She had to know if she'd find it there, Hermann Hesse's *Steppenwolf*. She didn't think she would find it. It wasn't one of those famous cliché books you mentioned in the middle of a conversation to look smart. It was more of a cult-following kind of book. It had actually been the black sheep of the author, who had known glory through his other novels, but met heavy backlash over this one due to widespread misinterpretation.

Steppenwolf was originally written in German, and seeing there was no such section, she looked for the English translation she had read herself. It was there. Her heart thumping, she retrieved the worn-out edition and held it close to her chest. Somehow this discovery had a huge impact on her. Someone, at some point, who lived in this very same house, bought it, read it, and liked it enough to leave wear-and-tear scars. That sole discovery gave humanity to this place. If someone like this could live in this house, maybe, just maybe, she could survive it.

Slowly, she landed back on earth and found that Olga hadn't moved from the doorframe, letting her have her moment, though sharing in her joy. Slightly embarrassed, she pointed to the book. "I'm so sorry… May I?"

"Of course, Miss Spencer, please go ahead."

"Thank you." For the first time, she said it out of gratitude.

After the tour of the house was complete, Olga advised Laura that supper would be ready at seven, as always, and asked if she would like to be fetched or meet Master Kayne directly in the dining area. "Now that you know how to go about the house," she added with a conspiring smile. As hard as she fought it, Laura's resistance to this kind woman chipped away, little by little.

Laura was a nervous wreck as dinnertime approached. She dreaded the thought of spending an entire evening alone with him. One part, intrigued by her recent discoveries, wanted to know more about her captor, and yet another part, all too aware of her nighttime disgrace, recoiled in horror at the prospect of his stares, the blushing that would incur, and the possibility that he could read her mind. But above all else, it was the *cage*, or the threat of it, that had her show up at seven on the dot to meet him. She chose to wear jeans with the loose-fitting purple hoodie, hoping to hide her femininity. Closets full of clothes were wasted on Laura.

He checked her out, restraining a smile. "Good evening, Laura."

"Good evening," she responded, her voice guarded.

"Take a seat." He pointed to the chair facing him. She obeyed. "Olga tells me you finally ventured out of your room."

"Yes..."

When he realized she would say no more, he leaned back in his chair, considering her. "No more 'sir' today?" he taunted her, a cunning smile on his face.

She turned bright red, cursing herself and her stupid nightmare. "Do you want me to call you that?" Her voice quivered, as she kept her eyes on the floor.

His smile widened at witnessing her discomfort, his eyes glowing with wickedness. He ignored her question. "Shall we eat?"

He served them generous portions of salmon and fresh garden salad. It was very simple and yet delicious. They ate quietly, her nerves thankful for the temporary respite. Every now and then, he looked at her, a sly smile on his face, causing her to look down every time. They kept up the dance the entire meal. When they finished eating, he reinitiated the conversation.

"So, tell me about yourself."

"What do you want to know?"

"*Everything.*" He put emphasis on the word in a mock threat.

"I don't know… I don't know what to tell you." She felt put on the spot, she hated that feeling. It made her nervous, even more so now. It was too broad, she had no idea how to answer him. She always did badly with too many options, did even worse under pressure. She had no fight-or-flight response, only *freeze.*

He sighed, throwing her an impatient stare.

"Okay… hmm… I was born here in Montreal. I graduated from Concordia, hmm… I don't know… I like soft music and long walks on the beach…" She threw him a sarcastic look.

He looked taken aback for an instant, then frowned with understanding.

Damn, he was upset. She often fell back on humor when uncomfortable or nervous and got in trouble for it. She didn't want to this time. "Sorry… it was just a joke…" she added sheepishly.

"I don't care about school and jobs. What do you like? … *Besides* soft music and long walks on the beach," he answered, the corner of his lips curling up.

A sound, somewhere between a chuckle and a sigh of relief, escaped her lips. "Well, reading. I love reading… and movies."

"What kind?"

"Books or movies?"

"Both."

"I don't know… very different types… Books, mostly fiction. I like mystery novels, fantasy, and coming-of-age stories, I guess. It's hard to say… Do you like reading?"

"Sometimes."

"Your library is amazing…" she said in wonder. "Do you speak all those languages?"

He hesitated before answering, as if realizing the conversation was turning on him, but deeming it harmless, he allowed it.

"My Italian is very basic. But I speak Russian and French fluently." He could sense the questions burning at the tip of her tongue and smiled indulgently, amused. "Go ahead, ask me what you want to ask."

Her brows furrowed. Of all the questions she was dying to ask, she was not sure which one to pick. She feared bringing up her brother would deteriorate into an interrogation, and her bleak vision of what lay in store for her warned against confirming her worst fears. She opted for safe, harmless chitchat.

"Are you Russian?"

"My father was. I was born here."

"Oh, I see."

"Any other question?" he added, an impish smile plastered on his face.

"Yes… many…" she said softly, more for her own benefit.

He smirked. "Well… you get one more."

"Okay… Did you… have it built? The library I mean."

"No. It was my mother's," he answered harshly, his eyes darkening.

She thought it was a safe topic, but she had thought wrong. She squirmed in her seat a little at his sudden change in mood. She couldn't help acknowledge, however, the smallest yet undeniably present relief she felt at the destruction of the pseudo-perfect girlfriend she had conjured earlier.

He was staring at her with an unreadable expression by the time she looked back at him.

"What about boyfriends? Do you have one?"

The question caught her off guard, and she just shook her head in response.

He smiled at her, pleased with her answer. "But you've had boyfriends before…"

"Yes, of course."

"How many?"

Her eyes widened in surprise, clearly uncomfortable with the turn the conversation was taking. "Two."

"Just two?"

"Well… yes… they were long-term kinda relationships…"

"Tell me about them."

"Okay…" Her discomfort was palpable. "I met Jarred in school when I was sixteen. We were high school sweethearts. We were together for two years, then he went off to college, and we broke it off." She shrugged her shoulders.

"Who broke it off?"

"It was mutual."

"It's never mutual. Who made the decision?"

She took a deep breath. "I did."

"Why?"

"I don't know, we were growing apart… He was a really nice guy. I just… we just grew apart."

"And the other?"

"Eric?" Her jaw tensed.

He nodded.

"Eric too was a nice guy," she responded mechanically, her eyes darting about the room.

"So you like nice guys," he remarked unconvinced, barely restraining a smirk.

"Well… yes… that's pretty normal," she replied defensively.

"You'd be surprised…" he purred, his eyes dark, his voice silky, then added in a commanding tone, "Go on, and what happened with *Eric*?"

"I met him in college. We were together for three years. It didn't work out." She stuck to the facts, steering clear of the painful emotions associated with his memory.

"Why didn't it work out?" he asked, intrigued by the distress in her eyes, and strangely, aggravated that another was the cause.

She took a long breath, closing her eyes, as if prepping herself. "He proposed."

His brows shut up in surprise. "And so you broke up with him? Maybe she doesn't like the nice guys so much after all..." he teased.

"No. It wasn't like that... I didn't want to break up," she confessed, fiddling nervously with her fingers.

His silent stare made it clear further information was required.

"He wanted children." Her voice cracked.

"And you didn't?"

"No... I couldn't... I can't... have children." She finally looked up at him, her shoulders slumped in defeat.

She expected him to badger her further, to laugh, to be cruel, but he remained silent, staring at her intently.

No one ever knew, not even Eric. She had wanted to tell him, but a voice inside of her warned her against it. He would have stayed. And she would have hated herself for making him give up his dream, and he would have resented her just as much for it. So she remained quiet when he called her cold and heartless, held back her tears as he threw the ring to the floor, and stormed off, slamming the door on his way out. She watched him leave, crying by herself in the one-bedroom studio. She picked up the gold band containing the tiniest diamond possible and wept. It had taken him months to save up for it. It had taken her one word to break its magic.

Only Peter ever knew. Always, Peter. It was him who made the appointment and sat by her side at the doctor's office. She was only fifteen, and her periods had failed to start. Blurry memories of that day, long tucked away in the recesses of her mind, resurfaced by pieces. A faceless white coat, white hair, white walls. Words like primary amenorrhea, congenital defect, failure of the ovary to receive or maintain eggs... They didn't mean anything to her then. If anything, she remembered feeling relieved at never having to go through painful menstrual cramps as so many of the girls her age did.

She recalled Peter's shattered face. His voice wanting to be comforting barely masked the pain. "Oh, Laura, I'm sorry, I'm so sorry..." he kept repeating, as if he was the cause of it.

She couldn't understand his sorrow. It would be years later, clutching at an engagement ring from the man who had just walked out of her life, that she understood the magnitude of it.

Kayne was looking at her. She seemed far away, as if she had forgotten about him. Usually, it would have aggravated him, and yet he felt like a privileged insider, looking in through the hourglass.

"You never told anyone?" he asked, a softness creeping in his voice.

She slowly shook her head in response.

For an instant, he felt for her, wanted to comfort her. Watching her head bent sideways, the errand strand of hair covering her face, he almost reached over.

"Have you been with anyone else since?" he inquired, seemingly unaffected.

She looked up, peeking through heavy lids. "What do you mean?"

"Casual dates, one-night stands… a fuck friend maybe?" he asked, playful wickedness back in his eyes.

"No." She shook her head vehemently.

"Such a good girl."

She blushed. "Do you… have a girlfriend?" she asked tentatively, trying to divert the attention away from herself.

He responded with a sardonic laugh, "No, Laura. In case you missed it, I'm not really the relationship type."

"Oh… I just thought… with the bedroom you set me in… and the clothes and all…"

"The clothes were bought for you. The room was my mother's. Does that satisfy your little curiosity?" he huffed impatiently.

It wasn't fair. He badgered her into answering all these personal questions, forcing her to scratch old wounds, not yet fully healed. Yet she noticed his mood change coincided with the mention of his mother. She would try to steer clear of that topic, though she knew her curiosity would eventually get the best of her. But then another thought came to her mind, and her face fell. He bought the clothes for her... That could only mean he had never meant to let her go. Her fate was sealed before she even went into that room, no matter what she would have said.

He noticed immediately, still in his tempestuous mood, and asked, "What's wrong?"

Her voice was strangled. She swallowed before she finally looked up to meet his gaze. "You knew all along... from the first night, even before you brought me in that room... you knew you would bring me back here, you even had clothes brought... You said if I cooperated I could leave... You... lied."

His eyes narrowed in quiet fury; his voice was calm, dripping with venom. "And you've come to this conclusion because... I was kind enough to make sure you'd be comfortable? If I remember correctly, what I promised was that you would get out alive, which you have. The *clothes* were brought to your room *after* I made the call. Don't you think I have the resources to get you a few pieces of clothing? I have contacts everywhere, Laura. And that's not a lie either. Maybe you should remember that in case you get other brilliant ideas," he hissed. "Never. Call me. A liar."

She was shaking with fear by the time he finished speaking. Before he even knew it, she dropped to his feet, her hands grabbing his jeans at the knees, sobbing erratically.

"Please, please, forgive me, I made a mistake... I didn't think you had it done the same morning. Stores are closed at this time... and there was just so much stuff... Please forgive me... I don't want to go to the cage again. Please..."

He felt confused, conflicted. Part of him still seethed with anger, wanted to leave her on the floor, drag her by her hair, and punish her for her careless words. The other part, even stronger than before, wanted to comfort and reassure her. Carry her in his arms and hold her until he could feel her tears fade away against his chest, and know he was the cause of it all, her tears and their death.

He was thrown off by his own reaction, by the emotion she stirred in him. His comfort always came as a reward well earned. Even then, given only so he could further savor the fruits of his victory and bask in the euphoria reached through absolute control. Genuine compassion was a foreign concept to him, and most likely, a major factor in his success in the Organization. It was not a desired trait in his world. He ground his teeth irritated at his passing weakness and quickly collected himself. He grabbed her chin between his fingers and raised her head to face his. When he spoke to her, his voice reflected the iciness in his stare. She could have never suspected the thoughts that ran through his mind.

"You will mind what you say and how you say it. Anything you do or say has consequences. Do we have an understanding?"

"Yes… sir…" she sniffled.

His eyes gleamed with an indiscernible emotion, between annoyance and excitement at the sound of the word, which came to her lips more naturally this time. He nodded his head. "Go to your room… before I change my mind."

* * *

He watched her as she made her exit, much like the first night, rushing to leave his side. He brought his hands up and rubbed his face, letting out a long sigh. He thought back to that first night. *What had he gotten himself into?* The girl was a mystery. He wanted to know so much more about her, he'd gotten some information tonight. Most, he could have guessed. So she was infertile, that he did not expect. He wondered if it was that fact alone that troubled her so or the loss of *Eric* because of it. Well, she wouldn't have to worry about that with him, he thought with an ironic smile. The situation suited him just fine. He'd never wanted children… or a wife for that matter. What he wanted from her, he wouldn't get by offering her a ring. She had no idea what he had in store for her, he thought, closing his eyes with devilish delight.

Clearly, she wasn't very experienced. He wasn't surprised she'd only been with the two boyfriends she mentioned. He wondered if she'd ever had an orgasm in her life, probably not with the nice guys she thought she liked so much. She definitely had a submissive streak, calling him "sir" twice, without his asking her to. The last time, in a manipulative effort to pacify him, which slightly annoyed him, but worked. Didn't it only speak to her submissive nature that she instinctively knew what to say to appease him? How she literally fell to his feet, appealing to his mercy? She craved the kind of power and control that didn't come from nice guys. It was written all over her. He sensed it in her from that first night at the club as she clumsily tried to flirt with him. It was quite endearing really.

She was a submissive, but she wasn't aware of it yet. He reveled in all the promises that came with this particular combination. A self-proclaimed submissive lost her appeal to him. He'd usually leave his whores, bored to tears, by the time they were all but too eager to please. *How delicious was the path to depravity, how he would love to show her.*

But there were other things that intrigued him about her, for one, her terror with the *cage*, as she called it. He guessed she was abused, but how? By whom? Clearly not by her boyfriends, or her brother. Was it her father perhaps? He had to know. He'd have to learn everything, from her deepest fears to her darkest desires, and only then, he could use them to his advantage.

Day-5

It was barely one in the afternoon when Olga rapped at Laura's door. Laura had decided to stay in her room after the previous night's incident.

"Sorry to disturb you, Miss Spencer, Master Kayne would like you to meet him in the living room."

Laura's heart skipped a beat, then pounded frantically in her chest. She had hoped against hope the incident would be forgotten.

"Oh? Did he say why?"

"No, he simply asked me to fetch you. He's waiting for you."

"Like now? … *NOW* now?" Her tone raised a few octaves, as panic slowly crept throughout her entire being.

"Yes, Miss Spencer."

"Okay…"

Laura obediently followed Olga into the living room to find Kayne sitting on the couch she had fallen asleep on, his legs open wide, and his head thrown back. He was smoking a cigarette. His expression was impervious as he motioned for her to sit down, his hand pointing somewhere between the available space on the couch and the adjacent La-Z-Boy. She chose the La-Z-Boy. He didn't speak to her right away as she sat nervously at the edge of her seat, playing with a loose strand in her jeans. He took his time, slowly inhaling and exhaling his last few puffs, before putting out his cigarette. Only then did he venture to speak to her.

"Can I get you anything to drink?"

She cleared her throat. Her mouth was dry from her faltering nerves. "A glass of water?"

He nodded, getting up to get it for her, and grabbed himself a beer.

He sighed, his expression grave. He didn't beat around the bush. "Laura, I have to ask you something."

"Okay…" She had initially feared he changed his mind regarding the consequences to last night's incident, but now she understood; it was about Peter. For how much longer did she hope to dodge further interrogation?

"Were you ever abused?"

"*What?*" Of all directions this conversation could have taken, she did not expect this.

"Answer me." His voice was quiet, his muscles tense.

"I don't understand… like… *sexually*?" She hated having to say the word, any word containing those three letters, in front of him.

"Have you?"

"No!" Her answer was unequivocal.

He closed his eyes as relief washed over him. He hadn't realized his hands were in fists so tight the blood had drained from them and wondered what made him feel so strongly about the issue. Granted, sex victims weren't ideal lovers considering his peculiar taste, *too many triggers*. He had neither the patience nor the mildest inclination to even hope to make it work if that had been the case. But it was more than that. Sheer rage blinded him at the thought of her being abused. The emotion was too strong to be explained away by his hope for sexual compatibility. Had she said yes, had she given a name, that name would have been carved on a tombstone not long after. He was surprised at how fast he had already claimed her as his. He was the possessive type, had never shared his whores with other men. However, even more than bare possessiveness, he recognized a strange feeling, one he hadn't often felt: protectiveness. This girl had strange effects on him indeed. He pressed on.

"Were you ever abused any other way?"

"What do you mean?" she stuttered, utterly confused with his line of questioning. She couldn't understand his reasons for asking such questions. Did he intend to sexually abuse her himself?

“Mistreated… Physically? Emotionally? Perhaps… locked in a *cage*?” He put emphasis on the last word. As expected, her face instantly paled.

“Yes.” Her lips thinned, her face down, she breathed the word.

“Your father?” he guessed.

Her eyes shot up, round with surprise.

It wasn’t such a difficult assumption to make from what she had told him. “Did he ever lay his hands on you?”

“Why are you asking me all this?” she asked, distraught, her voice barely above a whisper.

“Answer my question, Laura,” he warned.

“I just don’t understand—”

“I didn’t ask you to understand,” he interrupted her sharply.

She was beginning to know his moods, know how far she could push before he would push back, and this was it. “No, he never laid his hands on me.”

He nodded. “But he locked you… in a cage?”

“Yes.”

“How long did this go on for?”

“The cage?” Her face twisted with repulsion as she uttered the word. “I don’t know, years… Since I was a child. I don’t remember exactly when… for as long as I can remember.” Her voice was detached, robotic.

He could feel her retreat somewhere deep within herself. “What about your mother?”

“She wasn’t around.”

“Tell me about it.”

She let out a long sigh. “My father was a drunk, my mother too I suspect, but she left when I was still a baby. We lived in a dump. Peter…” Her voice wavered at his name. She glanced back at Kayne uncertainly, as if the enunciation of his name alone would suddenly remind him of why she was there, that he would jump on her at the realization and begin torturing her for further information.

When he didn't react, she continued. "Peter said that Dad wasn't so bad when my mother was around. He was still a drunk then... but I don't think he put me in the cage when she was there. I mean, she wouldn't have let him put her baby in the cage..." she said uncertainly, as if trying to convince herself. She looked up at him for approval, for reassurance in her shaky faith.

He didn't nod. Instead, he slid the cigarette pack over to her end of the table. Laura gladly took one. She hadn't had any since she got to the house. She hadn't even thought about it, but in this moment she wanted nothing more in the world. He held up the lighter but didn't hand it to her, forcing her to lean in close to reach the flame, closing her hand right above his to catch it, feeling his warmth.

"Go on," he said finally, after giving her the time to enjoy a few puffs.

"Not much to say. Dad would get drunk every day almost, but if you caught him sober, he was actually sweet. He used to buy me this chocolate cake I liked that they only sold in a shop at the other side of town. We didn't have a car, so he'd walk all the way there just to get it for me." She smiled tenderly at the memory, then quickly shook it off. "But most of the time, he was just upset with me. The worst time was when I got suspended." She smiled grimly. "I got in a fight with this girl at school who kept picking on me. I think it was the longest time I spent in the cage. He had to miss work and everything to stay home with me." She let out a bitter laugh. "It was just a stupid dog crate, you know? One of those big plastic ones for large-size breeds..." Her voice broke, the wound still fresh, her eyes gleaming with raw hurt.

"He had a lock on it, and he always kept the key on him. Peter would always find a way though. I just had to wait. I'd count up as high as I could, and then Peter would come and sneak me out when Dad passed out. It was the only time he'd get in trouble, because of me, *for* me. Dad always beat him afterward. You know, it's funny, we never once thought of sneaking me back in before he'd wake up… We were just kids I guess…" She shrugged her shoulders.

He watched her, fascinated, studying her every move. She was reliving every moment as she told it, tensing up at some memories, her eyes softening at others. She had no poker face.

"When I was ten, I don't remember why, but my father got really, like really mad at me. I think he saw me holding hands with the neighbor's kid or something like that? Anyway, he reached for his belt. He had never hit me before… I was *terrified*. Peter freaked out, he jumped in. Got the beating of his life. He left that same day. For three whole days he didn't come home. Longest days of my life. He was sixteen then. I just couldn't believe he'd leave me like that, you know? But he came back for me. In the middle of the night. Had packed my bags and everything. He snuck me out. I was still half asleep. He had gone out and bought a car. This old beat-up Tercel, you should've seen it…"

She broke into laughter, tears rolling down her cheeks. "It made this horrible sound every time you started it…" She wiped her tears away dismissively with the back of her hand as she chuckled some more. "And that was it, I never saw my father again after that." Her chuckle died down, her eyes dried up, her emotions settling, slowly returning to the present.

He had lit another cigarette and, for the first time, offered her a kind, sincere smile. He put out his cigarette and went over to the bar again without saying anything. He came back holding a glass of whiskey in each hand. He put one down in front of her before reclaiming his seat. He raised his own glass to her, a shadow of compassion softening his stare. "Cheers."

"Cheers."

In that moment, she almost forgot he was her captor. She had shared things with him she never had with anyone else, not even with her boyfriends. But then again, they had never locked her in a cage and forced her to open up about it. They hadn't even suspected what lay buried deep underneath. She had made it a point to play *normal* girl, for once not to be the victim, to act playful and carefree, to be *that* girl, and they all fell for it, even Eric. He never called her out once. Not when her stories were off or her responses suspiciously evasive, especially when it came to her family, or fear of closed spaces. He didn't want to scratch the surface; even he didn't want to expose the ugliness underneath. He loved *Playful Laura*.

Some part of her resented him for it, but with her pride came the burden of silence. No one besides Peter ever knew her, ever fully knew her, until now. She didn't feel vulnerable and exposed as she would have expected. She just felt relieved, like a huge weight was lifted off her shoulders. She was almost thankful for the coerced confession.

She looked at her unlikely confident and considered this fragile bubble of intimacy they had just created. Maybe because of it, she found the courage to voice the question that had been tormenting her. She cleared her throat, her fingers tracing the rim of the glass. She hesitated a few seconds.

"Can I ask you something?"

He nodded, his expression somber.

"Did they find Peter?" She rushed the words in a breath, her eyes fixing a spot on the floor.

He remained quiet for a while before answering her. "No."

She let out the breath she'd been holding in. She couldn't help smiling at him, half expecting him to smile back, sharing in her joy. He didn't.

"They did trace him back to Boston."

She mouthed *Oh*. Her relief was short-lived.

He leaned forward in his seat as if to tell her a secret, and she unconsciously mirrored his movement. In a conspiring tone, he added, "Want to know what I think, Laura? I don't think he's in Boston. I think he's already far, far away..." He leaned back in his seat, spreading his arms over the couch, a dark twinkle in his eyes. "But don't worry, your secret is safe with me."

Instant dread invaded her. She remained as still as a deer in headlights, powerlessly waiting for the blow to strike. It didn't. He leisurely took another sip from his drink and smiled knowingly at her panicked, questioning stare.

She blinked a few times, shifting uncomfortably in her seat, unsure of what to respond. "I didn't lie to you."

"I know."

She breathed a little easier. How she regretted ever bringing it up. "Are you going to kill me?" she blurted out, surprised at her own bluntness.

He stared her right in the eye, his voice betraying no emotion. "Only if you make me… But don't worry, I won't let you."

Her eyes watered, with sheer terror, with the relief and conviction that he was telling her the truth. She felt exhausted. Though the sun was still shining bright in the sky, she just wanted her bed. "May I be excused?" she asked, depleted.

He nodded. She got up, her movements slow and pained, and left his side.

* * *

He spent the day thinking of her. Time was running out. He'd received a call that night from Dimitri. The big boss himself wanted an update on the progress. Peter had betrayed them. He was seen talking with the police, but the worst offense was that he stole the file with all the information, damning information. He thought he'd use it as protection. How wrong he was. This act alone had cost him a high priority on Dimitri's hit list. Dimitri would not rest until he had his head. It was more than getting the file back; it was a matter of principle. He had to die. Traitors could not be allowed to live. Kayne knew Dimitri could wait, as long as it took. He would spend all the resources necessary, but he would hunt him down. He would never forget, never move on until justice was obtained.

The Peter that Kayne had met was very different from the one Laura described. Did she even know what her brother had become, or did she blind herself willfully?

She was a special girl, far beyond her years. He sometimes forgot she was only twenty-three. He never liked girls much younger than he was; he'd be turning thirty this year. He had learned a lot about her today. They had more similarities than he cared to admit. Both motherless. Although he'd never been abused, his father had a creative idea or two when it came to disciplining him as well. His father was a peculiar man. He made him the man he was. From his father, he had learned the value of words and the importance to choose them carefully. That any man worth his salt *commanded* respect, never demanded it. Lev Malkin laughed at clowns in flashy cars making ruckus whenever possible, to be heard and impress, and in the process, reassure their fragile egos. *Know who you are, and they will too* was Lev's golden motto. As a true disciple, Kayne steered clear of red convertibles and extravagant clothes. He appreciated beauty in its simplest form, always opting for understated elegance.

He remembered his tenth birthday. He had asked for a toy gun he had seen on TV. He received a real one. His father led him down to the holding cell where a man was tied up on a chair, beaten to a bloody pulp. It was his first kill. He remembered how nauseous he felt, he could still taste the bile rising in his mouth. However, when it was done and his father had patted him on the back as he seldom did, he felt a sense of well-being wash over him. He knew then he had done the right thing.

Kayne looked back at the postcard he was holding in his hands, feeling conflicted. He had Lucas go through Laura's mail and clear her apartment. It had taken them over six months before even discovering Laura. Peter had never mentioned a sister, *smart move*. In the two weeks he'd watched her, he hadn't noticed anyone close to her. He doubted anyone would raise too many questions about her disappearance. They'd assume she'd taken off. What a shame, he thought, she was definitely worth looking for. He hadn't mentioned the postcard to Dimitri. Placing it back on the table, looking at the jumble of random characters and scribbles, he knew he'd keep it that way.

Day-6

The day was rather uneventful. Laura made sure and asked Olga whether *Master Kayne* was around before she ventured out of her room. She went to the library and picked a few books before making herself a sandwich and settling in *her* living room, which she now baptized as her reading room. It was a rather pleasant day, all things considered. Olga came in only once to check if she needed anything and, as always, to confirm that supper would be served at seven, but she was otherwise left to her own devices. She even found a sealed pack of cigarettes left on the table in the living room where she had sat the day before with Kayne. She wondered if he left it on purpose for her. She had a cigarette or two during the day, making sure she smoked them in the living room, unsure if she was allowed to smoke anywhere else in the house.

As the clock hands moved toward the dreaded hour, Laura's nerves ebbed and flowed. She was unnerved, constantly looking at the clock. She felt fearful one moment, and the next… It was hard to describe, she didn't know what she felt. But that night, when Olga came to fetch her for supper, she was dressed and ready, her hair down, wearing jeans and a cute sleeveless pink top.

Kayne was already seated at the table as usual, in jeans and a grey sweater. He restrained a smirk upon noticing her different look, though an amused look remained plastered on his face. She blushed, inwardly cursing herself for straying from her drab attire.

"Good evening, Laura."

"Good evening." She kept her head up, as if unaware of the smoldering stare he threw her way.

"How was your day?" he added in a jovial tone.

"It was good, thank you."

"Olga tells me you borrowed a book from the library yesterday... *Yes, I ask about you,*" he teased in a mock romantic confession.

"She said it was okay. I asked..."

"Relax, Laura, I told you, as long as you obey my rules... Make yourself at home."

She wondered if he saw the paradox in his statement.

"I was just going to ask you which one."

"Oh... It's just this book... by Hesse... *Steppenwolf*... I read it a long time ago." He kept surprising her with his unpredictable conversation twists, she could never guess what would come out of his mouth.

"You like Hesse? Well... aren't you full of surprises, Miss Spencer..." he teased, *and she was.* Although he could better understand her fondness for such an author with everything he now knew about her.

Steppenwolf told the story of man torn from within, believing he was part man and part wolf. The man in him wanted to integrate into the world, the mundane society he lived in, even craved it. The wolf within despised his every attempt to do so. Realizing he couldn't reconcile his dual nature, he decided to end his life. He embarked on a mysterious journey and discovered the iconic *Magic Theater*, where the lines between fantasy and reality blur. It was an unusual and surreal story, filled with despair, poetry, and mystery, but in the end, with hope.

"You've read it?" she almost screamed in surprise and excitement.

He nodded, smiling benevolently. "My mother loved that book. It was hers." As with the few times before, his eyes darkened at her mention, his smile, however, remained intact.

"I see." She smiled back feebly. "Are your parents... still around?" she asked, treading uneasily on dangerous ground.

"No," he answered coolly, the smile wiped from his face.

"I'm sorry." She meant it.

"Don't be."

She wanted to ask more but knew instinctively she had reached the limit. They both remained quiet for a few moments, her waiting for his lead, him waiting to see if she would take her questioning further. When he saw she wouldn't, his face brightened again. He pulled out a box, gift wrapped beautifully with ribbon, and handed it to her.

"What is this?" she asked, turning the box in her hand suspiciously.

"A gift. Open it."

"Oh… thanks?" she replied, her tone suggesting uncertainty. She unwrapped the gift carefully, making sure not to tear the wrapping. It was a book, *The Kite Runner* by Khaled Hosseini.

"Wow… thank you," she said, the feeling sincere.

He smiled at her. "Have you read it?"

"No actually. I've been meaning to, just never got around to it. Have you?"

"Yes."

"Thank you, really." She held the book lovingly, looking him straight in the eye, wonder and gratitude in hers.

He nodded then gently commanded, "Let's eat."

Supper went relatively smoothly, discussing books, authors, but especially movies. It turned out they both shared a passion for film, though their tastes varied considerably. She bowed in awe at Peter Jackson's masterpiece, *The Lord of the Rings* and rambled endlessly on the many levels *Harry Potter* could be understood and appreciated. He preferred Korean action thrillers and Scorsese films. However, they both agreed, smiling at each other as if on a first date, *The Shawshank Redemption* was possibly the best stand-alone movie ever made.

After they both finished eating, he cleared their plates, refusing her offer to help, and casually asked, "I'm staying in tonight. Would you like to watch a movie with me? I'll even let you choose which one…" he added cajolingly.

She hadn't realized he'd gone out the previous nights. She was caught off guard, unsure how to respond. *Was it a genuine question or a subtle command?* She didn't want to find out, didn't want to break the mood. A part of her enjoyed his company, she had been spending her time mostly by herself. She realized she craved the human interaction, even if it was with a monster. But was he? She wasn't so sure anymore. What kind of monster could appreciate Hesse, see the beauty in *Shawshank*, and admit his favorite novel to be *The Little Prince*, by Saint-Exupery? Partly in fear of his reaction to rejection, partly out of the troubling desire to spend more time with him, intrigued by this unusual brand of monster, she accepted his offer.

He pointed to the couch as he told her to sit and handed her the remote after selecting the movie menu. As she scanned the menu, she began to feel chilly, cursing once again the cute but sleeveless top she had opted for. He noticed her rubbing her arms and offered her a throw.

"No, I'm okay, thank you," she automatically answered.

"Don't lie to me, Laura, even out of politeness." His eyes narrowed with the slightest hint of threat.

Her body immediately tensed. "Yes please, a blanket would be great. Thank you."

He nodded, satisfied, and left to fetch it for her. She wasn't sure what movie to choose. He did say she could pick whatever movie she liked, but she wanted to choose one they could both enjoy. Her eyes fell on *The Usual Suspects*. She had heard many good reviews about the film but never considered it as gangster flicks were not her thing. She asked him if he'd already seen it; he hadn't.

"Do you want to watch it? Apparently it's really good."

"Your choice." He offered her an engaging smile as he handed her the blanket and even a pillow, taking the seat next to her on the couch. The movie started. They had never been so close physically for such a long period. She cuddled up on the couch, trying to maintain some space between their bodies. She leaned her head on the pillow she had placed on the arm of the couch facing away from him, pulling the cover up to her chin. He sat with his legs spread apart, his arms wrapping the back of the couch, his knee brushing her feet. She could feel his warmth and was troubled by it, getting distracted from an otherwise captivating movie.

Halfway through the movie, his cellphone rang. He picked it off the table and read the caller ID, then resting his hand gently on her leg over the cover, he excused himself. "I have to take this." He walked out of the room to take the call.

She could still feel his touch where his hand had been. She felt her stomach knot, remembering her dream, *Yes, Master…* Moisture pooled between her legs. She squeezed them tight, mortified, and thankful for the cover.

He returned, a pleasant smile on his face, a disappointed look in his eyes. "I'm sorry, Laura, I have to get going."

"Oh…" She had paused the movie for him and was about to stop it.

"No, no. Finish it without me. I'll catch up later, okay?"

She was never sure when he seemed so benevolent if he was giving her an order or not, and as the time before, she decided against finding it out for herself. "Are you sure?"

He nodded. "I'll be home late." With a mischievous smile and a mocking tone, he added, "Don't wait up," before turning to leave.

Day-7

Laura slept deeply that night, grateful for a dreamless sleep. The next day, she went to her reading room and opted to begin reading *The Kite Runner*. As she settled on the couch, she looked out the window at the sunny day, seeing the security men guarding the premises. She wondered again about a possible escape. If she ever tried, it would have to be planned. She would have to earn his trust enough so he would let her go outside, *and maybe then…* Even so, she couldn't hope to outrun the gunmen from the house all the way to the gate. She fantasized about what she would do if she ever succeeded, where she would go. She knew they would be looking for her and shuddered at the thought. She then realized, against all logic and reason, she felt safer with him than she would on her own. She recalled a quote from *Gangs of New York*, one of her Scorsese favorites; Kayne's was *Raging Bull*. In *Gangs of New York*, Leonardo DiCaprio's character befriends his father's killer with hopes to eventually seek revenge. He describes their complex relationship in one scene: *"It's a funny feeling being taken under the wing of a dragon. It's warmer than you'd think…"*

She shook her head as if trying to throw the thoughts off. She didn't have the strength to look ahead, plan, and analyze. For now, her main goal was to get through the day, survive until the next, and, if possible, maintain her sanity throughout.

She opened the book decisively, opting for the safest escape at her disposal, within her mind. The story mesmerized her from the first line, and she didn't notice the hours go by. Sometime in the afternoon, Olga gently confirmed the usual supper time. It was almost seven when Laura looked up at the clock and realized she had under fifteen minutes to get ready. She decided on slim jeans in a darker hue and paired them with a beige long-sleeved fitted sweater. She left her hair in a ponytail and decided to forgo makeup once again. She realized with a twist in her gut that she *was* trying to look pretty, *for him*, but in a manner that wouldn't betray her desire. She showed at seven sharp on her own and found him sitting on a high stool by the kitchen island. He was dressed unusually casual, in grey sweat pants and a loose white T-shirt, his hair pulled in a low ponytail, loose strands tucked behind his ears.

He looked tired and weary, offering her a mirthless smile as she sat on the stool facing him. It made her feel uneasy, and she wondered if his murky mood had anything to do with her.

"Olga left early. I ordered us some Chinese." He pointed to the bagged cartons on the counter in explanation, a forced breeziness in his voice. Supper was unusually quiet. She looked down at her plate, throwing furtive glances when she thought he wouldn't be looking. He caught her gaze every time.

"So, how was the movie?" he eventually asked, a visible effort to lighten the mood. That was all it took. She dropped her fork and clasped her hands enthusiastically. She was dying to share.

"It. Was. Crazy! Wow! I can't believe I waited so long to watch it!" She was caught up with excitement. The movie was really good; she had loved it. And Laura always got caught up talking about books or movies she loved.

"That good, huh?" He softly chuckled.

"Yes! You definitely have to finish it!"

"Why don't you just tell me what happens?" He grabbed another bite, amused by her childlike excitement.

"No way! You're crazy if you think I'm going to tell you!"

His brow shot up. He calmly put his fork down on the table and leaned as if taken aback, his eyes narrowing, reflective.

She immediately regretted her candor and rushed to justify her words, panicky. "No, no, no… I didn't mean it like that. I just meant that… I mean…" She was frantically searching for words, her eyes watering. "I just didn't want to ruin it for you… I swear! I wasn't trying to disobey you or disrespect you or anything… I swear… I can tell you if you want me to… do you want me to…? Please don't be mad… please…" she pleaded again, having run out of things to say.

He crossed his arms, waiting patiently for her nervous ramble to end. "Are you done?"

"Yes… Please, sir…" she implored again, her voice cracking.

He turned his head slightly, half rolling his eyes. "Come here."

She got up, hesitantly approaching him, her walk shaky. He offered her his hand and gently pulled her between his legs; still sitting on the stool, they met at eye level. Her heart was pounding in her chest, she was almost hyperventilating.

He put his hands on her waist delicately. "Breathe, Laura… Breathe…" His voice was soothing, coming through lips curved in a roguish grin. He gently rubbed her arms, forcibly calming her down. "Don't you think I can tell the difference?" His voice was soft as he brought his fingers to her chin, forcing her to look at him.

A few tears slid down her cheeks. "Yes… I don't know… please, sir…"

She flinched as he brought his hand to her face, but he gently wiped her tears away with the pad of his thumb. There was a certain pleasure at the feel of his rough skin, touching her ever so gently. He caressed her cheek with the back of his fingers. Bringing her even closer, enveloping her with his body, he leaned his face to the side of hers.

"Tell me, Laura," he whispered huskily in her ear. "Why is it you always call me *sir* when you feel afraid?"

"I don't know…" she cried, biting her lip.

"You do know… tell me."

"I don't know… it just… comes naturally I guess… Please, sir… I don't want to go back… *there*…"

He pulled back so he could face her, his expression seemed sorry. "You think I would have locked you up just for that?"

“I don’t know…” Her eyes were glistening with renewed tears.

“You really think I’m a monster, don’t you? Answer me,” he added harshly. With a devilish gleam in his eyes, he then warned her with a deceptive softness. “Don’t lie.”

Her tears were flowing freely by now; he felt her crumble in his arms. She didn’t answer, just broke down completely. He sighed, standing up lazily, and pulled her to him. He brushed the tips of his fingers up and down her back, comforting her with one hand. With the other, he softly brushed her hair away from her face while he made shushing sounds in her ear.

He knew she thought of him as a monster. He smiled inwardly. *How right she was.* He looked at her with fondness as she closed her eyes, unconsciously, ever so softly leaning into his embrace. She *was* innocent, though not naïve. Life had not afforded her with such privilege. He began to understand that was precisely the key to her charm.

He was a monster indeed, the truest kind of monsters. He would not be satisfied to only make her cower in fear; he would also make her crave his comfort and render her desperate for his touch. He held and comforted her until her sobs died down and her breathing slowly returned to normal. He then held her shoulders and gently nudged her back to stare into her eyes.

“Better?” he asked half smirking, his tone patient.

She nodded sheepishly.

“Good.” Then as if remembering something unpleasant, his mood shifted again. “Go to bed, Laura, it’s been a long day.”

She staggered out of the kitchen but turned to face him as she was about to round the corner. “Good night…” She wasn’t sure if she was supposed to call him *sir* at all times, but she sensed he liked it when she called him that.

“Good night, Laura.” He sounded pleasantly surprised at her initiative.

She hesitated a little. “Should I always call you… sir?” she asked, avoiding his eyes, a faint blush coloring her face.

A wicked smile on his face, he quoted back her own words in response. "Whatever… comes naturally I guess…"

* * *

Kayne lay wide awake in his bed. He had received another call from Dimitri. He was throwing a party the very next day and wanted Kayne to bring the girl. He was curious, wanted to see her for himself. Kayne's words carried weight in the Organization. No one would contradict him or disobey him openly. Those who had were no more. But even he couldn't go head-to-head against Dimitri. He had explained his position as clearly and truthfully as he could. He wanted the girl for himself and would get the information out of her himself. He wanted to be given discretion to deal with it as he saw fit. Dimitri had consented, because he could understand his motives. Pretty women who unfortunately got involved in their world were often claimed once they had served their purpose. Just like in the old times, the victors claimed their spoils of war. The women were turned into personal whores, shared as sex slaves, or sold according to the whims of their holder. Laura was his to claim, and he had. But this time, it was different. She still had a purpose to serve. Dimitri was a reasonable man. He allowed Kayne to have his way, provided he got what he wanted in the end. But Kayne knew he was treading a thin line; whores were never put before business. He was apprehensive at how things would unfold. What if Dimitri wanted to have the girl interrogated again? Kayne didn't know what he would do. He would try to talk to him, buy himself, and the girl, a little more time. It was his only option. He knew Dimitri held a certain fondness for him, having been close to his father, even acting as a second mentor. If it came to it, Kayne would speak on her behalf, ensuring she remained under his care. He felt the same surge of animalistic protectiveness he had felt when he questioned her on whether she'd been abused. She was his, to do with as he pleased. He would not stand by and watch someone else have their way with her.

He tried to convince himself nothing drastic would follow. He would reason with Dimitri and have his way as always. He was earning the girl's trust. Soon if he played his hand well, she would tell him, of her own accord. He knew he could make her. Dimitri would have Peter's head, he would get Laura, and they would all live happily ever after. *Well, except for Peter.* He laughed sardonically in the dark at the fantasy. He derided himself, maybe he *was* in love with the girl. After all, for all his stoic appearance, it had taken just one look for Lev Malkin to fall helplessly in love with Elena Galiano. He had seen her at a park, sitting on a bench by a willow tree, wrapped up in a book. He pursued her relentlessly. She had dismissed his advances without a second glance, her nose buried in the book she'd been reading. He'd finally convinced her on a first date by presenting her with a signed first edition of her favorite book, *The Little Prince.* He proposed to her after their second date. Not with a ring, but by showing her the library he had built for her. What was it with women and books? Kayne wondered, then corrected himself, not all women, just the ones the Malkin men seemed unable to resist.

Day-8

Laura was cuddled on the couch in her reading room with *The Kite Runner* open pointlessly on her lap. She was having trouble getting into it, catching herself reading the same lines over and over again. She had an uneasy feeling she couldn't shake. She kept replaying the scene from the previous night. Kayne had seemed weird, troubled. Closing her eyes, she thought back to his embrace, his reassuring caresses, his gentle voice… how safe they made her feel. She shook her head and forced her eyes open. When Olga tapped at her door, it was around five. She was surprised at the random visit but welcomed the interruption.

"Sorry to disturb you, Miss Spencer, Master Kayne wanted me to inform you to meet him at seven in the living room… He said to dress formally… and to fix your hair and makeup," she finished, slightly uncomfortable giving such instructions. With a warm smile, she added, "I can help you if you like."

"So, no supper tonight?"

"I'm not sure what Master Kayne planned for supper. He didn't ask me to prepare anything."

"Okay, thank you, Olga."

"Well, please let me know if I can be of assistance," she offered again before leaving.

Laura was unsure what to make of this, wondered what he had in store for her. She headed back to her room and decided to take a long bath. She unconsciously began to shave herself, stopping at the realization, wondering why she was even doing it. It was such a meaningless action and yet so full of implication. *To shave or not to shave*, THAT was the question, to every girl anyway. She shaved her legs and armpits. Those were innocent enough, considering the request for formal wear. When she finished, she lingered, the blade resting below her belly button. The question begged to be asked, did she somehow hope he would see her, *there…*? Her inner voice responded with an emphatic *NO*, she had become completely delirious. She immediately got up and stepped out of the bathtub. However, on her way out of the bathroom, she couldn't help sneaking a quick peek in the mirror. The regrowth was still minor, she was shamefully glad to notice.

She opted for a seamless pink bikini and matching cotton push-up bra. She rummaged through the walk-in closet indecisively. Although she didn't want to look like she tried too hard, she couldn't look like she hadn't tried enough. She settled on a pair of skinny black pants, a beige silk camisole, and a matching fitted jacket. She found some black stilettos at the bottom of the closet and threw them on. She was no fashion expert by any means and looked at herself in the mirror, unsure. She thought she looked nice enough and turned her attention to the vanity. She straightened her hair and stuck to earthy tones for eye shadow, opting for a natural look. At six thirty she was ready, half an hour too early. She paced around in her room, constantly looking at the clock, half apprehensive, half excited. Maybe he was taking her out? Why else would he ask her to do all this? But then again, he didn't even let her out in the gated front yard. She highly doubted he was taking her to a five-star restaurant. She kept speculating, unable to come up with any logical explanation.

A few minutes before the clock struck seven, Laura took a big breath as she left her room. She realized she was anxious to see his reaction. He had never seen her dressed up… since that first night, she reminded herself, when he took her.

Kayne was sitting on the couch, dressed in a formal black suit, his hair slicked back, a glass of whiskey in his hand. He was staring at an invisible spot on the wall, consumed with thought, and didn't notice her come in. There was a large box on the table, gift wrapped with a ribbon, the kind that fancy stores used. She stood in the corner and cleared her throat to get his attention. Only his eyes moved toward her. His brows lifted upon seeing her, and he leaned his head slightly back as if he was surprised with what he saw. He then nodded slowly a few times in approval. She blushed but smiled at him, happy with his reaction.

"Come closer."

She took a few hesitant steps and stopped at the corner of the couch, just a few inches within his reach. He pushed the box toward her.

"It's for you," he said, his eyes penetrating, his expression somber. This had nothing to do with when he offered her the book. She had never seen him like this.

"Thank you…"

His strange mood disquieted her. She reached for the box uncertainly, opening it nervously, almost expecting a bomb to explode. It contained a gorgeous backless dark purple silk gown. It was her turn to lift her brows. She pulled the dress from the box, the rich material gently flowing down to her feet.

"Wow… it's beautiful! I don't think I've ever owned anything this beautiful, like *anything,* not just clothes…" She smiled warmly at him, realizing she was trying to make him smile too. He nodded again, offering her a smile that didn't reach his eyes.

"Try it on."

She didn't understand why he was acting the way he was, but kept smiling at him nonetheless. She turned to leave the room, holding the dress in her hand, when his voice stopped her.

"Where are you going?"

She turned back around, her brows furrowed. "You said to try it on…"

"I did." The corner of his mouth quirked upward.

"I don't understand…" she muttered, her eyes scouring the room in discomfort.

"Of course you do. Take off your clothes, Laura." His tone was callous; his eyes were fixed on her, a wolfish expression etched on his face.

She was shocked but remained in place, heart pounding, her breathing growing faster and louder.

"*Sir…?*"

"Sir me all you like, you will still do as I say."

Her eyes watered, and she nervously played with the dress in her hands. "Please, sir, please don't do this…" She berated herself for being so naïve. Of course he would rape her; she just wondered why he hadn't done it sooner. Why the whole charade? Then she thought back to her hesitation in the tub earlier. Oh how she wanted to slap that stupid girl senseless.

"Do what, Laura?" He leaned forward, his eyes fixed onto hers.

She remembered that first night, how he had earned her trust and betrayed it right after, how remorselessly he owned up to it, staring her in the eye unblinking as Maxwell shackled and hurt her. A shiver ran down her spine.

"Please… don't rape me…" She barely managed to finish the sentence, her voice thick with emotion.

He sneered at her, his eyes predatory. "You think I'm going to fuck you? Don't worry. I won't fuck you, Laura… Not until you ask…" he added with a seductive smile.

She felt relief at the reassurance and disbelief replaying his words. Did he just say *Until? Until!* Did he really think she would ask him to? She was hot with white rage. She opened her mouth and upon a second glance in his direction closed it right back.

"Laura. Take off your clothes," he reiterated, losing patience.

She gulped, lowering her eyes. She looked for a place to set the dress, opting for the La-Z-Boy, trying to delay the inevitable. He took another sip from his drink, lighting a cigarette. She looked around again, hoping for any excuse to delay, and caught his intimidating stare. Dejected, she first removed her shoes, then her jacket, fumbling nervously with the sleeves, then reached to place it next to the dress.

"Leave it."

She flinched at the sound of his voice and let it immediately drop to the floor. She hesitated between removing the top or the pants first, her hands moving from one piece to the other undecidedly. She looked toward him for instruction, unable to think, to make the call herself.

"Your shirt," he directed her, his eyes burning into her.

She was almost thankful to have the burden of decision removed. She slid off her camisole, then lingered for a few moments, playing with the band of her pants, unable to take the next step.

"Take off your pants, Laura." He understood. He understood her, her brain process. She would await his explicit instruction before removing each clothing item. Her pride wouldn't allow her to take any initiative, participating on her own. Her submissiveness, however, had her abiding hastily to his every command, albeit with clumsy jerky moves.

"Good girl."

She instantly blushed at his words, feeling her muscles down there contract in spite of herself. He smiled wickedly at her, all too aware of her conflicting emotions. He put out his cigarette, looking back at her.

"And now take off your bra."

Her eyes darted up to meet his, silently pleading. He only nodded his head to convey his order. Her eyes watered again. She obeyed, then tried to cover herself with her arms. He rolled his eyes.

"Put your arms down, Laura."

She did, slowly, fidgeting with her hands as if not knowing what to do with them. He shamelessly leered at her naked body, minus the panties he let her keep on. She squirmed under his smoldering stare. He enjoyed a few more sips of his whiskey, leaving her exposed and vulnerable, sadistically savoring every moment, her discomfort only adding to his thrill. She was truly a thing of beauty. She was looking up at the ceiling, blinking tears away.

"Don't, Laura, you'll only ruin your makeup. Why do you want to cry?" he added with slight irritation.

"Isn't it obvious?"

"Not from what I see," he answered, sneering at her, his eyes fixated with the moist spot on her panties.

She followed his gaze, then instinctively covered the spot with her hands, her eyes wide with terror. A chuckle escaped his lips. He finished his drink and languidly walked up to her, grabbing the dress on his way. He stood in front of her, without touching, just close enough so she could feel his warmth. He raised her chin, forcing her to look at him.

"Are you upset with me?"

"*Yes*," she hissed through gritted teeth.

"Hmm... You'll have to get over it. Get dressed. Lucas will be here any moment now."

She roughly reached to grab the dress from his hands, but he held it back.

"Easy now..."

She recoiled at the implied threat, all bravado leaving her. How he loved toying with her, so easily riled up, as easily calmed down. He let go of the dress and watched her as she slid it over her shoulders.

"Sit."

She immediately obeyed. He grabbed her stilettos and knelt in front of her. And for the first time that night, he offered her a charming, kind smile, though remnants of mischief still lingered in his eyes. He gently took her leg in his hand, his warm skin radiating against hers, and put the shoe on her foot, then proceeded with the other. He was all business again by the time he got up, staring down at her as she sat in the La-Z-Boy.

"We're going out tonight. Lucas will drive us. I don't believe I've introduced you... I expect you won't try anything stupid."

"May I ask where we're going?"

For barely a flash, she could see apprehension in his eyes, but in an instant it was gone, and they were back to their normal impassiveness.

"You'll see."

His cellphone rang. Lucas was outside waiting for them. Kayne offered his arm to Laura, which she accepted reluctantly. As they were about to leave the house, he leaned in her ear and whispered, "You looked beautiful."

She turned bright red at the insinuation… *looked*… not look… She understood him. He chuckled quietly to himself as he walked them to meet Lucas. He had mentioned him on the first day. He was the head of security if she remembered correctly.

Lucas Belfort was a handsome, mild-mannered man of biracial background. He was tall with a strong build, his green eyes standing out against his dark skin, his hair shaven in a military cut. He carried himself with dignity, his laughing eyes sparkling with intelligence. His deceivingly boyish good looks were reinforced with his deadliest weapon, his smile. It was a smile designed to instill trust and penetrate all the defensive walls erected by its recipient.

Kayne had met Lucas in elementary school. He had first noticed him in his ragged clothes, standing up to the school bully, twice his size, and accompanied by his two faithful trolls. Lucas had stared him straight in the eyes, unflinching, and threw the first punch. He got beaten to a pulp. A week later, his face still bruised, Kayne had seen the shame in Lucas's eyes as he faced the cafeteria lady, counting the spare change in the palm of his hand. He seemed more defeated standing in front of her than he had been lying on the ground, getting kicked around. Without a word, Kayne crept to his side and under the counter covertly slipped him the twenty-dollar bill his father had given him that very morning.

An alliance was formed then, one that strengthened over the years, deepened over shared experiences, and solidified over crimes perpetrated together. Lucas had spent his days at the Malkin residence since adolescence. His mother never asked questions. His father, he'd never met. When he was sixteen, he moved in permanently in the employees' quarters in the western wing. When he turned eighteen, Lev Malkin paid for his university tuition in criminology. Kayne studied business administration. They were twenty when Lev had finally lost his battle to cancer. After his death, Kayne stepped up and became the master of the house, following in his father's footsteps. Lucas began addressing him as *sir*, took over the security, and rallied all those remaining loyal to the Malkins, ensuring his only friend's ascent and control in the Organization.

"Good evening, sir."

"Evening, Lucas, I don't believe you met Laura."

"Ah, Miss Spencer, no. What a pleasure." He respectfully bowed his head to her then turned back to Kayne. "We should get going."

They embarked into the Audi, both sitting in the back with Lucas at the wheel. Laura remembered the first time she got in that car, how it changed her life. During the ride, Kayne seemed preoccupied, withdrawn. Her nervousness rose as the car sped away. Why was he acting so weird? Where was he taking her? It couldn't be anything good if it had even him upset.

"Sir…"

He turned to her, his eyes still absorbed in thought.

"Are you taking me to an interrogation?" she breathed, fear in her eyes.

That got his attention. *No, definitely not naïve*, Kayne thought to himself. He sighed then looked away from her, staring out the window. "We are going to a party actually. I suspect it's not your typical scene."

"Why not? What's at the party? Please tell me."

"You'll see. You won't like it," he said cryptically and turned his head away from her again. "My boss wanted me to bring you. He's the one hosting."

She paled. "So you *are* taking me to an interrogation…"

He turned back to her, keeping his composure. "I don't know, Laura," he finally responded, irritation tainting his voice.

He was nervous. That didn't happen very often to Kayne Malkin. The entire way, he tried to reassure himself. He would talk to Dimitri; it would all work out. It had to, there was no other viable option for him. He could not openly defy Dimitri, and yet he would not let him harm the girl, *his girl.*

Laura couldn't have suspected his inner turmoil. She only heard his fatalistic answer, the crushing response thrown callously at her. She wanted to jump out of the moving car, but they were going over a hundred kilometers per hour on the freeway, the doors locked under the driver's control. She started rocking herself back and forth, not knowing what to do, what to think, or how to feel. A firm but gentle hand held her by the arm, steadying her movement.

"Laura, look at me." He waited until she did. "Do as I say, and you will be fine. Okay?" Kayne's eyes burned into hers as he said the words. He knew them to be true the moment they came out of his lips. He would not stand and watch as they had their way with her. She was his and his alone. He had found and claimed her, and Kayne always protected what was rightfully his. He could feel her muscles relax. She nodded, her eyes vacant.

"Do you trust me?"

What a wonderfully ironic question. She laughed in her head at how ridiculous it sounded coming from him, and yet the answer was yes, *yes, she did.* She nodded again, this time meeting his gaze. He gently squeezed her arm, his smile brittle before letting go and turning back away from her.

* * *

The SUV finally turned into a driveway, not unlike Kayne's, though the mansion it led to was twice the size. There was security all over the premises, valet service, and even a doorman. Kayne turned to Laura just before exiting the car, fire in his eyes, his mood entirely changed.

"Ready?"

"Ready," a subdued voice answered back.

He led her to the entrance with his hand on the small of her back, right above where the material of her dress fell into graceful folds. Just the touch of his hand on her bare skin caused Laura to feel a knot in her stomach. She tried to walk ahead, ignoring the very pleasant burning sensation his hand was creating on her soft skin.

Before they got in the door, he leaned into her ear and instructed her in a hushed tone, "Stay close to me, don't speak to anyone, and keep your eyes on the ground." He then added, jeering at her, though not unkindly, "Last part shouldn't be too hard for you."

She just nodded, too nervous to be offended or embarrassed.

Words could barely express the sickening spectacle awaiting Laura. She froze in the doorway, refusing to take another step. There were hundreds of people. All the men were dressed formally in fancy black suits, much like Kayne's. As for the women… she was simply horrified. Some, which she assumed were strippers, were dancing in metal cages dangling from the high ceilings. Other women donned black latex underwear, some were completely naked. Most of them had collars, some with leashes, being dragged by a man, crawling on all fours. A very select few wore dark gowns like herself. She felt nauseated.

"I told you you wouldn't like it," Kayne whispered with devilish amusement in her ear before dragging her forward.

As they moved into the house, more explicit scenes befell her eyes. Orgies were happening all over the place. In one room, there was a group of men casually conversing with drinks in their hands while women serviced them, one woman serving only as a footrest. In another, five men were huddled by a naked woman, splayed flat on a table. One of them was carelessly thrusting himself into her mouth while another put her other orifices to good use. With her hands, she was pleasuring the others gathered around her as they fondled her generous breasts.

Laura looked around in panic, somewhere between revulsion and disbelief. It reminded her of the sex scene in the movie *Eyes Wide*

Shut, except there was no pretense to this, no need for costumes and occult hocus-pocus.

"You… you go to these things?" she asked him, in a hushed tone barely masking her disgust.

"Yes."

She let go of his arm, taking a step back, her eyes wide. He didn't reach out to pull her back to him. He remained still in his spot, his eyes boring into hers with a wicked gleam. As if on cue, a man drunkenly stumbled toward them, undressing her with his eyes.

"Well well... what do we have here?" He slurred his words, raising his hand to touch her hair.

In an instant she was back at Kayne's side, half her body hiding behind him, gripping his arm fiercely with both her hands, her nails digging into his jacket.

"She's with me," Kayne coolly warned the man.

"Oh, Mr. Malkin, I'm so sorry, I didn't know." And just as fast, the man scurried out of sight.

Kayne waited a few moments, then turned his face to Laura. He gently unclenched her firm grip on him, taking both her hands into his.

"So we're friends again…" he observed, a smirk on his face. Laura didn't respond, just tightened her hold on his hand.

As they walked around, Kayne ran into many acquaintances. They all checked her out shamelessly, some making lewd comments about her, mostly about how they couldn't wait for her to become available or about looking forward to seeing her in action. Kayne brushed off the comments dismissively, never letting them get too far, but no one risked approaching her. A shiver ran through her spine at every comment, every lingering leer. The thought of these men touching her made her feel sick. She understood; they thought she was his whore and that Kayne didn't share his whores with other men but that he'd let them watch sometimes… She wondered if he'd do this to her, if he'd make her strip in front of them as he had her do earlier at his home. The mere thought petrified her. It was bad enough she had done it for him, but in a way, it also made it okay, because it *was* him.

Her train of thought and frightful speculations were interrupted suddenly by a very present, very real terror. Maxwell Bane was standing right across the room from them, caught in a lively conversation with another man and a woman wearing a black velvet gown. Laura's face blanched, her hand squeezed his even tighter, if it was possible. "Kayne…" Her voice strangled.

He immediately turned to face her. She just nudged her head toward the back of the room, unable to say another word. Maxwell noticed, acknowledging them with a vile smile. The woman standing at his side turned her head in their direction. She was strikingly beautiful, tall and slender, a red mane slicked into an elegant side ponytail, contouring her delicate features and feline green eyes. She smiled brightly upon seeing Kayne, taking Maxwell's offered arm as they both made their way to Kayne and Laura.

Kayne was caught unaware, hearing his name from her lips. He was even more surprised at how much he liked it. She hadn't pronounced his name since he had brought her to Maxwell the night they met, when he betrayed her. He never allowed his whores to call him by his name; they would refer to him as *sir* or *master*, conveying the respect they owed him. But she wasn't his whore… yet, and he caught himself questioning if that was still his objective. Granted, he wanted her, in all the twisted ways he always wanted beautiful women. And yet he was at a loss explaining the emerging feelings she stirred in him, the protective way he looked at her, the slow seduction he instinctively opted for. Never before had he felt such pleasure from hearing his name uttered, never before was it spoken with such familiarity and urgent need. He wondered if that was the price to pay for holding her captive. The bond he inadvertently created, the responsibility he now felt toward a woman he would have otherwise just seduced and discarded without a second thought.

Kayne's eyes narrowed seeing the source of her distress. He turned his attention back to Laura, feeling her quickened breaths, her panic rising. He pulled her closer, brushed a strand of hair behind her ear, and softly whispered to her, leaning his face close but not too close as to enable eye contact. "Laura… Laura… Look at me, Laura," he patiently commanded her attention, snapping her out of the swirl of terror ensnaring her.

She looked up at him, dread in her eyes.

"Don't worry about him."

She nodded nervously, clearly not appeased.

He sighed, brushing her cheek with the back of his hand. "He won't hurt you. I won't let him."

At his touch, she relaxed a little, his words slowly entering her mind, fighting off her fears.

"Kayne! How are you? I see you brought the ever-so-lovely Miss Spencer." Maxwell turned to Laura, a reptilian smile plastered on his face as Laura shrank back.

"Oh my… she's a shy one," the pretty redhead said in a cutesy voice.

Kayne wrapped his arm around Laura's waist, pulling her close in a possessive gesture. "Maxwell, Tanya… How have you been?" he replied nonchalantly, annoyance perceptible in his voice.

"Good… good… I see you didn't waste your time with her… Can't say I blame you… She sure is a delectable little thing…" Maxwell licked his lips as Kayne's stare turned icy.

Laura couldn't help but notice that Kayne hadn't reacted the same way when other men made comments, he had merely brushed them off. She sensed Maxwell's convivial manners were affected. Kayne didn't even try to hide his hostility. There was definitely bad blood between the two. As for the woman smiling with such familiarity at Kayne… *Tanya, was that her name?* There was no doubt, from the first glance they exchanged, she knew the animosity she felt was reciprocated.

"So, Kayne… How long 'til we can play a little with her, huh? It's so unfair really, you're no team player!" Maxwell chortled loudly.

"Oh, come now, Maxwell, you know Kayne doesn't like to share his toys…" Tanya added in a singsong tone. "My guess is… hmm… two months? Maybe three… She looks *special*… But tell me, Kayne, if I promise not to break her, can *I* play with her?" She batted her eyes coyly at him as she raised her hand to touch Laura's face. Laura was already backing away when Kayne caught Tanya's arm midair.

"Don't," he said sharply, warning in his voice.

She glared at him for a moment but quickly fell back on a honeyed tone and a mock hurt look. "Not even me?" She pouted her mouth. "My my… Guess she *is* special after all…"

"Bah… no matter." Maxwell shrugged his shoulders. "In the end they're even better when he's done with them," and he winked at Tanya.

She let out a loud strident laugh, throwing her head back coquettishly, but her eyes, if only for a second, betrayed the hurt the remark just inflicted on her. And with that, they turned around and walked away, Tanya's chuckle still heard, Maxwell with his hand wrapped around her waist, his head barely reaching her shoulders.

The whole time, Laura had tried to keep her eyes on the ground, to focus on breathing, on Kayne's soothing hand gently rubbing her back, up and down. She tried to focus on the calmness it procured her and not shriek at the top of her lungs before stumbling into complete insanity.

The moment they were gone, Kayne leaned even closer to her. His hand still caressing her back, he whispered softly in her ear, "Are you okay?"

Her eyes watery, she shook her head. "Can we leave now?" she barely managed to say.

"Not yet… Not yet," he repeated, caressing her cheek again, his eyes soft, half smiling indulgently. "Come."

He led her to the back of the room where two doormen opened the double French doors giving way to a gorgeous terrace. There were a few tables here and there with waiters going about them offering beverages. A big illuminated water fountain stood in the middle, the whole of it surrounded by a magnificent garden. Laura couldn't help but take in all the beauty. What a lovely place it must look like from the outside. Kayne pulled her into a corner and offered her a cigarette, holding both in the corner of his mouth to light them, then handing her one.

Laura took the cigarette with shaky fingers. "You do this..."

"Do what?"

"This... to women..."

"Do you really want to have this conversation now, Laura?" His voice was calm. Though not threatening, it carried the implication that if she knew what was good for her, she'd drop it. In a way she knew he was right. In this moment, she didn't want to see him for the monster he was, to know the atrocities her only protection in this godforsaken place was capable of.

One of the doormen approached them, bowing his head with deference before addressing Kayne. "Mr. Malkin, Mr. Drugov is ready for you."

Kayne nodded, and the doorman left. He looked back at Laura. "Ready?"

"No?" She offered a weak smile.

He smiled back, wrapping his arm around her back, and with a grave voice added, "Let's go."

They went back in and entered a glass elevator that led them to the third floor. Dimitri Drugov was waiting for them in his office behind his desk. He was old, Laura guessed in his seventies, still had all his white hair, and divulged an imposing belly when standing up to meet them. He had a large nose, no facial hair, and pale blue eyes. His facial features, though severe, softened considerably when he smiled.

"Ah, Kayne, my boy! How are you?" He affectionately embraced him and smiled as kindly to her. "I presume this is the lovely Miss Spencer?"

She remained in the doorway, looking at the ground as instructed.

"Please, Laura. May I call you Laura? Come closer so I may have a look at you."

Seeing her hesitation, Kayne quickly interceded, "Come, Laura."

She obeyed, approaching the desk, her eyes still glued to the floor.

"Hmm… I see… very lovely indeed." He winked at Kayne, the latter remaining stoic. "Please sit down. Are you enjoying the party?" Dimitri then asked Laura.

She remained quiet, too terrified to do anything without Kayne's direct commands. They always managed to reach her, no matter how far lost in her thoughts she was.

"It's her first time, Dimitri," Kayne responded for her.

"Yes of course. You'll see, it's an acquired taste…" he added playfully.

She shivered at the implication. Was she expected to return?

"So, Laura, Kayne tells me that you've been cooperative. I like that, I like reasonable people. Suicidal heroics, what are they good for, huh? Only wasted blood…" He gestured his hand disdainfully at the notion. "I just wanted to make sure that we do have your full cooperation. Not that I don't trust Kayne's judgment. I just wanted to see for myself, I'm sure you can understand. I would like to ask you one simple question. Have you answered all of Kayne's questions truthfully?"

She remained quiet, unable to move a muscle.

"Answer him," Kayne commanded her.

Her eyes snapped up, then back down remembering her instructions.

"Yes, sir, I have."

"Hmm…" Dimitri considered her some more.

"May I have a word with you in private?" Kayne then addressed Dimitri, to which the latter nodded, waving his arm in consent.

Kayne then turned to her. "Laura, wait outside by the door for me."

She nodded but didn't move, her eyes imploring him not to make her. She dreaded the thought of being alone in this place, even for a moment, even on the third floor where none of the obscene party guests were present.

"Go!" he commanded harshly.

She flinched at the severity in his voice and rushed to the door. Patiently, she waited, every second seeming an eternity. When he finally came out to meet her, he flashed her a radiant smile, his demeanor more relaxed than she had seen it in the past few days.

"Is it okay? Can we go now?" she asked tentatively.

"Soon," he answered her softly, gently bringing his hand to her face and caressing her.

She closed her eyes at his touch, at the much-needed reassurance and pretense of tenderness she so desperately craved.

He led her back downstairs where everyone seemed to have gathered in a huge reception hall. A stage had been built in the middle. Tables, couches, even beds were spread out all around it. While the men sat comfortably, the women crouched at their feet as obedient pets, most of them being put to good use. Only the handful of other women in gowns were sitting on chairs at the tables with the men. A mattress lay on the center stage with a Dark Ages-looking pranger. A naked woman was shackled to it. She was hung by her wrists by a dangling chain, forced onto her toes. Bound with an iron collar, she remained very still as a shirtless man in a black mask and leather pants whipped her mercilessly, drawing blood with every stroke. The crowd cheered perversely with every blow that landed on her, ripping her skin, as she howled in pain, sobbing desperately in between every stroke.

"What is this?" Laura's eyes looked around wildly, like a frightened caged animal, ready to strike at the slightest movement.

Kayne didn't let her see his own sadistic smile. They could've left after meeting with Dimitri. They didn't really have to stay for the show. *He wanted to.* He had wrecked his nerves the past few days over her, for her; now she would return the favor. He wanted to see her reaction to it, test her boundaries. He knew very well she would be frightened and disgusted, but would any part of her, however small, be also turned on?

Ignoring her question, he picked a couch in a hidden corner and led her to it. Somewhere just far enough from the rest of the crowd so they could have privacy and that she would feel a safe distance from her environment. Just close enough so she couldn't disconnect herself entirely from what was going on and be forced to witness the show taking place in front of her eyes. He sat her next to him, wrapping his arm around her.

"What's going on…?" She was panting, panic seeping through her hushed voice. Her eyes were glued to the horrid scene taking place. His were on her.

"Relax, it's just a show." He gently rubbed her shoulder.

"It's not just a show!" Though her voice remained low, it rose a few octaves. "Kayne… Please… Please… I don't want to be here…" Her eyes darted in every direction.

He firmly took her face in both his hands, forcing her to stare at him. "Laura. Calm down, it's just a show."

By now the masked man had abandoned his whip, and another had joined him on stage. One of them began penetrating the woman forcefully from behind as the other fucked her mouth savagely, her gagging sounds echoing throughout the room.

Laura's eyes went back to the stage, though her face was still trapped in Kayne's hands.

"They're raping her…" she finally whispered to him, her voice broken, her eyes in agony.

"They're not raping her," he assured her dismissively.

"They are! They're raping her!" she insisted, her voice growing erratic.

Kayne closed his eyes, letting out a long sigh, his nostrils flaring. "Come with me."

He pulled her off the couch by the arm in one quick movement and dragged her out of the room, taking long strides as she struggled to keep up with him.

He turned a corner, then another, and stopped abruptly in the middle of a deserted corridor, pinning her wrists up to the wall. He leaned in close, his mouth barely a few inches from hers. They were both panting, Kayne, with a mix of aggravation and arousal, Laura from fear and the knot in the gut she constantly felt when alone and close to him. He pulled his face back, his breathing slowing to normal, but kept her pinned against the wall, maintaining his firm grip on her wrists.

"There. Out of the room. Feel better?"

She shook her head slowly, her eyes filling with unshed tears. He sighed again, though this time his features softened. He leaned his forehead against hers, closing his eyes for a few seconds, then pulled back. He let go of her wrists and just stared at her, somewhere between amused and fascinated.

"What am I going to do with you?" He shook his head at her, the corner of his lips quirking upward. "You're really convinced she is being raped."

"*Yes*." Her answer was emphatic, though spoken in a soft voice.

He shook his head again. "And what makes you so sure?"

"Seriously?"

"Tell me." He crossed his arms, a little annoyed at her stubbornness and yet amused by it.

"You want me to believe that this was *consensual*? Listen, I know all about S&M and bondage and stuff—"

His brow shot up with surprise, then smiling seductively, he interrupted her, "Do you now?"

She immediately turned red, stammering, unable to hold his stare. "Well… I mean… like… not firsthand…" and then with more conviction, she met his eyes again. "But yes, I do know about it, and this, *this*, was not role play. It was real, it was *very* real."

"Which still doesn't make it rape," he concluded flatly.

"This was NOT consensual!"

“And you know that… how exactly?” he asked patronizingly, clearly enjoying their little debate.

“You want me to believe she wants *this*?”

“What if I told you that I knew *for a fact* that she was into *this*.” He mimicked her disdain at the word.

“You can’t possibly know that…”

He didn’t answer, just lifted his brows in silent innuendo.

“You’ve done this to her…?” Her voice dripped with dread. She backed away from him, every inch of her body pressed against the wall.

He leaned in, putting his arms against the wall by each side of her shoulders, effectively caging her in, and wolfishly whispered into her ear, “Don’t ask questions you don’t want answered, baby girl.”

She gulped, the rest of her body remaining very still.

“Will this happen to me?” she asked at last, her voice so soft it was barely audible, her eyes filled with pain.

“What?” Genuine surprise marked his voice.

“You send girls here… when you’re done with them. Is that what will happen to me? If you never find Peter… it’s not like you’ll keep me in your house forever. And if you do…” Her voice cracked with pain. “It’s not like you’ll let me go. Is this where you’ll send me?”

He pulled back again, his eyes inscrutable. “No, Laura, I will not send you here.”

She lowered her head, shutting her eyes with relief. She remained silent, numbed by too many emotions lived through too little time. When she opened her eyes again, the tears she had been holding back fell freely down her cheeks.

He cocked his head, watching her beautiful face giving way to the flow of tears, her big grey eyes glistening, her soft pink lips quivering. He languidly grabbed her by the front of her dress and pulled her to him, arching her body toward him. She didn’t resist, looking up at him, her eyes filled with questions. He met her gaze. Slowly, he leaned in and kissed her softly on her lips.

* * *

Laura lay in bed, replaying the night in her head over and over again. She had never felt as confused in her life. She still shivered remembering the *show*, the way the women were treated, and then the image of Kayne appeared, overpowering all others. Kayne pulling her close protectively, Kayne whispering scary and yet seductive things in her ear, Kayne shamelessly leering at her naked body…

The last thought caused her body to react, and she felt the wetness pool in between her legs again. She squeezed her legs and opened her eyes in an attempt to banish the thought. And then she recalled his kiss. His sweet, gentle kiss. She had liked his kiss, realizing she was leaning into it when he broke it off. She remembered the sweet way he had looked at her after and held her hand to pull her out of that nightmarish place. In the car, he was silent, almost distant. She had glanced at him a few times hoping to catch his stare, but he never looked her way.

When they got home, he caressed her cheek as he had so many times that night and sent her off to bed while still standing in the doorway. He had somewhere else to go it seemed. She wondered if he was returning to the party. Tanya's image flashed in her mind. She could picture her greeting him on his own, making snide comments about her as she flirted away with him, taking him somewhere private. Laura chose not to pursue this line of thought, surprised at how fast her stomach turned with the vivid images in her head; her teeth clenched so hard her jaw hurt.

She couldn't understand why she felt that way. She was at a loss when it came to him. She couldn't reconcile the Kayne that kissed her so sweetly, that had protected her, even comforted her, with the Kayne who participated in these sordid parties, who admitted unblinkingly to the monstrous things he would do there… The same Kayne, she recalled her chest tightening, who had brought her into an interrogation room and had, by his own confession, interrogated countless others. Yet he had stepped in, had rescued her from the wolves he had delivered her to. What kind of monster was he? What kind of monster kisses like that? She caught herself wondering what it would be like to be with him. Would he be gentle? Would he be cruel as she knew him to be capable of? Or maybe… a little of both?

She felt an urge to touch herself down there, to soothe the ache building between her thighs. She resisted, unable to accept the effect he had on her. She had touched herself before, but never with anyone specific in mind, especially not a man, a *monster*, like him.

Day-9

The next day, Laura slept in. When Olga came sometime in the afternoon to take back the untouched breakfast, Laura was just waking up.

"Ah, you're finally up. Should I bring you a fresh breakfast? This won't do." She pointed to the cold food on the trolley, her smile as radiant as ever.

"Hmm... It's okay, I think I'll just have coffee for now. Thank you, Olga."

"As you wish." She was about to turn to leave then added, almost as an afterthought, "Master Kayne wanted me to inform you that he won't be home for supper tonight. Would you still like to eat at seven?"

"He *won't*?" Laura asked, a little too loudly.

"No, Miss Spencer."

"Oh... Yes, seven will be fine, thank you."

Laura could barely disguise the disappointment in her voice. He had never missed supper since he had brought her to the house. She used to dread it. She was even locked in a cage barely a week ago for refusing his company. Now, she felt a wave of disappointment, she almost felt rejected. Was he avoiding her? She couldn't help but wonder, feeling like a teenage girl waiting for a call after a first date. In a twisted way, it almost was, even ending with a soft kiss.

She shook the thoughts away, forcing herself to get through the day. Every so often she caught her thoughts treading a dangerous path, a path he had led her into, and now left her alone in.

Day-10

Laura dreamt of him for the second night in a row, waking up panting, her panties carrying evidence of the nature of the dreams. She woke up early, impatiently awaiting Olga's arrival. When she finally came in at nine to bring in her breakfast, Laura attempted to mask her nerves as she inquired about *Master Kayne*'s whereabouts.

"Thank you, Olga, it was delicious."

"It's my pleasure, Miss Spencer."

"Olga… Can you just call me Laura, if that's okay?" She smiled at her, her warmth genuine.

"Of course, Miss Laura, if you prefer."

"You can just call me Laura…"

"No, no, Miss Laura… that wouldn't be proper." Olga refused adamantly, waving her hands in front of her chest. Though Olga was old school, proper manners were more meaningful than tradition and culture to her. They were a lifeboat. She had convinced herself that keeping her head bowed and her eyes to the floor had kept her employer's hands away from her. She had suffered too much at the hands of men before being taken into the household. Once upon a time, she was young and thought herself invincible. She learned the hard way; the world rewarded the humble and spared only the invisible.

"Oh… Okay…" Unable to comprehend, Laura didn't insist.

"Well, will you be needing anything else?" Olga asked, her kind smile quickly back on her face.

"Hmm… actually... I was just wondering… Can I have supper in my reading room tonight?"

"Yes of course, wherever you like, Miss Laura. Any special requests?"

Her face dropped. *He was avoiding her.* Was it because of the kiss? She couldn't help but wonder. Did she do anything wrong? She could see Olga was still waiting for her answer, so she composed herself.

"Hmm… Nope, carte blanche." She smiled at her.

"Very well then." Olga reciprocated her smile, pleased with the vote of confidence.

Laura was grateful for Olga's presence in the house. She brought warmth and humanity to the place. She realized she had been the only person she'd had any type of human contact with… besides *him*.

She thought back to her old life, barely two weeks ago, it seemed like a lifetime ago. She wondered if anyone worried or asked about her, realizing, her throat choked with emotion, most likely not.

* * *

She woke up late at night in the reading room with the book still opened on her lap. She scrubbed her eyes, trying to read the time on the TV clock; it was past one in the morning. Still half asleep, she dragged herself off the couch, led by the prospect of the comfortable bed awaiting her, as a dangling carrot from a stick.

Once into the hallway, she could hear TV noises and see it cast shadows on the opposite wall. *He was there*, watching TV in the living room. She remained in place, hesitant. To her right awaited the safety of her bedroom. To the left, *him*, and all the implications that only word contained. Her heartbeat quickening, she took a few steps to the left. She wanted to see him, to know how he would react to her, what would ensue following their last encounter. She'd always had a morbid curiosity that pushed her forward to meet the storm head-on, to open Pandora's box, come what may. She'd almost turned the corner but lingered behind the wall, her impulses finally confronted with reason. *Shouldn't she just wait?* He could not possibly avoid her within his own house forever. It was madness to seek his company, alone, in the middle of the night.

"Laura." His voice resounded crisp through the distance.

Her heart beat even faster; she didn't move.

"You should really work on your stealth mode if you don't want to be heard..." he said playfully into the darkness while she still hid behind the wall.

She showed herself but remained lingering at the edge of the corner, almost childlike. "Hi..."

He was sitting in his usual spot on the couch, wearing jeans and a white shirt unbuttoned at the top. A bottle of whiskey was sitting on the table by his glass. He looked her up and down, a sensual languor in his stare. She was wearing a tight white cotton T, the V-neck showing just a little cleavage, and cute granite-colored yoga pants in a thigh-hugging cut that accentuated her curves.

"You're up late," he observed.

"Yeah... well no. I passed out in the reading room... I mean, that room with the red couch... I call it the reading room..." she rambled on nervously, then catching herself, offered an embarrassed smile and continued with more self-assurance. "I was on my way back to my bedroom."

"Wrong way," he pointed out with a smirk on his face.

"Yes... I heard noise..." she explained. "Well, I don't want to bother you..."

"You're not. Have a seat."

She took a few unsure steps before settling on the La-Z-Boy.

"So, did you finish that book I gave you?"

"No, not yet..."

"How come? You don't like it?"

"No, no, it's not that. I really do actually. It's just that—" She caught herself before finishing the sentence.

"It's just that..." he urged her.

She felt herself blushing. "Nothing. I guess I've just been a little… distracted…"

"And what has you distracted?" He smirked.

"Everything…"

He gave her an impatient look, which effectively untangled her tongue.

"I don't know… everything… the *party*…" She looked away with the latter admission.

"What about it?"

"May I ask you a question?" she ventured hesitantly, throwing furtive looks his way.

He waited for her to gather the courage and look him in the eye. "Ask."

"The women there… Were they… sex slaves?" she asked uneasily.

He let out a long sigh, getting up to get another glass, which he filled and set next to his, *not at her end of the table.* His eyes silently communicated the directive. She understood, got up, and settled on the couch uncertainly. She brought her feet up and wrapped her arms around them, simultaneously pushing herself to the furthest side of the couch and away from him, all the while under his scrutinizing stare.

"Some, not all," he finally answered. "Drink."

She took a small sip, already regretting taking the conversation down that path. But she had to know, had to know the extent to which her puzzling captor could cross the lines of right and wrong, the extent to which darkness resided in him.

"Do you… Do you do that?"

"Do what? Deal in sex trafficking?"

She nodded, apprehension in her eyes.

"Not personally." He leaned forward, resting his elbows on his knees, eyeing her sideways.

She sighed with the small relief that came with his answer, but persisted, already knowing the answer but needing to hear it vocalized, "But the people you work with do."

"Yes," he confirmed, his face showing no emotion.

"You don't… care?"

"No, Laura, I don't."

"But… how can you stand for it?"

"I don't *stand* for it… I don't stand *against* it," he corrected her, his tone rising with annoyance. "I'm not out to save the world, Laura." He leaned back in his seat, looking her in the eye. "Just protect what is mine."

She felt her stomach churn. "Don't you worry about catching anything? I mean…"

"The girls are closely supervised and regularly tested. They're clean," he threw dismissively.

"And… the others… were there by choice…?" she asked, still doubtful.

"The others were there because their masters wanted them there, and they want to please their masters." Though his voice was still annoyed, unapologetic delight danced in his eyes as he explained the last part.

It sent shivers down her spine. She thought of stories she'd read, where the willing prey lustfully bared their necks for the vampire's deadly bite. She'd been fascinated by those tales, by their cursed lovers damned to destroy whomever they loved, and by the men and women who loved them despite it all. Kayne had claimed he'd never had a relationship, and she wondered about the women who'd been in his life. What were they to him? What was he to them? Who were they? A colorful and highly abrasive image materialized in response. The redhead.

"What about that woman… Tanya I think?" She tried to conceal her disdain as she pronounced her name. Turning her eyes away, she could still feel him smile.

"What about her?" he asked, the corner of his mouth quirking up.

"She wasn't like the others... She doesn't have a... *master*?" She felt repulsion uttering the word.

"She belongs to Dimitri."

"Oh... I just thought..."

"And what did you think?" he inquired, a smile softening his features.

"I just thought... I thought you were together..." she admitted, her eyes constantly moving to the floor with discomfort and back to his face, seeking his reaction.

"She was mine. A long time ago."

"Oh."

He indulged her curiosity with amusement. He'd never let other women interrogate him like that, but her candid questions alone were more revealing to him than any answer she sought. So he let her ask away, divulging the nature of her curiosity, her fascination with the sinister world he had just introduced her to, his world, even betraying a pang of jealousy she could barely disguise.

A silence followed, while she took small sips of her drink, the one question she'd been wanting to ask, still burning on her tongue. She took another sip, liquid courage they called it. It did the trick.

"Are you a sadist?" she blurted, surprised at her own boldness.

He lifted a brow, seemingly taken aback as well, then offered her his most devilish, seductive smile. "What's your question, Laura? You want to know how I like to fuck?"

Blood rushed to her cheeks. She realized too late she had crossed the line. It wasn't about sex slaves, abuse, and female solidarity anymore. It was about *him*, and he knew it.

"No." She shook her head vehemently. "No, I just... I just don't understand... how any woman could want this... *consent* to it... That woman on stage, it was horrible... you said... you did this to her too..." Her voice trailed off, her courage long gone.

"Hmm..." He reached for her foot.

She instinctively tried to pull away. Her heart was racing, her nerves on high alert. In response, he wrapped his hand firmly around her ankle, though not hard enough to cause pain, his eyes conveyed the warning. She took short sharp breaths, panic overwhelming all other emotions as he calmly waited until she willed her body to relax and he could feel her foot loosen in his grip. Only then did he release his hold. He brushed the tips of his fingers against the bare skin around her ankles and the top of her foot, drawing little shapes on her skin.

"Sometimes what you think you want and what your body wants are very different," he finally said, his voice gruff as his eyes followed the little patterns he softly drew on her bare skin. He lifted his eyes to meet hers, but she remained silent, only her loud breathing being heard. "I think you can understand that…" he added, his eyes smoldering.

She shook her head in denial, her eyes bewildered.

"No…?" he taunted her, still playing with her foot. "Then tell me, Laura, why did you get so wet when I made you strip for me?" he goaded, his smile devilish.

She opened her mouth, then closed it right back in the face of his intense gaze, daring her to deny it. He chuckled softly at her unvoiced indignation. His hand lingered on her ankle a little longer, then in a flash he grabbed them both and pulled her, wrapping one leg behind him, the other on his lap. He leaned toward her, pinning her wrists over her head to the arm of the couch. His upper body towered over her, he could feel her frantic short breaths against him and smiled wickedly. "So many things I can do to you right now…"

She looked up at him, her frightened eyes silently pleading with him.

How he admired his captive prey. With a hungry look in his eyes, he brought his face close to hers, his mouth hovering over hers. She closed her eyes and, with a bitterness contradicting her fluttering heart, surrendered to his kiss.

He didn't kiss her. Instead, he moved his lips away. Slowly, his mouth traced the lines of her jawbone, on its unhinging journey down and up her neck, his own breathing growing louder with arousal.

"Would you stop me, Laura? Would you *consent*?" he huskily whispered into her ear.

She felt her stomach knot, the feeling so familiar now, her breaths growing even faster and louder than before, unsure whether from fear anymore. "Please… Please… sir… let me go back to my room…" Her eyes began to water. "Please…"

He pulled back, looking her in the eye, and shook his head, his smile predatory. If it had worked to her advantage before, she couldn't have picked a worse time to address him as such. He felt himself harden and brought her wrists together without haste to lock them in his left hand. He brought his free hand to her face, the tip of his fingers tracing its outlines, then softly down her neck and over her collarbone. "Bet you wish you would've gone straight to your room…"

He moved his fingers straight down the middle of her chest over her shirt, his eyes following the path his fingers traced. He lingered a little around her belly button. Then crooking his finger over the hem of her yoga pants, he caressed her bare skin with the back of his finger, following the hemline.

She was panting and didn't utter a word, overwhelmed with conflicting emotions dominating her. She could feel the moisture build between her thighs, her apprehension mixing with a very different feeling.

He continued his way down over her pants, at a maddeningly slow pace, taking his time and savoring every moment. When he finally reached his destination, he didn't touch her there, where she was aching for his touch and dreading it at the same time. His fingers circled around it, making her ache only grow. At last, he delicately rested his fingers there, barely touching her.

She unconsciously whimpered at the contact. Desperate for him to press harder, to move his fingers over and around her bundle of nerves and give her that release she wouldn't allow herself on her own. She blushed with shame at her own animalistic thoughts, deeply disconcerted at her responses to his sordid ministrations. Her thoughts incoherent, she whimpered, "Please..."

He began moving his fingers. At first, very slowly, unnervingly so, his fingers barely grazed her. Without will or awareness, her body arched to meet his touch.

He let out a soft chuckle, applying more pressure as he picked up the rhythm. "Please what, Laura? Please... stop? Please... continue? Please... *make me come*?" he coaxed her, his voice hoarse, whispering into her ear.

A soft and surprised "Oh" escaped her lips as her muscles contracted and quivered against his fingers. He pulled his head back barely an inch so he could have a better look at her. Enraptured, he watched her horrified eyes turn hazy with pleasure as her body slackened underneath his, and smiled triumphantly at her. She was still panting, distress gaining her eyes at the realization of what just happened.

"You may be excused," he leaned back close and whispered teasingly, just as she had asked him time and again before. He freed her wrists, watching with open amusement as she staggered to her feet flustered and disoriented. He caught her by the waist when she took a false step and lost her balance. She blushed, muttering a hushed impersonal "Thank you," her eyes roaming in every direction to avoid his, then she rushed out of the room without ever turning back.

"You're welcome," he called out after her, his troublesome snicker underlining what he was referring to.

* * *

Kayne poured himself another drink. He stared at the TV blankly, his mind consumed with thought. He was still horny as hell, considered making a call but decided against it, feeling lazy and pensive. The girl surprised him. She was gutsier than he gave her credit for. He still couldn't believe she had come to meet him on her own. *Crazy girl*, he shook his head with an amused smile. She had been terrified but still spoke her mind, he could respect that. Had he noted jealousy when she asked about Tanya? He wondered. It was almost too easy. *I thought you were together...* He laughed inwardly, that's one way to put it.

He thought back to his time with Tanya, when she was still his. He could still see her defiant stare as she'd obey unblinkingly his most degrading demands, crawling on all fours with her head held high. She was something else, brought out his most sadistic side. He felt himself stiffen. He had loved to hurt her, humiliate her, always pushing her further. But what he wanted most of all was just to make her bow her head, feel her break and crumble at his feet.

He remembered when it finally happened. It was neither whips nor canes that ended the long duel. It was cruel words whispered softly in her ears that had sealed her fate. She was shameless and thick skinned, but like most women, her heart was her ultimate demise. He remembered how she had crawled to him, her belly flat on the floor, and latched on to his foot, kissing it, again and again. "Please, Master... I love you..." she had finally confessed, breaking into a sob. He stood over her, looking down with disdain at the dewy-eyed creature he could barely recognize. He knew it was over right then and there.

"How incredibly disappointing of you," he had callously answered, before shaking his foot free from her clutching hands. Then he walked away, leaving her heaving on the floor. Before exiting the room, he had turned his head back. "You're free. Find another master."

He had received the courtesy call from Dimitri barely a week later. That was three years ago. She had come a long way since, even becoming one of Dimitri's favorites. Her status as the favorite had been further reinforced when Dimitri gave her permanent quarters in his second mansion. It was where he hosted all his parties, where Kayne had brought Laura barely two nights ago.

Then his mind went back to Laura. He felt that same urge, that unwholesome need to dominate, to conquer and destroy. And yet the girl stirred something else in him. Unlike Tanya, she cowered and easily bent to his will, though unlike all the others, she managed to hold on to herself. What a fascinating creature, he thought. He wondered how much longer it would take. She would have let him inside of her, he suspected, but he wanted more, much, much, more. He wanted to get inside her head, to turn her against herself, to hear her utter the words *Yes, Master.* He wanted to break her apart so he could put her back together again, over and over again.

* * *

Laura cried all night long, curled in a little ball under the sheets. She didn't cry from shame at what happened. She cried from despair at what was to come. This man had a hold on her. This man, holding her captive, hunting her brother. This man who'd most likely killed and tortured in cold blood. A man who stood by idly as women were being sold and abused. This was the man she knew would eventually have her. What if he had tried that night, could she have cried rape?

She cried over the life he took from her, the life she would never have. She cried over Peter, not once blaming him for her ordeal. *The betrayal was hers.* She could no longer get his postcards and wondered if he had sent one, if it was still waiting for her in her mailbox. Wouldn't they have sent someone to go through her stuff? If they had found one of his postcards, wouldn't she have been interrogated? Was he still in Boston? Was he still alive, riding a convertible into the sunset, or huddled by a gutter looking for his next fix? Would they get to him first, or would life simply catch up with him? How long do junkies really live? She cried over what he had become, over what he had once been. She cried over the Peter she loved, the one that already died, long ago.

Day-11

She barely had a few hours of sleep and woke up with a start. It was still early in the day when Olga came in with her breakfast. She was already dressed in jeans and a warm grey sweater. Even with the sun shining bright outside, Laura felt cold, big circles under her eyes framing her vacant look. Olga, concerned, inquired about her well-being. Laura absentmindedly reassured her, confirming with a withdrawn smile she would attend supper at seven.

She spent the day in the reading room, unable to read or even watch the television, just looking out the window, trapped in her mind.

* * *

At seven, Kayne was already sitting at the table. His mischievous smile immediately dropped upon seeing her dejected expression.

"What's wrong?" he asked, his voice grave, his face hard.

Laura advanced slowly and took the seat facing him. She looked up at him, her eyes weary, and her voice toneless. "I would rather not talk about it, if it's okay."

His jaw tensed. "What's wrong." He wasn't asking anymore.

"Have you found Peter?" she asked, her voice strained.

He sighed, then nodded his head very slightly a few times, as if confirming his inner speculations. "No, Laura, we haven't."

She breathed in with relief. "Will you ever let me go?" she asked quietly, her directness not emanating from actual courage but with the carelessness of one who had nothing left to lose.

This was not the supper he had in mind. He felt somehow rejected, a rather new and unpleasant feeling. She should be blushing and squirming under his stare after what he'd done to her last night, not stare him straight in the eye, her face haggard, asking about freedom, *from him*.

"I don't know," he finally answered, his voice cold.

She lowered her eyes, resigned. "What about my stuff, my apartment, my job…"

"It's been taken care of."

She nodded, her eyes still fixed on the untouched plate in front of her.

"Eat," he commanded.

They spent the rest of the supper in silence. She played with her food with no appetite, tentatively bringing a spoon or two to her mouth every now and then.

"Will you… will you let me go outside?" Her soft voice reached into his turbulent thoughts.

"What?"

"Just out in the backyard. I just thought I could read outside…"

"No."

"May I ask why?" she asked, her eyes glistening.

"So I won't have to hurt you when you try something stupid," he cautioned, his eyes penetrating.

"I won't. I swear… I mean, how could I even… there's guards everywhere…"

"You think you won't, now. But you will, believe me, you will."

"No… I swear… I just wanted to read… You can't lock me in here forever…" Her voice quivered, unshed tears filling her big grey eyes.

"Try me."

They finished the meal in an oppressing silence. She waited until he finished his plate to ask to be excused to which he nodded, his expression inscrutable. As she picked up her plate, ready to bring it to the sink, he stopped her.

"Leave it," he barked.

She jerked at the command, then quietly exited the room under his unnerving glare.

* * *

Laura fell into a deep sleep as soon as she shut her eyes, mentally drained, physically exhausted. She had a horrible nightmare about Peter. They were in a Roman arena. She was sitting next to a faceless king with a crown on her head, an uneasy feeling in her gut. There was a skinny daunted gladiator in the arena facing a lion. The crowds cheered and roared dementedly as the lion circled the defenseless gladiator shakily holding his blade up, turning around on himself in a futile effort to keep the lion in view.

The gladiator then threw his blade to the floor and ran in the queen's direction. "Laura! Why won't you help me?" he screamed, his face distorted with emotion.

She recognized her brother too late. The lion broke into a run and jumped in the air. She howled in pain, screaming his name over and over again.

She woke up still screaming, her face wet with tears. Someone was shaking her awake.

"Laura... Laura... wake up." Kayne was sitting on the bed by her side, a darkness in his eyes contrasting the softness in his voice.

She blinked a few times, slowly coming out of her dream-induced haze.

"You had a nightmare. You were shouting in your sleep."

She brought herself up to a sitting position, her eyes looking deep into his. "But it wasn't just a nightmare... Peter..." Her voice cracked, tears returning to her eyes.

He held her gaze, remaining quiet.

"Peter..." she repeated and broke into desperate sobs.

He pulled her to him, carefully, as if afraid he might break her. Burying her head in the nook of his neck, he ran his fingers through her hair, making shushing sounds in her ear. She wailed against his strong chest, letting herself be caressed and comforted while he placed gentle kisses on her forehead.

"I don't want him to die..." she sobbed in his arms.

With his lips still pressed against her forehead, he responded, in a hushed tone, a hint of affection softening its inflection, "I know."

She leaned back, turning her big grey eyes to his, the last shred of hope threatening to abandon them, never to return. "Help me..."

They remained in this loose embrace for what seemed like an eternity, silently staring into each other in the middle of the darkness that surrounded them, which was slowly becoming a part of them.

He finally nodded his head, slowly, resolute, his eyes boring into hers. Without another word, he got up and walked away.

Day-12

Kayne sat in his office across from his bedroom on the second floor. It was already past one in the morning. He had just returned home. He opened his desk drawer and pulled out the postcard. He turned it over in his hands pensively. *He was already helping her.* He just didn't know to what extent he was willing to go and began to wonder if his intentions were still purely selfish. His talk with Dimitri had been tense but successful.

Dimitri knew right away the girl knew more than she let on. He had questioned him about it, displeased. He felt the need to remind him what they stood for; it was far more than getting the information back. If Peter wanted to use it, he would have. It was about righting the wrong. Betrayal cannot go unpunished, he reiterated. He reminded him of his father's teachings. Kayne did not take kindly to being lectured but remained quiet nonetheless. Dimitri wanted to take back the girl, have her interrogated right there and then. He had assured him the girl would be returned to him still attractive, *still useful.*

Kayne had stood his ground then. It was about much more than the girl; it would undermine his position. If they took the girl from him, Dimitri would openly disgrace him, deem him incompetent in the eyes of all. He would not tolerate such insult. The mood got tense.

Kayne made his arguments, carefully choosing his words. Peter had been on the run for over eight months now. He would be found, and his head, along with the information, would be brought to him, he assured Dimitri. He had never failed him before. Was Dimitri ready to jeopardize a lifelong relationship to gain a few days? If betrayal could not be forgiven, disrespect would not be tolerated, Kayne asserted. He drew the line in the sand and hoped for the best. Dimitri finally broke the strenuous silence that followed by waving him into an embrace, chuckling.

So proud, just like your father you are. He'd given him one more week. That was four days ago.

Things with Laura were unpredictable. One moment she was eating out of his hand, the next acting like a terrified prisoner. Then, just last night, he felt her shatter in his arms, looking up at him as a savior, *Help me.* Her desperate plea resonated in him. He'd never been the person you turned to for help. Hunt, track, destroy. Those were his talents, his very identity. But he had acquiesced. In that moment, he had meant it.

Even now, he knew, he wouldn't turn his back on her. And yet he had to find Peter. He'd have to make her tell him, within the next three days. Tomorrow, he thought, tomorrow he would put an end to the Peter saga. He would find a way, and she would tell him all he needed to know.

He put back the postcard on the desk and leaned back in his chair. He reached for the phone, exhausted and disgruntled. He needed an outlet for all this pent-up frustration.

A female voice answered, "Master..."

"Hello, Pet." A sadistic smile promptly chased away his morose mood. "You have twenty minutes."

"Yes, Master."

* * *

Laura hadn't seen Kayne for the day. She so desperately wanted to. Had she dreamt it all? Had he really walked into her room last night and consented to helping her? Had she imagined all of this?

She had spent the day pacing around, unable to set her mind to anything but awaiting his return. Olga had informed her early on that he would not make it home for supper. She waited in the living room for him all evening, scared to miss his return.

She had finally retreated to her bedroom around midnight and tried to go to sleep unsuccessfully.

She realized she had been asleep, waking up to clicking sounds coming from down the hall. She looked at the time; it was almost two in the morning. Intrigued, she threw on the first pair of jeans she found by her chair, threw a T-shirt over it, and tiptoed out of her room. By the time she made it into the main parlor by the front doors, the sound was gone. She wondered what it could be. It made her think of a woman's high heels. Could there be another woman in the house? *With Kayne?* The idea deeply disturbed her. Rattled, she looked for the unwanted intruder all over the first floor, going in and out of every room, finding nothing. She went back to the small living room by the kitchen, *their* living room. She couldn't shake off the betrayal she felt. How could he bring another woman here? While she was here. It was ridiculous, she knew. Shouldn't she be relieved he had spared her his sordid sexual penchants? He had agreed to help her and didn't ask for anything in return. Wasn't that the best-case scenario she could have hoped for? And yet the unrelenting twist in her gut disproved her efforts at reason. *Kayne was here, with another woman.*

She then remembered the cage in the basement. He had taken her left as soon as they had reached down the stairs, but wasn't there a corridor going to the right? Her trepidation grew. Before she even realized what she was doing, Laura retraced the steps that had taken her down to that cursed room. She opened the back door carefully, her heart beating faster as the spiraling stairs reappeared. She remembered too well how she had felt going down them the first time. But as if in a trance, she was unable to stop herself, taking one step at a time, careful not to make any noise. She had a vision of Walt Disney's *Sleeping Beauty*, when Aurora, under the spell of the wicked witch, climbed the winding stairs leading to the spinning wheel and, to the hypnotizing music of Tchaikovsky, brought the dark prophecy to fruition.

When she reached the lower ground, she shook off a shudder as the holding cell emerged to her left. She quickly looked away, facing the corridor swerving right. She wasn't even sure what she was hoping to achieve.

There were closed doors on each side. She turned right, following the corridor that curled to the left. She could hear female moans and loud cracking sounds followed by low manly grunts. At the very end of the corridor, a metallic door was left ajar. Through it, she saw a woman, hog-tied on a metal table facing away from her. Laura could only see her long black hair cascading down. The woman moaned and whimpered as harsh whips fell unto her back, ass, and thighs. Laura was frozen in place, fixated on the woman, on her throaty "*Yes, Master… Thank you, Master… Please… More…*" The male voice was low and gruff. She couldn't make out the words, but she knew it was Kayne's. She could recognize his voice anywhere, his commands, his own brand of brutish force and sensual persuasion. He took a step forward toward the woman, and she could finally see him. He was topless, wearing only black dress suit pants, revealing his muscular torso, toned abs, and broad shoulders. His hair was tied back, though loose strands fell on his face as he leaned to whisper something into the woman's ear.

Laura gulped, fascinated and frightened to death by the shocking scene, by the dangerously alluring and simply dangerous man standing in front of her. Hearing the small sound she had just made, Kayne, while still bending down to the woman's face, lifted his head, barely an inch in Laura's direction. His eyes rounded with surprise upon finding her, then narrowed with fury at the realization.

Laura took a few steps back, terrified, mouthing *No, no…*

His eyes piercing into hers, he brought himself up to his full height. She didn't wait an instant longer. She broke into a run, up the stairs and all the way to the front doors, trying the handle frantically, but it was locked electronically. She banged on the door with frustration, in complete panic, which only attracted the attention of one of the guards posted outside. She fell to her knees and wept on the floor. There was no way out. Any moment now, he would come. God only knew what he had in store for her. There was nothing else for her to do but to get back to her room and powerlessly await the ramifications of her impulsive actions.

* * *

Kayne was livid. He almost chased her up the stairs but talked himself out of it. He would have to calm down a little before finding her, or else he didn't know what he would do. He dismissed his whore unceremoniously and went back to his room for a hot shower to help collect himself. After throwing on a pair of jeans and a white shirt, he went to his office and picked up the postcard. Carefully folding it, he put it in his back pocket, took a few long breaths, then headed to Laura's room.

He opened the door slowly, finding her crouching on the bed, her back against the stand, hugging her knees, visibly shaking. He didn't walk straight toward her. He inspected the room, looking around, familiarizing himself with her environment. He had always avoided this room. *His mother's room.* He lingered by the vanity, picking up and placing back a few things, all the while under Laura's petrified stare. He then grabbed the chair facing the mirror, moved it close to the bed, and casually sat in it. He spread his legs, leaning back, making himself comfortable before addressing her. His eyes acerbic, he commanded harshly, "Speak."

She broke into uncontrollable shaking. She began rocking herself as tears rolled down her cheeks.

He leaned forward in his seat, resting his elbows on his knees, his soft voice dripping with threat. "You have willfully disrespected and disobeyed me in my own house. I am being kind enough to give you a chance to explain yourself. You would be wise to use it."

"No… no, no, no, no…" she repeated hysterically, shaking her head.

"Explain yourself!"

She had a complete meltdown. "Please… please… I swear… I didn't mean to… I didn't mean to disrespect or disobey… please…" she desperately cried.

He remained impassive, if not a little annoyed. He stood up. "I will count to five. If you don't start talking by then, I guarantee, you will wish you had."

She wanted to speak, wanted to explain, but she could barely understand her actions herself. She threw herself at his feet.

"Please, sir… Please… Please forgive me… I didn't mean to."

He looked down at her, irritated. "Get up."

She supported her weight by holding on to him. This time, he didn't help steady or support her. He remained stoic and cold against her fragile body. She finally managed to get to a full standing position, keeping her eyes fixated on his chest, too terrified to meet his stare.

"Look at me, Laura." His voice was cold, but calmer.

She was dry heaving but finally brought her eyes up to his. He grabbed both her arms, slowly, and pushed her back against the wall. Her body was threatening to give out any moment, held up only by his firm hold on her.

"Why did you go downstairs?"

"I don't know… please… I'm sorry…"

He kept one hand firmly grabbing her arm, the other he slowly brought up and closed around her neck. A gasp escaped her lips. But he didn't apply pressure, just left his hand there, the threat hanging.

He leaned into her ear. "You don't know?" Cold rage echoed in his voice. His hand tightened just a little bit on her throat.

"No… please, sir… please… I don't know why I went downstairs… I heard her come in… I don't know why I went… I'm sorry… Oh god, I'm so sorry…" she sobbed against his cheek.

"Yes. You will be sorry," he whispered menacingly into her ear before letting go of his hold on her. He was about to turn around, but she grabbed his arm with both of hers, desperate, knowing if she let him walk away, it was over.

"I was jealous!" she almost screamed in agony, then softly as the realization dawned on her. "I was jealous…"

His face stoic, he lowered his gaze to her hands holding his arm so desperately. She let go of her hold immediately at his silent command. He then raised his eyes to meet hers, his expression inscrutable.

"Why were you jealous?"

She looked down, remaining quiet. He let out a long exasperated sigh.

"You know why." Though her voice was hushed, bitterness tainted her words.

He smiled, wickedly. "Tell me."

"Please, sir… please… don't make me say it."

His sardonic laugh resonated in her ears. He took a step forward, towering over her, their bodies at an unsettling closeness, his face so close she could feel his breath against her skin.

"Tell me," he commanded, his voice gruff.

She shut her eyes, unable to face the shame of admission. Her voice quavering, she confessed, "I wanted it to be me."

He exhaled slowly as she looked up sheepishly at him. He brought his hand around her back, his fingers gently working their way up, through her nape and into her hair. She sighed in relief, closed her eyes, and leaned into his caresses. He fisted her hair into his hand, very close at the nape, and tugged slowly, forcing her head backward and up toward his. She whimpered, opening her eyes with surprise.

"You want me to fuck you, Laura, is that it?" he whispered huskily, bringing his mouth to her ear.

An incoherent sound, between a moan and a cry, escaped her lips. He pulled her head further back, forcing her body to arch into his, making her feel even more vulnerable in this unnatural position, while allowing him a full view of her face. Using his free hand, he caressed the outer side of her breast, could feel her nipples hardening against his chest, hear her breath becoming ragged.

"Answer me," he commanded yet again, his voice raspy.

"Yes…" she breathed.

"Yes. What?"

"Yes… I want you… to fuck me…" she finally conceded, her eyes half shut, with pleasure and shame.

He emitted a low guttural sound, feeling himself harden. He pulled her back to a standing position and, with a devilish smile, cautioned her, "I still have to punish you for your behavior."

Her eyes opened wide with instant terror. "Sir, please, *no…*"

"Hold your arms up," he ignored her plea.

She obeyed. With gentle fingers, he lifted her T-shirt over her head and threw it to the floor. She watched it fall, her bare breasts now exposed, then looked back at him. "Please, sir, please don't…"

He continued to ignore her and proceeded to unbutton her jeans, pulling down the zipper, while looking her in the eye with a wolfish grin. Her heart pounded in her chest, her eyes desperately pleading her case. Unaffected, he bent down to lower her jeans, then, kneeling on the floor, commanded her to raise one leg after the other to remove them.

"Sir?"

Still kneeling on the floor, he looked up at her inquisitively.

"Please… don't hurt me…"

He let out a soft chuckle, then stood back up under her terrified stare.

"Are you going to hurt me?" she asked softly as a defenseless child.

With an amused smile, he grabbed her by the waist and pulled her to him. He kissed her, very softly, his lips savoring hers. When he pulled back, her eyes were still closed, her chin lifted toward his, still lost in the moment.

"You will do what I say, as I say it, without question, hesitation, or delay. Is that understood?"

She nodded repeatedly, her eyes conveying the conviction of a drowning man whose been thrown a rope.

"Good girl," he whispered, his voice hoarse.

He kissed her again, his hands still on her hips. With his lips still pressed against hers, he commanded her to open her mouth.

His tongue invaded every inch, his kiss turning voracious as he brought her arms up and wrapped them around his neck. Then he brought his own down her back. His fingers grazed her ass, drawing little circles over her underwear. In a firmer grab, he picked her up, forcing her to wrap her legs around him for support. He carried her to the bed without breaking the kiss, kneeling on the mattress and gently laying her on her back. She opened her eyes, stared at him intently, consumed with excitement and apprehension. He responded with an indulgent, reassuring smile. His body over hers, he unwrapped her arms from his neck and directed her to grab the posts on the headboard.

"Keep your hands there, no matter what."

"Yes, sir."

He leaned back, still kneeling between her legs. His fingers traveled the length of her body, barely grazed every surface, lingering on her breasts, circling her hardened nipples. He then lowered her underwear, very slowly, his fingers tracing the outlines of her thighs and legs, and bent her knees together to remove them. Her panting only increased as he gently deposited the palms of his hands on her knees to wedge them apart, and she resisted the pressure.

"Open your legs."

She blushed, feeling the juices flowing in her private parts, already missing the cover of her panties. She obeyed, exposing herself, and felt self-conscious with the moistness dripping from her.

Kayne remained still for a few moments, savoring his willing prey. He was in awe, of her beauty, of her vulnerability. In knowing that she was irrevocably his for the taking. He let his fingers glide across the surface of her soft skin, on the outside of her legs up to her thighs and back. He removed his shirt and threw it to the floor before leaning forward, hovering over her naked body with a feline grace.

"Close your eyes," he breathed in her ear.

He wanted to offer her the cover of darkness, ease her into the exhilaration he knew he could bring her by demanding her complete submission. He moved down her body, kissing every inch of her, taking her breast in his mouth and swirling his tongue around her nipple as she moaned in response. His fingers then dipped down her belly and touched her wetness as he continued to kiss and nip her firm soft breast. He felt her panting increase, her moans coming closer together, and he brought his face close to hers.

"I know you want to come," he hoarsely whispered into her ear. "Don't you dare without my permission."

A loud moan escaped her lips.

"Do you understand?"

"Yes… yes, sir," she panted.

"Good girl."

He brought his mouth to her slit, his tongue continuing the sweet torture his fingers had initiated. He could feel her tension building up, her wetness on his lips, as she unconsciously wreathed under him. He steadied her limbs, firmly pinning her hips on the mattress.

"Sir… Sir, *please*," she cried out.

He didn't respond. He wanted to hear her say the words.

"Sir… please… can I… come?" she panted.

"Come," he commanded gruffly, as his middle finger penetrated her entrance. He felt her muscles clamp with her orgasm, her whole body spasm then go lax, as she almost screamed her release. He licked his lips with delight, staring at her hungrily as he removed his jeans and then lay his body over hers.

"Look at me."

She opened her eyes, her face still flush. She wished she hadn't upon seeing his warm smile. It cut right through her. She could barely accept the effect he had on her body. She couldn't face the turmoil his smile brought about in her shattered world.

She could feel his erection rubbing against her, bringing the ache back. However, this time it went deeper. Her body didn't simply want physical release. She felt the need to have him inside her, to fill her up.

"Ask me," he commanded as he continued to rub himself on her.

Her eyes watered with shame. "Fuck me… please, sir…"

He grunted, resting his elbows on each side of her head, his fingers caressed her face. His first thrust was slow, entering her inch by inch, until he could feel her inner wall. He pulled out slowly and reentered her, his rhythm picking up with every thrust.

She could feel a second orgasm building up, now that she knew what it was. She had made herself come before, but he was the first man to give her an orgasm. Realizing she could no longer hold back, she panicked at the idea of coming without his permission, and mad with pleasure, she screamed out, "Sir! Sir, please…"

"Again?" he taunted her, his smile devilish.

"Yes…yes…" She was beyond shame, in a place where only physical pleasure existed.

"Come for me, Laura," he whispered in her ear as he fucked her relentlessly.

Her moan was low and long, immediately followed by his guttural growl as he found his own release. He collapsed on top of her, both panting against each other.

He finally raised himself on his elbows, cocked his head to the side, eyeing her playfully. He planted a kiss on her forehead before he rolled himself over to her side. She was still breathing fast, looking at him through a haze of confusion.

He then turned on his side to face her and turned her around as he brought her to him, spooning her affectionately. He kissed her hair and caressed her arm as she nestled against him.

"Laura..."

His voice came to her disembodied. She was still lost in the moment, trying to make sense of everything that had just happened. "Hmm?" came her absentminded answer.

"Laura." His voice was stricter, demanding her attention as he stopped caressing her.

The slightest shift in his mood was enough to snap her back to reality. "Yes, sir."

"You asked me to help you…"

"Yes…" she answered wearily. She didn't expect him to bring it up, in this moment, as she lay in his arms, naked and spent.

He moved behind her, then placed a very familiar-looking postcard in front of her. Her heart clamped, and she felt her chest tighten. She instantly jumped out of his embrace, reaching for it.

"Where did you get this!" she almost screamed, as her fingers lovingly caressed the postcard. She turned back to him, sitting up, eyeing him with terror as she awaited his explanation.

He sat up on his elbow; his voice soft, he ignored her question. "Where is he, Laura?"

Her heart skipped a beat. It was all a scheme to get her to speak, the seduction, everything. *He only fucked her to get her to talk.* She felt as though she got punched in the gut. Betrayed, used, enraged, and hurt, she didn't know how to feel or which emotion was worse.

"You used me…" she finally said, her face expressing the repulsion she felt toward him. "You really are a monster."

He sprung up and pinned her back on the mattress. "*Am I*?" he growled. "Who do you think has been protecting you all along? Huh? Who do you think stopped them from interrogating you? Your guardian angels?" His voice was low but jerky. "No, Laura… It's a *monster* that's been keeping you all safe and warm in your ivory tower," he hissed. "I could've left you. Dimitri wants you. Maxwell wants you. Do you think they would have shown you the patience I have…?" He laughed sardonically in answer to his own question.

Then his tone softened, as did his hold on her wrists. "I *am* helping you, can't you see that?"

Tears fell to the side of her face, drops forming on the pillow. She remained quiet, turning her gaze away from him.

"Look at me, Laura."

She did, her eyes holding a resigned intensity. He rested his forehead against hers and breathed a long sigh before meeting her gaze again.

"They will find him… soon. We tracked him down to Chicago. It won't be long now." He broke the bad news, his voice soft.

She closed her eyes to the flood of silent tears rushing down her cheeks.

"Trust me, Laura, you would rather I find him first. I will go alone."

"To kill him…"

"To retrieve the information he stole. I'll make sure he doesn't suffer. Believe me, Laura, it's the best option you have."

"No! No!" she sobbed. "You can't kill him!"

"I can't let him walk," he admitted, his face grave.

"No…" she repeated in broken sobs.

"It will be quick and painless. I give you my word."

"*No!* I can't… Please…" She was gasping for air.

"Even if I could, Laura, it would just delay the inevitable. When they find him, it won't be quick. They will torture him. He will be *begging* for death. Do you understand what I'm telling you?"

"No… no... But he would still have a chance… They've been hunting him for eight months. He's good, they won't catch him..." she pleaded desperately, her whole body convulsing with uncontrollable sobs. "Please... Kayne… Please…"

He considered her for a moment then leaned closer, kissed her temples, and brushed her hair away from her face.

"Okay."

"Okay?" she asked, disbelieving, waiting for the confirmation that she had finally lost touch with reality.

"Tell me where he is. I won't kill him," he asserted, his eyes locked with hers.

He reached for the postcard and handed it back to her. He rolled off her, sitting up, while she pushed herself up and leaned her back against the headboard.

Her fingers traced the little patterns on the card lovingly, and she brushed her tears away with the back of her hand.

"Promise me." She finally looked up at him.

"I promise." He nodded, his eyes solemn.

She gazed at the card, the fatality of it dawning on her. She felt numb, felt herself going out of her body and witnessing a stranger dictate the address, down to the street and apartment number.

"How do you know?"

She proceeded to explain the infantile and yet complex coding system her brother had invented, interchanging letters and numbers following math equations to determine the city and state, their arrangement dictating which characters stood for which. A square meant a residential building, a rectangle a motel, characters within a circle determined a room or apartment number, and so forth…

He sighed, slowly getting off the bed and reaching for his shirt.

"Are you leaving… *now*?" she asked, her voice growing shrill with panic.

He leaned down and kissed her on the forehead in response.

"Wait… *wait!*"

"Try to get some rest. I'll be back as soon as I can." He offered her a weary smile, and just like that, he was gone.

* * *

Laura remained still, in shock. Everything had happened so fast. She was unsure of what happened, so much, too much, in one short night. She looked back at the card, realization creeping up on her. She took it in her hands and kissed it over and over again, as tears rolled down and fell on the thick paper, diluting the blue ink. But he promised, *promised*, he wouldn't kill him. She clung to this promise, to the only hope she still had that kept her pieced together. She slid herself under the covers, bringing them over her head just as she had when she was a little girl, and stared into nothingness, her mind completely blank.

Day-13

Kayne found himself in a messy, dirty apartment. It was past eleven at night, and he was tired, going on almost forty-eight hours without sleep. He had driven all day. It hadn't taken him long to retrace the given address. He removed a heap of dirty clothes off a beat-up armchair. Wearing a suit and black leather gloves, he dusted the seat before sitting, pulled his silencer from its holster, and rested it on his lap. Patiently, he waited.

The door unlocked, and a man walked into the living room, looking disheveled. He was wearing dirty clothes, his face gaunt, and his body impossibly thin. He was carrying a grocery bag, containing everything but groceries. Twitching, he deposited it on the only remaining space on the table as Kayne remained silent, waiting for the man to notice him.

The man finally turned around, his look of shock quickly dissipating into resignation. "I should've known it would be you…" Peter smiled bitterly.

"It's been a long time," Kayne conceded. He had actually gotten along with Peter back then. There was a mutual respect between the two. Kayne never forgave Peter for his betrayal, took it even more personally due to their closeness at the time.

"Yup. How did you find me?"

"Take a seat, Peter." Kayne waved the gun toward the sofa. Peter looked around, sighed, then dropped to the sofa facing Kayne.

"Laura," Kayne explained with this one word.

Peter instantly snapped up, his eyes full of venom.

"What have you done to her?"

"Sit down, Peter."

"Answer me, you son of a bitch!"

"She's fine." Kayne raised his voice. "Sit down."

Peter hesitated; he knew Kayne. He knew he didn't lie. For the first time, he felt shame. He hadn't felt shame when he begged for money, stole, and mugged, when he squatted and went through trash. But now, hearing his sister's name from that man's mouth, knowing he was the cause of it, he realized the scum he was.

"She's fine, Peter, no harm has come to her," Kayne reassured him, his tone softer.

"She gave me up that easy, huh? Good on her..." He smiled sadly as he reclaimed his seat.

"No. She hasn't."

"Okay…" Peter added, confused.

"I gave her my word I wouldn't kill you."

"Then why are you here?"

"The case file."

Peter nodded, went rummaging through a heap of broken things and dirty laundry, then pulled out a USB key.

"Here, it's all there. I destroyed the folder. I transferred it onto this key." He handed it to Kayne. "Where is she?"

"She's at my house, under my protection."

Peter exhaled the breath he'd been holding, relief washing over his face. "So that's it? You're just going to let me walk?" He laughed, disbelieving.

"You know I can't do that."

"Yeah... Dimitri can sure hold a grudge, can't he?" He chuckled bitterly, his eyes defeated. "I just couldn't, Kayne, I mean, I know I'm no fuckin' Captain America, but the women trafficking… I just couldn't…" He shook his head. "I kept thinking of Laura, you know? What if someone did that to her?"

Kayne gave a small nod.

"What about Laura? Dimitri will want you to get rid of her… a *liability*…" he uttered, disgusted.

"I won't. I'll keep her safe."

Peter considered him a moment. "You… care about her…" He wasn't asking; he was just voicing his incredible realization. Turned out, *Kayne Malkin did have a heart after all.*

Kayne remained impassive as Peter smiled at his old friend.

"You promised her you wouldn't kill me?"

Kayne nodded again, this time the move more deliberate.

"But you have to."

Kayne reached inside his pocket and brought out aluminum foil and a syringe. He deposited them on the table. "It's good stuff."

Peter laughed, his face surly. "And if I don't… You let me walk?"

"If you don't, Dimitri will have her interrogated. In two days. That's all the time I could get."

Peter's face dropped; he understood. Kayne meant to keep his word. He wouldn't kill him. Peter would have to do it all by himself, or Laura would pay the price. The two men stared at each other in silence. Peter finally nodded, his face somber, his body relaxing, finally accepting his fate. He stood up and reached for the package.

"You know... I was trying to quit… shit is bad for you," he joked, disheartened. They quietly chuckled together. "What about Dimitri? Doubt he'll be too pleased with an overdose…"

Kayne simply waved the gun in response.

"You thought of everything, huh? Well… can you wait 'til after the high?"

It was such an unusually morbid conversation, undertaken with calm pleasantries. Peter, much like his sister, always resorted to humor, even in his darkest hour.

"I'll wait until it's all over. The gun's just for the pictures, for Dimitri's benefit."

Peter threw his head back, smiling tight-lipped with understanding. "Can I write her?"

Kayne closed his eyes in acknowledgment, and Peter went scavenging for a paper and pen, then began cooking the heroin. He scribbled away on a paper he handed to Kayne, then went back to filling the syringe.

"Take care of her."

"You have my word."

They nodded at each other, their eyes grim.

"Well… Cheers, mate!" Peter raised the syringe.

Kayne smiled back at his old friend one last time.

Day-16

It had been two days since Kayne left. Laura had gone through every emotion possible. *What's taking him so long?* She kept imagining the worst, hoping for the best, caught in the limbo between. She asked Olga constantly for news of Kayne's whereabouts. It seemed Olga was in the dark as well. Olga fretted over her, checking in on her constantly, almost force-feeding her in bed. She stayed by her side, watching over her while pretending to busy herself with other things.

It was late at night. Laura had asked Olga to keep her company, and the latter was glad to oblige. She was reading in the chair by her bed when sounds coming from the entrance made them both jump up.

"Kayne!" Laura exclaimed and leaped to her feet, rushing out of her bedroom. The door opened as she reached for the handle, and she ran into him.

"Kayne..." She smiled up at him, her eyes full of hope.

His expression was inscrutable. He kept his eyes locked in on her then turned to Olga. "Would you give us a moment?"

"Of course, Master Kayne, I'll boil some tea." Though happy to see him, Olga left the room feeling uneasy about his tense expression.

"Kayne?" Laura asked, her voice quavering, her high hopes slowly evaporating. "He's okay? He's okay, isn't he?" She already knew the answer from his severe expression but refused to believe it.

He shut the door behind him, led her gently to the bed, and made her sit. He knelt in front of her and shook his head.

"No! No! You promised! You promised!" she screamed.

"It was suicide, Laura."

“No… I don’t believe you... Peter would never, NEVER!”

He closed his eyes and nodded his head in acknowledgment. He then handed her a paper note that was tucked in his front pocket.

“What is this?”

“Read it.”

She grabbed the paper from his hand, eyeing it suspiciously, then immediately recognized the handwriting.

My Sweet Laura,

I fucked up. So bad. I failed you in so many ways. Please forgive me. You will be safe now. I love you, always and forever.

Peter

“No…” She shook her head in denial. “NO!” she then screamed forcefully, falling to the floor, the sound almost inhuman.

Kayne had dreaded the reunion. He had remained true to his word, though he couldn’t shake the feeling he had betrayed her nonetheless. He put his hand on her shoulder, wanting to comfort her.

“Don’t you fuckin’ touch me! Do you hear me? Don’t you fuckin’ dare!” she bellowed hysterically.

Kayne was taken aback, unsure what to do, how to deal with all this pain. He stood up, hovering over her as she wailed on the floor, lowering her body over her bended knees.

“You did it… I know you did… It was you.” Her voice came out eerily soft. In an instant, she was up on her feet, staring him down, a demented gleam in her eye. “Tell me. Tell me to my face you didn’t kill him.”

“I didn’t kill him.”

She could see the pity in his eyes. She snapped. Raising her arm to slap him, she called out, “LIAR!”

He caught her hand midair, holding her wrist so tight it hurt. He maintained his calm, though his eyes betrayed his anger. “I know you’re upset, but I didn’t. He overdosed. I have a picture if you would like to see for yourself. Don’t you fuckin’ call me a liar,” he hissed. Then raising his voice, he added, "And don't you *EVER* raise your hand at me."

But she knew. She knew in her heart he was lying. His denial felt like salt being poured over her wound. With blind rage, she looked at him defiantly, then spit in his face.

His hand twisted her wrist even harder, his eyes narrowing with silent fury. But she held his gaze, challenging him, with the courage that's granted to those who've lost reason. He didn't bother wiping his face. He lifted his other hand and struck her, slapping her hard across her face, while still holding her wrist.

Her entire body quavered on impact, only held up by the wrist he was still holding. She fell to the ground the instant he let go.

She crawled back away from him, terror in her eyes, backing away until her back hit the wall. She wrapped her arms around her knees and started rocking herself, her eyes vacant.

Within seconds, he wanted to go to her but immediately cooled off, still feeling her saliva dripping on his face.

"When you're ready to talk about it, you can come to me," he said coolly after he wiped his face. He then walked out, leaving her behind, shattered on the floor.

Day-24

It had been almost ten days since Kayne returned. Olga, very upset that first night, had chased him down to the living room as he poured himself a glass of whiskey, drinking it standing by the bar. He was in one of those scary moods, and she could see his father staring out of his eyes. She didn't let up. She'd seen the girl's face, all red and swollen, but he simply snapped at her to leave it alone.

Ever since that night, she stayed by the girl's side. She brought ice for her face and fixed meals she liked, but Miss Laura wouldn't eat. The girl was shrinking in front of her eyes. She wouldn't get out of bed, she wouldn't even cry. She just stared ahead, her eyes vacant, all day long. She allowed Olga to dress and undress her, even bathe her with no resistance. Olga's heart broke for her. She would tell Master Kayne about it every evening. She could see how he listened attentively but then shrugged it off, his eyes cold.

In the evenings, she'd pull a chair by her bed and stay with her until she fell asleep. She gave up trying to make her talk. She racked her brain trying to find a way to snap her out of her catatonic state. On the third night, Olga was recounting to Laura one of her favorite fairy tales from her childhood when her eyes moved, barely, but they moved. Olga knew she had found a way to reach into her. She continued telling her a different story each night, recounting old Russian folktales her own mother used to tell her when she was little. Laura turned to her, listening enraptured. She would close her eyes sometimes, as if imagining the tale in her mind, but remained quiet.

It was during one of those evenings that she first spoke again. Olga had just finished telling her the tale of Alexei and Aniska, two orphans, brother and sister, wandering through the Russian wilderness.

In the tale, the two siblings meet all sorts of characters throughout their journey, from friends and foes, to evil men and enchanted beasts. They learn the secrets of the Winter Woods, befriend a traveling bear, and even escape a murderous huntsman. Their journey leads them down the path of the Great White Wolf Witch. The cunning Witch lures the children into her realm, wishing to use them as sacrifice to undo the curse that had bound her spirit to that of the White Wolf's. Unlike all their previous encounters, they can't get out of this situation with wit and bravery alone. The Witch is strong, powerful, and most cunning of all. Yet a human part still remained in her heart. She had been a mother once, long, long ago. Her human heart would not let her forget it when the time came. Incapable of carving out the innocent children's hearts to free herself, the Witch pierces her own. She dies alone in the snow, forsaken and unwept. It was a sad story.

"I love wolves, I always have," Laura said simply, her voice childlike, at the end of the story. The next night, she asked Olga to retell her the story of Alexei and Aniska.

Following that night, Olga established their new routine. Every morning, she would drag Laura out of bed and bring her to the solarium. They had never gone there before, she'd barely shown it to her. It was Elena Malkin's domain, and like so many traces of her, it was shut out and forgotten.

It was really a beautiful place, though a pale comparison to what it had been in its glory day. Olga thought Laura would like this place. In so many ways, she reminded her of Mrs. Malkin, and she frowned inwardly at the association.

Olga spent the days doing her crochet, talking about everything and nothing, telling funny anecdotes she remembered from childhood, back in her homeland, her Russia. She even made Laura's lips widen into a sort of a smile a few times, though her gaunt eyes foretold of the long battle ahead to recovery.

They would have their breakfast together there. Laura would only nibble on hers, shivering away regardless of the warm weather and layers of clothes. Olga would cover her with the thickest comforter she could find. Sometimes they would just sit together silently, comfortable and comforted by each other.

It took a few days for Laura to begin participating in conversations, dropping sentences randomly here and there. In response to another one of Olga's fond childhood memories involving a mischievous dog the family had, Laura just said, "We had one when I was really young, but after my mom left, my father got rid of him. He didn't like dogs."

Laura didn't mention that the dog crate, however, remained. She wondered if Kayne had told Olga about it. He hadn't. She had gone over that night in her head over and over again. She wanted to believe him; he had given her his word. He had never lied, he hadn't lied in other circumstances where he easily could have. But the coincidence was too much. Then she thought maybe Peter had become aware they were on to him, noticed the men who had tracked him down to Chicago. The men *she* had led to him. *Maybe she was the one who killed him.* Or maybe it just got too much. Maybe the darkness that always gnawed at her had greedily swallowed him. *Was it really that surprising?* She rubbed a faded scar on her wrist unconsciously. Maybe it was just the Spencer curse, she thought. The Spencers, they would be no more. Peter's death ensured it. She recalled her father's comment when he found out about her infertility: *Good. You should be celebrating! Spencers... rotten blood. I told your mother she should have aborted you. Damn bitch was so stubborn...* She had thought her father cruel at the time, but always she forgave him. She knew of his own hard childhood, of the abuse he survived, denounced, and, so unwittingly, reproduced. The Spencers, the cursed. For the first time, she understood her father, and she felt relief at knowing her family line would die out with her.

Olga, for her part, obviously treasured her family and to this day fought back tears when reminiscing about her time in Russia. For all the heartfelt memories she willingly shared of her childhood, she remained suspiciously evasive about all that followed when she reached Canada as a young teenager.

Laura had tried asking her about her time with the Malkins, but Olga proved as equally secretive. She admitted to being with the family long before Kayne's birth, but she wouldn't go into any detail. But she did confirm Laura's suspicions. Olga was no fool, she was well aware of the family business and knew of the life Kayne lived. She was quick, however, to add that light and darkness existed in all of us. To support her statement, she reluctantly offered her one personal secret Laura could never have suspected.

Olga was homeless when Lev Malkin found her. He took pity on his fellow countrywoman and took her under his wing, offering her shelter and employment. She had been young and beautiful once, and men preyed so easily on the defenseless. Master Malkin hadn't and for that alone earned her loyalty. Years later, when she was in her thirties, a man she didn't know had come to the house on business. Master Malkin rarely mixed family and business, but it was an emergency, and this man was sent to retrieve a package instead of the usual pick-up guy. He had leered at her openly all night and made vulgar comments out of earshot. Master Malkin had finally asked her to show him out when the business was concluded. But the man forced her into a corner on his way out, the moment they were alone. He had forced her mouth shut and legs open. Master Kayne had witnessed the scene, came at him like a madman, and he *stopped* him. He was only sixteen then.

Master Malkin didn't give his son grief about it; they got rid of the body. The Malkins looked after their own. They instilled fear to ensure obedience but knew only gratitude could earn loyalty.

Day-26

Kayne sat alone in his office pensive. Olga gave him daily updates on Laura. He looked forward to them. The truth was he missed her company, her shy glances, and her inquisitive ones. He missed her bashful smiles, her nervous chatter. He even missed her annoying curiosity. He was passing by the solarium one day and heard laughter, actual laughter. He envied Olga in that moment.

That night he made another call where he was particularly cruel, and the following night, and the night after that. He whipped and caned mercilessly, made them cry, made them beg, and made them come. He came too but found no release.

Day-30

Laura had heard, night after night, the clicking of heels. She had wept bitterly in her pillows, knowing Kayne was having sex with another woman at that very moment. She had no tears left. She felt the change in her, however subtle. From the shadows, she didn't return fully the same. She never did. Every now and then, since she was a little girl, from the cage to Peter's suicide, darkness would claim her but never keep her. Even when she went willingly. Every time she returned, a little piece of her was lost. She was done crying.

She wondered about her puzzling captor who treated Olga so kindly, who had protected her, killed for her. Her captor who hurt women for pleasure, who killed and tortured for a living. Her captor who terrified her, who fascinated her, who captured her, in every sense. She hadn't seen him since *that* night, when he got back and changed her life forever. *Didn't he always?* From their very first encounter, he took her freedom. Then he took her body, turning it against her. Then he took Peter. She wondered what else he could take from her, if she even had anything left worth taking.

She asked Olga that day if he would be home for supper. He would. Her heart beat faster as she asked if it was okay if she joined. It was, Olga assured her happily.

* * *

In her usual jeans and a soft pink top, leaving her hair loose, she nervously went to meet him. He was already seated, staring at her, his expression unreadable as she hesitantly pulled the chair facing him.

"Hi..."

He nodded in response, his sealed lips even more telling of his murky mood. They remained in silence, their eyes locked on each other as he reached over and served them.

"I believe you…" she finally said in her softest voice, her eyes fixing the plate in front of her.

He didn't answer, keeping his eyes on her, scrutinizing her.

"What happened to his… body? Is it just… rotting there?" She looked up to meet his gaze, her voice quavering as her eyes glistened with unshed tears.

"No. The state provided for the funeral," he finally said, his eyes softening.

"Oh… I was just hoping to say good-bye…" Her voice broke, and a few tears rolled down her cheek, which she quickly dried off with the back of her hand.

He kept looking at her, not saying anything.

Her voice went steady then, her eyes fixing far ahead into a nonexistent distance. "I tried it once… when I was sixteen. He had started doing the harder stuff. Sometimes he'd be gone for days. This one time he didn't return for two weeks. I was freaking out. I wouldn't leave the house. I was so scared that I'd miss him when he came back. I stopped going to work. I didn't go to school anymore. I'd literally run to the store when I needed something and run back home. I just knew he'd come back for me, you know?" She shook her head, hurt in her eyes.

"At least for my birthday… he never missed my birthdays, no matter what. I even baked a cake and everything." She chuckled bitterly. "I waited 'til midnight. When he didn't come back… I slit my wrist. On my sweet sixteen." She finally looked up at him, offering a sad smile that didn't belong to a twenty-three-year-old. "But he did come back for me. He found me. He saved me… *And I didn't.* I didn't save him… I didn't…" She choked, tears rushing down her cheeks.

Before she knew it, he was by her side, pulling her up into his embrace. He held her close, rubbing her back, running his fingers gently in her hair while she sobbed uncontrollably against his strong, comforting chest. They hadn't been so close in a long time. She could feel him all around her, warming her, calming her. She remembered how good it felt; she just wanted to close her eyes and get lost in him, disappear completely into him, and have him carry the load that was to be Laura Spencer.

He waited for her sobs to fade, her breathing to slow, then pulled her away just a little. He grabbed her wrist and lifted its palm facing up, where a little faded scar could still be seen.

"You will never try this again," he commanded her, his voice assertive though not harsh, his eyes boring into hers.

She returned his gaze, studying his expression, and took a few seconds before slowly nodding her head.

"Good." A faint smile crossed his face. He leaned in and placed a soft kiss on her scarred wrist.

Day-31

Laura awoke to a peculiarly excited Olga, carrying a picnic basket into her room.

"How about breakfast outside today?" She lifted the basket, grinning from ear to ear. Confused, Laura was not sure how to respond.

"But… Olga…"

"Master Kayne said it was okay. Actually it was his idea," she affirmed as a proud mother.

"Are you sure…?" Laura had learned too long ago the truth behind the adage *If it's too good to be true…* Even if that meant taking fifty steps out the entrance.

Olga nodded confidently, her smile growing even wider. "Come on, let's go. It's a beautiful day."

They set a red checkered blanket on the grass by a weeping willow tree. The security guards left them on their own. Laura had brought *The Kite Runner*, intent on finishing it. Olga had her crochet, weaving an impossibly intricate design she'd been working on for as long as Laura could remember. She constantly undid whatever advancement she had just achieved, muttering through gritted teeth in Russian. But she was a stubborn woman, waving Laura off dismissively when she had suggested choosing another design.

Laura sat in silence, unable to read, just taking in the moment. It truly was a beautiful day. She felt the sun on her face, the warm breeze dance in her hair. She took off her shoes and rubbed her feet in the grass and she smiled gratefully, tearing up with emotion. In that moment, she was happy. She wondered if she had the right to be; she shrugged her shoulders in response. Sometimes, particularly in those times, a moment of clarity would come to her. Past the pain, past the despair, she would reach a place where nothing could hurt her anymore, and she felt only submerged in a feeling of inner peace. This time, it came in the shape of a green leaf carried by a warm breeze, falling gracefully to the earth as the sun shone behind it, of the same warm breeze that played with her hair, made her shirt flutter against her skin and the grass wiggle wildly under her feet. In this moment, she got it, *the secret.*

They stayed outside all day, watched the sunset with glasses of red wine under warm blankets, content. It was past seven when they headed back to the house. They crossed paths with Kayne who was deep in conversation with Lucas, on their way up the stairs. Lucas was speaking to him in a hushed tone, waving his hands about excitedly, when Kayne stopped, turning to Laura without saying a word. She held his stare, a modest smile on her lips as she mouthed *Thank you*. Without openly smiling back, he nodded, slowly, his eyes conveying the understanding they shared in that moment.

Day-37

Laura had gone outside every day since. Even on rainy days. She hadn't been with Kayne since their last supper and felt a rush when Olga came to fetch her outside to advise her that Master Kayne was inside and would like to see her.

He was dressed in a silver suit, looking dashing as he sat on *their* sofa. Laura felt silly in her denim short shorts and purple T-shirt. There was a familiar-looking carton box, gift wrapped with a ribbon, on the table, and her heart beat a little faster at the memory.

"Hey…" He leered at her exposed skin, grinning mischievously.

"Hi…" She smiled nervously, her eyes fixated on the box.

"How are you?"

"I'm okay… you?"

He smiled, tapping his palm on the arm of the La-Z-Boy, motioning her to sit. She did, her eyes constantly reverting to the box, terrified at what it could mean.

"Laura." He waited for her eyes to rest on him before he went on. "Would you like to accompany me to a wedding?"

She was stunned. "I don't understand… You're not taking me to a *party…*?"

He shook his head, smirking, but kindly, the way only he could.

"A wedding… like outside?" she asked, still feeling suspicious.

He nodded.

Her eyes brightened up at the thought. *Outside, she would leave this house.* "Yes… definitely yes!" She smiled again, a smile he had been forbidden for too long, genuine, warm, and meant for him.

He picked up the box from the table and handed it to her. She smiled coyly at him, at the déjà vu. Opening it, she found a gorgeous long ocean blue chiffon dress, strapless with a sweetheart neckline.

"It's beautiful… Thank you…" She held it close to her chest, smiling away.

Kayne watched her silently, taking in her radiant smile, her childish joy. He had kidnapped her, locked her up, made her cry and beg, and had enjoyed every second of it. And now watching her smile, he realized just how much he reveled at being the cause of it. Her tears made him want to do things to her, her smile made him want to do things for her. He didn't know which he liked more.

He got off his seat and, caressing her cheek, informed her to be ready at three sharp. She stayed in her seat long after he left, feeling dejected and confused as she realized her disappointment at not having to try on the dress for him. *In front of him*. Did he not want her anymore? She caught herself worrying.

She showed up at three, her hair up in an elegant bun, donning drop diamond earrings and silver sandals. She got the reaction she wanted. She felt her insides swarm with excitement. She was leaving the house, with Kayne, as his date.

He offered her his arm, and as they reached the door, he took her hand and pulled out a jewelry box, which he deposited in her open palm. She lifted a brow in question to which he responded by nudging his head toward the box.

It contained a diamond platinum bracelet. It was perfect, so simple and so beautiful.

"Thank you…" Laura breathed, unsure what else to say.

He smirked, turned it around, and showed her the engraving, *From Your Monster*.

She didn't react. She stared at him, just fighting the urge to lean and kiss him, *her* Monster. He would've let her, she knew he would have. But she couldn't muster the courage, so she stared, trying to communicate what her body couldn't, knowing he could read her mind, *hoping* he could read her mind.

He didn't lean in. He took the bracelet out of the box and put it on her, securing the elegant screw that held together this unusually beautiful design.

"There, now you can't take it off… even if you want to," he cautioned teasingly.

* * *

They took a private jet there. Laura threw him side glances the whole way, trying to read him, to pick up anything and decipher the puzzle that was Kayne Malkin. She didn't know what to think. *Who was this man? Who was the man that held her life in his hands?* Every now and then, he would catch her stare, and he would shake his head at her, a knowing smile advising her to give up the futile quest.

The wedding was quite an elegant affair. It was set outside in a big green open space, the blue sea for a backdrop. There was security everywhere, important celebrities, men and women dressed as royalty. Kayne introduced Laura around, keeping close to her, his eyes locked on her when she wasn't on his arm.

Mrs. Drugova had lured her to the group of women chatting away by the bar. Natasha Drugova was the matriarch and left no doubt about it. She had maintained her beauty, her distinction shining through her posture and elegance, her piercing gaze only contrasted by her indulgent but reserved smiles. Laura didn't want to leave Kayne, feeling nervous at being surrounded by strangers. But Natasha Drugova had a reassuring authority about her, and Laura had followed her obediently, though she looked back often and found Kayne staring back at her, every time. She would smile at him, feeling safe under his enveloping gaze.

The women relentlessly questioned her, about her, about Kayne, about their relationship. She became nervous, trying to stay vague, which only heightened their curiosity. Apparently, she was very different from his previous dates.

Mrs. Drugova smiled somewhat compassionately at her before pulling her away. "Shall we take a walk…" It wasn't a question;

it was a polite order. She started walking away before Laura even answered.

"Don't worry, child, he feels the same."

"Excuse me?" Laura uttered nervously.

"It's obvious. He's been watching you like a hawk, from the moment you left his side." She smiled knowingly.

Laura was grateful to escape the beautiful hyenas badgering her. She wondered what Mrs. Drugova would think if she only knew why he watched her constantly. It wasn't sweet young love, it was a captor supervising his prisoner, knowing that at this very moment, she contemplated walking out of the place. As simple as that. *Keep walking, never turning back, walk past the fancy garden, past the unsuspecting security, or were they?* But Laura knew she wouldn't. It was more than a fear of reprisal that kept her locked in his world, more than a sense of safety in her captivity acquired through conditioning, more than Stockholm syndrome. Laura looked out the open gated entrance, considered the scary and beautiful world awaiting her past these doors, and knew she wouldn't walk out.

"These women are idiots," Mrs. Drugova proclaimed once they were at the safe distance from the pack. "But you're not, are you?" She looked at Laura and smiled before pursuing, "You know exactly the kind of man he is." She waited for Laura to concede, the latter barely nodding her head uncertainly.

"It's a gift and a curse to be born a woman in this life. You're neither his date nor his girlfriend," she remarked.

Laura's eyes watered, feeling trapped, caught in a lie she was forced into. She shook her head, looking down.

"But you want to be."

Laura's head snapped back up, shaking it repeatedly, with forced conviction, to which Mrs. Drugova smiled indulgently, amused.

"I know Kayne. I've known him since he was a little boy. He cares for you. If he didn't, you would be dead, Laura. Or worse..." Mrs. Drugova gave her the once-over, sizing her up.

"Men like Kayne..." She shook her head. "When I met Dimitri, I immediately fell in love with him. But I wasn't a fool about it. I did what I had to do to be with him, in a way that was tolerable for me. Do you understand what I'm telling you?"

"No..." she breathed, terrified.

"Don't be naive and dream up a romance. He will have you, and I don't just mean physically. I can see in your eyes how you feel about him. Be smart enough to make it on your own terms. That's the best advice I can give you."

"No... I can't... It's not like that..."

"So you'll be his whore then, and you'll be discarded when he's done with you," she stated with finality.

Laura's eyes widened with shock, at the crude word coming from that regal woman's mouth, from the truth of it. Everything felt surreal, the beautiful sunny day, the beach, Kayne watching her with his unique smile, this intimidating woman she never met, who knew all about her, giving her advice.

Her words were still playing in Laura's head, when they rejoined the others. Mrs. Drugova smiled at her and nudged her head, indicating to Laura to turn around. Kayne was already walking to them and, embracing Laura from behind, exchanged a few pleasantries with Natasha.

"She's a special girl. Hold on to her," Mrs. Drugova finally said, gently squeezing Laura's hand before she excused herself. A slow song was playing, and Mr. Drugov approached them to steal her away onto the dance floor.

"Don't worry, she's not going anywhere," Kayne replied in a silky voice, more for Laura's benefit.

Still in his embrace, Laura felt a shiver run down her spine. She turned her head sideways toward him, her apprehensive stare landing on laughing eyes.

He stepped back and took her hand, leading her to the dance floor as well. They danced with his hands on her waist, her arms around his shoulders, and their eyes locked on each other. He smiled kindly at her intense gaze.

"Why are you being so nice to me?"

He smirked mischievously. "I'm always nice to you."

She snorted humorlessly in response. "I thought you never lied..." she then said, bitterness creeping in her soft voice.

He answered with a devilish smile, pulling her even closer, cheek to cheek. With his arms around her, he whispered in her ear, his tone surprisingly serious. "Believe me, Laura, I've been nice to you."

They remained like this for the remainder of the song, cheek to cheek, in silence, until her eyes welled up with tears; she was unsure why. She hid her face in him, resting her head on his shoulder.

"Have you thought of running away?" he asked her softly in her ear.

"Yes..." she conceded, shamelessly, softly, her head still on his shoulder.

"Why didn't you?"

She didn't answer, he didn't insist.

He caressed her back, the entire song, and the next as they remained locked in this embrace.

"What will happen to me?" she eventually asked him in a childlike voice, her face still hidden in the nook of his neck.

He didn't answer, she didn't insist.

* * *

That night Laura heard again the clicking of heels and felt her heart tighten. She didn't cry.

Day-40

Laura was going through her room, from boredom, from a relentless feeling of anguish and a desire to belong, to know every corner of the only home she would ever have. A bedroom. She went through every drawer, every closet, pulled out all the clothes and put them back.

It was in a top drawer she found the picture. A beautiful brunette was smiling back at her, her hair curled up like they did back in the day, her hazel eyes vibrant, gleaming with mischief. Laura couldn't stop looking at the picture, recognizing the familiar traits in them. *Kayne's mother.* Who was she? What happened to her? What kind of woman gives birth to this kind of man? Was she like Mrs. Drugova, pragmatic and jaded? Like Olga, seeing goodness wherever she could find it? Or was she like herself, just seeking refuge in fantasy from a world she wasn't armed to face?

That night, she brought the picture with her, tucked into her back pocket, and went to meet Kayne for supper. She stopped, taken aback at finding his seat unusually empty, and looked at the time. She wasn't early. She took her seat, her unease only increasing.

She was lost in thought when two big hands gently grabbed her shoulders. She jerked, stunned, hearing a gruff chuckle behind her, before the warm hands abandoned her. Kayne took his seat, smiling devilishly at her.

"What's going on in that little head of yours?"

She just pulled out the picture, without saying a word, and handed it to him. He seemed curious at first, then his eyes instantly narrowed upon recognition.

"Where did you get this?"

"In my room..." she stammered, feeling her heartbeat quicken.

He looked at her, then back at the picture, his eyes hard.

"Is it… your mother?"

He didn't respond right away, keeping his eyes fixed on the picture. "Yes."

"You look like her…"

"I look nothing like her," he snapped, his eyes lifting to meet Laura's.

"Why are you upset?" she breathed, her eyes watering.

His eyes softened, though the darkness remained. "Don't worry about it," he reassured her, his tone still hard, and deposited the picture far away on the table, and out of sight.

"I don't understand... Do you hate her?"

"Drop it," he warned, his face menacing.

She squirmed in her seat. She couldn't link such a violent reaction to the sweet face she had looked at all day.

"Let's eat," he said after a moment, his eyes still tempestuous. They ate in silence, Laura throwing cautious glances his way, looking back down every time her gaze landed on the pools of darkness staring back.

They finished their supper with the heavy silence still weighing on them. He then got up and went digging for something in his jacket. He came back to the kitchen, leaning back against the island counter, watching her, as she remained in her seat, unsure what to do. She looked so pitiful, fidgeting nervously in her chair, and that sight alone was enough to pacify his temper. "Come here."

She looked up at him, as if assessing the situation. Apprehensively, she approached him, constantly gauging his reaction with each step that brought her closer. He waited patiently, arms crossed, his expression betraying his amusement as she embarked on the dangerous journey that led her to him.

When she finally got to him, he reached for her wrist and pulled her close. He could sense her maddened pulse and reveled in feeling her underlying panic. *Poor Laura*, he thought patronizingly, *how wrong you are this time*. He smiled inwardly, knowing she reacted exactly as he'd trained her to, always fearful, always on edge, always seeking to please. This behavior will be rewarded. He pulled out an envelope and handed it to her.

"What is it?" she asked, her voice low and raspy, her breathing hard.

He leaned into her ear, his expression playful. "Happy birthday."

She seemed confused at first, then closed her eyes as the fact dawned on her. She was turning twenty-four. It was her birthday.

"Do you want me to open it?" she asked, still not reassured by his positive mood swing.

"It's yours. Do what you want." He smiled indulgently.

She opened the envelope wearily and found two tickets to *The Swan Lake* premiere from Les Grands Ballets Canadiens for the following evening. Her eyes were round with surprise.

"You're taking me to *The Swan Lake*? How did you even know?" she gasped.

"Happy?" He smirked.

A tear clung to the corner of her eye. "Yes," she breathed. "Thank you."

They remained close, their eyes locked on each other. She felt lost in his eyes, in his presence, in his world. Adrift in this swirl of madness where he was the only thing left she could hold on to. She closed her eyes, cautiously raising herself on her toes, and closed the small distance separating them. Her lips barely grazed his, for the length of a second, her sweet lips tasted the saltiness of his. She felt her heart sink in her chest, just like the roller coasters when she was a child. She quickly pulled back and, avoiding his gaze, turned to walk away.

She felt his hand grab her arm from behind, slowly making her turn around and pulling her back to him. Her heart was racing, and she kept her eyes to the ground, feeling his piercing gaze on her.

He brought a hand to her shoulder, letting his fingers run the length of her arm; and feeling her shiver, he sighed. He pulled her into him and brought his mouth to her ear. His voice hoarse, he whispered, “Don’t play with fire, little girl.”

Her face flushed, she nervously nodded her head. Without ever looking at him, she rushed out of his embrace and away from him.

* * *

That night Kayne didn’t make any calls. His mind was fixated on his captive, on the soft kiss he could still feel on his lips as he ran his thumb over them. How could anything so sweet, so innocent turn him on to such an extent? He wondered. He’d wanted to take her, knew he could have, but pulled back, though he felt his desire reciprocated. He knew she didn’t want him to take her the way he wanted, though she would have let him. He wondered what stopped him. At the last second, he changed his mind, let her walk away. It was her birthday after all; she could have her sweet chaste kiss. He shrugged his shoulders, smiling to himself. Next time, there would be no mercy.

Day-41

All night Laura dreamed of the following evening. She barely got any sleep from excitement. *The Swan Lake*, not just any ballet, she was going to *The Swan Lake*. She wondered how he knew and remembered mentioning something vague about it to Olga. She had spent her childhood watching an old VHS tape her mother had left behind of the famous ballet. It was performed by a world-renowned Russian troupe at the time. She had danced in her living room imitating the graceful prima ballerina, albeit clumsily, more than once breaking things, landing her in the cage.

None of it mattered now. She was going to watch it, in person. No more lines running through the screen against colors faded to different shades of grey. She had closed her eyes and smiled from the images playing in her head. *A red carpet, a white limousine, cameras everywhere, Kayne and she would be greeted like royalty. All the women would envy her. Kayne wouldn't even notice them, because she would look gorgeous, not cute and pretty. And Kayne would know it, seeing her for the woman she'd become, and he'd want her above all else. He would hold her by her hand, lead her inside. He would act protective of her as he always did, be in one of his lighthearted moods, constantly smiling at her in his indulgent way, caressing her cheeks, kissing her hand…* She fell asleep, a smile plastered on her face.

She spent the day outside. It was a beautiful sunny day. It seemed as if the entire universe was conspiring with her, for once, on her side. She smiled, finally finishing *The Kite Runner*. It was a great novel, she wondered what took her so long to finish it. Another of Kayne's gifts, she held it close to her heart, kissing the cover. She remembered kissing him the night before and blushed at the memory, though she couldn't help smiling. She didn't know what came over her, but she didn't regret it. She remembered his warning and brushed it off as it fit so inconveniently with her immediate contentment. She would have let him take her, part of her wished he had. She wasn't playing with fire; she depended on it. She could only survive off its warmth, off its sole source of light in never-ending obscurity. She would withstand its inevitable burns.

She got back to her room on light feet. Kayne had told her to be ready by six thirty. It was only four, but she wanted to take her time preparing, enjoying each step of the way. There was another gift-wrapped carton box on her bed, which by now had become very familiar. She rushed to the bed, her heart leaping with excitement.

Laura couldn't help grinning dumbly and opened the box to find a black satin gown, as majestic as she pictured in her wildest fantasies.

At six thirty sharp, she entered the living room, almost expecting a corsage. Kayne was in a black suit, his back turned to her, he was looking out the window. She shyly cleared her throat, and he turned around, smiling at her. He walked to her, took her hand, and pulled it out, giving her the once-over.

"Beautiful."

"Thank you." She smiled brightly back at him, though she flushed, lowering her gaze with modesty.

"I can't make it tonight," he said softly.

"Oh…" Her heart tightened in her chest, she felt as though someone just kicked her in the ribs. She could still see the night in her mind as she had pictured it, the renegade images now coiling around her lungs, suffocating her.

"Something's come up," he explained, looking intently into her eyes, a certain melancholy creeping into his smile, though he would not apologize. "Lucas will take you."

She tried to smile. *She was still going.* He only said *he* couldn't. She wanted to say more and project breezy indifference, but the lump in her throat advised her to keep her answers very short. "Okay."

He brushed her cheek with the back of his hand, his expression soft. "He's waiting for you at the door."

"Okay," she barely managed to get out as she quickly turned from him to head for the door, her eyes threatening to betray her very shaky composure.

Kayne watched her leave. He was sorry, he had meant to go with her. But Tanya called. She had an update on the Maxwell situation, and that took precedence over anything else. He had maintained a good relationship with her or, more likely, used her weakness for him to his advantage. Though she never let him have her after that night, she made sure to remain in his entourage, always trying to remind him of what he lost, what *he* gave up. Dimitri had no qualms about sharing his whores, so Kayne had asked her to get close to Maxwell and report back to him. He didn't trust him; there was something about the man. Maxwell, it seemed, was up to something. That didn't surprise Kayne. What surprised him was how easily he played into Tanya's hands, but she was good, you had to hand it to her. She even made you wonder who the whore was, with Maxwell following her around at gatherings like a lapdog. Kayne shook his head with disdain.

* * *

Lucas was dressed for the occasion. He smiled lightheartedly at Laura as he offered his arm and helped her into the car. The entire night, he was very attentive, constantly making sure she was okay and enjoying herself. He was refined, cultured, and very pleasant company, inspiring ease and well-being. She felt like she'd known him all her life, an old friend whose spot-on observations never failed to amuse her.

Finally over her initial deception, once the ballet started, she was submerged in the magic of the show. She realized what an unforgettable night it truly was. She felt safe with Lucas like she did with Kayne, though with Lucas, she didn't feel the lingering menace that always kept her on edge around Kayne. It truly was a magical evening. She rushed to her feet at the end of the show to join the standing ovation, clapping away and tearing up with emotion.

When they returned home, she was still glowing, the euphoria lingering in her senses. She couldn't go straight to bed, didn't want to wait for tomorrow to tell Kayne all about it. She wished to thank him again, for quite possibly the best night in her miserable, short little life.

She ran into the kitchen and the living room, in and out excitedly, finding him nowhere. She shrugged her shoulders, defeated at last. *He must still be out.* She wondered what could have come up. *Work obviously.* Was he out interrogating someone this very instant, while she stood in the empty house looking for him in her black gown, still high off tutus, sorcerers, and spellbound princesses?

A shrill laughter pierced through the air and into Laura's thoughts. Though having only heard it once, at the *party*, she could recognize this high-pitched voice anywhere. Her face dropped. Was he *here*, with *Tanya*? Is that why he couldn't go with her? She almost wished he was out interrogating, whomever, she didn't care.

Her heart pounding in her chest, she followed the echoes of the hated sound, passed the west wing corridor and into the reception hall, slowly lowering the handle of the right side double white door.

Kayne was sitting down on a massive couch, the top of his shirt unbuttoned, and his hair messy. A woman in a black thong and heels was kneeling on the floor between his legs. She was taking him in her mouth, her face hidden by her long curly black hair, as her head bobbed up and down sensually. There were glasses of alcohol and a half-empty bottle of whiskey on the table near them. Tanya sat next to him on the couch, in a short tight black dress, her whole body turned toward him. Her legs slightly apart, caused the dress to lift even further up her thighs. Her hands were intertwined on his shoulder, her head resting on them. She was whispering in his ear, smiling devilishly as he smirked, looking straight ahead while his hand rested on her inner thigh with intimate familiarity.

Laura gasped, bringing her hand to her mouth, her eyes horrified as the two faces turned her way. Tanya's eyes glistened with carnivorous thrill. Kayne's expression was predatory, his stare callous and condescending, his alcohol-induced state reflected in his eyes.

Laura shook her head, her hand still covering her mouth. She took a few steps back, then turned around. It was all a dream, she walked into a dream, a horrible crazy dream she just wanted to wake up from. Her heart was pounding in her chest, her mind racing with incoherent thoughts. More than the woman going down on him, it was the image of him and Tanya that kept playing over and over again in her head, keeping the constant pain shooting in her chest. He abandoned her for Tanya, had pushed her away the night before when he could've had her. She remembered the kiss she gave him, the fantasies she entertained. *Don't be naive and dream up a romance*, Mrs. Drugova's words came back to her. She felt her heart shatter, the pain, physical. She wondered how many times a soul could break apart before it ceased being itself, becoming something else.

She walked to the front door, her feet carrying her of their own accord. She heard voices calling her, they'd seemed to be coming from another world. She kept walking, out of the front door and onto the paved lane. The gates were open; they were never open. She kept walking, past the open gates and the security men. Though looking at her, none tried to stop her. She walked into the street. The moonlight was shining brightly, illuminating her way. She removed her heels, carrying them in her hands. She kept walking, in her evening gown, bare feet on the asphalt. Cars passed by, honking. She kept walking.

* * *

Kayne's cellphone rang.

"Sir, Miss Spencer is heading toward the front gate." Lucas waited for instructions.

"Is she still wearing the bracelet?"

"Yes, sir."

"Good. Let her."

Kayne hung up and pushed the whore off him. Tanya's face was glowing as she feigned concern, not even bothering to restrain her delighted smirk. "Oh, what's wrong? Did the little bird fly away?"

Kayne shot her a cool warning stare in response, turned around, and walked away. "You know the way out," he threw back, his voice hard.

* * *

Laura kept walking, numb, her mind blank. She didn't know how long she'd been walking for. She didn't know where she was heading.

* * *

Kayne met up with Lucas in the office upstairs. Laura couldn't possibly know that at the very moment, her chip-encrusted bracelet was popping up as a little red spot on their monitoring system.

"Where is she headed?" Kayne asked coolly.

"Nowhere in particular, I think. She seems to be just walking along the highway. Could be dangerous, sir. Are you sure you don't want me to retrieve her?"

"No." His reply was instant. "I want to see where she goes. Have Kiev follow her. Only intervene if she gets close to a police station."

"Yes, sir."

Kiev, a slim dark-eyed man with a crooked nose, was also part of the security team. Proudly from Kiev, he took the name of his home city for his own when he left the motherland. He was well into his fifties now. Though fit as they come, his body and posture still reflected the military training received during his early years back in his homeland. He specialized in interrogation techniques and executions no one else wanted to perform. He had been with the family for as long as Kayne could remember. He was very loyal to the Malkins, had helped Lev, and Kayne after him, get rid of unwanted obstacles and ensure their position in the Organization. Kiev wasn't a sadist, just an unblinking soldier. Kayne could trust him to follow instructions.

* * *

Laura saw the flashing red neon of the open sign at a shabby local bar and headed straight toward its wooden door. There were only men at the tables, a few waitresses past their prime, donned outfits suggesting they refused to acknowledge it. They all stared at her in an awkward moment of silence. She didn't realize the absurdity of the situation as she walked straight to the counter on her dirty, bloodied bare feet and her dusty expensive gown.

"A whiskey, straight up please," she asked the barman, as he openly checked her out with curiosity.

He lifted his brow, kept playing with the dirty towel on his shoulder. At last, he obliged, pouring her a glass, which he set in front of her. She threw her head back and downed it in one shot. She felt a head rush, the burn in her throat, the slow numbing of her senses. She smiled, smacking the glass back on the counter.

"Can I have another please?"

"Sure, three dollars for the first, unless you want to open a tab?" He eyed her suspiciously.

"Oh…" She had no money. How silly… it hadn't even crossed her mind; such an everyday worry. When did one of those cross her mind last?

A man approached her and stopped by her side.

"May I?" He offered her a charming smile. He didn't wait for her answer and gave the man his credit card. "Two more please."

She kept staring ahead, refusing to acknowledge him. When the barman brought the other round, the man reached for both glasses before she had a chance to take hers. He handed her the glass, forcing interaction, and raised his own to clink it with hers.

"To beautiful mysterious ladies appearing out of nowhere."

She didn't return his smile. Looking at him, she cocked her head and sized him up. He was kind of good looking. Brownish hair, beautiful green eyes, but his teeth were crooked. They weren't yellow or nasty, just crooked. *Kayne's teeth are perfect*, she thought.

They both swallowed the drink in one shot. She finally smiled at him, gripping the counter as she felt herself getting light-headed.

"And she smiles…" he teased.

* * *

"She's at a bar, sir. Kiev is in the parking lot. She's been inside for over twenty minutes."

"A bar…" Kayne licked his lips, pensive. "Okay. Let's go."

* * *

Laura stood against the stone wall in the back alley by the bar. She felt comfortably numb, smoking a cigarette as the man leaned against her, one arm on the wall by her side. He'd been rambling on about himself nonstop, bragging about his career and ambitions. She wasn't sure what else, she wasn't listening anymore. She felt annoyed by his presence, by his obvious moves and sweet mannerisms. But seeing Kayne and Tanya in her mind, imagining them together, she let this unknown man get near her. She cringed as he caressed her cheek but allowed it. He leaned closer, kissing her on the neck. This was it. It was as far as she would let it go. She put her hand flat on his chest and weakly tried to push him off her, as she turned her head away from him.

The man flew away, landing on the ground a few feet behind. She turned her head back to find Kayne staring at her, his eyes, open slits of fury.

"What the f—" The man dusted himself off as he stumbled back on his feet.

With his eyes still fixed on Laura, Kayne pulled out a gun and pointed it at him. "Stay down."

The man immediately raised his arms but remained on his knees. "Hey! Easy—"

"Shut up," he spat, disgusted.

Laura could see two black SUVs blocking each side of the back alley, Lucas on one end, a man she noticed around the house at the other. Kayne's eyes were still boring into hers.

"Has he touched you?"

"No, man... I didn't… I swear… Listen, I don't want any trouble…" the man mumbled, panicked.

"Be quiet," Kayne hissed, throwing him a quick but threatening glance that had him cowering further down on his knees, crooking his arms behind his head.

Turning back to Laura, Kayne addressed her, his voice deceptively calm. "Laura, have you let him touch you. In any way?"

Laura shook her head violently. Everything felt surreal. Kayne, *here*, the man, on his knees, the gun, Lucas…

"Don't lie," he cautioned her, a wrath in his eyes she'd never seen.

She was too petrified to even cry, shocked into silence. She finally stammered, her voice hushed, "He... he kissed my neck—"

She was interrupted by a deafening popping sound. Warm liquid spurted on her face, and she recognized only what it was when she saw the blood on Kayne's face, the red spots all over his white shirt. She remained very still, in shock, in denial, looking at the limp body on the ground, its head blown off. A body that was standing not a few minutes ago, breathing into her ear, annoying her.

Kayne's eyes remained locked on her, venom seeping through them. He pulled out a handkerchief and wiped his face, slowly, never breaking eye contact. She felt herself shiver, her teeth chattering uncontrollably. Kiev approached them and began to drag the body, rolling it up in plastic.

This isn't real, it can't be real. Laura was gasping for air as she watched Kayne turning away from her and walking back to the car.

"Miss Spencer..." It was Lucas, his voice soft. He was trying to get her away, gently pulling at her arm. "Miss Spencer, we have to go."

The black SUV had pulled up to them, and Lucas led her to the backseat, where Kayne was already seated.

She shook her head in terror. "Lucas… no, please no..."

"We have to go, Miss Spencer." He gently but forcibly pushed her into the car.

Kayne didn't look at her; his eyes were cold as stone. He looked straight ahead as she cowered in the corner, pulling her feet up on the seat. She hugged them, her entire body shaking with convulsions.

"Do this again, and I will kill you," he finally said, still staring straight ahead, his voice deadpan.

She broke down crying and began rocking herself, waiting for the nightmare to end. The entire way back home, she wondered if it ever would. They got back to the house and Laura saw the gates close behind them. Was that how the nightmare would end? Would those gates be the last thing she would see before dying? Was he going to kill her? Or maybe just lock her in the cage until she went completely insane and died her own way? She was lost in morbid thoughts, when his harsh voice snapped her back to reality.

"Get out," Kayne hissed, waiting by the open door.

"No… please no…. please… please…" she sobbed.

He grabbed her arm and pulled her out roughly. She stumbled and would have fallen if it weren't for his firm grip. He dragged her into the house, unresponsive to her desperate pleas. Olga was waiting inside, her face instantly paled as they walked in, covered in blood. Once inside, Kayne pushed Laura so hard she fell sideways on the floor. With her hands behind her, she crawled backward to Olga, grabbed her leg, and looked up at her pleadingly.

"Master Kayne—" Olga began, her voice shaky.

"Leave us," he warned in a low growl.

"Master, I beg of you—" She used her remaining courage to face his wrath.

"Leave!"

She looked down at Laura, offering her a reassuring smile, though her eyes conveyed the shame she felt as she obediently retreated to the western wing, closing her bedroom door behind her.

Laura crawled further back until her spine hit the wall, until there was nowhere further to seek refuge. Her eyes were wide, as she panted like a wounded animal. She looked mad, shaking uncontrollably, while her eyes turned at the slightest sound or movement.

Kayne stared at her, his own breathing loud.

"Is this how you repay me?" His voice was controlled, his eyes blackened with rage.

She shook her head furiously, unable to speak, unable to move, frozen with fear.

"Do you have *ANY* idea what I've been through for you?" His voice was sharp, growing louder with every word as his self-control faltered. After a pause, he then added, his voice back to hair-rising softness, "Dimitri… wants you dead. Maxwell… wants to sell you… Had I known you were just dying to whore yourself, I wouldn't have busted my balls over you."

"No… no… Master… I swear…" She pained to get each word out, her sobs unstoppable.

"Oh, it's *Master* now? Quite the manipulative little thing, aren't we? Well… Master is not happy, *Pet*." A sadistic gleam merged with the rage already present.

"No… please… please…"

"No…? You didn't let this man put his dirty paws on you? You didn't let him kiss you?" he pronounced every word, his eyes burning.

"You were with your whores!" she wailed, shouting at the top of her lungs. "What do you want from me?" Her voice broke.

He grunted, a diabolic smile matching his menacing eyes. "Don't worry, Pet. I'll show you."

Her eyes snapped to meet his, panic and pleading, fear and despair mirrored all at once. She opened her mouth to beg but didn't have the time to utter a syllable. In an instant he was by her side, holding her up by her hair. He dragged her kicking and screaming, all along the hall, down the stairs, and into the dungeon.

He led her to a bed and let go of his hold. She fell to her knees on the ground, her face and arms landing on the soft mattress as she wailed, caught in a nightmare she couldn't wake up from. His eyes malevolent, he cocked his head and watched her, enraptured by her distress.

He tugged her hair again, bringing her up to his lips, and whispered softly in her ear, "Why did you do it?"

She sobbed, vainly throwing her arms about, trying to free herself from his hold. He pushed her on the mattress.

"Were you… *jealous*? … *Again*?" he asked her, his voice raspy, as she lay flat on the mattress, her cries swallowed by the comforter. "Whores don't get to be jealous," he callously threw at her.

He then climbed on top of her, kneeling with one leg on each side of her body and ripped her dress off her back. She gasped, her body freezing for a moment, before her sobbing came back, even more desperate than before. He caressed her back softly, reached for her arms, and brought them to the bedposts where handcuffs awaited. He locked each of her wrists.

"Please… please…" she implored, her voice throaty from all the screaming and crying. She panted, out of breath, her little body drained.

He leaned close to her ear and made shushing sounds. "Tell me why you did what you did, and I might go easier on you," he whispered softly in her ear, kissing her earlobe.

"I don't know… I saw you with her… I couldn't…" Her voice was calm, numb. "I *was* jealous. *Again*," she admitted, the words tasting sour on her tongue.

"So you whore yourself to a stranger?"

She lay her head down on the pillow, her eyes filled with bitter surrender. "I didn't. Believe what you want."

A sardonic chuckle escaped his lips. "I *believe* I've been too soft with you." He left her side, coming back with a whip in his hand. He cracked it on the floor. She jerked and screamed at the imagined pain, making him chuckle. She barely had time to compose herself, when the whip cracked down on her. It cut her breath, the pain unbearable. She was in shock, couldn't even scream. It sank down on her again. This time, she bellowed with everything she had, her scream lingering in the air. He struck her again, again, and again. She hollered and shrieked with every strike. She thought she would pass out from the pain, convinced he'd drawn blood and that she'd be scarred for life.

She wasn't. He'd been careful not to break her skin. He liked her pristine skin and kept the intensity at a minimum, controlling the impact as it landed on her ass and back.

"The only man who will ever touch you is me."

"Yes, Master," she responded, her voice deadened.

"Who do you belong to?" he hissed, unhappy with her response.

"You…" she cried, the truth of her words resonating in her.

A guttural sound escaped his lips. He caressed her, brought his hand down, and reached between her legs, growing hard at finding her wet. He spread her wetness through her slit, all the way back, wetting the tight little circle as he spread her ass cheeks apart.

"You're mine..." he said, almost to himself. "And you will never forget it."

He entered his finger. She gasped in response, contracting her muscles at the unpleasant feeling.

"Relax."

"I can't," she panted, lifting her head in panic. He pushed his finger all the way in and used his other hand to continue playing with her sensitive spot. He wanted her to relax despite herself, to get lost in the pleasure he provided her, despite the pain he had inflicted on her. She moaned, rocking her hips against his fingers.

"Just like a bitch in heat..." He chuckled sadistically, knowing how deep his words cut her.

A whimper escaped her lips, her eyes tearing at the sting of his words. Yet she couldn't help rubbing herself against him, insane with the pleasure she craved so much, desperate for any pleasure she could get from him. He pulled out his finger and laid his body on top of hers. She could feel his erection rubbing against her ass, lingering at the entrance his finger had just violated. She wanted to plead, beg him not to, but he continued to play with and tease her pulsating nerve. She could feel his body surrounding her, his fingers driving her mad. She understood in that moment just how deep his power over her truly went. With his touch alone, he had more control over her than all the values and principles she clung to her entire life.

"Beg me," he commanded, his voice wolfish in her ear.

She whimpered.

He grabbed her hair, pulling her head back. "Beg me to make you my whore."

"Make me your whore... please, Master," she sobbed.

She cried out at the sharp unnatural pain as he penetrated her ass. He thrust slowly, as he entered her completely. He moved in and out leisurely inside of her, enabling her to get used to the sensation. Once he felt her muscles relax, he picked up the rhythm, pulling out completely and reentering her with each thrust. She sobbed under him, crying in her pillow, but he kept his fingers on her bundle of nerves, never letting her forget the pleasure she was getting regardless of anything else he did to her.

Laura was caught in a foggy haze, where pleasure and pain coexisted, where blood and tears paved the way to her haven. She was no longer herself, she was a body reacting to sensations. Kayne… Kayne… Kayne… She repeated his name over and over again in her head. She couldn't admit to herself the distress she had felt facing another man, facing the normality of the life he took from her. She would have given everything to be back with him then, to have him be the one standing in front of her trying to kiss her. Then he was, and she was terrified. A man was murdered, in front of her, *because* of her. And all she could feel in this moment was the sweet numbing relief of belonging to him, her Monster, *her* Kayne, surrendering completely in the face of this unavoidable, irrepressible force.

She came as he fucked her ass, claiming her, asserting his ownership over her body. He came not long after, in a growl. He got up and unshackled her without saying a word. As she lay on the mattress, she felt emptiness invade her. He had threatened her life, killed a man, and taken her body without consent. He whipped her, used her as his whore, and she let him; she even came from it. She had thought she had nothing left to lose after Peter died. *There's always more you can lose.* She brought her knees up to her chest and stared vacantly into the open space.

He walked away and opened the door but stopped in his tracks at the last second. He looked back at the broken body he just left behind. He got irritated, feeling trapped. He didn't want to go back to her; she ran away, deserved any punishment he saw fit. Worse than that, he found her in the arms of another man. He could've massacred an entire village. But he knew, looking at her face, if he walked out on her now, the Laura Spencer he knew would be no more.

He slammed his fist on the wall, yelling out "Fuck!" in frustration. Her naked frail body jerked at the sound. He exhaled slowly, lowered his head, and closed his eyes. His walk resolute, he went back to her and scooped her in his arms. She looked up at him, terrified, and he smiled kindly to reassure her, sadness in his eyes. He picked up a blanket from the bed with one hand, while still holding her with his other, and covered her body. Then he carried her to her room and gently laid her down on the bed under the covers. After removing his own clothes, he climbed in next to her.

She stared at him, her eyes carrying the weight of the world. She kept her arms protectively closed over her chest, her hands in fists under her chin. He rubbed them gently, stroked her back, bringing her close into his embrace. He could feel her little heart pounding furiously against his chest, and for the first time, bore sorrow.

"Laura..." he said softly, as he caressed her face still covered in blood. "Do you want to tell me off? Yell at me? ... Curse me? … Hit me?"

She didn't answer but kept her eyes locked on him.

"Want to spit on me? … *Again*?" He chuckled softly at the memory.

A lonely tear rolled down her face.

"Laura…" He shut his eyes and wiped her tear. "Laura…" He didn't know what to do. He had only been taught how to break, never how to mend. In this moment, he would have given anything to have that power, to have her lean in and kiss him softly again, her eyes sparkling with innocent expectation.

"Anything. Ask me anything," he commanded, his tone gruff, solemn.

"Make love to me."

Her voice was so soft, he wasn't even sure he heard her right.

Laura fought hard. Darkness, her old friend, had come knocking on her door again. But this time, she knew if she went with it, she wouldn't return. She'd been used and abused, by the one person who could do this to her. She didn't care about wrong and right anymore, could still feel the dried blood itching on her face. She felt her back burning with marks from the whip, her heart still reeling from the cruel, demeaning words. All she wanted, all she needed, was for him to undo what he did.

He closed his eyes and gently placed her on her back. Leaning his body on top of hers, he rested his forehead against hers, caressing the dried blood on her face. He softly kissed the wet path of her tears, down to her quivering lips. With utmost care, he pulled her arms apart and lifted them over her head.

She felt his hands possessively reaching for her wrists, beginning to pin them on the mattress then pull further, his fingers intertwining with hers. Every time, his caresses started out soft, every time, they grew possessive, only to finish as softly as they had started. She could feel him restraining his urge to dominate her, forcing his moves to be gentle. He kissed her down her neck and rubbed himself against her. Her body responded immediately. She couldn't stop her tears from falling, her excitement from building. She felt torn apart and yet serene in the face of all the destruction, the fatality of it. No more anguish, no more questions. She had opened Pandora's box and now faced the evil she had unleashed. She sobbed into his mouth as he passionately kissed her, swallowing everything: her tears and pain, her despair, her hopes, and her desires. He took it all, relieving her of everything she couldn't carry anymore. He penetrated her slowly, every inch of his body touching her, his face inches from hers, and she gasped at the pleasurable intrusion. He broke the kiss to bring his mouth to her ear and continued to thrust inside of her sensually as he gruffly whispered, "Maybe I am a monster. But I'm your monster. I'll fight for you. I'll kill for you. You're mine. Always. Wherever you go. I'll find you. Always. There's nothing I wouldn't do for you."

She squeezed his hands, her eyes hazy and intense at the same time, lost in his. His words felt like medicine on her wounds, his touch, the only anchor in her godforsaken world. The last barrier keeping the darkness at bay.

Her body shattered beneath his, and he kissed her again, swirling his tongue slowly in her mouth, and picked up the pace to reach his own release. He came in a grunt, collapsing on top of her. He planted soft kisses all over her face, then turned her around so she lay against his chest. Lying on his back, he stared at the ceiling deep in thought as he ran his fingers through her hair.

She curled up against him, into him; she would've slit his chest open and crawled into it if she could.

"What happened to your mother?" Her voice sounded so soft, so fragile.

He could feel her little fingers trail on his chest. He exhaled slowly. "She betrayed my father." He guarded her in his embrace, speaking with a soft voice, his hurt for the first time coming through for what it was, and not the cold rage it had festered into over the years.

"With… another man…?"

"No." He took a long pause before exposing his old scar. "Because of me. After I was born. She wanted to *protect* me from him."

"Oh…"

"She went to the cops, Laura. She was ready to sell him out, take me from him, to take everything away from him."

"But… she did it out of love… for you."

"That's not love. *My father* loved her. He did everything for her, *everything*. He never lied to her. She knew the life he was offering her. She *married* him, carried *his* child. Then she betrayed him, for no other reason than the fears in her head. My father took good care of me. He was there for me, always. She didn't even give him a chance. She just turned on him."

"Is that why she died?"

"Yes."

It was tragic, and horrible. Kayne didn't blame his father for the murder of his mother. She had given her life for him, and he held it against her. She felt her heart break for her, for Kayne, for herself, for all the suffering that happened between those walls. She understood the message in the cautionary tale of Mrs. Malkin's life and death, grasped the deadly warning given to her earlier in the car. "I wasn't going to the cops. That's not why I left…"

“I know.” He kissed her forehead.

Their voices soft, their wounds bare, they opened up to each other under a silvery moonlight.

“My father… he told me he loved me… all the time. He would pull me onto his lap and watch the same Disney movies with me over and over again. I think I made him watch *Beauty and the Beast* every Sunday for a whole year.” She chuckled softly, and Kayne responded with the similar smile he had given her earlier, filled with warmth and heartache. “Sometimes, I thought it just made it worse, you know? Sometimes I wished he could just… *be* a monster and not make me forget every time, make me trust him again. The pain would be so much worse… *every time.*” Her voice quavered.

He considered her, understood the depth from which this cry came, the hurt buried deep within. He’d never known another woman to such an extent, never knew any other person so deeply. He understood the plea that came from her confession. Her plea, to *him*.

They fell asleep with their bodies intertwined, Kayne spending the first night of his life in the arms of another.

Day-42

Kayne was already gone by the time Laura awoke. Olga sheepishly came in to greet her, her discomfort apparent. Laura wasn't resentful. Of all people, she could understand the terror of facing a wrathful Kayne Malkin. She smiled kindly at her, trying to make her understand there were no hard feelings. The previous night felt like a blur. She kept replaying the events in her head. Kayne did not come home that night. Laura wondered if she was on his mind as well and spent the whole day in a dizzying haze.

* * *

Kayne was with Tanya. They were going over the details for the following night. Dimitri was throwing another party, and they suspected Maxwell wanted to use this occasion to touch base with possible detractors. Tanya was to remain by his side and give Kayne the names of all the men Maxwell interacted with. It was not enough; they needed to know what his exact plan was. Tomorrow would just be about getting names.

"So… will our little bird be joining us tomorrow?" Tanya tossed, her voice playful, her grin devilish.

Kayne smirked, shaking his head. He would not play this game with her. It was already late when he left her quarters at Dimitri's mansion. On the ride home, he thought of Laura, remembering when he brought her to the party, and smiled to himself. He thought of the previous night, of her naked sweaty body against his, of her soft pleas, her ragged moans as her body shattered underneath his. Of the special way she had of reaching into him and bringing out something he didn't even know was there.

Day-43

Laura was on her way back in after spending the day outside. Olga had advised her Master Kayne would not be home for supper, and she felt butterflies in her stomach when she unexpectedly ran into him on his way out. She hadn't seen him since they spent the night together.

"Hi…" She smiled shyly at him, her face bright with the happy surprise.

"Hey…" He smiled, somewhat tenderly, his eyes penetrating hers.

She lowered her gaze, though her smile remained. He pulled her to him, caressing her cheek with the back of his hand. She blushed, raised her eyes to meet his, bashful and decadently sensual at the same time, in a way that was entirely hers.

Her fingers lingered on his arms, as she suddenly noticed the formal black suit. It was the same he'd worn that night, when he took her to the *party*. Her heart began pounding faster and faster; her face dropped.

"What's wrong?" he asked softly, concerned with her sudden mood change.

She shook her head silently. She didn't have the courage, was unsure if she wanted to know as she already felt her chest clamping.

"Laura, what's wrong," he inquired again, irritation quickly replacing concern.

"Are you…. going to a party?" she whispered, her eyes fixed onto his chest, avoiding his gaze.

He sighed, understanding dawning on him. Though not harsh, his voice betrayed no emotion as he stared intently into her eyes. "Yes."

She closed her eyes with the pain his answer caused her. She wanted to back away from him, but he grabbed her arms, gently pulling her back against the wall by the front door. She refused to look at him, keeping her head turned as she fought the tears welling up in her eyes. After everything they'd just been through, how could he do this to her? … How could she think he would've done otherwise? She didn't know at this very moment who was really the one to blame.

"Look at me."

She shook her head, keeping it turned to the side as one tear spilled over, running down her cheek.

He shook his own head, a discouraged smile on his face. "What am I going to do with you…"

Her face still turned away, she shrugged her shoulders, refusing to meet his gaze. He grabbed her chin and forced her to look him in the eye.

"Don't be jealous. It always ends badly when you do…" he cautioned her, a devilish grin on his face. Leaning in, he kissed her sensually on her cheek, so close to her mouth the corner of his lips grazed hers, and then he walked out.

* * *

Laura waited until she couldn't hear his footsteps anymore. She wanted to scream at the top of her lungs, but no sound came. She wanted to break everything, wanted to set the house on fire, set the world on fire, and watch it burn with everything in it. She didn't cry, didn't make a sound, just wondered how much more of this she could take. *Not much.* Using the wall for support, she dragged herself back to her room. She laid her head on the pillow and stared at the bracelet he had given her, *From Your Monster.* But he wasn't hers. He never would be. With that realization, her tears finally came.

Hours had passed as she lay on her side looking out the window, her eyes now dry, and her body still in the same position. The moon was particularly bright that night, reminding her of their night together. He had held her all night long, and Laura, who always froze awkwardly in such intimate moments, had felt at home in his arms. Tears welled up again at the thought.

It was late in the night when her door cracked open, letting in the light from the hallway. She sealed her eyes shut, feigning sleep as she heard him walk in, feeling him moving about. He removed everything down to his boxers before climbing in bed with her and then wrapped his arm around her, a smirk on his face.

She remained very still, holding her breath as he leaned closer to her. "I know you're awake."

"I know," she responded, her voice soft.

He sighed and pulled her into him even closer, spooning her. She tried to ignore the warmth his embrace triggered, focusing instead on fighting back the tears building in her eyes.

"I didn't fuck anyone," he softly reassured her.

"Just blow jobs then…" she answered, bitter though subdued. She remembered walking in on him with Tanya… and the other woman, and cringed. The next moment, he was flipping her on her back as he pinned her wrists down. They stared into each other, her eyes glistening with tears, his conveying exasperation.

He watched her silently, studying the pain in her eyes. What did she want from him? What did she expect? He didn't fuck anyone, *for her*. Did she also expect him to turn down the whore making rounds as he sat with his associates? Excuse himself politely because of a lover at home? Show weakness, show any softness, and it would be the last thing you did. Did she not understand the world he lived in, *still*?

Her innocent expectations aggravated him to no end, and yet he liked that she was jealous, over him. No woman had ever been. His whores accepted his terms without question, never negotiating, never demanding. There she was, shattered by the mere thought of his being with someone else. For this reason alone, he knew they could never be together. For this reason alone, he knew he would never want anyone as much as he wanted her.

"You really can't help it, can you…" He shook his head at her. With a condescending sneer, he added, "What did you think would happen, Laura? That I would quit everything? *For you?* Turn my life around? Marry you? Start a family?"

Her eyes widened, as if even she hadn't expect such cruelty from him. She stared him straight in the eye, her eyes burning with an intensity he'd never seen. "Fuck you."

He chuckled softly, lowering his face to breathe down her neck.

"Get off me!" she screamed, wiggling wildly under him in an attempt to free herself. "Get off me!" she shouted again hysterically, fighting him off with all her strength.

His whole expression gleamed with animalistic excitement as he easily subdued her, and she panted under his body, her face flushed.

"What am I going to do with you…" He smirked at his helpless prey. Pinning both her arms with one hand, he reached between her thighs with the other, biting his lower lip at finding her wet.

"Missed me?" he taunted her, licking his lips, his eyes predatory.

"I hate you," she breathed through clenched teeth.

He grinned wickedly and moved his fingers around her wetness. "But you don't, Laura… isn't that why you're so upset?"

She closed her eyes, unwilling to admit, unable to deny.

He kept stroking her, watching her anger dissipate and transform, her head falling backward as she gasped with pleasure.

"How long are you going to keep fighting me? Don't you *know* you're going to lose?" he whispered wolfishly, then slowly penetrated her with his middle finger. "Every time."

A soft cry escaped her lips. "Fuck you," she panted.

He chuckled. "Not unless you beg…"

"Fuck you."

His brow shot up. With a wicked gleam in his eyes, he released her wrists and wrapped his hand on her throat, applying some pressure. Her eyes snapped open in terror. He applied more pressure, his grin devilish, and she gasped for air, beginning to feel light-headed. She wrapped her newly freed hands around his arm in vain, she had no strength left. She panicked, feared she might pass out.

He kept fingering her, rubbing her with the palm of his hand. She gasped for air that never came, only more pleasure, mind-numbing waves of overwhelming pleasure. Her entire body was reduced to the sensitive spot he kept stroking, to the muscles clamping uncontrollably around his finger. She was dripping wet. Her eyes rolled back, as her entire body stiffened. He knew she was on the brink, and let go of his grip as her entire body convulsed in a loud orgasm, gasping desperately as the air rushed back into her.

He lay back down by her side, leaning lazily on his elbow, and watched her as she came down from her high. She turned to him, still dazed.

"What the *fuck*?" she gasped, terror building in her eyes.

He kept staring at her, the corner of his lips quirking up. "Thought you might like that."

"You could have killed me…" She reached for her throat, her voice now soft, though terror was still very present in her eyes.

He half rolled his eyes, amused with her indignation, and languidly pulled her back to him. She didn't resist as he spooned her again, brushing her hair and kissing her on her temple.

"Kayne…?"

Her voice reached him, so fragile, so small, he just wanted to pull her even closer. Hold her so tight he could make her *understand*. Understand what exactly, he wasn't even sure himself.

"Yes, Laura…" His voice came out amused, even mockingly patient.

"Was she there?" Her voice quavered.

"Who?"

She didn't answer.

"Tanya?" he guessed and felt her body tense at the mention of the name.

"Yes."

He smirked behind her, reveling in her jealousy. But in this moment, while she lay so sweetly against his chest, naked and vulnerable, her breathing soft, he didn't want to toy with her emotions, didn't want to hurt her more than he already had.

"I'm not fucking her, Laura," he answered her, his voice soft, then, before she had a chance to twist his words in her head, responded to her fears. "There is *nothing* going on between me and her."

"Okay…" she voiced hesitantly, other worries still obviously on her mind.

He turned her around to face him and looked into her eyes inquisitively, trying to read into the pools of sadness that wearily returned his gaze.

"What is it?" he asked her, caressing the side of her face with the tip of his index finger.

She shook her head.

"Tell me."

She sighed, defeated. "I hate… that you bring her here..." Her little voice broke at the confession. She lowered her gaze, not wanting to know how he would respond, what cruelty he had in store for her. She didn't think she could survive it. She waited in limbo for his response, like her life, her entire world depended on it.

He remained silent for a while, gazing at her. He couldn't understand why she fixated on her. She'd seen him fuck a woman in the dungeon, seen another give him head in the reception hall barely two days ago, and yet it was Tanya she despised. Another part of him though, understood, very well.

He gently lifted her chin and shook his head, a tolerant smile on his face. He leaned in and kissed her softly on the lips. "Okay. I won't bring her here anymore."

He felt her entire body ease with relief. She didn't let him break the kiss; instead, she pulled back into it, holding on to him with urgency. He was slightly taken aback by her ardor for a second. He opened his mouth and felt her tongue swirl around his with desperate passion. He kissed her back, sitting up on the mattress, and helped her up on top of him as she lifted herself to straddle him. She ran her hands through his hair, never breaking the kiss, digging her nails in his shoulders and chest. He grabbed her wrists, holding them together behind her back.

"Fuck me… I beg you, Master..." she panted against his lips, rocking herself against his growing erection.

He grabbed her hair and pulled her head back, breaking the kiss. She still pulled toward his face, trying to find his lips again. He pulled her hair even harder and heard her gasp, somewhere between a moan and a cry. He licked his lips, his stare voracious; never had another woman looked so beautiful. She was hypnotizing. Panting, desperately reaching for his lips, rocking against him while ragged breaths escaped her moist lips, her eyelids heavy with wanton desire. She was a far cry from the scared little girl he had brought to his house. He saw the woman in her, *his woman*, claiming her man, with no shame or modesty.

"Fuck yourself," he commanded her, his voice husky, still pulling her hair.

She raised her hips and tried to place him at her entrance, struggling as he kept her hands pinned behind her back. He chuckled softly at her vain efforts. He tilted his hip and placed himself at the right angle, then pulled back every time she brought her hips down to take him in. She cried out in frustration as he chuckled loudly, exhilarated. He brought his mouth to hers and kissed her as passionately as she had, pulling her into him. He rubbed himself on her, feeling her juices flow down on him. She met his movements, rocked her hips along his, and kept trying to take him in. When he could no longer hold it, he let her have her way. He struggled to resist his building orgasm from the first thrust, while she moaned in his mouth. He pulled her head back again, hearing her pant *fuck* over and over again.

He came with a loud growl and kept fucking her. He pulled her hair further down her back, twisted her wrists in, and forced her back to arch completely into him, exposing her delicate neck. He leaned in and bit the hollow of soft skin above her shoulder. She cried out, in pain or pleasure, he wasn't sure anymore.

"Come for me, Laura."

She gasped, her cry loud and long, as she obeyed him. *Her Master. Her Monster. Her Man.*

She didn't collapse but kept straddling him with her back straight. No one uttered a word. They remained as they were, their eyes locked on each other, a wicked smile on both their lips.

Day-44

Kayne faced Tanya.

"Everything is set then?" he asked.

"Yes. In the black Lexus. Just like you said." She half rolled her eyes.

"*Where*... in the black Lexus?" he insisted, his patience forced through gritted teeth.

She exhaled, just as aggravated. "I slid it in that little gap near the stick. Then I made a huge scene the next day about losing it," she added, somewhat proudly. "*If* he ever finds it, he'll just be happy to give me back my earring," she brushed him off dismissively.

"Good. And those are all the names?" He lifted the folded paper in his hands.

She nodded, exasperated. Then her energy shifted, and her eyes grew wanton. "I could come over tonight... We could test our little GPS Tiffany earrings." She grinned at her own joke. "I think he's meeting someone. We could see if it's one of the names on the list... Besides, there's this adorable little blonde I just found..." She smiled wickedly before biting her lip. "Maybe you could return the favor and test *her* for me before I present her to Dimitri?"

He considered her for a second, then answered her, his face impassive, "No need. Lucas will handle it. I'll come see you from now on."

"What?" she snapped. "Why?" she then demanded, her eyes blaring.

His eyes ablaze, he smirked at her, then turned around, ignoring her question. "I'll see you tomorrow."

"It's because of her? That new whore of yours?" She lifted her face, her eyes defiant.

He stopped in his tracks and turned around swiftly, irritated. He didn't answer, just narrowed his eyes at her.

"It is!" She let out a sardonic chuckle.

He slowly walked back to her, his menacing expression contrasted with his soft voice and seductive smile. "Have to keep the vultures away from the little bird…"

She laughed humorlessly. "Then *you* should stay away," she added, her eyes boring into his.

He didn't answer, restraining a smirk.

A subdued smile crossed her lips. "You and I. We're the same. Do you really think that scared little puppy can survive you?" She paused. "If you care about her at all, let her be. You will take everything from her, and when she has nothing left, you will leave her, and you will come back to me. You always do."

The truth of her words stung him. He didn't want to acknowledge them. "I will do what I want with her," he growled.

"Is she worth it? Is she worth throwing away your only friend?"

He sneered at her, then slowly wrapped his hand around her neck, his thumb turning her face to his. His voice husky, he replied, "*Friend?* We're not friends."

She smirked devilishly at him, her breathing ragged with arousal, her voice throaty. She taunted him, "Do you want to fuck me, Kayne?"

She waited for his expression to change, for his animalistic desires to emerge, then added with disdain, "Too bad your whore won't *let* you. Is that why you were being such a *good boy* at the party yesterday?" She chose her words carefully, her tone mocking him, willfully provoking him.

He knew she was, knew her little games all too well, but they worked nonetheless. He exhaled slowly, flaring his nostrils. He wanted to choke the life out of her, wanted to fuck her senseless and wipe that smirk off her face.

Keeping his hand on her neck, he grabbed her hip with the other and pulled her sensually to him. "Does it hurt, Tanya? Does it hurt to know that I prefer the *little puppy* to you? Tell me... do you still think of me every time Dimitri whores you around...? Still wish it was me every time a man touches you...? Does it hurt to know that I never will again? Regardless of what whore I take."

She closed her eyes and remained very still, only her loud breathing betraying her emotions. Two can play that little game, he thought. She should have known he was better at it. He let her go and turned around, heading for the exit.

"Have *her* fuck Maxwell for you then!" she screamed behind him, hot rage burning in her feline eyes.

He was already at the door, turned his head back, and slowly nodded his understanding. They stared defiantly at one another, willing to meet in a battle neither truly wanted and neither would back out of.

Day-50

Kayne avoided Laura all week. He needed Tanya. He expected she would react badly but hadn't foreseen how badly and quickly things would escalate. He blamed Laura for it. He knew he was being vindictive and unfair but couldn't help it. The few times he ran into her, he ignored her, barely looked her way indifferently. He could tell how it hurt her. The first time she was walking toward him, a bashful smile on her face. She didn't say anything, but her eyes widened as he walked past her, barely nodding coolly her way. After that, she had avoided him as well and returned his icy indifference the few times they'd crossed paths. He was alienating the one person he pushed Tanya, and her resources, away for.

Natasha Drugova was organizing a brunch in a few days and had requested Laura's presence. He would make it up to her then, he thought.

Day-53

Olga had advised Laura the previous evening that Master Kayne requested she meet him in the living room at nine in the morning, dressed and ready.

She thought of not going. She couldn't understand him, anything about him, about the way he was with her. He had come into her room after the party that night, had been cruel, had been kind, and in the end held her in his arms all night. He was even still in her bed when she woke up. He had lazily smirked at her, his eyes half closed, catching her as she watched him fascinated, thinking him still asleep. She could have watched him all day. She was happy then. He had grabbed her abruptly and flipped her on her back. He was in one of those playful moods, and she giggled under him, thrilled and terrified.

The next time she met him, he was entirely different, colder than he'd ever been. She couldn't understand. She felt the burn, would've preferred facing his wrath over this indifference. But she didn't cry, didn't crumble; she could handle the burn. She'd been forged in fire.

She was wearing beige linen pants, sexy nude stilettos peeping out the front. Along with a white silk shirt, she felt feminine and elegant. She approached him, her walk confident, her eyes cold, and greeted him, "Good morning."

He was leaning against the wall in jeans and a white polo, his hair tied back. He smirked when he saw her. He didn't answer, just walked languidly over, making her think of a tiger creeping up on its prey. She kept her head held straight, refusing to lower her gaze.

He took her hand and brought it to his lips, his eyes smoldering. It completely threw her off. She would've expected anything from him, not this simple sweet gesture.

"Ready?" he asked, his eyes mischievous, as he held her hand in his. She could feel the burn his lips left on her hand and wanted to pull it back. Returning his gaze, she nodded, forcing herself to feign detachment.

He was still holding her hand when they got into the car. Lucas was already in the driver's seat. She wouldn't even ask where he was taking her and betray any sign of insecurity or concern. They didn't speak to each other the entire ride. Even so, she felt his gaze undressing her, could see with the corner of her eye the wolfish grin on his face.

They pulled into a mansion almost identical to the one he had taken her to for the party. This was the official Drugov residence though. While the other projected lustful opulence, she was the good sister of the twin mansions. Strong, straight, and beautiful, she would not offer dark hallways for secret rendezvous with beautiful strangers.

As soon as Lucas stopped the car, Laura reached for the handle. She didn't wait for Kayne, heading straight for the mansion. She didn't care what awaited her. Whatever hell he was bringing her to, she could face it.

Kayne was staring at her the entire way. She was definitely not the scared little puppy anymore. He wanted her so much. In this instant, he didn't regret anything. Let Tanya bring all she had, he didn't care. He could handle Tanya, and Maxwell.

In one continuous movement, he reached for her arm and brought her into him, kissing her hungrily. He felt her resistance, her open palms on his chest trying to push him away. But he pulled her in even further, deepening his kiss until she opened her mouth and let him in, until her entire body gave in and melted into his.

When he pulled away, her brows furrowed. She sighed, somewhat exasperated, her face flushed. He smiled at her, mischief gleaming in his eyes.

Though her eyes softened for a moment, she didn't say anything. She just turned her head and kept walking. He chuckled softly, reached for her hand, and forced her to walk with him, hand in hand.

"You must've made a good impression on Natasha. She specifically asked that I bring you," he threw at her playfully.

She smiled thinly and continued to look straight ahead.

The doorman advised them the brunch was taking place outside on the top terrace. There was already quite a crowd gathered. The men were on one side, the women giggling away on the other. Kayne and Laura exchanged a glance, she finally smiled at him, and they separated.

She headed for the table where Mrs. Drugova was. The latter stood up to greet her, bringing her affectionately in her arms. She introduced her to everyone at the table before pointing to the empty seat next to hers.

"I saved it for you," she said with a discreet smile.

As Laura listened absentmindedly to the conversations, she felt Mrs. Drugova squeeze her hand on her lap.

"We should go for a walk after lunch. It is such a lovely day."

Laura nodded, a genuine smile on her lips. They finished their meal, leaving the women in a heated conversation about renovation and interior design.

"Idiots." Mrs. Drugova smiled at Laura, shaking her head disapprovingly. "How have you been, Laura?"

"Thanks for inviting me." She nodded, smiling back.

"Of course," Mrs. Drugova answered dismissively. "I'm glad to see you heeded my advice. You look positively radiant, my dear."

Laura cocked her head to the side. "I don't know, Mrs. Drugova… I don't know that I have."

"Please. Call me Natasha. All my friends do."

Laura smiled again. She liked Natasha. She was everything she wasn't and hoped to be. Then she remembered what Kayne told her… *Dimitri wants you dead…*

"Natasha, can I speak candidly with you?" Laura stared her right in the eye, her face somber.

"You always do. That's what I like about you." Natasha smirked, her expression all-knowing. She seemed larger than life to Laura.

"Mr. Drugov… Dimitri… wants me dead…" Laura's voice came out low and grave.

"Yes. So would Kayne if he wasn't infatuated with you," she added, the smirk etched on her face. "You're a loose end, Laura. The point of the matter is, it would just be simpler to be rid of you, permanently."

Laura's eyes grew round. She hadn't expected such bluntness, spoken so casually from Natasha as she discussed her life.

"Which is why I know you've taken my advice. Kayne wouldn't have put his neck out for you if it weren't the case," she finished.

Laura couldn't help smiling to herself, replaying the words in her mind. He cared, regardless of *parties* and other women. He cared about her, in his own twisted way. "May I ask you something?"

She nodded.

"Last time… you were telling me about… being with… Dimitri…. In a way that was tolerable for you… I don't think I can…" she confessed, remembering her hours spent in bed crying, her heart scorched with images of Kayne and other women.

"You don't have a choice. It's that simple. Most women lie to themselves, prefer spending their time discussing *interior design…*" She let out a condescending chuckle. "But you can't, you're like me. You remind me of myself when I was younger. It's no way to live, Laura, you will suffer tremendously.

"My husband has whores. And that's all they'll ever be. There is only one Mrs. Drugova. Every now and then, one of them will stand out from the rest. That one, I keep close. If she steps out of line, she pays for it, with her life."

Her eyes austere, Natasha imparted her wisdom to Laura. She liked the girl, had leaned in Kayne's favor when Dimitri was still on the fence. Dimitri couldn't afford alienating both of them, so the girl remained with Kayne. Natasha could see herself looking in Laura's eyes, reminiscing about the trembling young girl she once had been. Brought into a world she didn't understand, making sense of all the good values her parents had dutifully imparted on her. For her to survive, the young girl had to die. She never once regretted the loss. She carried her fondly in her heart but never shed any tears over the sweet naïve girl she left behind.

Laura was deep in thought. Could she ever become this way? Just the thought of another woman touching Kayne sickened her. Part of her envied Natasha, her realism, her pragmatism in the face of a seemingly impossible situation, and yet she seemed to come out on top. *Keep Kayne's whores around?* They wouldn't survive the day. She'd gladly ship them back to whatever hell they came from. She remembered when not too long ago, she'd seen them as victims. Her heart had gone out to them. Kayne was the monster then, abuser of the innocent, the weak, and the helpless. She wondered what changed. The answer came back quickly and resonated within her. It was just a word really, a mere preposition, but it changed everything. He was no longer the monster, he was *her* Monster.

Natasha pulled her out of her thoughts, gently squeezing her arm. A woman was anxiously waving her down from up on the terrace.

"If you'll excuse me, Laura dear, I believe there must be an appetizer emergency, given her state of panic..." she added sarcastically.

She left Laura to her introspection and weary conscience. Laura remained by herself for a while, wondering about it all. The difference was that Natasha had a choice, had willingly picked this life. Laura didn't have the luxury to hold on to her values and leave Kayne behind. She would remain his prisoner, willing or not. Bitterly, she realized, no matter what he did, no matter how hard she fought him off, she would end up drained, in his arms, somewhere in an abyss of pleasure and pain.

"Hey..." a singsong, gratingly familiar voice snuck up behind her.

She snapped around, her whole body tense. “What are you doing here?”

Tanya offered her the most condescendingly sweet smile she could conjure. “Natasha invited me. *Silly.*” She shook her head, a saccharine smile on her face.

Keep your friends close… Laura quoted *The Godfather* in her mind and smirked to herself.

Tanya seemed dissatisfied with her reaction but shook off her aggravation instantly. “I saw you talking with her earlier. Don’t you just love her?”

Laura didn’t respond. She felt like she was walking into a trap. One part desperately wanted to walk away, and the other didn’t want to retreat, wished to stand her ground, showing Tanya she was not the least bit intimidated.

“Well… she really likes you...” Tanya added, her tone pleasant, her expression carefree. “I know she does, she told me.”

“Did she…” Laura replied, her expression both disbelieving and irritated.

“Of course. We’re quite close actually. She talks about you *a lot*. Has a lot of respect for you.”

“Sure…” Laura sighed, annoyed. Her heart was racing, though she kept her eyes cool as she returned the haughty look. “Well… she never mentioned you… In any case, *Kayne* is waiting for me…” She excused herself. “See you around.” She threw back with forced pleasantness before turning around.

She smiled gleefully, wanting to pat herself on the back. She’d never had frenemies to practice with, but from Tanya’s pursed lips, she knew she hit her mark.

Tanya held her arm. “Wait… Listen… I know we got off on the wrong foot. I guess I just wanted to apologize… I don’t want you to hate me.” She looked her in the eye and seemed sincere.

“Okay,” Laura conceded, though suspicious. She was about to turn around again. She had just won the last round, couldn’t they leave it at that?

"I just... I would like it if we got along..." Tanya offered her a tentative smile.

Laura lifted her brows in response. Even she wasn't that naïve.

"For Kayne..." Tanya explained, picking up the weapon Laura brought out to use against her. "I care about him, a lot. I mean, we've been through *so much* together. And he cares about you... so..."

She cursed herself, realizing too late she would be David in the battle. In real life, Goliath always wins. She already burned with the petty jealousy Tanya tried to incite in her, but she was ready for it. She was ready for whatever Tanya threw at her. This was a woman's war. No guns, knives, or torture devices required.

"I don't think he's ever cared about anyone like you." Tanya's eyes darkened for an instant, but her composure quickly returned, as it always did. "Honestly. I'm happy for him, Kayne and me..." She shook her head, a devilish grin on her face. "But you two go well together. You obviously love him very much."

Laura felt her patience wearing thin. "Well, thank you for the well-wishes." She smiled tight-lipped before turning around, ready to walk away.

"I mean... That you can just forgive him like that... I don't think *even I* could have..." Tanya added, Laura's back already turned to her.

It was in that moment, Laura knew her next decision would have more impact than she could deduce. She could walk away and ignore her obvious jeers. Or she could stay and fall prey to Tanya and her pettiness, just to know what she meant to use against her, reveal the sword dangling over her head. She stayed, she always did. She would open Pandora's box yet again. She wondered what it could be. Had he been sleeping with her? He swore he hadn't, that nothing was going on... more women at parties, other whores? Laura prepared herself, covered her heart in stone, and waited. She would smile at whatever words came out of this woman's mouth, *condescendingly if possible.*

Laura crossed her arms, a forced bored look on her face.

"I mean... your own brother..." Tanya shook her head, disbelieving, her whole demeanor theatrical.

"What? What are you talking about?" She did not see that one coming. Her heart was pounding furiously in her chest, sensing the imminent danger, far too late.

"I mean when I saw the pictures... with his head blown off... to know Kayne did this to him... How could you even look at him? Weren't you like very close with your brother too? Peter? Was that his name?" she asked, her brows furrowing. "He had it coming, mind you... Anyway, guess love does conquer all, huh?" She smiled, satisfied with herself.

Of all things, Laura hadn't prepared her heart for this. She stared at Tanya, trying to read her face. She felt strangely calm, like she was leaving her body, rising above, far above everything. Tanya was saying it all to hurt her, just to hurt her... And yet she knew it to be the truth. Hadn't she known it all along? Hadn't she known it in her heart, from the first night Kayne came back? The timing too coincidental, the suicide too convenient, hadn't she known deep down inside Kayne was responsible for Peter's death?

She walked away from Tanya and her triumph without saying a word. She focused on breathing, struggling with every breath, fearing her shaky legs would give out any moment.

Her face aghast, she stumbled forward in the blur of sunshine and greenery. She walked straight past everyone on the terrace and headed to the driveway. Lucas was leaning on the car, a cigarette in his mouth. His eyes were closed, his face turned up, bathing in the sun.

"Lucas... Lucas... take me home."

"Are you okay, Miss Spencer? Should I get Mr. Malkin?" He seemed concerned. Laura was white, her body shivering under the sun.

"No!" she replied instantly, her eyes wide. "Please... please, Lucas... take me home," she pleaded, not waiting for the answer, and climbed in the car.

Lucas was unsure what to do. He took his instructions directly from Kayne, but he could sense the urgency of the matter. He decided not to make her wait and confirm with him; he got in the front seat and drove. The entire drive, he kept looking at Laura through the visor, worried by the reflection he saw. She'd never looked like this, not even the night they fetched her from the bar.

Laura walked in like a zombie, ignored Olga, and went straight to her bedroom. It was the calm before the storm. The perfect storm brewing in her blood, poisoning every cell, membrane, and nerve in her body. She paced in circles; she was suffocating, wanted to pull her hair out, find a way, any way to get the venom out.

Olga was in the kitchen when she heard a chilling scream echo throughout the house. It wasn't human. She was drying the dishes, dropped the one she was holding. She felt a shiver run down her spine and froze on the spot. The sound of glass shattering and furniture breaking snapped her back to reality. Panicked, she rushed to Laura's room.

Everything was destroyed. Laura stood in the middle of the mayhem, a demented gleam in her eye, holding the foot of a broken chair. She screamed at Olga to leave and threw the wooden piece in her direction. Olga rushed out of the room, picked up the phone, and reached Lucas.

* * *

Lucas was already parking the car back at the Drugov mansion when he received Olga's frantic call. He went inside, quietly approached Kayne, and addressed him discreetly.

"Sir. There's a problem at the house."

Kayne turned his head in response, his eyes instantly darkening.

"It's Miss Spencer. She wasn't feeling well. She asked me to bring her back—"

"*What,*" Kayne hissed, barely containing his anger.

"She didn't look well, sir. I thought it was wiser to bring her back straight away, thought you'd approve."

Kayne narrowed his eyes. "And what's the problem now?"

"I'm not really sure. Olga called, panicked, saying Miss Spencer had gone mad... destroyed her room..."

Kayne rushed behind the wheel with Lucas in the passenger seat. He was livid. It seemed no one had any idea what triggered Laura's meltdown. He would deal with her and her tantrum. *He would deal with her all right.* Grinding his teeth, breaking every speed limit, Kayne screeched the car to a full stop before walking in and slamming the door.

The house was quiet. Olga was sitting on a couch in the living room, playing with the towel she had been using to dry the dishes. Her face was white. She just looked up at Kayne, her eyes distressed.

"Where is she?" he bellowed.

"Still in her room.... She's quiet now..."

He nodded, his eyes ablaze. His walk determined, his hands in tight fists, he made his way to her room. The bedroom was completely trashed, broken glass everywhere on the floor, all the furniture broken, turned over in pieces, but no Laura.

He turned his gaze to the closed bathroom door, walked slowly to it, and tried the handle. "Laura. Open the door." His voice was eerily calm.

Nothing.

"Laura! Open this fucking door before I do it for you!" he threatened, raising his voice, his façade of coolness long gone.

Nothing.

A demonic smile crossed his lips. *She will pay for this.* He kicked the door in.

Laura lay in the bathtub, her eyes closed, the water surrounding her, an unwholesome tint.

His eyes widened, his anger evaporating instantly. He was by her side in a second. He reached for her wrist and covered the gash with his hand, blood seeping through his fingers.

"Lucas! Get Iman! Now!" he shouted, urgency in his tone. He picked up the limp body and deposited Laura carefully on the bed. Then he removed his shirt, bandaging the wound as best as he could.

"Laura! What the fuck!" he screamed to himself enraged, knowing she couldn't hear him. Knowing in this moment, he had no control, over her, over himself, over anything. For the first time in his life, Kayne Malkin felt the stab of powerlessness.

He paced around like a madman until Iman arrived. Iman, a slim brunette with olive skin, was in her late thirties. She had been a surgeon in her country, in Palestine. Like her father before her, she had a fascination for medicine, felt a calling to save lives, regardless of what side of the border they belonged to. Until she saw her world come crashing down. Until she saw her entire family die in front of her eyes, blown to pieces due to a strategic hit by military forces. Their neighborhood had been deemed hostile. Iman, whose name meant faith in her mother tongue, understood that day there was no greater good, only monsters fighting for power. She left her country, her life, and her memories. Only a scar on the left side of her face kept her linked to the hopeful hazel-eyed beauty she had once been.

Upon arriving in Quebec, she worked as a cleaning maid in a hotel. She pretended not to speak French or English, shutting herself off from the world. She walked in on Lucas bleeding in one of the rooms one night. Without saying a word, she removed the bullet and stitched him back together. She'd been with the Organization ever since. Iman accepted the world for what it was, who populated it; she would at least control which monsters got her help.

Day-55

It had been two days. Iman assured him the girl would live. She gave him pills for Laura and advised him to let her get all the rest she could get and that she would return to check up on her. Kayne had not left Laura's side, for two days and two nights. He kept watch from the La-Z-Boy he had dragged to the side of her bed.

He wiped the sweat from her forehead, heard her cry in her sleep, tossing and turning, uttering his name. He cringed, knowing he was the monster in her nightmares. He couldn't know she was calling for him, lost in a daze, calling for him to save her, her tears coming from despair, not fear.

Day-56

It was evening when Laura's eyes fluttered open. Kayne immediately put the laptop away and turned his attention to her, not uttering a word. She looked around, her eyes weary. When she noticed him, she closed her eyes right back.

"You should have left me…" she uttered weakly, eyes still closed.

"Laura… why? You promised me, *you promised*, you would never try this again." His voice was contained, though raw with emotion.

A bitter subdued snort escaped her lips. She opened her eyes, staring right ahead. "You promised you wouldn't kill Peter. Guess we're both liars."

"*What?*" His expression instantly changed, his eyes blackened.

She didn't answer, just turned her gaze his way. There was no anger there. There was no more place for anything but the limitless grief that inhabited those haunting grey eyes maintaining his gaze.

"What the fuck are you talking about?" His voice was gruff and heavy, his eyes concentrated on her.

"You shot him."

He shut his eyes, exhaling slowly. "Who told you that?"

She responded with a sardonic chuckle. "*Tanya.*" She met his gaze, a wicked humorless smile on her lips.

"Are you fucking kidding me? And that's it? You just take her word as the cold hard truth. *Hers?* A goddamn whore… who hates you…?"

"But *it is* the truth..." She remained calm, lifting jaded eyes to his.

"It's not, Laura. I had given you my word," he responded, a flicker of hurt flashing in his scornful stare.

"So you just happened to find him dead, from an *overdose*… the moment I sent you to him."

"No," he conceded, his expression unreadable.

She closed her eyes again, bracing herself for the piece of the puzzle he'd been holding back. The one she was dreading to hold in her hands and yet knew it was the only way she could finally lay her brother to rest.

"He was alive. But I didn't kill him. I waited for him in his apartment. He wasn't that surprised to see me. I explained the situation to him… It was you or him, Laura. Dimitri had given me another week that night at the party. He wanted to interrogate you... right then… but he gave me another week. I gave Peter the drugs. He made his choice. I shot him after… For Dimitri's benefit… He was already gone..."

Tears spilled over from her closed lids. "You might as well have shot him. It would have been more honest," she spat at him, her eyes still closed, her voice as cold as ice. She didn't know if those hurtful words were meant for him, she didn't even know if she meant them. She just felt the need to hurt him, to bring him into her pain, to hold him there, and never let him go.

"Let me go,… or let me die," she pleaded, all malice gone.

He remained quiet, taking her words in. In the oppressing silence that followed, he turned around and left her room. She broke down, the moment he closed her door.

Day-58

Kayne had gone to Dimitri and requested to meet with Tanya privately. Dimitri had listened, seemed vexed with the whole ordeal, but nodded his consent nonetheless to Kayne's request. He understood it to be a request only as far as it would be granted. Kayne Malkin, like his father, was not one to cross. Dimitri was very displeased with Tanya himself. Not only did she reveal privileged information to an outside source, giving more weapons to a loose end he already wanted to be rid of; she did it out of passion, for another man. Sharing her with other men was one thing. To have her openly infatuated with another, betray his confidence out of jealousy for another, *that* he could not accept. He would let Kayne deal with her, let her have her moment with him.

Tanya Malone. Kayne reminisced how he had met her. A party, very similar to the one he had taken Laura to. Tanya, however, was all smiles, clearly in her element. She had come willingly, unclaimed and actively looking. He had spotted her while she was surrounded by admirers, her demeanor closer to Scarlett O'Hara at the fancy picnic than a woman aware of the future awaiting her. She looked magnificent, dressed in long dark blue gown with crystal embellishments, flirting back with only those she deemed worthy, men of high rank. She was not prey, she was baiting solicitors, and she would go to the highest bidder. Kayne knew, from that first encounter, he'd make her his.

He had crept up behind her, wrapped his arm around her, pulling her close to him. He left his hand on her stomach, leaning in, his voice silky, and whispered in her ear, "I can play or I can fight… whichever you prefer…"

She turned her head coquettishly to him, her eyes fiery. "Aren't they the same?"

"Only to the winner."

Her eyes bored into his, challenging him; she nodded. The deal was struck.

He shook his head remembering their torrid affair, remembering their last night together. Tanya Malone, the one person who brought out the worst in him, to have loved him, because of it. Though he knew his father had loved him, knew Olga's devotion to him. Tanya was the only person to ever utter the words.

He remembered his disappointment at feeling nothing, the moment anticlimactic. He hadn't wanted her love, had only felt contempt toward her when she finally bowed in defeat.

He wondered if she had ever meant it. A woman like Tanya couldn't love, he thought, though she could feel. The only thing Tanya ever loved was power, even when used against her. He realized that even in doubt, he still carried a fondness if not a repressed admiration for the fiery seductress. It didn't matter anymore.

He was sitting in a small private living room, leaning his head back, his eyes closed when he heard her heels clicking toward him. He opened his eyes to find her in a fancy green cocktail dress, her silky curls tied in a high ponytail. Regardless of the occasion, Tanya would always be red carpet ready. She sat in the adjacent chair as they stared at each other in a silence that said it all.

"I told you you'd come back to me," she finally said, her playfulness forced.

He stared at her some more, his face weary as he returned a crestfallen smile. "You know why I'm here."

Her eyes glittered with bitter understanding. With a defiant smile on her lips, her voice willfully mocking, she mimicked concern. "The little puppy couldn't handle the truth?"

"What did you think would happen?" He leaned in on his elbows, his eyes boring into hers.

She chuckled humorlessly, she had expected a retaliation from Kayne. Had imagined him storming in, wanting to strike her, his eyes furious, his body lashing at her. She would have gladly welcomed it. His grave attitude however unnerved her, and she felt her mask dropping.

"I really don't know what you see in her. What I do know is what she *doesn't* see in you. If she can see what I see, the real you, all of you… and still want you... Then fine, she can have you."

He bobbed his head in understanding, his face somber. He then reached for her knee, gently brushing his thumb over her skin. He'd never been gentle with her. In that moment, she understood from his sweet caress what she'd done, what she brought upon herself. She closed her eyes and felt a shiver run down her spine. When she reopened them, there was no trace of malice, of wicked playfulness. For the first time in his life, Kayne faced the unguarded, uncensored, Tanya Malone.

"Dimitri gave you the okay?" she asked, her voice low though unwavering.

He nodded.

She closed her eyes, inhaling deeply. "Did it come from him? … Or you?"

"Me," he admitted, holding her gaze.

She snorted bitterly. "Li'l pup has bite…"

A half smirk crossed his lips. "Was she worth it? Was she worth throwing away your only friend?" he quoted back her words.

She grinned, playing along, one last time. "Friend? We're not friends."

They stared at each other in silence, a subdued smile on their lips.

"How do you want it?"

She took a deep breath. "With your hands on my body."

He nodded, solemn, got off the couch, and slowly made his way to her. He brushed her cheek with the back of his fingers, his eyes burning with restrained emotion.

"I really did love you, you know?" She looked up at him, for the first time, her voice breaking.

He nodded again, he believed her. He wrapped both his hands gently around her little neck and began applying pressure. She closed her eyes, maintaining her body as still as she could. He could feel her heart beating frantically, feel his own twist and tighten in its guarded fortress. It didn't stop him; he'd learned to live with that feeling long ago. Just like his father before him, Kayne kept applying pressure. Until he felt the life drain from her, the woman who had loved him and, ultimately, betrayed him.

Day-61

Laura was in the solarium looking out the glass wall, lost in her thoughts. Kayne stood in the entrance, watching her, watching her bandaged arm rest lifelessly in her lap. She turned her head tiredly to the sounds of his footsteps. He took the seat Olga usually sat in, when she used to bring her every day. Laura realized just how much she missed it.

"What do you want?"

Her voice did not carry the bitterness he expected. It was the voice of the condemned to his executioner, accepting of his plight. He eyed her wearily, pulled out a small jewelry box, and placed it on the table next to her.

"What is this?"

"The best I can offer you," he answered, his tone flat. "I'll see you at supper."

With no other words, he exited the room. Laura eyed the box for a long time before her fingers finally reached for it. It held the most beautiful engagement ring she had ever laid eyes on. A round sapphire stood on a platinum band, surrounded with a thin layer of diamonds. It wasn't the flashiest; it was just the perfect one, for her.

She remembered the modest pear-shaped diamond gold band Eric had offered her. How different the two rings were. How different the men. Eric who wanted to offer her everything, even what he couldn't afford to, had never really known her. It showed in the pear-shaped diamond he chose, the gold band he opted for, oblivious to her modest and yet exclusively white gold jewelry collection. Mostly, it became palpable when describing his love, bestowing on her flattering traits she did not possess. Not once had she corrected him. She liked the Laura he saw and worked tirelessly to maintain the illusion. She had liked the pear-shaped diamond, just because he picked it, thinking she would.

Then her eyes reverted to Kayne's ring. It was unfair to even compare the two. His ring was beautiful, simple, and chic. Yet it was off-puttingly cold, its design too perfect to be lovable. It was chosen by a man who clearly knew her taste, who knew her inside out, wanting to please for failure to love.

She closed her eyes, feeling tears already glistening. How could a proposal from the man who meant everything to her be so heartbreaking? She had never, even in her wildest fantasies, thought he would propose. Let alone get down on one knee, his eyes full of hope as had been Eric's. Kayne's ring didn't come with promises of love and hopes for a family. His was a cold and calculated decision, from the man who couldn't love, to the woman who'd never bear him children. It was a trade-off. *The best he could offer her.* To her, it was everything. She spent the afternoon staring down the blue velvet box.

The little box carrying her deepest desires and repressed hopes, from the man who was responsible for her brother's death. The man she still wished would get down on one knee to propose.

* * *

She met him for supper in drab attire, wearing no makeup to conceal the dark circles under her eyes, and no ring on her finger. His eyes set on her, but he didn't say a word. She took the seat facing him, served herself, and held his silence.

"Where's your ring?" he finally inquired, anger creeping into his tone.

She met his gaze. "Didn't match my outfit." She gave him a thin-lipped smile.

Kayne returned her smile, his full of threat. "Go get it."

"No."

He snapped up and was at her side in a second, pulling her out of her chair.

"Did you somehow think you had a say in this? That it was a request? ... A *proposal*?" he asked in a low growl, their faces inches apart.

"Wouldn't it be easier to just kill me?" She met his stare, her voice cool.

He snorted sardonically, then brushed his thumb against her cheek. "It would..."

She closed her eyes, unconsciously leaning into his hand.

He exhaled slowly, feeling his anger dissipate despite himself. "You will wear the ring. Tomorrow you will meet with Natasha. She will help with the preparations. In three weeks, we will be married."

"Why are you doing this?" she asked, her voice soft. She could feel his body heat against her, dreamed of a different conversation in her head.

"And here I was thinking you'd be jumping for joy," he answered with bitter sarcasm.

"I can't... give you children... " Her voice finally cracked.

His eyes softened as he let go of his hold, taking a step back. "Make sure Natasha never finds out."

It would be the only answer she would get. She watched him leave, retreating to the upper level of the house. Did he not want children? That was a mild relief, but why was he marrying her? *So you may live*, answered a voice within. Which was why Natasha should never find out, to ensure Dimitri wouldn't. He had no choice; he only did what was necessary to protect her from Dimitri. Unlike her, she thought with a twist in the heart, he didn't have visions of a little boy. A young and beautiful boy, with her eyes and his smile, running around the house, filling its halls with laughter.

* * *

Kayne lay awake in bed. In three weeks, he would marry Laura Spencer. He would ensure her safety with that alone. Dimitri was not happy at all when he told him, questioning him relentlessly. He had no answer for him. What could he have said? How to explain what he felt? He could never let her go, even if he wanted to. Even if he trusted she would never go to the police, and he didn't, Dimitri wouldn't stand for it. The cops would pursue her relentlessly, could force her to testify, even against her will, unless she was his wife. Dimitri would have her taken out the moment she stepped off Kayne's residence, and protection. Laura Spencer was a liability. Mrs. Laura Malkin, however, would be out of reach, to everyone. He'd thought it through. Marriage was the only freedom he could ever offer her. He'd even asked Dimitri to walk her down the aisle, ensuring his public display of support, which he would be forced to uphold. He'd spoken to Natasha too, knowing her fondness for the girl, and she had delivered.

It wouldn't change anything, he told himself. It wouldn't be a real marriage, just a cover, a means to an end. Yet he fumed at her reaction, at her refusal to wear the ring he had carefully selected for her. The ring he pictured on her delicate finger, smiling inwardly at the thought.

Day-75

Laura looked in the mirror. She couldn't find herself in the reflection of this mysterious bride. Her hair had grown and was curled for the occasion, flowing loosely down her back. Her bangs now reached her chin, her face had slimmed, making her cheekbones more defined. Her makeup was dramatic, with smoky eye shadow enhancing her clear grey eyes. Though it wasn't gaudy, her dress was worthy of Cinderella's ball gown. In the true princess fashion, it had a sweetheart neckline, straps that went round the top of her arms, and crystal embellishments embroidered in the chiffon skirt. She kept staring at herself. She wanted to reach out beyond the mirror and embrace this melancholic princess, comfort her, tell her she was not alone, that she understood.

Laura had been threatened by the makeup artist not to cry. She hadn't. She stood alone and thought back to everything that happened leading her to this day. It was still early in the morning. Natasha had explained to her that the wedding ceremony would be held according to their tradition. Kayne and Laura would be betrothed in the morning at the Orthodox Church; the rings would be exchanged then. A crowning ceremony would follow, though no vows would be exchanged. It wasn't a contract to be upheld until death released you of your promise. It was a solemn commitment, made in front of God, a union even death was powerless to break. The reception would be held at the Drugov residence, and the decorators had arranged the gardens for the occasion. White lanterns and veils were hung up on trees, white lights installed in the fountain and the surrounding water. Laura felt she had walked into a hazy fantasy, where only she was aware of the illusion. Everyone else just wanted to play along.

Natasha had fussed over her. Olga even shed a few tears when she had finally stepped out in her gown. Only she would not get caught in the spell. She had barely seen Kayne in the past three weeks. Lucas drove her to meet with Natasha every day. Natasha planned, barely looking her way for an opinion. Laura understood that Natasha lived this event as the wedding she would never plan for the daughter she never had. Catching a glimpse of her maternal instinct, Laura wondered about the causes behind it, could almost picture herself standing in Natasha's shoes one day.

Laura was glad for Natasha. She doubted she would have survived the whole ordeal without her taking charge, with an iron fist, always, in a velvet glove. For the past three weeks, Laura would come home late at night, exhausted and past supper time. Olga would wait for her, then they'd sit outside together. Laura would smoke a cigarette, as Olga sipped her tea and made her recount all the detailed planning of the day. She would be too tired to speak and only dreamed of her bed but didn't have it in her heart to disappoint Olga's excited face. So she would tell her everything, staying up past her bedtime, only to wake the next day even more exhausted and go through it all once again.

She had started wearing the ring the day after her last supper with Kayne, had spent countless moments staring at it, admiring its simple and elegant beauty, trying to unlock its mystery. She had somehow convinced herself this one piece of jewelry held all the secrets to Kayne Malkin's heart. But the ring remained silent, loyal to her one true master.

The one encounter she had with Kayne leading up to the big day had been tense. She was wearing the ring. He smiled when he noticed, but things quickly dissolved as he announced that Dimitri would be walking her down the aisle. She pled with him, begged him even, for one request, only one, for it not to be him, the man who wanted her dead. Even that simple request was sharply rejected in a tone that left no room for negotiation, nor the slightest compassion.

Dimitri walked into the room, carefully closing the door behind him, and opened his arms, pulling a reluctant Laura into a warm embrace.

"Laura, you look stunning! Never has a bride looked so beautiful. Now don't go telling Natasha I said that." He winked at her playfully.

Laura remained guarded, smiling weakly.

"What's wrong? You should be happy! Has anyone troubled you?" he asked with concern.

She couldn't understand the man. He seemed genuine in this moment, an involved father figure. Three weeks ago, he wanted her dead.

"I'm fine. Thank you, Mr. Drugov," she answered, her voice subdued, her weary eyes looking down.

"Dimitri. We've gone through that already," he corrected her. "Laura, my dear, if something is wrong, you must tell me."

"I feel so alone," she admitted, for lack of better words.

His expression changed, and sounding sincere, he addressed her distress. "I understand. You have no family, no friends present. But what you have to understand is that now, you have a new family Laura. And family is everything, especially to those who have none. We look out for our own, we watch out for each other, and now you will too. Let go of the past and embrace the family that has opened its arms to you. You will never be alone.

"I was against this marriage, I know you know. You're no fool. But Kayne wants you. He's made it clear, he wants you for a wife. He asked for my blessing, asked me to walk you down the aisle. I have nothing against you. I am just an old pessimistic geezer." He smiled. "I see the worst in people. But… Kayne trusts you, so does Natasha actually. They can't both be wrong..." He smiled again, his expression softening. "Leave Laura Spencer to her ghosts. There is a bright future awaiting Mrs. Kayne Malkin."

Laura remained quiet for a few minutes, taking in his words, drinking up the temptation. The same Scorsese quote came back to her mind. It would be warmer *under the wing of the dragon*, imagine a whole cohort, for once flying by her side, on her side. For once, not being the lone warrior facing the army. She let the sweet thought rock her in a calming daze.

Staring into his eyes, she gave the faintest nod, acquiescing. A dim smile crossed her lips, an echo of her visions of a dragon family protecting her, keeping her warm, the dragon king himself, Kayne Malkin, at her side. Still lost in the sweet fantasy, a smile still on her lips, she felt a little pinch in her chest, an indistinct heartache. She understood, too late, this was the price to pay, the betrayal of Laura Spencer. Laura Spencer, who was slowly, painfully dying within her, reaching out in a last cry from behind the mirror as she lay trapped by the mysterious princess who had emerged and claimed her body.

Dimitri nodded back to her, satisfied, his stare heavy with understanding. He folded the veil over her face, offered her his arm, and led her out of the room and into the first limousine in a black procession.

* * *

Kayne Malkin looked dashing in a black suit. With Lucas at his side as his best man, he awaited his future bride at the entrance of the church. Her heart skipped a beat when she stepped off the dark horse, taking the final steps to join herself to the bewitching Prince of Darkness waiting for her, his eyes smoldering, fixed on her. She felt a shiver run down her spine and looked at the crowded streets, noticing the bystanders stop and smile pleasantly at the grandiose ceremony taking place. She thought, for the briefest of instants, to break into a run, keep running, and never look back. But even with her face turned away, she could feel his eyes on her, exercising their influence, silently summoning her to him, their pull magnetic, their power over her, absolute.

She climbed the few steps under his piercing gaze, her limbs pulled forward as if by a string. A priest met them at the entrance and blessed the young couple. A few prayers were recited by the priest, who then took the rings and exchanged them on the couple's fingers three times, in symbolic homage to the Holy Trinity. Laura witnessed the whole ordeal, disoriented. Lost in a dream, or nightmare, she wasn't sure anymore. She hung on to the enveloping gaze of the man standing next to her, the one thing keeping her feet on the ground, her head on her shoulders. They were each given a candle, to light each other's paths in the hour of darkness. They were then led to the center of the church, to begin their new journey from flawed fractions to a complete, perfect whole.

The priest recited more prayers in Russian. Laura kept her eyes trained on Kayne, finding solace in the flames dancing in his eyes, mirroring the ones burning within her. She felt her heart flutter when the priest finally joined her right hand to Kayne's.

When the crown was finally placed on each of their heads, she sensed her inner transmutation nearing completion and with a tender heart waved off Laura Spencer. Their right hands intertwined, candles in their left, Mrs. Kayne Malkin stood next to her king, proud, willing to stand by him, rule with him, in whatever kingdom he offered.

They still hadn't exchanged a single word when the priest instructed them to share the wine from the common cup, symbolizing their commitment to share equally all burdens, all treasures, all of themselves. She squeezed Kayne's hand as they followed the priest around the sacramental table. He quickly looked her way, an indiscernible expression on his face before turning away.

The final blessing was uttered, the crowns removed, and they headed back to the waiting limousine, still holding hands, still silent, surrounded by countless blessings from the attending guests.

At last alone, Laura turned to Kayne and smiled. She wanted to tell him something, everything, but didn't know where to start.

"Don't worry, Mrs. Malkin, I've arranged a separate room for you."

The first words her husband spoke to her cut through her like a knife. She recoiled from him, didn't respond, and didn't look his way for the rest of the ride. They spent the entire time looking out their windows in an oppressing silence neither acknowledged.

Kayne knew the day would be horrific to Laura, knew it was the furthest-possible scenario she could have ever dreamed of. He felt a pang knowing he even managed to betray a young Laura, a Laura he'd never met, who fantasized about Prince Charming and romantic happy endings.

He knew she deserved far more than he could ever offer her, far less than he would inflict upon her. In an isolated selfless impulse, he vowed to himself the marriage would only be a cover, just for her protection, for her freedom, for her. He would not drag her down to his debauchery, would not take what he manipulated her into offering willingly.

He could sense her hurt as they rode silently to the Drugov mansion. He resisted the urge to reach for her, take her into his arms, and kiss her with desperate passion until there was nothing left of her.

Hundreds of guests cheerfully greeted the newlyweds as they arrived in the gardens for the reception. Both offered a plastered smile to the countless faces smothering them in unwanted embraces. Separated by the sea of anonymous arms reaching out, they went their separate ways, neither looking for the other.

The celebrations began with an orchestra playing traditional Russian folk music. A beautiful singer offered a haunting rendition of "Oy da ne Vecher," which Olga explained to Laura was a popular folk song that told the story of a famous soldier and his premonitory dream of his own death. In his dream, he envisioned his horse going wild, a dark omen, and the loss of his head. That soldier, who had truly existed, was later decapitated in battle. Laura felt her tears well up, enraptured by the captivating melody. She felt she'd known it all her life, somehow understood the lyrics, the tragedy behind them, without understanding a single word.

Eventually, the couple was called to the banquet. According to tradition, they had to down a shot of vodka and wash away its bitterness in a lingering kiss. Facing each other, Kayne clinked his glass to Laura's. They threw their heads back and consumed the first toast. The wedding guests cheered "Gorko" in unison, crying the word "Bitter" in Russian, egging on the first kiss.

His eyes smoldering, Kayne pulled Laura possessively to him. Before she could realize what was going on, she felt his lips crush hers, his tongue prying her lips open. Her heart beat madly in her chest, her senses both numbed and awakened simultaneously.

The second toast, usually reserved for the parents, was made to the Drugovs. The couple was to open the dance floor with the latter. The whole dance, they stared at each other in silence, swaying in unison, their mouths unable to speak the truth their bodies shouted. Loud applause finally reached into their haze. They had not heard the music stop, still facing each other in complete silence, oblivious to the world around them.

As more upbeat music broke through, families and couples took over the dance floor. Kayne nodded to Laura, solemnly excusing himself, without a word. His hand abandoned hers, and she didn't see him for the rest of the night.

The sun had long since set, the moon was reclaiming its throne. The celebration raged on. Some of the men had retreated to a private party. A few had remained at the reception, along with all of the women and their children, still awake. They danced, they drank, and always, they laughed. Sometimes children's cries and screams were heard, under the watchful, loving eyes of their parents. The atmosphere was uniquely alluring, the chaotic bursting of life contagious, to all but Laura, and Lucas, whom she found while trailing off on her own.

He was hanging by the side of the house, far from the crowd and ongoing celebration. His knee folded against the wall, he was smoking a cigarette nonchalantly when Laura approached him.

"Would you have an extra one of those?" She smiled despondently, pointing her head toward the cigarette.

He smirked, pulling his pack out. With his finger, he lifted one so it stood out in the pack and flicked the lighter once the cigarette was between her lips.

"How are you holding up?" he asked with a knowing smile.

She just shook her head, warning him she would not answer, would not follow this line of questioning.

He chuckled. "Frankly, I think it was a beautiful wedding. Though you might just be the saddest-looking bride I've ever seen."

"You've been to many weddings?"

"No," he conceded, which made them both share a chuckle.

"Were you ever in love, Lucas?" she asked, out of the blue, without staring at him, watching the dancing, celebrating crowd, further ahead. The groom was long gone, having retreated to the men's private party. The bride was nowhere to be seen, but the guests didn't ask. With music, vodka, and some good food, the feast would never end.

He considered her for a moment. "Yes. I believe I was."

"What happened?"

"Well… I didn't marry *her*…" He replied, trying to get his message across.

"Kayne doesn't love me..."

Though she still avoided his gaze, he could sense the pain in her eyes at the admission. He lifted his brows, considering her statement.

"Do you know Tanya?" she asked, her voice flat, her stare fixed in the distance.

He snorted, shaking his head. "Yeah… I knew her."

"I think he loves her." She felt the stab in her chest pronouncing the words but somehow felt immune to the pain.

Lucas's expression betrayed his surprise. "Loves her? I highly doubt that…" He shook his head again.

"I hate her."

"I could see why," he answered, a telling smile on his face. "But... you know... she's gone… Kayne *took care* of her."

"What?" In a second, he commanded her full attention.

“He didn’t tell you, did he?” He shook his head in indulgent disapproval of his friend. “Yeah… you were still bedridden...”

“He... killed her…” Laura reiterated, more for her own benefit, realizing it was the third time she had caused someone’s death. For the first time, she fought the urge to smile.

Lucas nodded, his gaze meeting Laura’s.

“Because... of what she said to me?”

“Maybe you should ask your husband that, Mrs. Malkin.” He smiled.

She returned the smile, she liked the sound of that. Even if Mr. Malkin was currently at a private party, and she could only imagine what he was doing there. Her eyes hardened. “How come you’re not at the party with him?”

“Not really my scene.” He shrugged his shoulders.

She smiled bitterly at him. *Just her husband’s.*

“I’m no angel.” He was quick to add. “That’s just not my poison. The real question is, how come *you*’re not with him?”

Her eyes shot him daggers for an answer.

He chuckled softly. “It’s none of my business… But… if I were you, of all nights, I wouldn’t want to spend my wedding night chatting it up with the head of security.”

“The best man,” she corrected.

“Just go get your man. *With all due respect, Mrs. Malkin*,” he added, in mock politeness.

She considered him for a second, then her eyes lowered. “You know I can’t go in there.”

“You’re *Mrs. Kayne Malkin*. .Who would stop you?”

She nodded slowly, a sad smile on her face. She already knew she would not follow the advice.

It was already past midnight when they parted ways. She withdrew to her room and remained sitting on the couch in her wedding dress, watching the hypnotic fireplace. She didn’t know how long she stayed like that. The whole day had felt surreal. She replayed the kiss in her mind, could still feel his lips against hers, feel his gaze boring into hers. She opened a bottle of red wine and started drinking alone, her cold bitterness coming to life with each sip, her cold rage enflaming along with the fire burning in front of her. She would not spend her wedding night alone. She would find him, in hell if necessary, and bring him back to her.

She left her room and walked straight toward the forbidden private party, her walk resolute, her feet carrying her despite her frantic heart. The doormen eyed her apprehensively.

"Mrs. Malkin. It's a private party," one of them stuttered uncomfortably.

"Step away."

"Mrs. Malkin, I'm really sorry about this. Our instructions are clear—"

"I need to speak with my husband. Move… or answer to him."

They looked at each other, disconcerted.

"Maybe we can get him for you?" the other added, his uncertain tone already betraying his weakness.

"Move!" She raised her voice, her eyes cold as stone. They stepped aside, each pulling open one of the doors.

She walked past them, her head held high. The party was held in one of the lower-level reception halls. There was a vast room with many corridors leading to smaller private rooms. It was lit by thousands of red candles spread throughout. Everyone was dressed in black, most wearing capes. Men and women swayed their bodies to Khachaturian's spectral masquerade waltz, bonded in the same lustful opulence. All were wearing masks; some being held in place by a stick, others secured with an elastic band.

It was very different from the party Kayne had brought her to. There was no established hierarchy, no organized sexual abuse and degradation. This was pure chaos. Men and women equally partaking in hedonistic decadence. A woman was riding a man on the floor who neighed wildly like a pony. Another was dripping wax onto the chest of a blindfolded man strapped to a table. One was being showered with champagne, while black-caped men leaned over her body like vampires and drank it off her.

Orgies were happening left and right. Everywhere she turned, masked faces looked her way, stopped for a moment, and cackled at her horrified face. She had thought she could handle it, but her head began to spin. Everywhere, masked faces, everywhere, madness, and no Kayne to be found. She stumbled forward in her white gown, with every step separating the black sea of masked faces, which would gather back behind her, like a drop of oil seeking itself, finding itself. She wanted to scream for him. Couldn't he sense her presence? Why didn't he come for her? Why couldn't *he* find her?

She finally leaned on a wall for support, gasping for air that made itself scarce. She felt uncomfortably hot and light-headed. Her eyes glistened with unshed tears. She'd come all this way, crossed the River Styx, and paid the ferryman, only to land in a Kayneless hell, her one true hell.

As her tears finally spilled over and she felt her knees give out on her, she was pulled backward by a strong arm hooked around her waist. She wanted to scream in panic but couldn't make a sound as she wrestled vainly out of the firm hold.

"Laura. It's me."

His voice was hoarse, vibrating so close into her ear. In an instant, her whole body relaxed against his. Her tears flowed with relief, air finally reaching her lungs.

She could feel his heat radiating behind her; she could breathe now. *Everything is going to be okay. Master is here.* She closed her eyes, could finally see the shore, and knew she would reach it safely.

"What are you doing here?" His voice was calm, though intense, did not threaten.

She didn't know what to say, didn't even know if her voice would obey her command. She was still gasping for air, having spent too much time underwater. She turned in his embrace to face him. It wasn't his beautiful devastating face she found; it was the mask of the Beast. A mask that revealed his true nature more than his spellbinding features ever would. She was ready to face her beautiful monster, not the beast she knew lurked underneath.

She covered her eyes with her hands in a childlike gesture. Kayne exhaled slowly, feeling her shoulders shake with her soft sobs. He lifted his mask, letting it rest on the top of his head, and gently nudged her hands away.

His beautiful bride, in his cruel world. Tanya was right, he thought, she would not survive him. Maybe he needed someone like Tanya, who would've gladly accompanied him to the parties, who would've offered him women and watched with animalistic hunger as she forced their heads onto him, forcing them to take him in completely. Who would've whipped a woman bloody at his single command and would've devoured every instant of overpowering other women, avenging her own treatment at his hands.

Laura… his beautiful bride, his innocent girl. He had stolen her, had fought for her, killed for her, all because of her. Laura, who to this day managed to surprise him, who showed strength and resilience, who sacrificed everything, because of him. He wondered how she did it. The more he took from her, the more power she held over him. His little white lamb, who willingly penetrated the lions' den, for him. He would slaughter them all for her, would paint the world red and lay its carcass at her feet.

She looked up at him, her eyes tentative, and smiled feebly at finding the familiar face. Tears fell down her face as she held his stare; she didn't bother to wipe them.

His eyes penetrated hers. He wiped her tears with his thumbs, cradling her face in his hands. He took her hand and, without a single word, led her away from his world of depravity.

They walked in silence, hand in hand, as he led her to her designated room.

"Take me to your room," she whispered softly as they reached the third floor, approaching her room.

He stopped for a second, looked her in the eye, and kept walking. He pulled her along, past the door to her room, all the way to the end of the corridor.

He opened the door and motioned her in. His room was huge, far bigger than hers. She walked to the center of the room and stopped in the middle, between the couch and the burning fireplace. She looked around, watching as Kayne entered, and walked past her. His eyes remained fixed on her as he made his way to the bar and poured two whiskeys. He walked up to her, his body so close, almost touching hers, and handed her a glass. They tipped their glasses to each other without clinking them.

She felt the alcohol burn in her throat, liquid fire rushing through her veins. She carefully placed the glass on a table nearby, then turned back to Kayne, still silent, still watching her intently. Without a word, she placed her hands on his chest, looking up to see his reaction. No help would be found there, his expression remained inscrutable. With shaky fingers, she began to unbutton his shirt. She felt his chest rise and fall under her fingers, felt his ragged breath on her neck, yet he remained silent, not moving a muscle. Once his shirt was completely open, she leaned in, softly kissed his chest, and with subtle fingers, removed his jacket then pushed his shirt off his shoulders.

She moved to his belt and struggled with the buckle. With a smirk, he patiently waited, letting her discover his body, and watched her furrowed brows, amused, as her trembling fingers tugged and pulled on his belt.

The belt unlocked at last. With utmost care, she unbuttoned his trousers and pulled the zipper down. She met his gaze as she pulled his briefs down and over his growing erection, lowering herself to the floor. Her eyes were determined and hungry as she leaned in and took him in her mouth. She wet the skin first, covered her teeth with her lips, and wrapped her hand around him, slowly taking the whole length of him.

A rough groan escaped his lips. He brought his hands down on her shoulders and closed his eyes, consumed by the pleasure she gave him. But it wouldn't take long for his nature to break the spell, forbidding him a pleasure he did not control. His hands wrapped around her wrists, pulled them apart and away from him.

She looked up inquisitively, afraid she'd done something wrong. He pulled her to her feet and gently caressed her, reassuring the nervous face in front of his. He circled around, his eyes on her, once again, reminding her of a tiger on the prowl. She felt her stomach knot, her heart flutter in her chest, as she lay waiting, trying to anticipate his next move. He settled himself behind her and impatiently unlaced her gown. He tore the dress off her back, pulling it roughly to the floor. When he came around to face her, she shivered in her white corset and garter, feeling shy and vulnerable under his wicked stare.

He picked her up and carried her to bed the way he knew grooms did; he could at least give her that. Her eyes never left his, her nervousness creeping in. He leaned in, gently kissed her on the lips, and swiftly turned her around, laying her flat on her stomach. He stripped her naked and used her garter to tie her wrists together above her head.

Her breathing quickened, she turned her head and kept her eyes on him, not as a loving bride, but as fearful prey realizing the trap was set, carefully monitoring her predator's movements. He removed his remaining clothes and returned her gaze with unabashed hunger. He smirked at her nervousness, at the desire he knew overpowered her apprehension. He missed their old games. Tonight, lion and lamb would meet again.

He laid himself by her side, his body turned toward her, and let his fingers glide on the soft skin of her back.

"What are you afraid of?" he asked her, his voice husky with carnal desire.

She panted but, keeping her eyes locked on his, didn't answer.

"Laura…" He shook his head reproachfully, a wicked smile on his face. "Why do you keep doing this to yourself?"

Her eyes widened, panic rising to another level, but still, she kept silent.

He turned her on her back; his naked body hovered over hers, his fingers trailing her every curve. "Tell me. Tell me what you're so scared of," he whispered in her ear.

One night, all she wanted, was one night, of pleasure, with her husband. She would get it, she would always get her pleasure, if she was willing to accept the cost. She closed her eyes, a lonely tear falling down her cheek. She would always accept the cost, no matter how high. She would not only accept it, she would willingly seek it, regardless of the tears, fears, and pain that inevitably came with it. No cost was too great. In a perverse way, she thought, weren't they perfect for each other? Who else but her Monster could truly understand her broken soul, meet her in her madness, find her in the depth of her despair, and somehow, alleviate her from it.

His fingers found the pulsating nerve between her legs. His face remained close to her, his nose and lips tracing every line of her face, breathing her in, leaving sensual kisses on their path.

"You," she gasped, as tears tumbled down her cheeks. She closed her eyes and felt the gates open, her last fortress fall. "You... I fear you... I'm afraid of all the ways you can hurt me…" Her voice was jerky, her breathing frantic as his fingers maintained the sweet torture.

The high was stronger than any drug, the euphoria more addictive, as she lay terrified and helpless to the unwholesome pleasure, baring her all, releasing all the monsters under her bed, to the one she knew could fight them off.

Kayne kept playing with her, kept the rhythm slow and steady, felt his fingers dripping with her juices. He pulled his head back and stared intently at her face, knowing that in this moment, he walked the secret path to the darkest recesses of her soul.

"I'm afraid… I'm afraid of… how much you can hurt me… I'm afraid of…" Even in her state, the last words came to her lips with a twist in her heart. "When you'll stop..."

She cried as her body shattered in a mind-numbing orgasm. He did not smirk as usual, when he'd make her come on his twisted terms. His eyes were dark and intense, resting on her drained body. He lay on top of her.

"Look at me."

She didn't want to, not after her confession. She wanted to remain in the sweet oblivion engulfing her. She obeyed.

He cursed his sealed lips. He only opened them to kiss her with the hopeless passion of a cursed lover. Wordlessly, he willed her to understand what his guarded heart wouldn't allow him to betray.

He pulled and tugged at her, possessively manipulating her body to quench his thirst for her. With a guttural sound, he collapsed on top of her. He pulled her body close, keeping her face to his. With his hand, he caressed her face, watching her eyes close serenely under his touch.

She opened her eyes again and brought her own hand to his face, then clasped her fingers shut at the last instant.

"Do you not like it when I touch you?" she asked softly, lowering her gaze to his chest.

He sighed, lifted her chin, and leaned his head, seeking her eyes. "Of course I do."

"Why did you stop me?"

He shook his head, sensing the hurt in her innocent question. "Because I'm a fool."

She looked back down, a sad smile forming on her lips. Her voice hushed, she met his eyes again. "You killed her…"

This time, he knew exactly who she was talking about. Holding her stare, his eyes inscrutable, his answer was remorseless. "Yes."

"Why?" she breathed, hearing his voice in her head. *For you, because of you, because she hurt you, because… I love you.*

"She betrayed me."

Laura closed her eyes, feeling the bitterness in her smile at her foolishness. "Did you love her?"

He considered her question. Of all people, how could *she* think that? He waited for her to open her eyes, to meet his intense gaze. He shook his head. "No, Laura. I didn't love her."

She nodded, bitterness still lingering in her expression.

"Natasha knew about her... and Dimitri... She befriended her. She told me... she... befriends her husband's whores..." Her voice broke. She looked up at him, pain twisting her features. "I could never do that..."

He kept watching her, sharing in her pain, knowing he was the cause of it, knowing he couldn't stop it. "I don't want you to do that."

"Then what?" she pleaded, her voice quavering with emotion.

He shut his eyes, could see the impasse awaiting them. Dimitri had spoken to him at the party earlier. He'd promoted him, a wedding gift he called it. Kayne was now to overlook all aspects of the operation, act as his counselor. He knew Dimitri too well to be honored. It was a test, a chance for him to prove his loyalty, to prove that his marriage would not be a threat to the Organization. He could no longer benefit from being the lone wolf; he would now be directly responsible for all the trades, including the prostitution rings and sex trafficking. The implication was way beyond his participation at some morally questionable parties. His very survival would now depend on his capabilities as the counselor. Having other women was the last thing on his mind and was now ultimately inevitable as new *merchandise* had to be sampled and tested by the counselor, representing the boss's interests.

How could he explain this to her, how would he break this new reality to her? Tomorrow, he would tell her; tomorrow, he would step in as the underboss. Tonight, he would just be her husband.

Facing his silence, a silence more revealing than any answer, Laura turned away from him, staring vacantly at the ceiling. There was no answer, none he could give to appease her and remain truthful. Kayne Malkin didn't lie, so he remained silent in the face of her despair. She felt her heart harden. *Why delay the inevitable.* Without looking at him, she carelessly declared, "You should go back to your party."

His eyes narrowed. Did she think she was the only one to suffer? That her pain allowed her to dismiss him as he did his whores? He wanted to strike her, to strangle her and holler his own torment at her. He swallowed his anger and simply nodded, his eyes dripping poison. Without a word, he got off the bed and picked up his pants and shirt thrown carelessly on the floor, not bothering with the jacket. He was still buttoning up his shirt when he calmly closed the door behind him. He heard her break into a desperate sob on the other side of the wall.

Laura regretted her words the moment she felt his weight shift on the mattress, felt the emptiness of him heavier, more tangible than any other truth. She wanted to jump off the bed and throw her naked body in his way. Instead, she watched him leave while pinned to the bed she had made and now had to lie in by herself, in her oppressing solitude. Why *not* delay the inevitable? Why had she forbade herself this one night with him, their wedding night? Tomorrow, he could have his whores. Tomorrow, he could slaughter and destroy. She would even wave him off and send kisses from the port. Just let her have him for this one night, she prayed with all she had, to heaven and hell, to whomever would answer first. She would trade it all, for this one night.

She jumped from the bed, frantic, reached for the torn wedding dress, and pulled it hastily over her shoulders. Her bare back fully exposed, she rushed for the door. Maybe it wasn't too late, maybe she could still find him, maybe, maybe, maybe…

She swung the door open wildly and stopped right in her tracks, feeling her heart shatter, her chest collapse. He was there, leaning on the wall facing the door. He just stood there watching her, his face impenetrable.

"Kayne…" she cried, relieved, crazed. "Kayne…Kayne…" she repeated his name over and over again, as if uttering an arcane prayer with healing powers.

With whatever strength she had left, she threw herself in his arms. "Forgive me… forgive me…" she cried softly in his ears.

He tightened his hold on her, feeling his chest swelling with hurt. "No. Forgive *me*."

He was apologizing for it all. For everything he already put her through. For everything he would still put her through, knowing he was too selfish, too rotten, to ever push her away. Knowing she would always come back to him, no matter what he did. Knowing he would always be there, waiting to collect her, all the pieces of her, and put her back together, until the next time she broke apart in his hands.

Their lips frantically sought each other, their tongues mingling with desperate hunger. He dragged her back into the room, kicking the door shut behind them. He slammed her bare back against the wall and felt her cry out with pain in his mouth. She wound her arms around him as he lifted the skirt of her dress and unzipped his pants. He wrapped her legs around his, and he fucked her, mercilessly, with all the raw emotion he felt. With anger and passion, lust and regret, with the animalistic hunger she ignited in him and the cursed desire afflicting him.

They fell asleep clinging to each other, every inch of their bodies touching, with no other words needing to be exchanged. Morning come, he was gone.

Day-76

Kayne left before sunrise. He could never face her following those stolen moments of intimacy. The Kayne who fell asleep in her arms was not the one who would awaken by her side. He'd been at peace with himself before Laura. Now the wild wolf bared its teeth to the emerging dog wanting to be domesticated. The fight was unbalanced, raging on the wolf's long-established territory. He reluctantly let go of his sleeping bride, kissed her on the forehead, and saw her smile in her sleep before he left her side. Just like in her beloved book, Kayne could never fully embrace his conflicting sides, though he would not let one destroy the other.

Every kindness, every moment of tenderness would inevitably be followed by his own retreat into the wilderness, into his domain. Kayne belonged to the Organization, not to a loving home. Yet he belonged to Laura, not the faceless women who pleasured him in ways he would never get from Laura, ways he would never want from Laura.

He had asked Lucas to drive his new bride home, and stayed behind at the Drugov residence. A party was being thrown at the second mansion in his honor, for the promotion. Dimitri and he would go together; the announcement would be made.

* * *

Laura felt a pang at waking alone, looked, without belief, for a note she didn't find. When Lucas drove her home, it was already getting late. She hadn't seen Kayne all day, had spent it with Natasha who informed her that Kayne was busy with Dimitri, but did not go into further detail.

Upon exiting the car, she noticed the security guards who'd always ignored her previously bowing their head in respect as she walked past them. Olga was already waiting for her. She brought her into a warm embrace and wouldn't let go or hide her disappointment when Laura, explaining she'd had supper with Natasha, turned down the fancy meal and dessert she had prepared for her.

She just wanted to head straight to her room and fall back on the familiarity of her bed. As she gently pushed Olga aside, her eyes fell on the staircase leading to the forbidden upper level. But she was *Mrs. Kayne Malkin now, who would stop her?* Lucas's words came back to mind. Her eyes burning with a conqueror's determination, she set forward.

"Mrs. Malkin?" Olga's voice faltered behind her.

Laura turned, defiant, and remained silent as she climbed the first step.

Lucas nodded to her, an encouraging smile on his face, and pulled a tense Olga away.

Laura's heart sank with every step she climbed but continued her journey, her head held high. As a true Malkin, she would not let her fear show, even with no witnesses around.

There were only two doors, one on each side. She tried the left first to no avail. She turned around, her heart pounding, and felt the handle give way. For all the ways he invaded her life, her body, and her mind, for the first time, Laura would penetrate Kayne's world, his inner and most private world. It lifted the hairs on her skin. She stepped inside and felt as though she'd violated a sacred temple.

His bedroom reeked of him, no woman had left her mark, no other being had left a trace. It was purely him, a mixture of boldness and elegance, the classic touch to the modern feel, simple yet chic. Laura swirled around, her arms wide open, and her head tilted back, her eyes closed. She was in the heart of it, she could feel it, could almost feel rain on her face like in the movies she had seen.

She opened her eyes and went about scavenging the only helpless version of Kayne she would ever encounter. No stone would be left unturned. Her first action was to open the drapes on the wall made entirely of glass, which gave way to a terrace. As always on those unusual nights, the moon was shining bright, bathing the sleeping world in its silvery glow. Laura smiled, she liked this moon. It was a wolf's moon, her and Kayne's moon, the benevolent light in their darkness.

She opened drawers, finding everything neatly folded. She penetrated the walk-in closet, which in itself could contain a small-sized room. She turned on the spotlights, found more drawers, rows and rows of suits and all the clothes she recognized seeing him in. She let her fingers glide lovingly down the sleeves, lifted them to her nose, and breathed him in, feeling herself tear up with emotion. She never made it to the bathroom. When she reached his bed, she wearily opened the end table, expecting all sorts of sordid paraphernalia, but found one item, only one, a worn-out copy of *The Little Prince*.

With solemn deference, she pulled it out and opened the cover. On the first page, she found the note written in elegant cursive, *Property of Elena Galiano*. She turned the pages carefully, understanding the value of what she held in her hands. There were little side notes written all over the margins, highlighted quotes everywhere. She smiled when randomly landing on one: *"What makes the desert beautiful," says the little prince, "is that somewhere it hides a well."*

Just like that, another piece of Kayne Malkin was revealed to her. His favorite book had been his mother's. She closed her eyes and kissed the cover, tears rolling down her cheeks. She would not give up. Her desert contained a well. She knew this with certainty, from the elusive kindness she'd seen in his eyes, from his all-consuming caresses when words failed him. How could she not believe in the well, having tasted its water?

In a world that was all Kayne, in desperate hunger for him, she removed her clothes and put on one of the shirts carrying his scent. She laid herself on the mattress, still cradling the book against her chest, and fell asleep, feeling warm, kept safe by an invisible bubble surrounding her.

* * *

Kayne returned home very late and was surprised to find Olga still waiting up for him. Nervously, she advised him that *Mrs. Malkin* was upstairs, unconvincingly adding, "I think it's good that she wanted to wait for you in your room."

He grunted, his eyes shining with the too many beverages in his system, with information he was still unsure how to react to. Laura's first act as his wife was to break his rules, invade his privacy, and enter a room no one besides himself was allowed in. He weighed in quickly. He was not happy, not happy at all.

He calmly made his way to the room and opened the door slowly, hoping to catch her unaware, expecting to find her on her knees on the floor, tearing his drawers inside out. That's what he got for being soft with her, he thought, a situation he would remedy, immediately.

His sadistic sneer faded from his lips as he found the sleeping lump on his bed, in his shirt. He took a seat in the black leather club chair facing the bed and watched her sleep in the darkness. Her sleep became agitated under his gaze. Her eyes blinked open. Slowly, she raised herself on her elbows and smiled tentatively upon finding him, only his black eyes emerging from the shadows.

"You're back..." Without fully seeing him, she could sense his brooding mood and felt herself stiffen.

"Come here." He pulled out his arm to her, his voice low and gruff.

Wearily, she got up on her feet, recognizing the shift in his demeanor. It wasn't the sensual call of her lover; it was the calm before the storm.

He sat her on his lap, caressed her arms, and tucked her hair behind her ears as her heart fluttered with emotion.

"It suits you," he said, playing with the cuff of his shirt, in a soft voice that contrasted his serious face.

Blood rushed to her cheeks, she stared at him inquisitively. "Are you mad?" she breathed, her heart pounding in her chest.

He exhaled deeply before returning her gaze. "Had you asked, I would've said yes."

She could see it, the water retreating around her feet, the sea pulling back only to unleash its fury, could see the monstrous wave heading her way.

"But I'm your… wife," she uttered, her voice breaking.

"So you felt entitled to disregard my wishes?"

She shook her head in response, pleading reflected in her eyes.

"Get up," he commanded, his voice remaining calm.

She apprehensively took his offered hand and followed him out of his bedroom. She imagined he would take her back to her room, and felt a stab of rejection, feeling like a dog being kicked off his master's bed to be led back to his kennel.

He didn't take her to her room. Instead, he turned into the western wing that led to the spiraling stairs. At the top of the stairs, she lost her resolve. Nothing good ever came from going down those stairs.

"Master… please no… I'm sorry… I didn't think…"

His anger was quiet as he led her gently. He then turned to her and affectionately caressed her cheeks, shushing her softly.

"You did think, Laura. You just didn't care. You're right, you are the lady of the house. But I'm the master. Never forget that."

She bowed her head; a few tears rolled down. He was right, she hadn't cared, and truth be told, she would do it all over again given the chance. She didn't want his permission. She didn't want her own bedroom either.

"What are you going to do to me?" she asked, her eyes on the ground, her voice carrying the pain she knew was coming. "Please… don't whip me." She broke into soft sobs.

He lifted her chin and nodded, his eyes piercing hers. Her sobs only increased.

"Don't you trust me, Laura?"

"I trust you will hurt me..." If not the whips, what had he planned for her? She thought of the cage; the thought terrified her.

He smirked wickedly but didn't reply. He took her hand again and led her into the dungeon. She felt mild relief as they stepped away from the cage. He left her hand at the entrance, walked to a big leather chaise, and sat in it. He eyed her devilishly for what seemed an eternity.

"Get on your knees," he commanded, his voice hoarse.

She did, keeping her eyes locked on his.

"Crawl to me."

Her eyes grew round with bewilderment, she hesitated. He could feel her inner dilemma; knowing how proud she was, he knew this unusual punishment would be far worse than all the physical pain he could've inflicted on her.

Clenching her teeth, her eyes narrowed with pure loathing. She got down on all fours and, slowly, painfully, crawled to him. His shirt lifted above her ass with every step, taunting him. Her eyes bore into his with silent rage. One he knew would be swallowed only momentarily.

He could see it in her eyes. She only survived this because she knew she would make him pay for it, somehow. He smiled, his beautiful bride, his fallen angel, how far she'd come, how far she'd descended. A decent person would've felt remorse. He looked at her with pride and admiration. Laura Spencer had adapted to her environment, had survived it, becoming Laura Malkin.

He realized he would never break her, that she would always bend, but never break. It was just as well. He would gladly spend his life breaking her, always getting closer and never reaching his goal. He wanted to watch her transform, always rising from her ashes. He also knew that she was just as hooked on this sick game. She would lose countless battles, never the war.

When she reached him, he stared her down, his eyes glowing with sadistic pleasure. "Kiss my feet."

She snapped up instantly. "*What*," she hissed through gritted teeth.

He cocked his head to the side and, with a mock sorry expression, shook his head disapprovingly. "Tsk-tsk-tsk."

"You're fucking out of your mind if you think I'm going to do that." She glared at him, her voice calm, dripping venom.

He broke into a loud chortle, throwing his head back. When he faced her again, his eyes were wicked. He lifted her to her feet and, with a devilish grin, pulled her backward.

Her heart was racing, she could only imagine what was coming next. He lifted her arms and bound each one to a metal ring dangling from the ceiling. He then walked back to his leather seat and just watched her, the grin never leaving his face.

It was too easy, she thought, there had to be more, but he remained quiet, simply watching her from his comfortable seat. Soon, her muscles began to cramp, her discomfort increasing with every second. But she would not beg, would not plead. She would never lower to this. He could whip her if he wanted, but kissing his feet? No way. It wasn't just the act that was repulsive, it was all the meaning it carried, more than submission, worse than pain. It was the humiliation. That, she couldn't stand. Scars on her back would heal, but the ones carried in your heart, the ones that kept you up at night, that gave you nightmares and made you resent yourself, those she'd had enough. She had obediently went into a cage like an animal when she was young and helpless. To this day, she fantasized of scenarios where she fought back, where she didn't simply take the abuse and bowed her head in shame. She had vowed to herself, *never again*.

"The pain will only get worse," Kayne informed her, making a point to stretch his arms and readjust his position to maximize his comfort.

She remained quiet, her eyes set with a determination that fascinated him.

"You know… some women would be glad to please their master, whatever way he wanted."

"Good. Then have one of them lick your dirty feet," she spat back without thinking.

He considered her for a moment, his eyes shining with something twisted, then he licked his lips, weighing his thought. He looked at her, his eyes boring into hers, and slowly nodded his head. He took out his cellphone and called a number on speed dial.

He saw the emotion change in her eyes. She had grasped too late the domino effect of their little confrontation. He waited for her to speak up, willing her to stop him as the phone rang. She didn't, simply staring in horror as he spoke on the phone.

"Ten minutes." That's all he said before hanging up.

Ten interminable minutes passed, each waiting for the other to stop the monstrosity about to unfold. Their staring contest ended with the sound of clicking heels.

Laura watched in disbelief as a beautiful blonde entered the dungeon and quietly removed her trench coat, wearing nothing but a black choker matching her lingerie and stiletto heels. Without being told, she got down on all fours, bowed her head, and waited for instructions. She displayed no reaction at seeing Laura tied up.

Kayne was watching Laura and decided to give her another ten seconds, to speak up, say anything, just make a sound, and he would send the whore packing. But she didn't see him, she was watching the whore, horrified, repulsed, and silent.

The ten seconds passed. He inhaled deeply. *So be it.* He finally turned toward their unwanted guest.

"Come here, slut," he threw at her callously.

She immediately got moving, crawling on hands and feet, somehow making it sensual, not demeaning in the way Laura thought.

When she reached him, Kayne looked at Laura before giving his next instruction. She met his gaze, her breathing heavy, her eyes fixed in that horrified state.

"Kiss my feet," he commanded the woman kneeling by his side.

With deference, the woman removed his shoes and socks, placing them carefully one beside the other, then proceeded to obey his instructions with such ardor, Laura could not believe it was genuine.

He reached for a thin black leash on a table near him and, in a harsh tone, commanded her to stop and raise herself.

"What do you want, my pet?" He finally smirked at her, as he brushed her cheek with his thumb, cradling the side of her face in his palm. She rubbed her face to his hand like a dog seeking his master's touch. The association sent shivers down Laura's spine. She hated her and pitied her at the same time, burned with jealousy and recoiled in repulsion simultaneously.

"I just want to please you, Master," the blonde answered in a low sensual tone.

He shot a fast glance in Laura's direction. He realized how sick this was and yet could not be more turned on.

"Please me with your mouth."

He felt himself growing even harder as she took him into her mouth, lathering him with her expert tongue. He kept her head down, pulling her hair while he stared at Laura, who watched helplessly the twisted spectacle. One she requested, one he knew killed her inside. Yet still she remained silent, did not turn her eyes away, and returned his stare as his whore pleasured him.

He came with a groan in the woman's mouth as she swallowed his seed with no required instructions. He took a few breaths with his eyes closed. When they reopened, they automatically fell on Laura.

"Beat it." He dismissed his whore without looking her way.

She scrambled to her feet and was gone in a moment.

Kayne slowly got off his chair, zipped up his pants, and languidly walked up to Laura whose eyes followed his every movement.

When he reached her, he let the tip of his fingers glide down her back and over his shirt. She shivered at the contact, grounding her teeth as she shot him daggers.

He moved to her side, letting his free hand rest on her thigh. Slowly, he moved his hand up, toward the inside. She let out short rapid breaths, but still no sound escaped her lips.

"Bet you wished you had asked for the whip instead..." he huskily whispered into her ear, his fingers making their way to her wetness. A strangled scream came out of her in response. He hardened instantly at finding her wet. *Fuck*, he bit his lip. His perfect woman, his goddess. He wanted to whip her, fuck her, please and worship her.

He fell to his knees and forced her legs apart as her body twisted and turned in his grip. He held her firmly, bringing his lips to her wet core. He licked her engorged flesh and felt her juices on his tongue. She screamed and cried out her pleasure, her torture, as she felt the world around her subside. Her pained moans only increased his hunger. He licked, kissed, and teased until he pushed her over the edge. Her orgasm came out in one long, loud wounded sound. She broke into a hysterical sob as her whole body gave out, being only held up by his arm as he unbound her. The moment he freed her wrists, her arms came crashing down on him. She hit him, over and over again, her fists raining down on his chest as she howled in pain and fury.

He let her, stood still as she expelled the poison. He let her hit him until she had no strength left and fell to the ground slowly. He lowered himself with her, never letting go of his hold. Her sobs didn't fade. Every now and then, when she regained enough energy, she hit him again, then pushed him away. He kept holding her as they lay on the floor together. He would stay, for as long as it took.

Laura fell silent at last with Kayne still by her side, holding her. She stared up at the ceiling, her eyes now dry, her breathing even. She finally pulled herself up, not wanting his help to pull her up or carry her, regardless of how much she craved it.

"I'm going to bed," she said flatly.

She felt his hand on her arm and turned around to find him already standing behind her. Without a word, he offered his hand. She considered it but wanted to walk out on him, for once to be the one to leave him behind. He didn't give her the chance to bring her threat to fruition. In her hesitation, he grabbed her hand. Gently, he led her up the stairs and all the way to his room. It was bittersweet. Her heart wouldn't let her walk away. Its fresh scars wouldn't let her savor the moment.

Kayne had never brought anyone to his room. The moment felt almost surreal. He kept looking at Laura, wondering what she was thinking. This cold and collected Laura disgruntled him. He felt their bond so fragile, hanging by a thread pulled so tight, any rough moves and it would break. He pulled the covers, his movements slow and cautious. She got inside on her own, avoiding his touch whenever possible. As he lay beside her, she could feel his deep breath, the entire night, could sense his desire to reach for her.

Kayne fell asleep thinking of the woman lying next to him. He woke up not long after, feeling uneasy, and immediately looked to his left to find her side empty. He snapped up and, scanning the room, found her huddled on the floor in the corner. She was hugging her legs, staring straight ahead. When he put his feet on the ground and moved toward her, he felt her body tense, saw the panic in her eyes. It killed him, but he understood. He wouldn't go to her. This Laura he faced was wild. He would have to tame her all over again, earn her trust, and for once hope to be worthy. He slid himself to the ground, his back leaning against the bed as she watched him like a hawk. He made no more moves toward her, maintaining the distance she had deemed safe. He stayed on the ground, never shifting from his uncomfortable position, and he just stared back at her, his eyelids heavy from sleep. Noticing her shiver in his shirt, he slowly reached for the cover on the bed, brought it to the floor, and, with cautious moves, slid it over to her. She reached for it tentatively, covered her legs, and went back to watching him.

The sun was creeping up as they remained on the floor. Too afraid to move, too afraid to sleep. She feared closing her eyes and finding him break their established boundary to reach for her. He feared closing his and finding that she'd pulled away even further.

Day-77

They were awakened by the sound of a cellphone ringing. Both stared at each other, surprised at having fallen asleep, relieved at finding the other exactly where they were. Tiredly, he reached for the phone on his end table, rubbing his eyes as he picked up. He exited the room to take the call. When he came back, Laura was gone.

* * *

It was already well into the afternoon when Laura quietly snuck out of Kayne's room to find refuge in hers. She was exhausted, could not sleep by his side, constantly wanting to go to him, feeling the burn the moment she tried. She'd wanted to go back to her room in the middle of the night but only found the strength to crawl the ten feet away. Even in that moment, she found comfort in knowing he was near. She wished he had whipped her instead. Physical pain could be contained; what she felt was pure chaos. There was no cure for that, only a coward's way out.

She got ready for supper in a trance, unconsciously reaching for a black dress befitting her mood. She fixed her hair and makeup as if preparing for a night out. She smiled back at her glamorous reflection. She had never been one to pride herself on her looks or invest the time and effort required to enhance them. She understood now the motivations behind the art of beauty. It was a necessary mask to hide the emptiness inside. She already felt stronger hiding her weakness behind smoky eyes and lifted her chin to face the tête-a-tête she was not ready to attend.

* * *

Kayne was dressed as elegantly in a black suit and greeted her in a somber mood. Following the rushed greeting, no other words were exchanged as they ate their meal in heavy silence.

"I'll be leaving for a while." He dropped the bomb after finishing his plate. He stood up and went to her side. They hadn't yet exchanged a smile. They wouldn't.

She simply looked up at him but didn't say a word as he placed a few items on the table next to her plate.

"A bank account has been opened under your name, credit card, and cellphone. Lucas will leave with me. Anything you need, anywhere you have to go, see Kiev. He will take care of you."

She would not ask him for how long, would not ask him why he had to go, where he would be. She would not ask him if his departure hurt him as much as it hurt her. She simply nodded her head.

She thought he would put his hand on her shoulder for a second. Instead, he brought his hand down on the table, tapping his fingers.

Was that it, was that all he had to say? she thought bitterly. "Well… Bon voyage," she said at last, staring straight ahead, her voice betraying no emotion.

He closed his eyes, nodding quickly. He opened his mouth, then closed it without saying anything, only inhaled deeply. "While I'm away, you may go wherever you like... inside the house… or out. All I ask is that you take Kiev with you when you leave the premises."

A jaded smile crossed her lips. She barely nodded her head. She watched him leave, the man she realized with a twist in her heart she loved, the man whom to this day still didn't trust her. She watched him walk away until he became a little black speck and disappeared into the distance. She didn't call out to him. Silently, she prayed he would return to her.

Day-126

Kayne looked out the window of his fancy hotel suite, staring at the full moon. It made him think of Laura. It had been almost two months he hadn't seen or spoken with her. He'd traveled to many countries with Lucas, met with business associates, had all types of orders carried out, left countless bodies behind. He'd attended underground parties and shows, had more women than he could account for. The moment he was alone, his mind always traveled back to Laura. When Dimitri had called him, advised him of the travel, he'd been reluctant to leave Laura the way things were, but he had no choice. He realized with a sting that she, however, would only be too glad to be rid of him. He feared he'd lost her forever. He hadn't called her directly but made sure to program his number into her cellphone should she want to reach him. She hadn't.

Sometimes when he lay alone in bed, especially on those nights when the moon was particularly bright, he would think back to an old Russian folktale Olga use to tell him, when he was still a child. He would imagine Laura and himself as Alexei and Aniska, the two of them against the whole world, two parts of an unbreakable whole. With bitterness, he realized he wasn't Alexei. Laura had her Alexei; he'd taken him from her. He was the murdering huntsman, the wicked white wolf. He was no hero. He would always be the villain in the story.

* * *

Emptiness. It filled Laura's world. Not the type of emptiness that left you bedridden, depressed, and alone, seeking solitude and dying from it. It was the loneliness of a clown, hiding behind laughter and noise. Laura Malkin didn't sulk. She hired a full staff to fill the house with life, went out as often as she could, spending her days shopping away, her nights hosting endless gatherings.

She dressed in the finest gowns, laughed the loudest, and danced the night away. She was always the last one standing, pushing the inevitable lonely nights as far as she could. She would crawl back to her bedroom and look out the window, thinking of Kayne. Her life was rendered meaningless. For all the things she bought and people she surrounded herself with, nothing could fill the void his absence left. Every once in a while, the moon would call out to her. She would slip upstairs into Kayne's room, wear his shirt, and fall asleep on his bed. Those nights she would dream of him, those mornings, were the hardest.

* * *

Kiev had helped hire the new staff; they were all approved by the Organization. Olga was very happy for the help, and the company. Most were of Russian origin except the two youngest, who were barely in their twenties. French Canadians, Louis Lavallé and Genevieve Roy were as thick as thieves, always giggling together in the corners of the house. Olga felt weary of the young blonde beauty, and even more so of the protective way Louis always eyed her. She wondered why Laura accepted her. She didn't like the defiant way Genevieve took orders. She was a flirt with all the men, rebellious and arrogant with the women. *Never a good combination for an employee at the Malkin household.* But Olga knew her place. She didn't breathe a word of her concern to Laura but kept a close watch on the French Lolita.

Day-145

Laura had just received the news. *Master Kayne was coming home.* She could barely contain herself. She paced around all day, went shopping for another outfit that she carefully laid on the bed, and changed her mind a few dozen times before returning to the initially selected new grey chiffon dress. It reminded her of the one she wore the first night she met him. So much had happened since, and yet her heart still fluttered in her chest at the mention of his name, at the thought of finding herself alone with him.

She asked Olga what his favorite meal was and insisted on preparing it herself. They spent the day in the kitchen, Laura laughing heartily under Olga's supervision and resigned headshake after her third burned batch of knish and kalduny, Russian versions of dumplings.

She set the table smiling away and sat patiently in her grey dress, constantly looking at her watch. Hours passed, and Laura fell asleep with her head resting in her palm. She woke up to the clock striking midnight, a cold untouched meal, waning candles, and no Kayne in sight. With a bitter taste in her mouth, she smiled coolly back to the empty room, lifted her chin, and headed to her bedroom in her unseen dress.

* * *

Kayne delayed his return as much as he could. He'd been looking forward to it for so long; now that it was here, he felt apprehensive at facing the reality of Laura's welcome, of having his fantasized reunion shattered mercilessly. Dawn was creeping when he stumbled home with Lucas holding him up. He was greeted by a sexy young blonde who boldly introduced herself as Genevieve, looking him straight in the eye with a seductive smile. She was putting away a cold meal he assumed Olga prepared for him and smiled dejectedly at recognizing all his favorite foods as a child.

He realized he was hoping to find Laura in his bed when he walked in to his empty bedroom. He passed out on his mattress fully clothed, thought he recognized her scent on his pillow.

Day-146

Laura avoided him purposefully, quietly sneaking out at the crack of dawn, and stayed out as late as possible. She had sheepishly hoped her cellphone would ring, that an infuriated voice would beckon her home. It hadn't happened. Kiev had been her companion for the past two months. She had initially preferred to have Lucas by her side. He would have found a way to make her laugh, to see things in a different light. She learned to appreciate Kiev's quiet strength, and found comfort in his morally blind devotion.

She had fantasized about walking with Kayne down the colorful streets of Montreal, had imagined them swaying their heads during late nights spent drinking too much at jazz clubs. How she loved her city, Montreal, there was no place like it on earth. Not that she would know, having only discovered other worlds on paper and screen. But she knew in her heart, none would match its magic. Montreal didn't fan her feathers for the world to see, was no star next to the likes of New York and Paris. Montreal was a jewel to be discovered, delighting only the eyes who could recognize beauty in its simplest form. Was there any feeling like walking down the cobble streets of the Old Port on a warm summer night, its full terraces announcing the end of the long winter and its ever-present artists offering you back a piece of your lost childhood? Montreal was Laura's gate 9 ¾; it contained all the magic and wonder she would ever need. But even Montreal couldn't dazzle her out of her lonely truth. Crossing Pont Jacques-Cartier to the night skyline in the dark Audi, Laura could only offer a brittle smile to Kiev.

* * *

Louis had been watching the interactions between the newly arrived master and Genevieve. All day, he caught sideway glances and sly smiles. Genevieve was a flirt. He'd learned to accept that in his best friend. He knew her every move, her subtle way of leaving a lingering hand on a shoulder, of brushing her fingers on your lower back when passing behind. Her touch, although always seemed innocent, was anything but. He spent years suffering in silence because of it. She had perfected her seduction skills on him, from the first kiss she'd given him when they were only twelve. They had been neighbors and best friends, often mistaken for twins with their matching blue eyes and sun-kissed hair. He was in awe of her; she was strong-minded and outgoing when he was just a little shy boy afraid of his shadow. He had no friends. She had the entire third grade at her feet. Of all the boys pining over her, of all the girls pretending to be her friend, she had picked him. They'd been inseparable ever since.

He had followed her to summer camps, had taken up smoking with her, dropped out of school, and got trashed with her on their prom night, celebrating alone in the backseat of a car looking over Mount Royal. They'd lost their virginity to each other. He had thought they would be together forever. She had told him he was the best friend she'd ever had. He wore the badge with honor, taking his role very seriously, regardless of the heartbreak that followed her every conquest. She was wild, and he loved her for it. When things got out of hand and he couldn't save her from her hell, he followed her into it. They had all given up on her, thought she was too far gone. It was him and no one else who was able to convince her to go to detox. Sweaty, feverish, and vomiting, she had cried in his arms, told him she loved him, that no one else had ever loved her. He thought he was the luckiest person in the world. When she felt better, she never mentioned the *incident* again. He knew better than to bring it up and face her cruel laughter.

When two short months ago she mentioned the new job her friend told her about, he knew it was bad news from the get-go. He didn't like that friend of hers. Another of her conquests, heavily into drugs, gambling, and any bad thing you could imagine. He couldn't get her to change her mind, the money was good, and there was no way she was going to end up working the counter at a fast food joint. Genevieve Roy liked the shady aspect of the job. She reveled in danger. She knew she'd be safe; she knew Louis would come with her.

Day-147

Laura was on her way out when Kayne first saw her. He barely recognized the distinguished lady facing him. He stared at her, like the first night, willing her silently to turn around.

The air changed around her, she could feel a tingle down her neck. Slowly, she turned her head, knowing beforehand he was there, her body sensing his presence before her eyes could confirm it. Her eyes lit up for a moment, then falling on his sardonic smirk, they instantly narrowed.

"You're back…" she observed, her voice cold, smiling tight-lipped.

"You're leaving," he countered just as coolly.

Her heart pounded in her chest. She had prayed for his return, had even pleasured herself with his face in her mind. Now that he was here in the flesh, she froze. She would have forgiven him all, would've gladly run to meet him if only he would have greeted her with his warm smile, if it was her Kayne who would have come back to her. It was the other, the cool arrogant one. The one who seduced and tortured her. She wondered if she would always have to go through that Kayne to end up in the comforting embrace of the other.

Her Kayne, she was powerless to, this one, she resented. This one had taught her the lessons she would use against him.

"Well… I'll see you around I guess," she threw indifferently.

He smirked arrogantly. "I'll see you *tonight* for supper. Seven sharp."

"Oh... sorry, I can't make it for supper. I have plans..." She held his narrowing eyes and smiled arrogantly herself to the fury dancing in them.

He licked his lips, predatory instincts kicking in at her challenging him. "Cancel them," he commanded, his voice restrained, his gaze swaying between threatening and entertained.

"It's with Natasha—"

"She'll understand," he interrupted sternly.

They stared at each other in silence for a long moment, each sizing up the other. He took a few long strides to come face-to-face with her. He could see the fear in her eyes mixing with excitement, the alertness in her muscles. She didn't fool him. Behind her proud stance and daring eyes, he could still see his little girl. Could still bring her out by shattering her mask with one touch. He got off on the power he held over her. He loved his ability to terrify her with one look, to soothe her with a whisper. He wanted to be her savior, but it was the villain who always dragged her to bed, kicking and screaming, until she moaned and gasped, powerless in his grasp. But his very ability to manipulate her into wanting him at any cost held a darker truth. She would never love him, he thought. Not on her own, nor through the strings he'd skillfully attached to her, and constantly pulled to his selfish designs. He could twist, bend, please, and break her body, but he could never reach her heart. He disregarded the stabbing pain of an unattainable Laura, focused instead on the adrenaline rush of a helpless Laura splayed on her back, spread eagle, fear in her eyes, slowly turning wanton.

The mental image was enough to get him hard. He wanted to pin her to the wall right then and there. He brought his face closer to hers and cocked his head to the side. "Anything else you want to say?"

She exhaled slowly, her mouth in an "o" shape. She gathered her composure before responding words spat with venom. "No, Master. Your wish is my command."

Her heart skipped a beat when he stepped toward her. She held her breath unconsciously. She had counted the days, down to the seconds, until the moment she would see him again. He, on the other hand, had preferred to spend the night out, presumably in the company of other women. She knew he'd been with many others during his time away but that he chose to extend his time away from her that extra night, to still choose to be with someone else, cut right through her. That was the injury. The insult came in the form of a seductive Kayne lurking in the shadows calm and collected when she was at her wits' end, commanding her as his secretary to make herself available the moment he sought her company. She could've rebelled but knew her indifferent submission would hurt his pride more. She wouldn't admit to herself that this strategy suited her desire to be with him just as well.

With that said, she turned around and walked away. She left and stayed out for as long as she could. She preferred the loneliness she felt when he was away to the one that ripped her apart in his presence.

* * *

He busied himself all day and caught himself constantly looking at his watch, impatient for supper, hungry for his wife. At seven sharp, he entered the empty dining room and sat alone, impatiently tapping his fingers on the table. At a quarter past seven, Olga came in to check up on everything and was dismissed immediately by a cranky Kayne.

By seven thirty he was pacing in the living room, furious at Laura's disobedience, maddened by her rejection. He knew he didn't deserve her love, that he was barely worthy of her company. It didn't matter; he had never craved anything as much. He retreated to the reception hall, poured himself a whiskey, drank it too fast, and refilled another. By the fifth glass, he could barely stand his own reflection in the mirror.

He hated her for turning his world upside down. He hated himself for wanting her so desperately and still not being able to offer her the slightest requirement to ever hope to earn her love. In victory as in defeat, Kayne smirked arrogantly, this time at his own reflection, falling victim to his own hubris. He cursed the cocky smile, disdainful of his distress. In blind rage, he punched through the mirror, annihilating his tormentor.

Genevieve, lurking nearby, jumped at the sound of shattering glass. For two days she had shadowed her new employer, had flirted shamelessly, and fantasized remorselessly about the married older man. She had always liked them older; married was even better. Her therapist had called her *a classic case of father abandonment issues*. Her pious mother had called her the spawn of Satan, her girlfriends, a slut behind her back. Her dismissed conquests, a cold bitch. The only person in the world who ever knew her and cared for her was Louis. She loved him with all her heart, yet she pushed him away, knowing she would never be worthy of such a noble man. She didn't want love, devotion, or worse, admiration. Guys her age fell to her feet effortlessly, each more of a disappointment than the last. The first man who understood her needs, who didn't melt like putty in her hands, was twice her age, married, rich, and very handsome. He'd used her and discarded her. For the first time in her life, she felt yearning and heartbreak; she recognized them as love. She sought them out ever since.

Genevieve cautiously opened the door to find the handsome dark figure staring at his bleeding hand, surrounded by broken shards of glass. In the shattered mirror, his reflection was monstrous, his features beastly. The man facing her, however, could have been Apollo's evil twin.

"Sir, are you all right?" she asked in her soft voice, her French accent pronounced.

He simply turned his face her way, his dark stare sending shivers down her spine.

She cleared her throat. "I'll clean the mess. Can I see your hand?" She walked toward him. She was at his side before he could even answer, reaching for his hand.

"What's your name again?" he asked her haughtily.

"Genevieve… at your service, sir," she added coyly.

He snorted, amused by her blunt flirting.

"If you allow me, sir, I could clean it up for you."

“There’s no need. I’m fine, Genevieve.” She was cute, and her flirtatious ways did appease his bruised ego, but only Laura had the power to heal it. It was now seven forty-five, and she was still a no-show. He refused to call her, to hound her as a forlorn husband, especially when such a delectable thing tried so hard to divert him.

“But, sir, it is my job. To take care of you… See to all your needs...”

He chuckled this time, entertained by the tackiness of her amateur seduction.

“How old are you, Genevieve?”

“I’m legal.” She grinned.

“Answer me,” he commanded, slightly annoyed.

“Twenty.” Her face dropped instantly.

“Twenty… you wouldn’t even *know* how to see to all my needs…” He turned away from her.

“With all due respect, *sir*, you grossly underestimate me.”

The corner of his lips quirked up with devious intent. “Do I? All right. Five minutes. If you can get me hard without touching me, I’ll graciously recant,” he added mockingly.

“I do love a challenge.” She met his luscious gaze. She walked to the table and slowly undid the top button of her tight uniform, exposing her black lace bra. Seductively, she sat down, slowly opened her legs, and revealed black nylons held up by matching garters. She pushed the skirt of her uniform up, looked at him longingly, and swayed her legs on each side.

“Four minutes,” he called, his voice deadpan, and saw nervousness creep into her eyes.

“You think I’m just a kid.” She fixed her eyes on his and slowly brought her hand around her neck, down her chest, lusciously caressing her breasts, down her belly. “I’ve wanted you since the moment I saw you. I know you want me too.” She began to touch herself, pushed her G-string to the side, and widened her slim legs apart. It was enough to hold his attention. He took a seat facing her and remained silent, encouraging her to go on.

Her voice became raspy, her breathing quickened, as did the rhythm of her fingers. "Don't you want to fuck me? Use me like a little slut? Look at what I'm willing to do for your cock." She slid a finger in and began rocking herself against her own hand. "I want you to make me come so bad. Don't you want to make me your little fuck-toy?"

Kayne got hard, with less than a minute to go on the countdown. He would recant, *graciously*.

"Don't come."

She immediately removed her hand.

"Did I say to stop touching yourself?" he asked, a wicked grin on his face.

"Sir…" She brought her fingers back, very slowly and cautiously rubbed her engorged flesh, barely holding back her building orgasm. "Will you make me come?"

* * *

It was past eight when Laura walked back in. She had aimed for fashionably late, waved off Kiev's warning they should leave downtown before traffic hit. As a result, they were caught in bumper-to-bumper traffic, as she nervously looked at her watch.

She walked in the house terrified, and over an hour late. She breathed in and out a few times before making her way to the dining room, forcing a breezy smile on her face. She wasn't that surprised to realize Kayne Malkin had not patiently waited for her arrival. She wondered where he was, what the consequences would be. Her pride would not allow her to seek his presence. Her heart could not tolerate his indifference, and so like any neglected child, she preferred acting out, preferred his reprisal to his neglect.

She searched for him, with cool dread running through her veins, and heard the moans coming from the reception hall. Jaded and disgusted, she pushed the door open and looked on disdainfully as Genevieve lay flat on her stomach on the high table, while Kayne held her down with both hands on her back, thrusting himself slowly in and out of her. He barely stopped moving at the interruption. Genevieve, still bending over, lifted her head and stared back at Laura, a supercilious look on her face.

Laura snorted, unfazed, and walked in. She bent down to meet Genevieve at eye level and addressed her in a condescending tone, "Genevieve, sweetheart. Would you kindly get off my husband's *dick*? I would like a word."

Genevieve was thrown off by the calm and collected cuckolded wife. She stumbled to her feet as Kayne lazily pulled his zipper up. She glanced at him inquisitively, nervousness straining her features. He just nudged his head toward the door before returning his attention to his wife. He didn't seem nervous. A half smirk was creeping on his face as he watched his wife. She left the room as quickly as she could. She felt used and cheap, like the tables had somehow been turned on her. She'd dealt with women who knew of their husband's affairs, but even the most tolerant ones always lost their cool when facing her. Genevieve prided herself on being the mistress, the one the husband betrayed his wife for. The one he would jeopardize everything for. It felt very different this time, as if the joke was on her. It was clear from the moment Mrs. Malkin had walked into the room that she commanded her husband's attention with a mere look. Genevieve wasn't a threat, merely a distraction, easily discarded without a second thought. She could almost hear them snickering about her behind closed doors. For the first time, she admired her rival; for the first time, she hated *the wife*.

* * *

Laura and Kayne stared at each other silently, fighting the duel with their eyes alone. Eventually, she turned from him, a bored look on her face.

"Really, Kayne… The help? How appallingly cliché."

He smiled. "Sorry to disappoint. I could take you down to the basement again and call that blonde you liked so much…"

He hated her cool composure, hated her calm in the face of his tactless infidelity. It only strengthened his crushing suspicion; if she once cared, she no longer did. He knew his words were cruel but needed to provoke her. Needed desperately to know if he could still reach her, stir anything in her, even if it was loathing.

He got the reaction he wanted. She turned her face back to him, her eyes round with shock. She exhaled in response, disbelief and horror on her face. He smirked. He could almost hear her say the words again, *You're a monster.* But she didn't, her eyes said it all. With disgust, she turned away and resumed her walk.

"Where the fuck do you think you're going?" he called out, his voice cool.

She picked up her pace in response, and he could sense her desperation to reach the door in her quick steps. He caught up to her in an instant, pulled her arm, and turned her around.

With fury, she wrestled vainly out of his hold, keeping her head down to hide her face. He pinned her wrists behind her back with one hand; with the other, he lifted her chin, forcing her glistening eyes to meet his.

His eyes softened. This Laura, he couldn't hurt. He exhaled deeply. *She still cared.*

"Why were you late?" he asked, his voice low, his eyes boring into hers.

"Why were you fucking the help?" she snapped back bitterly.

A soft snort escaped his lips, sad and jaded at the same time. "Answer me."

She shrugged her shoulders. "I was caught in traffic… Why do you even care? You don't care..."

"I don't care… Is that what you think?" he asked, his voice guarded, his expression indiscernible. "I married you. I killed for you. I risked *everything.* For *you.* I asked about you while I was away… *every night*… Apparently, you were doing great. Shopping away, throwing parties… Having a blast, it seems," he threw bitterly. "Did you even once think about me? Or were you too busy showing off your new wardrobe for other men to gawk at?"

Laura had felt her chest tighten at the beginning of his confession, for a naïve moment thought this might be it. The moment they would let it all drop, bitterness and pride, masks and old scars. That he would pave the way for her terrified little heart to come clean as well. Today would not be the day.

She chuckled just as bitterly. "I thought about you all right. Should I have asked about you as well? And what should I have asked? Who you interrogated? Had killed? Or been fucking?"

He let go of his grip, stung with the truth in her words. He looked her up and down, his wife, his girl, and yet she would never be his. How he wished she could have been more like Natasha, to understand his world, to accept it. But he knew he wouldn't have loved her any other way. The thought resonated within him, coming as a revelation. He loved her.

"Laura…" He spoke her name softly.

His tone reached deep into her. She felt her heart tighten in her chest, recognized the voice of her Kayne. She looked up at him, her eyes sad, waiting.

The words choked in his throat. Even in love, or especially because of it, Kayne Malkin wouldn't expose his vulnerability. He had thought he wanted to be her savior. Now he understood, even if he ever was, he would willingly want to still be perceived as the villain.

Seeing he wouldn't say anything else, she accepted his olive branch. She smiled at him, a heavy, broken, and honest smile. In the silence that followed, they continued to stare at each other, for the first time, with a tenderness enveloping their gaze. The roles had been confused; they weren't even sure themselves who was executioner and who was victim anymore. The only truth that now faced them was that they both suffered, that they both cared, knew it to be hopeless, and hoped nonetheless.

Day-148

Genevieve lingered behind the door hoping to eavesdrop on the aftermath of the interruption. She had expected the woman to lose her cool the moment she faced her husband alone, to fall into a nervous heap of tears and insecurity. For him to reassure her halfheartedly, apologize insincerely, and give concessions begrudgingly. None of that had happened. It was not a hysterical female voice that she overheard; it was an inflamed deep and manly one. *Why would the cheater lash out?* she wondered. She couldn't understand words through the closed doors but could still recognize the passion in his heated arguments. It unnerved her further, only solidified her growing suspicion: Mrs. Malkin was not your typical housewife or Mafia wife for that matter. She could tell she was very young, barely a few years older than herself, she guessed. But there was something about the way she carried herself, like she'd lived it all, knew it all. There was some indiscernible quality, which made her look far beyond her years. Genevieve hadn't paid much attention to it before.

She was caught in her thoughts when Louis tugged her arm at night; he urgently wanted to speak to her, seek her advice. She was in no mood, so much had happened. She simply couldn't focus her energy on anyone else. Louis knew of her little selfish streak. She suspected it made him love her even more. Selfish people were simply more desirable; it was a sad truth. One she understood at a young age, ever since her estranged father rescheduled much-awaited getaways for last-minute fishing trips, or whatever activity was better suited to his current mood. Her mother was devoted, always available. She despised her, yet she adored her father.

Kiev, whom she referred to mockingly as *Le Grognon*, came to fetch her sometime in the late afternoon. "Boss wants to see you." She felt a tingle, quickly looked at herself in the mirror, and approved of the reflection before following him out of her room.

He led her to the reception hall. She smiled inwardly, recalling her session with her employer from the previous night. She played with her hair, adding a little pop to her hips the moment they stepped into the room. Her face immediately dropped at realizing it was not the boss she had in mind.

Laura flashed Genevieve a radiant smile.

"Genevieve, come in. Please, have a seat."

Unsure, and quite suspicious, Genevieve obeyed instructions. She seated herself on the nearest chair, keeping her eyes fixed on the boss who had summoned her.

"Would you like anything to drink?"

"No… thank you," she stammered.

"Tea, coffee, juice… water? Nothing at all?" Laura asked, a suspicious kindness to her tone.

"Coffee… Let me get it. It's my job," Genevieve replied somewhat bitterly. "What would you like, Mrs. Malkin?"

Laura chuckled. "Nonsense. Kiev, please bring us two mugs of coffee, milk and sugar on the side."

She turned her attention back to Genevieve once they were alone. She took a seat facing her, crossed her legs, and, placing her hands on her knees, sighed in a pleasant mood.

"So, Genevieve. Do you know why I hired you?"

Genevieve hated that feeling of awkwardness, like she was the butt of a joke everyone was in on. She was off her game but was slowly regaining her ground.

"Because I'm so pretty?" She mockingly guessed, her face conveying her immature, petulant temperament.

Laura chuckled, her expression haughty. "Actually… yes."

"Okay…" Genevieve mumbled, thrown off.

"You like seducing men, don't you?" Laura inquired, an amused smile on her face.

"Is this about your husband? He came on to me..." she lied, lifting an eyebrow defiantly.

"How awful..." Laura smirked wickedly at the naïve girl in front of her. For a moment she felt bad for her but then remembered the look on her face as she walked in on her and Kayne, the vulgar arrogance with which she met her eyes. "And you seem like such a *sweet innocent* girl..." she mockingly added a tsk-ing sound.

"What do you want, Mrs. Malkin?" Genevieve put an end to the jabs and pleasantries, all too aware of the trap being set by the woman facing her. She hadn't realized Kiev had walked back in and stood idly in the corner until Laura waved him in. She handed her a mug and instructed her to drink before she resumed their conversation.

"I'm afraid there's nothing I want from you anymore, Genevieve. You've served your purpose." For the first time, her face grew severe.

"You hired me to fuck your husband?" Genevieve asked, disbelieving. "I think you're *firing* me because of it."

"Oh no. You're not fired." Laura's honeyed reply was instant. Her eyes gleamed with the same wickedness endured, then learned, from the man who had single-handedly changed her destiny, down to the very core of her being.

Laura considered her young rival. From the moment she had laid her eyes on Genevieve at the interview, she knew she would be perfect. A young Tanya, a Tanya she could control and use for her own benefit. She would dangle her in front of Kayne, because she needed to know the extent he could hurt her, betray her. He could fuck all his whores while he was away. Would he also disgrace her in her own house? The answer came too fast, and yet she understood it as retaliation from him, a reaction, as unhealthy as they come, to his perceived rejection. She was sick of playing games. She didn't need to test him anymore. She knew what he was capable of, *everything*. Understanding his twisted logic didn't make it any easier to tolerate.

Late at night, she had tossed and turned in her bed. She hated herself for what she'd become, hated him for what he could still stir in her. Was there no line he would cross that she wouldn't forgive? As long as he was alive, he would hold this power over her. She had a thought, too terrible to formulate, that was dismissed just as quickly as it sprang. She could never kill Kayne, not out of a basic sense of right and wrong; those had long gone with the wind.

As much as he hurt her, she was too aware of just how easily she could hurt him as well. The broken mirror and his bleeding hand were not lost on her. Even as he fucked the maid, it was all about her, and she knew it. There was something terrifying, repugnant, and yet exhilarating about it all, *to hold sway over a monster.*

"Mrs. Malkin? So you're *not* firing me?" Genevieve asked tentatively, snapping Laura out of her haze.

Laura shook her head. Her acquired facade of pompous superiority faltered, her eyes revealing the hostility kept at bay. She could see Genevieve's eyelids drooping.

"A wise woman once advised me to keep my friends close, my *husband's whores* closer…"

"Je ne comprends pas…" Genevieve mumbled more to herself.

"I say six feet under is better." Laura's hard face matched her icy tone. She stood up as Genevieve's movements became sloppy, her words slurred.

"Qu'est-ce qui se passe..." Genevieve managed to utter as she fell to the ground.

Laura stared coolly at her as Kiev approached and picked up the body.

"Have you decided, Boss?"

She nodded. She'd wanted to have her sold, put her seductive skills to good use. In an infinitesimal redeeming compassion, she changed her mind. "Make it quick, and painless."

* * *

It was almost ten at night. Laura was in a backless silk nightgown, brushing her hair at the vanity in her room when she heard a gentle knock on her door. Without awaiting permission, Kayne entered her room.

She only turned her head to greet him. "Hello…" she murmured in a deep voice, more from nerves than seduction.

He nodded, his expression hard to read.

"And to what do I owe the honor?" She turned her face back to the mirror and continued to brush her hair.

"Laura… what have you done with Genevieve?"

His face was serious, his tone grave, and yet she could swear she glimpsed an imperceptible smirk in his question. She took a deep breath and turned her entire body to him this time. "Tell me, Kayne, what would *you* have done if you had walked in on me fucking another man in your house?"

His eyebrows shot up, his voice was soft as he uttered, "She was just a kid…"

Her eyes shot him daggers. "Didn't seem to have stopped *you*…" Her stare growing cold, she added, "Wouldn't be worthy of calling myself a *Malkin* had I spared her."

The corner of his lips quirked up as he nodded a few times in concession, and slight admiration. "Kiev?"

She nodded.

"Her friend, the blond one, he's been badgering Olga all day. He won't believe she just quit and left without a word. She just came to see me about it."

Laura shrugged her shoulders, disinterested. "Have Kiev take care of him too."

Kayne furrowed his brows disapprovingly. "Laura!"

"Am I shocking you? *You*?" Her voice went shrill. "YOU! Of all people. You made me this way…" Her voice cracked. In that moment, it all hit her. She brought her hand to her mouth, in horror at the reality of her actions, of the path she had embarked on. "Oh my god…. Kayne... what have I done? What have I done?" She broke down.

He stepped closer to her, pulling her to him. "You did what a true Malkin would have done." He looked her in the eye and asserted his undying devotion to his wife, the only Malkin queen he'd ever known, the only one he deemed worthy to carry his name.

Her breathing slowed, her twisted features eased. She had just killed someone, over him, over the man she had bartered her own soul for. He might never love her, but she knew he would stand by her side no matter what. It made it all worth it. She would meet him at the gates of Hades and never look back.

"What about the boy?" she finally asked, her voice soft.

"I'll handle him."

"Will you hurt him?" An echo of her kind heart worried.

"I'll handle him," he reiterated, closing the discussion. He would face the consequences of her actions. He'd led her down the path of darkness, but unlike him, there was still hope for Laura. There was no price he wouldn't pay to wash the blood off her hands. He would slaughter lion and lamb alike, let their blood rain down on him to keep her coat white as snow. From hell his laughter would echo all the way to the heavens he would have secured for her.

She nodded, relieved of her burden.

"To think all this would have been so easily avoided if you would have just shown up on time." His expression turned wicked all of a sudden. He leaned into her ear. "You do realize I still have to punish you for your disobedience…."

She literally jumped out of his embrace.

How he loved toying with her, how he loved the flames in her eyes that made her look wild, that sweet surrender he would always extract from her. The serenity he found in her eyes in this moment would quiet his own chaos. She could bring him peace with one glance, could ground him with it, and bind him to her with just a kiss.

As he approached her, she stepped back, her eyes fixed on him. She walked around him, cautiously making her way to the door. It amused him.

"Do you really think you can outrun me? That there's anywhere in this house, on this earth, where you can be safe from me?"

She didn't respond, kept walking backward toward the door.

He chuckled loudly, looking forward to the hunt. His eyes devilish, he added, "Fine. I'll even give you a five-second head start. Don't let me catch you," he warned seductively.

She hadn't meant to run, did not want to lower herself and display such fear, but the moment she heard him count up, her legs snapped of their own accord. Before she even knew it, she was sprinting down the hall. She felt him catching up too soon, turned into the kitchen, and stopped behind the island.

She panted out of breath as he stopped nonchalantly on the other side and stood casually facing her. She could see from his posture, from his smile, the sadistic mood he was in, how the chase only ignited it further.

"Kayne…" she pleaded. "Please don't do this. I beg you." It hurt her to beg. But she couldn't handle any punishment he had in mind for her, not with the emotional mayhem she was in.

He smiled, entertained; it was part of the game for him.

"Please… Master… I'm begging you… I don't think I can handle it."

"You don't give yourself enough credit, baby," he replied, his tone sinister.

She broke down and in utter despair wailed her final plea, "Kayne… I'm begging you! Please! Haven't you tortured me enough?"

His expression changed, his smirk disappeared as his eyes studied her. She thought she succeeded, found a way to reach into him, to bypass the sadist to her Kayne. She exhaled with relief.

He was calm when he addressed her, his voice soft. "Laura… You know this is who I am. Must you act horrified every time? This is it. This is what you'll get from me. Always."

Her whole world came crashing down. There were no two Kaynes, no Dr. Jekyll and Mr. Hide. It was his voice, *her Kayne*, who had put into words her worst fears. She felt like in those horror movies where the hero thinks he has finally escaped the nightmare in the end only to realize that it was just another trick and that he was back exactly where he started. Then the credits roll, leaving a bitter taste in your mouth, a sickly feeling turning your stomach, having just lived for the past two hours with the protagonist still caught in the hellish loop.

Slowly, he took a step to the right. She took a step left. He smirked, taking another step.

Her heart raced, she pleaded again, "Please, Kayne, please." She was weeping.

He stared back at her, his eyes intense and yet kind. It made her heart melt. She felt weak in the knees. She wondered if she *wanted* him to catch her.

He took another step.

"Please… stay away…" Her voice jerked with emotion.

He smirked and took another step.

Frantic, she reached for the first weapon at her disposal and grabbed a butcher knife off the counter behind her. With shaky hands, she held it threateningly with her arms stretched out in front of her. "Stay away from me… I don't want to hurt you," she managed in between broken sobs.

His smirk widened; he stepped closer and over to her side.

She took a hesitant step backward. "Stay away… I'll hurt you if I have to."

He just cocked his head to the side then closed the distance in one swift move. He grabbed her hands holding the knife and brought it to his throat. "Do it then," he taunted her, a dark gleam in his eyes.

He took the last remaining step, wrapping his free hand behind her back, and he pulled her to him. "Do it," he dared, his voice husky in her ears.

"Stop…" she wailed, as the point of the blade pierced his skin. "Stop… I'm hurting you…" she pleaded in torment, tears raining down her cheeks.

He didn't care. Ignoring the pain, he let go of her wrists and pulled his face closer to hers. When his lips were almost touching hers, he commanded, his voice gruff with desire, "Kiss me."

She didn't kiss him; she let the knife drop to the floor instead and closed her eyes as tears continued to roll down her face and sobs escaped her lips.

He took her into his mouth, forcing her lips open with his tongue. Her body didn't resist the intrusion. She obeyed like a rag doll as he brought her arms around his neck and pulled her waist against his. He kissed her with the built-up hunger that had brewed in his blood for over two months. His wife, his favorite toy, his obsession.

He wedged his knee between her thighs, forcing her legs apart, and felt her panting in his mouth. He broke the kiss to stare into her eyes. There was no conflict there, only unbearable pain. He recognized the sweet young girl he had met a lifetime ago in those tormented pleading eyes.

"I… can't…" she sobbed, each word uttered with seemingly enormous effort. "I can't do this anymore..."

She wasn't crying hysterically. She looked him in the eye, defeated. It wasn't a plea anymore. She was stating the truth she had accepted with calm finality. Kayne unconsciously responded by loosening his grip, though his eyes remained locked on hers.

"I can't... I have nothing left. You've taken it all. I have nothing… Nothing..." she repeated in a soft though resolute voice. Emptiness replaced the pain as bitterness crept in her voice. "I look at myself in the mirror…. I don't recognize that girl. I *hate* that girl… And I have to live with it. *Every day.* You will never hurt me more than I've already hurt myself. Punish me if you have to… I won't fight you."

The iciness in her words traveled through the air, rendering the room a frozen wasteland, and like an arrow, right into him, paralyzing him.

It took him a few seconds to snap out of the hypothermia engulfing him. He stared at her blankly. Her words still echoed in every corner of his mind, making their way through his whole body, like venom seeping into his veins. His expression was unreadable as he let go of his grip completely, turned around, and exited the room.

How long she stayed by herself staring at the abandoned knife on the floor, she didn't know. She went back to her room, took off her sophisticated makeup, and for the first time in a very long time, pulled out the grey yoga pants and purple hoodie that used to be her daily uniform.

She curled into a ball and cried without restraint into her pillows. In that moment, crying shamelessly in her beloved attire, she almost felt like her old self again. She smiled through the watery curtain on her face. She missed *her*. Scared, awkward, clumsy little Laura, she missed her so much. She missed seeing the world through her eyes, loving Kayne with her devoted innocence. Laura Malkin had brought her the strength to survive Kayne; only Laura Spencer allowed her the frailty to be with him.

She was cried out. She continued to rub her already puffed-up red eyes and stared at the ceiling as the idea rooted itself in her mind. She could not, would not fall asleep on her own, knowing he was but a staircase away. She would find neutral ground where they could both meet. She would conjure it from willpower alone if she had to.

Tiptoeing up the stairs, Laura couldn't help but think back to another story Olga had told her. It was the story of two porcupines in love. They got lost in the middle of the coldest winter night and could not find refuge. All night they suffered. When they remained too far from each other, the claws of the cold ripped through them. When they sought warmth by each other's sides, their own spines pierced and bled them. All night they bled and froze, constantly adjusting and readjusting. By the crack of dawn, a little girl found two porcupines asleep peacefully, close enough to ward off the cold, far enough not to hurt one another.

Upon reaching his bedroom door, Laura took a few long breaths to calm her trepid heart. Her knocks were so subtle, she hoped they wouldn't be heard. She wondered if she would find her beautiful monster asleep and nonthreatening or awake and on his guard. She didn't wait for her courage to leave and softly pushed the door open.

Kayne was sitting up on his bed, his back against the headboard, one leg bent up, the other flat on the mattress. His hair was loose and tucked behind his ear; he looked dangerously calm and nonchalant in his undershirt and khaki cargo shorts. Once again, he reminded her of a lion or tiger, licking his paws peacefully before he bared his claws for the kill.

She froze at the door.

He didn't move a muscle. Only his eyes turned to her, his face showing no reaction. Cautiously, she took a step in. His eyes were glued to her, following her every move with animalistic curiosity, yet his body remained lax.

She took another step toward the bed, her eyes returning the intensity of his gaze, though hers conveyed the turmoil raging within. She stopped at the foot of the bed, a tentative coy smile taking shape on her features. She played with the hem of her pants and hesitantly reached for the bottom of her hoodie then moved back to her pants, awaiting the instructions she hoped to get.

He understood her, he understood her brain process. He would take the olive branch she offered. *His* beautiful Laura, she had somehow brought her back and would sacrifice her at the altar, as a peace offering.

He remembered the first instruction he had given her, the reaction it provoked. The wetness on her face contrasting the one betraying her at obeying his command. *Take off your clothes, Laura.*

He wanted nothing more than to utter the command and wash away the bitterness of her earlier words, and yet he couldn't bring himself to. In this moment, the jaded lover overpowered the insatiable sadist. For the first time, he felt tired. For the first time, Kayne lived in a world that didn't bend to his will and laughed openly at his bare wounds. To a Malkin, the only response was to laugh even louder and cut off the wounded limb.

Faced with his vindictive silence, Laura exhaled and pushed the limits that had long been broken. She met his gaze, with determination, and removed her pants. She took her time, making sure to sway her hips left and right as she wiggled them off her legs.

By the time she lifted her head to meet his, she was not fooled by his cool composure. Something wickedly promising was already taking shape in his eyes as he shook his head in disapproval.

"Get the fuck out of here," he spat at her with a disdainful smirk, his voice still carrying the bitterness he had willed into condescension.

Laura shut her eyes. When she reopened them, they still carried the entrenched heartbreak he had seen earlier. The sadness in them, however, was unlike the cold surrender that inhabited them in the kitchen; those eyes suffered, were willing to suffer, and dared to hope.

"No." Her voice was soft as she held his stare with pure eyes. They contained no remorse or regret, no blame or rancor. It was not a negotiation or an act of juvenile defiance. It was just Laura, with all her walls down, still standing.

He stared her down, making her heart race, but she didn't look down. She remained standing tall as Kayne snapped to his feet and planted himself right in front of her. He could sense her fear and, like a dog responded with heightened senses, every nerve tingling with arousal. A desperate dog howled inside of him, reached with all its might toward his loving mistress. To him, there were no past scars, no dead ends waiting, only a beloved body within reach and the promise of a touch long yearned for. His pained howl was heard, awakening the beast that was asleep.

Kayne narrowed his eyes, he would not surrender to the abyss of pleasure calling out to him. This would be his biggest punishment to her yet. *Nothing*. Rejection, it was cancer to a man's soul, death, to a woman's.

He exhaled deeply, studying her face, her controlled breathing, her terrified eyes holding his gaze. How he loved her in this moment.

"Get out, Laura… before I make you," he whispered close to her cheek, his voice, an animalistic growl, warning and seductive.

She didn't even blink. "If that's your *order*, I will leave. But you will never see me again, and you know I would never *dare* lie to you." She avowed her own warning through gritted teeth.

Kayne smirked. *Ultimatums, always a bad idea*. What did she think would happen? That she would pull a knife on him, then meet him in his room and have him fall at her feet? That the mere mention of her leaving would tear his world apart? It did. That point, he conceded. What she failed to realize, however, was that he would tear his world, his own body apart with his bare hands before ever laying it at anyone's feet.

He would not stop her. For the first time, Kayne wished she would lie to him. He remained silent, daring her to walk out with his eyes, supplicating her not to from his very core.

She waited, pushed her ill-fated faith for as long as she could. She could sense the conflict in him. Once more, believed in *her* Kayne, willing him silently to reach for her, to utter anything, just make a sound, and she would stay.

Her response came only from silence's deafening buzz in her ears. She lifted her chin, already held high, with dignity and understanding. She lowered her head, somewhere between a nod and a bow out. She turned around and lifted her pants, slowly. She had no tears to fight back, no sorrow to hide from her tormentor. She had come full circle. She could see the injury, acknowledge the frightening gash oozing blood out, and yet felt nothing. Death. It was not the end, it was liberation. An unwholesome smile tainted her face as she walked out of the room regal-like.

Kayne fell back on his mattress and watched her leave in disbelief. Minutes turned to hours as Kayne remained immobile in his bedroom, looking out his glass wall pointlessly. He waited for her return. The waning moon in the dark skies retreated under his very eyes, mourning Laura's departure.

Ominous clouds claimed the sky. In the humid night, a lightning flash illuminated Kayne's room, while tropical-like rain ensued, big drops banging violently against the glass. He felt release at the fury unleashed around him. For a moment too quick to truly grasp, he lost himself in the sweet folly of Mother Nature. It seemed to him, she held her arms out, cried the tears he'd never be able to shed.

By the time thunder boomed in the electric sky, Kayne had already banished the grief-stricken boy. His harsh facial features spoke of cool self-control and unbreakable determination. He had made a promise, with this promise alone had taken the life of Peter Spencer. *He would keep Laura safe.*

He rushed to the office, calling Lucas for assistance.

"Where is she?" Kayne's voice was harsh. He remembered the last time he tracked her. His heart beat at the thought of finding her hurt, or worse, safe and sound, in the arms of another man.

"I don't know… it's weird." Lucas seemed perplexed. "She's… in the middle of nowhere."

Conflicting emotions strained his features, no other man… no safety either. "*WHERE* is she?" he hissed.

Lucas shook his head, concerned himself. "She's… in the woods."

In the middle of a thunderstorm, it was the single worst place she could be, and he had pushed her there. He ground his teeth with sheer wrath. He couldn't let his mind run away with the sinister scenarios already playing in the back of his head.

"Keep tracking, I'm going after her."

Lucas nodded, his face grave as he watched his boss storm out into the tempestuous night.

* * *

Laura had been walking pointlessly for hours. She was dripping wet, her teeth chattering from cold. She had strayed off the beaten path, had refused to meet the civilized world it led to. She was no longer part of it. She was no longer part of anything. Once she had been a sister, it had defined her identity, her very reason for being. That was taken from her. Then she became a prisoner, had even willingly played her part. She had remolded her entire being to survive her new cage, forsaken all for her jailor. Then the jailor gave her up.

She didn't feel human anymore. She was a wounded animal, instinctively returning to the wilderness. Crouching on the earth, with a dripping hoodie over her head hiding half her face, she let her tears mix with the rain. She hugged her knees and rocked herself, just as she had as a kid. As a young girl, her worst fear had been to be locked in the cage like an animal. Alone, hurt, cold, and scared, she realized there was worse: to be set free.

Hours passed, she longed to see her brother again, wondered if he'd be waiting for her when freedom finally came. Wondered if he'd ever forgive her. She thought of Kayne. She recounted their story to herself, her eyes closed. She pictured a young Laura listening enraptured, sometimes terrified, somewhat hypnotized by the twisted tale that would become her life. A serene smile softened her features; she wouldn't change a thing. Not all fairy tales were meant to end well. She felt the cold penetrating her clothes, her body, down to her bones. She didn't fight the slumber that had already invaded her limbs. As she drifted to the realm of the wise and silent, she wondered if Kayne would ever find her, if his kiss held the sorcery to wake her.

* * *

Kayne had abandoned the Audi on the side of the road. With Lucas on the phone directing him, he made his way into the foreboding woods. He could barely hear him under the vehement thunder. He called out to her, screaming her name repeatedly as he beat away the sinister-looking branches blocking his path. In the dark of the night, the beast helplessly sought his redemption.

* * *

It seemed as if it came from another world. She tried to ignore the sound, the incessant call pushing away the peaceful shore awaiting her. She thought she recognized her name, saw the glow retreat back into the void, felt the warmth dissipate. She heard her name, louder and louder, closer and closer, recognized the strained voice that had brought her back.

By the time she blinked her eyes awake, she felt the warmth of his hand against her cheek, could see the beloved features facing hers. He seemed tired, his face was dripping, his hair unruly. He looked wild, scary, and comforting at the same time. Her Kayne, he was there, his eyes boring into hers.

"How did you find me?" She was still dazed, struggling to force a sound out of her hibernating body.

He lowered his head, bringing their foreheads together. He exhaled deeply as relief softened his features.

"Oh, Laura…" His smile was brittle as he reached for her sleeve and crooked the bracelet with his finger.

"I don't understand…" Her voice was soft. She feared she was dreaming.

He turned the bracelet around, showing her the engraving. "For as long as I'm your Monster, I will always find you."

He brought her to her feet, removed his jacket, and draped it around her shoulders.

"Let's go home." He didn't wait for an answer. He simply took her hand and started walking away. The little hand slipped away, and he turned around to find Laura standing still.

"Laura. We have to go," he commanded irritated, apprehension in his voice as he looked to the angry skies.

She shook her head. She looked at him and felt the strings on her limbs pull her to him. Never had a man or beast looked so terrifyingly beautiful. She knew this for certain as she watched his wet shirt cling to his body, his eyes glowing with emotion, his clenched jaw warning of its deadly bite. She didn't want to return to the ivory tower. She would cast away its safety and solitude, would rather perish in the dark forest, devoured by her beast.

“We’re going to die out here! Is this what you want?” he yelled, his eyes narrow.

“YES!” Her scream was long and pained.

Looking at her face, he knew not all the drops came from the rain. His body relaxed, he considered her for a moment. “So be it,” he said with finality.

His walk determined, he took the few steps leading him back to her and, in one fluid movement, grabbed hold of her.

He captured her in his arms, his elusive prey. His lips met hers with ferocious lust. The world growled around them, lightning illuminated the sky. He didn’t care. Their story had claimed too much blood. The Monster and his captive, their happy ending awaited them in the underworld. Side by side, they would laugh at the all the happily ever afters agonizing in the routine of the mundane.

He lowered her to the ground and pulled her wet clothes off as she struggled to rip off his shirt. He left the bundled hoodie around her wrists and held her down with one hand, while the other pulled her pants down to her knees. He unzipped his jeans, didn’t take the time to tease and seduce. This fuck wasn’t for her. It was a selfish fuck, meant to appease his own desperate needs. He took her savagely on the ground, sliding himself in and out roughly, though he found her entrance wet and ready, her body willing, intuitively opening up to its true master.

“No more, Laura,” he half growled in her ears. “No more bullshit. I’ll mind fuck you until you get it.”

Laura gasped, knowing the threat to be true, fear and desire, almost impossible to dissociate. She felt her muscles clamp around his hardness, felt the buildup rising deep inside of her. She had surrendered her body long ago. That wouldn’t be enough to appease the beast’s hunger. He wanted more, he wanted her total submission. He *could* mind fuck her into insanity, into becoming an obedient rag doll he could exercise his complete control over, she realized with a pang.

She could resist in vain, hold on to her reeling pride, to her wavering individuality. She could stand on her own and fight a losing battle. She didn't have the strength left; more so, she didn't have the desire to. How tempting the sweet surrender to her Monster seemed. He would fight all her fights, would vanquish any and all threats. He would keep her safe. He would keep her happy. Her pride could have pushed her to fight nonetheless, screaming that the price was too high. But Laura knew, in the end, he would have her, just as he wanted her, submissive, forsaking her pride for the sweet oblivion of his touch, for the intoxicating comfort of belonging to her Monster.

Her voice raspy, her lids half closed, she allowed herself the truth she long felt, and even longer, resisted. "I'm yours. Do as you want with me."

Day-149

It was nearing dawn when Kayne led Laura back to the car. The storm had ceded to clear blue skies, birds could be overheard in the distance. They hadn't said anything else to each other. On the ride home, he left his hand on her thigh. Every now and then, he turned and offered her a knowing smile below tired eyes. This was as close to a normal couple as they would ever get, Laura thought.

When they reached the house, he dragged her to his bedroom, removed her wet clothes, and prepared a bath for the both of them. Obediently she followed him and sat in between his legs as silently instructed. She let him bathe her body and brush her hair. She felt at peace, felt the release of being utterly under his care and control. After he dried her, he took her hand and led her to bed. He caged her body with his legs and wrapped his arms around her. She felt his kiss on her temple before she drifted off. In this moment, she didn't understand why it couldn't always be that way. In her last waking thought, she murmured a *thank you*, to whatever had her lying in his arms again, feeling his chest against her back, building a home within his arms.

She dreamt of a warm summer day, picnicking out in the fields. She was dressed elegantly as they did in the fifties, in a black dress, complete with the long matching gloves and veiled hat. She was sitting on a blanket, looking up at the clear blue sky with her legs folded together on her side, resting her weight on her left arm. She felt light, very light.

She turned her head back to the blanket and noticed a black crow had just landed. It was standing still, just watching her, its clear blue eyes strangely human. It sent shivers down her spine.

Laura woke up with a start, sweaty and feeling uneasy. It was well into the afternoon and the setting sun drew its pinkish hue behind. She let her fingers trail along the empty space by her side, yearning for the body still indented in the folds.

* * *

Louis had been going mad as the silent hours passed by. He called Genevieve's cellphone nonstop, filled her voice mail with unanswered messages. He reached out to all their acquaintances, hoping to find her, though apprehensive that she might have found refuge elsewhere. He refused to believe she would turn her back on him. For all her fickleness, he was the one constant in her life. Not out of love, but out of mere selfishness, he knew she would never abandon such a faithful companion.

No one had heard a word. He lowered himself further and began calling all her part-time lovers. If she lay in their bed, they remained silent about it, some even laughed in his face before hanging up on him. In only two days, Genevieve Roy seemed to have vanished into thin air. For the second day in a row, he went to the nearest bar and got as drunk as his wallet allowed.

He replayed the discussion he had with the master of the house. He had demanded to see him and did not lower his gaze when formulating accusatory questions. Kayne Malkin had remained calm, even showed some concern, was patient and tolerant facing the inflamed young man. Louis hadn't fallen for it. He knew something bad had happened to Genevieve. He could feel it in the eerie calm and peacefulness her absence left. He was convinced the Malkins were behind it.

It was in this bar that he ran into Carlyle, the beat-up thug who recommended the job to Genevieve. He was tall and beastly looking. Genevieve hadn't picked him for his looks, Louis suspected. It was the air of danger that followed him everywhere, his connections with the Mafia that had lured her to him.

With a height of five foot seven and all of one hundred and fifty pounds, Louis marched with the determination and courage found at the bottom of a whiskey bottle to confront the gold-toothed sneer of the two-hundred-and-fifty-pound mass awaiting him.

"Have you seen her?" he spat at him as he still walked closer.

"Gen? That your girl, isn't it?" Carlyle responded with a malevolent calm.

"Just answer me."

"Nah, man…. Haven't seen her face in a month… saw her back though… last week in the backseat of my car…" He broke off snickering. A few thug attired look-alikes snickered along, their eyes looking to one another for cues.

Louis reddened. Further words were exchanged. He was not even sure who threw the first punch. He only remembered being pulled away and dragged out of the club. He remembered the blonde policewoman being rude and aggressive. The policeman with her was a tad more civil as he pushed him into the backseat of the cruiser.

Louis hated the police. He had been part of too many peaceful protests ending in indiscriminate pepper spraying and mass arrests to see them as anything else but government lapdogs. He suspected a good 70 percent of them were incompetent, arrogant, and on a power trip. They seemed more like glorified bouncers than officers sworn to serve and protect. The other 29 percent were corrupt; those he actually preferred, the Mafia dogs tended to leave you alone. He didn't like to generalize, so he allowed for a 1 percent margin to be composed of decent cops.

He had learned an invaluable lesson from his years of protesting and public pot smoking: dodge the female cops and the short male ones. They were always the worst. They reminded him of little Chihuahuas barking away excitedly, *asserting their authority.* He cackled alone in the backseat at the thought.

Louis was still drunk when the officers interrogated him. He was barely coherent. He managed to shout out his indignation. *The Malkins! It was them! They did it! The Malkins!*

He was ushered out with eye rolling and more force than necessary. After, he was placed in the holding cell and forced to share it for the night with a homeless man. The man's teeth were completely rotted, but he managed to present reassurance through his kind smile. He insisted on offering him the same suspicious-looking banana every now and then. Louis graciously declined the offer and considered his strange bedmate. He didn't seem much older than himself. His mind went back to Genevieve. They could have ended up the same way. He wondered where she was. He knew it was all linked to the Malkins somehow. He hadn't expected the cops to take his plea seriously. If the Malkins were behind it, there would be nowhere to turn to for help. If the Malkins had hurt her, they would pay, he would make them pay. With sweet thoughts of revenge, sweeter thoughts even of Genevieve's miraculous return and their passionate reunion, Louis fell asleep with a pleasant smile on his face.

Day-150

Kayne was with Dimitri. He had spent the night at their mansion revising shipment strategies. Dimitri was a man of vision. When he had inherited the leadership, the Quebec branch was disorganized, with big tempers, bigger egos, and little-result. With Kayne's father by his side, they expanded, united separate fractions, and diversified. Kayne remembered only one occasion of raised voices between the two. Lev Malkin preferred the cautious money in his pocket, while Dimitri only saw the money to be grabbed. True to his nature, Dimitri was still unsatisfied, they were losing out on big operations, and he wanted in.

It was almost supper time when he headed home and his cellphone rang. Upon seeing Maxwell's name blink on the screen, he ground his teeth.

"Maxwell," he called out, his voice already impatient.

"Kayne."

Maxwell's grave voice, the lack of insincere joviality surprised Kayne.

"Louis Lavallé. He's one of yours, isn't he?"

Kayne exhaled. "What about him?"

"He's a problem."

"I'm aware."

"Really? Are you also aware that he spent the night in holdup? That Riley got hold of the report? That your name was in it? Something about a missing girl?"

Maxwell had his attention now. Maxwell and Kayne's mutual dislike for each other was almost instant. He reminded Kayne of something reptilian. Maxwell had shown up at his promotion, even at his wedding with his wife and young boy. He had shaken his hand with a venomous smile. He knew he would relish any opportunity to make him look bad, especially since his promotion.

Once again, Thomas Riley had proved to be a worthy investment. He had been bought and his loyalty secured for a long time. He reported to Maxwell, however; it was his man, his contact. Riley was a man of values, forged in an unyielding character guarding a kind heart. He had never looked down on anyone from his towering height and massive build. He entered the police force as women joined the convent long ago, with the humility of the faithful. He believed he could make a difference. With unconditional devotion he served to make the world a better place, for his better half. For the way she held her growing belly every morning as she sent him off with loving kisses and hot coffee. Late at night, after all his coworkers left, he stayed behind, looked at the framed pictures in his cubicle, and knew he was fighting the good fight.

Fifteen years later, the only difference he had made was to ruin his marriage and alienate his beloved daughter. To this day he constantly reached out to his ex-wife, badgering her with angry calls placed during lonely nights, pleading with her in apologetic ones stemming from shameful mornings.

His daughter wouldn't show him her mother's forgiveness. She already resented him as a child. As a teenager from a broken home, she resented the entire world and blamed him for it all. She held him responsible for her mother's heartbreak. She hated him for all the nights he wasn't there for them, all the nights he spent saving others. Upon the divorce, she took her mother's name, avoided his calls, and missed all their appointments.

In the past five years, he'd gotten one call from her. His elation was short-lived. She was in the bad kind of trouble, with the worst kind of people. He had run to her side, fixed the problem, and paid off her debt with money he didn't have. For the first time, he'd seen gratitude, even love in her eyes. She didn't see a corrupt cop, a failed missionary; she only saw the father she always needed and never had. He traded his soul for it but never regretted it. Ever since, he'd been Maxwell's man.

Kayne considered the new revelation, the implication it carried. He recognized Maxwell's honeyed tone he despised so much, could only presume the pleasure this incident triggered in him, to have one up on him. He remembered seeing Louis pacing around the house like a lost puppy dog; he'd barely paid him any attention. His mind was on the sleeping body that unconsciously resisted when he carefully removed his embrace. His mind was on Dimitri who had summoned him.

"Yes. Thank you, Maxwell. He'll be taken care of." It was all the gratitude and information Kayne would impart.

"Kayne, I will be at the cabin with Carlo. Some other business... You already have enough on your mind with the shipments and all. Not to mention your beautiful bride..."

Kayne's hands tightened around the wheel. How he hated hearing her mentioned from his mouth, he could picture his toothy smile.

"Just get him here. I'll take care of him for you. Tell him we have his girl. He'll believe you. He so desperately wants to," Maxwell added with gleeful cynicism.

In another circumstance, he might have considered it. He knew Maxwell too well to ever accept any resemblance of favor. He knew him too well to expect him to handle a duty and not prolong his twisted pleasures indefinitely.

The boy needed to be dealt with. He understood his life was moot the moment the word *police* was uttered. Once upon a time, he might not have cared for innocent blood to be shed, and yet he felt his gut twist. He sympathized with the boy. Not long ago, he himself stood against Dimitri for Laura, for her safety, then to have her, and finally, to keep her.

Kayne found himself in the villain's shoes once again. He could not spare the boy's life. He would at least ensure him a quick death.

"I'll bring the boy. I'll handle him myself. You can take care of the cleanup," he commanded dismissively, asserting his authority while reminding Maxwell of the established hierarchy. He would not let him come off as the savior, merely an errand boy.

It was Kayne's turn to showcase his malevolent smile. He could imagine Maxwell's face turning burgundy, his pursed lips on a strained face as he muttered, "Very well," before hanging up.

* * *

Louis returned to the Malkin residence and avoided Mrs. Malkin's inquisitive stares. He kept mostly to himself, his head low, his movements agitated.

Laura saw him checking his phone constantly, realizing with a guilty conscience the futility of it. He would not get the call he was pacing around for. His presence became intolerable to her, his anxiousness, a constant thorn in her side. She hoped to linger around until Kayne came home, but her shame vanquished her desires. With bitterness, she acknowledged her own cowardice as she flew the scene of her crime.

* * *

Louis fidgeted nervously on the couch in the reception hall. Obediently he awaited Mr. Malkin, as instructed by Lucas. It seemed to him like hours had passed until the door finally swayed open. Kayne, followed by Lucas, walked in, their mood somber.

"Louis. Thank you for waiting." Kayne approached him.

Louis jumped to his feet and nodded his head as he offered a clammy hand to shake Kayne's.

"It's about Genevieve." Kayne paused.

"Yes." Louis's face was apprehensive. It was evident from Kayne's grave tone that this story would not have a happy ending. Louis's mouth twitched unconsciously.

"I know where she is."

"Where?" Louis almost screamed, his voice rough with emotion, his energy aggressive.

Kayne nodded his head, somewhat compassionate. "I'll take you to her." He didn't want to see the relief in the boy's eyes, the calm returning to his body. The words carefully chosen only alluded to the boy's death sentence. It was his one ethical code. Through this one trait he had built a reputation, had bought himself some resemblance of morality. Covered in blood, surrounded by dirty money, he had held on to this one truth. He was not a liar.

"Is she okay?" Louis asked without conviction, the pain in his eyes reflecting his awareness of the grim answer awaiting.

"No."

Louis's eyes moistened. He defensively lowered his head and blinked his eyes dry. When he looked back up, his eyes were hateful, filled with unspoken accusation.

"Let's go," Kayne commanded, his eyes boring into the hostile face. He maintained eye contact until Louis folded and brought his eyes to the floor. His head bowed, he followed Kayne silently to meet his fate.

* * *

The trap was set. Maxwell would be awaiting him at the cabin with Carlo. Kayne would proceed with the interrogation alone, retrace all the different paths the boys' inflammatory words could have taken. He would be shot in the temple using an unmarked firearm and his body placed in a manner to suggest suicide. The case would be overseen and ultimately signed off by Riley.

The drive was long and eerily silent under a moonless sky. At last, Kayne turned into a gravel road and drove deeper and deeper into the wilderness, until pulling up to a cozy-looking wooden chalet.

"We're here," he declared with finality.

Louis looked around suspiciously but voiced no concern at the unusual meeting point. He nodded and rubbed his sweaty palms against his jeans before reaching for the door handle.

Once out of the car, Kayne took the lead. It would have been wiser to follow behind, and for this reason alone, he turned his back to him, suggesting a climate of trust.

They walked straight into the kitchen area from the back door. Maxwell was already there, his slimy features twisted in what he thought was a smile.

Kayne walked up to him and reached out his hand. They nodded to each other knowingly. Kayne flashed him his darkest stare. Maxwell returned it with wolfish hunger.

"And this is Mr. Lavallé, I presume?" Maxwell bent his body sideways to look behind Kayne at the fidgeting boy who only nodded in response.

Kayne leaned into Maxwell and in a hushed tone inquired, "Everything is ready?"

Maxwell's eyes burned with malevolent jubilee. His voice louder than expected, every syllable pronounced distinctly, he responded, "Oh yes. Everything is ready for you."

It was in that moment, Kayne's eyes grew round with bewilderment. By the time he heard a gun cock behind him, he already understood, too little, way, way too late.

Louis Lavallé, the invisible man. No one ever saw him, no one but Genevieve. She breathed life into him. There was nothing before her; there would be nothing after her. He'd known it from the moment she disappeared. He could sense she was no more from the emptiness he felt in his chest. The Monster and his Babylonian Whore were behind it. He knew this as well, without proof or hint. He knew it as a woman recognized her rival when all others saw charming innocence, or as a mother could hate one of her child's friends after one look.

He wallowed in holdup, was laughed off as a conspiracy theorist. He vowed he would not let them get away. His prayers were answered in the form of an auspicious black Lexus waiting for him upon his release. It seemed the Monster had made more than one enemy, even within his own organization. He was not surprised. He was terrified.

He was to return to the Malkin residence and await the call to get the go-ahead. The call would confirm that Maxwell had spoken with Kayne and that Louis's suspicions had been confirmed and the hit set up. All day he paced around, checking his phone a hundred times a minute under the curious stares of Mrs. Malkin. All evening, he resisted his urge to confront the Monster. Under no circumstance was he to show suspicion and inquire about Genevieve's situation. He couldn't help asking one question, see if the Monster would lie to his face; he hadn't.

He got the call and received Kayne's instructions as predicted by Maxwell. He followed the Monster and found the gun hidden behind the flower pot as advised. He would get his vengeance, as promised.

The moment Kayne turned around, his shaky fingers pulled the trigger of their own.

"She's dead! She's dead!" Louis screamed hysterically.

Kayne looked at his chest, saw his own blood coloring his shirt. When he looked back up, his eyes seemed to be carrying the weight of the world, a crooked smile curving his lips.

"You killed her! She was everything! Everything! You used her as a whore! And you killed her!" Louis yelled insanely, his sweet face distorted in that of a manic clown.

Kayne growled at the sharp pain, felt his own blood rising in his chest, turning on him as well, choking him. He struggled to breathe, coughing blood with each breath, and slowly let himself fall to the ground. A part of him felt at peace, a part of him always knew, this was the only end befitting a Monster. He felt no resentment toward the boy. In his shoes, he would've done the same. Hell, he would've tortured him for days and laughed when he would have begged for death. He would have brought him back to life just so he could do it all over again.

"She was everything…." Louis's voice cracked, his fury dissipating, abandoning him to his unbearable pain. He let himself cry. He was about to speak again when another gunshot was heard. He didn't have time to react. The shot was precise, aimed right between his eyes. He fell instantly to the ground.

"How could I resist? Bringing the two lovebirds together… Ah! I'm just a hopeless romantic." Maxwell's slithery voice concluded.

He dragged a chair to face Kayne. With a gleeful smile and dignified air, he sat down.

Kayne coughed again, remaining silent.

"You know…" Maxwell carried on conversationally, "I do owe sweet little Laura a special thanks. I barely had to convince the boy. I think he was ready to take on the both of you at your house. You have to admire youth's fervor. But I would have missed all this…"

Kayne's eyes narrowed with murderous threat, his menacing air broken as he heaved on the floor.

"Shall I get you some water?" Maxwell asked with concern in his voice before he broke off into loud laughter.

Kayne remained silent, holding his stare.

"Ah well... Anyway. As I was saying… I think it's almost poetic… We will all die and murder. Not for money. Not for glory. *For love*." Maxwell's eyes finally narrowed, his hatred blazing through. "You have killed for the woman you love. You will die because of it. I bet you think I've been planning this for years, that there is nothing I wouldn't do to get ahead. You're right. And yet right now, looking at you, pathetically drained of your own blood. You know what I'm thinking of? *Who,* I'm thinking of. A goddess. A goddess with fiery hair and emerald eyes. She is worth murder and betrayal, she is worth everything. I want you to die knowing this. You died because of her. My Tanya will be waiting for me. Your sweet little Laura, you will never see again. Not where you're going."

Kayne lay immobile on the floor. It was a funny feeling to be on the other end. He thought of Tanya. Tanya did win the battle, from beyond the grave, threw her last arrow, straight into his chest. He smiled bitterly. It was a good fight. He would shake her hand down below.

But his last thoughts were with Laura. This was his cruelest act yet, taking everything from her and leaving her behind. He thought of all the movies he'd seen where lovers facing death prayed to be taken, to have their lover's life spared. They were nothing but selfish cowards. The real sentence was endured by the survivor. He deserved to die; he wasn't sorry for himself. The unrest he felt as his vision darkened was for Laura. He failed her, as her lover and as her master.

He wondered if she would remain true to herself, pure, beautiful, and untainted by him. He prayed for it and feared it above all. He was not a noble lover. In this moment, facing death and the prospect of never laying his eyes on her again, he knew the truth that lay in his dark heart. He wanted her to burn in hell with him, for eternity. His Laura, he'd loved her with the ferocity of a mother and her defenseless babe. He'd loved her with the awe that brought you to your knees in the presence of the divine. With his entire wretched being, he'd loved her, as a man hopelessly loves a woman.

She would never know, she would never hear this from him. This one regret burned him alive as his heart bled out.

Maxwell could have never guessed the heart-wrenching thoughts ripping his victim apart. When Kayne gathered his remaining strength to spit his last words, he looked victorious, his smirk condescending.

"Where I'm going, I'll be fucking your bitch."

Maxwell's fury turned his cheeks beet red. He raised his arm but restrained himself. He had to wait for Kayne to stop laughing, oozing blood. He had to wait for his last painful breath to leave his body. The scene had to remain intact.

* * *

It was past two in the morning and still no word of Kayne. Lucas had repeatedly tried to reach him with no success. He had reassured Laura unconvincingly, before retreating back to the office. Kayne had asked him to gather all information regarding the next shipment while he handled the Louis issue.

Laura had returned home around midnight. It was not unusual for Kayne to come home in the wee hours of the morning, and she felt at a loss by the uneasy feeling gnawing at her in his felt absence. She roamed the lonely corridors, not knowing what to do with herself, unable to sleep, unable to think.

* * *

Maxwell looked with disdain at the inert body lying on the floor in front of him. He had expected the long-awaited victory to drown his senses with euphoria, the sustained nirvana to last for days. He fantasized of a pitiful Kayne, groveling before him. Kayne had once again deterred his bliss. Now he was gone, and Maxwell would never get his vengeance, not the way he envisioned and devotedly poured himself into it.

Maxwell had hated Kayne from their first meeting, as he had hated all the other Kaynes that came before him. He knew all too well his sort, born under a lucky star. Blessed with looks, showered with money, gifted with charm and confidence. The Kaynes of the world had every need met before the desire was even born.

The Maxwells of the world were born ugly, usually short and stocky, destined to bald prematurely. They were the ones who pined after the girls the Kaynes took carelessly and dismissed ungratefully. They were the ones who worked twice as hard for half the result, and none of the recognition. The Maxwells of the world were called snakes, thought of scornfully to play dirty, deemed to have no virtue. The Maxwells of the world learned young that virtue was the luxury of the strong. Deceit was the only defense of the weak.

But no one roots for the ugly duckling, lest he become a swan. He had met a swan. She'd been an ugly duckling too. When all others recoiled in front of his so-called sadism, his devious thinking, she had smiled proudly at him. She understood him. Not his frigid, politically correct wife. Tanya Malone, his bloodthirsty goddess. His ugly duckling in the skin of a swan.

Tanya Malone would not have died in vain.

He reached for his cellphone. "Mr. Drugov. I apologize for disturbing you so late."

"Maxwell?" Dimitri's voice was alert, even when dragged from sleep.

"Something has happened."

"Yes. I assumed that much," Dimitri snapped impatiently.

"Kayne. Kayne Malkin is dead," he announced in a somber voice.

"*What,*" Dimitri hissed.

Maxwell sighed. "He's been shot."

"*How*?" Dimitri growled on the other end.

"Louis Lavallé, an insignificant servant boy. He'd been running his mouth. Kayne had his girlfriend taken out... He was supposed to bring him here to the cabin. We made him believe he was going to meet her here. I was to handle him with Carlo. You know... I'm not sure how it happened... The boy had a gun on him. I don't understand how he slipped it past Kayne.... Anyway, when he figured out the girl wasn't here.... He shot him, Kayne came unarmed. Luckily *I* had my gun. One can never be too cautious."

"Have you touched anything?" Dimitri asked, still taking everything in.

"No, sir."

"Don't. I'm on my way." Dimitri hung up immediately after.

Maxwell knew his word wouldn't be enough, not when it came to Golden Boy's head. With pride, he looked at the bodies lying around him. Their silence would support his story.

Carlo came in behind him. "So is it over, Boss?"

The trap had been set, had played out perfectly. Dimitri would confirm the story for himself. Most likely, Maxwell's gun would be placed in Kayne's hands. An anonymous call would be placed in the morning to the police. They would find two bodies placed in what looked like a shoot-out. The case would be overseen and ultimately signed off by Riley.

"Yes. It's all over."

Day-151

Laura hadn't shut an eye. All night she paced around Kayne's room with ever-increasing angst. Like the madwoman in the attic, she could be heard below, an eerie presence lurking in the shadows.

By noon the next day, her anxiety caught on, spread throughout the household like mass hysteria. Even the always-composed Lucas Belfort could barely hide his growing concern. Olga ran around the house like a headless chicken, beginning a chore and abandoning it to begin another. Kiev was the only one rendered apathetic by his disquietude. He sat alone in the solarium, his eyes brooding, with a tall glass of vodka, straight, sitting in front of him untouched.

Laura was still in her nightgown when she heard a gentle tap on Kayne's bedroom door.

"Yes…" Her voice came out strained, unrecognizable to her.

"It's Lucas. May I come in?" His voice was soft, his tone grave.

"Lucas…" Her voice cracked with emotion. "Come in."

He opened the door but remained standing in the doorframe. "I've just spoken with Dimitri. Natasha wanted to call you. I preferred telling you myself... I'm so sorry, Laura." His eyes were deadened.

She swallowed. Her eyelids fluttered for a moment. Lucas advanced, thinking she was about to faint. She didn't. She looked at him, her eyes cold as stone. "He's dead," she muttered, acknowledging the truth that had tormented her all night.

Lucas nodded, his jaw tense. He proceeded to summarize the story recounted by Dimitri.

"Louis Lavallé… that little piece of shit would have killed *Kayne*... KAYNE MALKIN?" she blasted.

"It would seem so." Lucas could barely look her in the eye.

"And… *Maxwell* saved the day?" she hissed, her eyes ablaze.

"Dimitri went down himself, checked the story out."

She broke into a loud humorless laughter. She stopped almost as suddenly, her eyes narrowed, and her lips pulled thin. "Maxwell is behind it. Find the link," she commanded coolly. "Find me the link, Lucas," she reiterated, wagging her index finger, her tone almost playful, and her eyes glittering with something unholy.

In this moment, he almost feared her. He nodded respectfully and walked out.

The moment she was alone, she collapsed to the ground. She opened her mouth and bit her arm, screaming as loud as she could, in complete silence. She refused to believe it. She shook her head in denial. Kayne couldn't be dead. It was all a sick joke. She had just slept in his arms… was it last night? Or was it the night before… He had brushed her hair, he held her. She had whispered I love you… Was it *I love you…* or *thank you*? She couldn't remember to save her life. It was silly, but it really bugged her. She decided she said I love you. Kayne Malkin couldn't have possibly died without having heard her tell him those words. Kayne Malkin, gone. She looked out to the radiant sun. She almost laughed. *Hadn't the sun heard?*

First Peter, and now Kayne. The two loves of her life had snuck out through the back door, like thieves in the night. She felt numb, strangely calm. Kayne Malkin, her Master, her Monster, had gone where she could not follow. She looked at the scar on her wrist, felt the old itch again. Laura Spencer would have done it. Laura Spencer would have been unworthy of her Master. Mrs. Malkin would rise. Mrs. Kayne Malkin would meet her cursed life in her best attire, with her eyes dry and her hair perfectly set. She would understand the necessity to survive, to remain strong. Mrs. Kayne Malkin would devote the rest of her life to avenge her Master. Laura Spencer writhed inside her from the intolerable pain. Mrs. Malkin reached in, lovingly, held her in her arms. She rocked her and caressed her hair, like a doting mother hushed her incessant howling. "He will pay… We'll make him pay," she lovingly whispered in her ears.

Maxwell Bane would pay. He would learn the price of Kayne Malkin's head. She hung on to this one single thought to lift her heavy limbs off the floor.

She received the official visit from two curt policemen not too long after. Once again she was subjected to the gruesome details, though noted the slight and telling differences of the official report. She acted blissfully ignorant when questioned about Kayne's work. She only allowed her bleeding heart to show when questioned about their marriage. When they left, she knew she had cried her last tears.

* * *

Lucas returned not too long after. He found Laura awaiting him in the reception hall. She was sitting straight in a high-back chair, calm and collected. She was clad in a black body-hugging dress and matching hat, a retro chic look about her. She looked far more glamorous than in mourning. Before he even opened his mouth, she silenced him with her palm.

"Where's Kiev?" She loved Lucas. He was a good consolation for the brother she lost. But she had come to depend on Kiev. He incarnated the irreplaceable father figure she never had.

"I'll get him."

The two returned dressed in formal black suits, usual for Lucas, an appreciated gesture from Kiev.

She looked at Lucas and simply nodded her head to give him the go-ahead.

"You were right."

Laura's cool face came to life upon the affirmation. Something sinister inside of her had taken residence. It resonated in her eyes.

"We'd been tracking him. We had a chip in his car…" Lucas continued.

Laura looked down at her bracelet. “Just like this one?” she asked, lifting her wrist.

Lucas offered her an apologetic stare. “Similar. It was an earring, made from the same jewelry maker… We’ve dealt a lot with him. Maxwell even knows him… Kaminski. He’s old as a mummy but silent as a tomb.”

“And Maxwell wasn’t suspicious of receiving earrings from Kayne?” she inquired, her tone sarcastic.

Lucas cleared his throat. “They were Tanya’s. She was working with Kayne… spying on Maxwell. She hid them there.”

“I see.” Laura felt the sting at hearing her name. Even from the grave, Tanya still managed to rub her closeness with Kayne in her face. “Please go on.” She feigned indifference.

“Maxwell was at the police station sometime late at night yesterday.”

“Okay…”

“His man Riley was on duty that night, so that’s not that suspicious. But… Louis Lavallé was also there… spent the night in holdup. The chip shows Maxwell drove around until dawn…. And then awfully close to here… about two streets down… sometime in the early morning… Not long before Louis came home…”

Kiev shook his head. “Yes... yes…. Listen. You know Maxwell did it, Boss knows it, and I know it. But that shit won’t fly with Dimitri. You say he went to check himself? We can’t go to him with that. It’s not enough.”

“We won’t go to him with that.” Laura’s calm voice echoed in the big hall.

Both men turned to her, having forgotten about her for a moment. They would not make that mistake again.

Lucas’s emotions finally took over. “She’s right. Fuck Dimitri, he probably knows something is fishy. He’ll keep quiet just to save face and, obviously, keep the shipments on schedule. I say we go after Maxwell ourselves. Just say the word, Mrs. Malkin, and he's a dead man."

Laura smiled with all the hatred in her heart.

"Thank you, Lucas and Kiev." She bowed her head, regal-like. "I don't want him a dead man."

"Laura!" Lucas screamed, infuriated. He'd thought he'd seen a glimpse of a woman he could follow, one worthy of his service, worthy of the memory of his best friend.

The look she shot him both reassured him and silenced him.

Her voice was as calm as ever. "Maxwell Bane…." She looked above and around her, as if pleasantly tossing an idea in her head.

"He's married… with an adorable young boy, isn't he?"

Lucas nodded.

"Kiev, take the men you need. Find the wife and child. Bring them to me. Lucas. You get me Maxwell. *Alive*, and unharmed."

The men looked at her. She looked back, but clearly she didn't see them. She smiled wickedly to the vision playing out in front of her.

"You're right. What we have is not enough. We'll get our confession straight from the dragon's mouth. Let's see how *he* holds up in interrogation… Let's see how he holds up to his wife's… and that of his precious little boy."

Kiev and Lucas exchanged a stare.

"That will be all. Thank you, gentlemen."

They nodded their head in unison before turning around and leaving her alone.

She watched them leave. Once alone, she returned to her sweet fantasy.

Maxwell had stolen her Master away and any chance she had to ever prove her love to him. His grotesque and mutilated body would be her shrine for her Monster. The horror she would inflict on him would be heard of by gods and demons alike. Little children all over the world would tremble in their beds at night, having heard the tale of the Monster's wife and the aftermath of her broken heart. And Kayne, wherever he dwelled, would know how helplessly Laura Spencer loved her Master.

* * *

Kiev and Lucas walked side by side in the hall, their walk resolute, and their faces bleak.

"The king is dead," Lucas muttered, mostly to himself.

"Long live the queen," Kiev completed.

They stopped to look at each other. After a long pause, they nodded, bowing their head one to another in quiet complicity. Their allegiance was pledged.

Out into the beautiful sunny day, two grim reapers set out on their macabre mission. Up in the clear blue sky, a crow circling overhead cawed along. It followed the two men all the way to the front gate then returned to the Malkin mansion. Atop the grand entrance, it perched itself, watching the opening gates, its clear blue eyes strangely human.